Penelope Douglas is a writer living in Las Vegas. Born in Dubuque, Iowa, she is the eldest of five children. Penelope attended the University of Northern Iowa, earning a Bachelor's degree in Public Administration, because her father told her to "just get the damn degree!" She then earned a Masters of Science in Education at Loyola University in New Orleans, because she HATED public administration. One night, she got tipsy and told the bouncer at the bar where she worked that his son was hot, and three years later she was married. To the son, not the bouncer. They have spawn, but just one. A daughter named Aydan. Penelope loves sweets, The Originals, and she shops at Target almost daily.

Visit Penelope Douglas online:
www.facebook.com/PenelopeDouglasAuthor
www.twitter.com/pendouglas

There is in every true woman's heart a spark of heavenly fire, which lies dormant in the broad daylight of prosperity, but which kindles up and beams and blazes in the dark hour of adversity.

Bully

A Fall Away Novel

PENELOPE DOUGLAS

PIATKUS

PIATKUS

First published in the US in 2014 by Intermix, an imprint of The Berkley Publishing
Group and New American Library, divisions of Penguin Group (USA) LLC.
First published in Great Britain in 2014 by Piatkus

15 17 19 20 18 16

A CIP catalogue record for this book
is available from the British Library.

ISBN 978-0-349-40593-3

Printed and bound in Great Britain by
Clays Ltd, Elcograf S.p.A.

Papers used by Piatkus are from well-managed forests
and other responsible sources.

Piatkus
An imprint of
Little, Brown Book Group
Carmelite House
50 Victoria Embankment
London EC4Y 0DZ

An Hachette UK Company
www.hachette.co.uk

www.littlebrown.co.uk

For the ladies . . .

Acknowledgments

First, to my husband for all of his patience and support. He endured countless nights and weekends alone as I locked myself in our bedroom to write this story. I promise the investment will pay off ... eventually.

Next, to my friend Bekke for ... well, everything! Without you, I would have been fumbling along with Word, HTML, and yes, writing in general. I have no idea where this book would be without you!

Finally, to all of the readers out there who find their escape in the realm of books. Your time and feedback are the best gifts you can give an author. Thank you for reading!

Bully

Chapter 1

"No! Turn here," K.C. shrieked in my right ear.

The tires of my dad's Bronco screeched with the sudden, short turn onto a car-packed street.

"You know, maybe you should've just driven like I suggested," I blurted out, even though I never liked anyone else to drive when I was in the car.

"And have you bury your face in your hands every time I don't launch myself through every yellow light? Not!" K.C. responded as if reading my mind.

I smiled to myself. My best friend knew me too well. I liked to drive fast. I liked to move fast. I walked as quickly as my legs could take me, and I drove as speedily as was reasonable. I rushed to every stop sign and red light. Hurry up and wait, that was me.

But hearing the pounding rhythm of the music in the distance, I had no desire to rush any further. The lane was lined with car after car, displaying the magnitude of the party we were crashing. My hands clenched the steering wheel as I squeezed into a spot a block away from the party.

"K.C.? I don't think this is a good idea," I declared ... again.

"It'll be fine, you'll see." She patted my leg. "Bryan invited

1

Liam. Liam invited me, and I'm inviting you." Her calm, flat tone did nothing to ease the tightness in my chest.

Unfastening my seatbelt, I looked over to her. "Well, just remember . . . if I get uncomfortable, I'm gone. You catch a ride with Liam."

We climbed out and jogged across the street. The party ruckus amplified the closer we got to the house.

"You're not going anywhere. You leave in two days, and we're having fun. No matter what." Her threatening voice shook my already unsteady nerves.

As we walked up the driveway, she trailed behind me. Texting Liam, I assumed. Her boyfriend had arrived earlier, having spent most of the day with his friends at the lake while K.C. and I shopped.

Red Solo cups littered the lawn, and people filtered in and out of the house, enjoying the balmy summer night. Several guys I recognized from school lunged out of the front door, chasing each other and sloshing drinks in the process.

"Hey, K.C. How's it going, Tate?" Tori Beckman sat inside the front door with a drink in hand, chatting with a boy I didn't know. "Drop your keys in the bowl," she instructed, returning her attention to her company.

Taking a moment to process her request, I realized she was making me surrender my keys.

I guess she wasn't letting anyone drive drunk tonight.

"Well, I won't be drinking," I shouted over the music.

"And you might change your mind," she challenged. "If you want in, I need your keys."

Annoyed, I dug into my bag and dropped my set into the bowl. The thought of giving up one of my lifelines irritated the hell out of me. Not having my keys meant I wouldn't be able to leave quickly if I wanted to. Or needed to. What if she got drunk and left her post? What if someone accidentally took my keys? I suddenly remembered my mom, who used to tell me to stop asking "what if" questions. *What if Disneyland is closed for cleaning when we get there? What if every store in town ran out of gummi bears?* I bit my lip to stifle a laugh, remembering how annoyed she would get with my endless questions.

"Wow," K.C. shouted in my ear, "look at it in here!"

People, some classmates and some not, bounced to the music, laughing and living it up. The hair on my arms stood on end at the sight of all of the bustle and enthusiasm. The floors echoed the beat coming from the speakers, and I was speechless at the sight of so much activity in one space. People danced, horse-played, jumped, drank, and played football—yes, football—in the living room.

"*He* better not ruin this for me," I said, the force of my voice sounding more forceful than usual. Enjoying one party with my best friend before I left town for a year wasn't asking too much.

Shaking my head, I looked to K.C., who winked knowingly at me. I motioned towards the kitchen, and we both slithered our way, hand in hand, through the thick crowd.

Entering the huge, every-mom's-dream kitchen, I spied the makeshift bar on the center island. Bottles of liquor covered the granite top along with two liters of soda, cups and a bucket of ice in the sink. Blowing out a breath, I resigned to keep with my commitment to stay sober tonight. Getting drunk was tempting. *What I wouldn't give to just let go for one night.*

K.C. and I had sampled our parents' liquor stashes here and there, and I'd been to a few concerts out of town where we'd partied a bit. However, it was out of the question to be off my guard around some of these people tonight.

"Hey, Tate! Come here, girl." Jess Cullen grabbed me in a hug before I reached the bar. "We're going to miss you, ya know.

France, huh? For a whole year?" My shoulders relaxed as I hugged Jess back, my muscles less tense than when I walked in. At least one other person here besides K.C. was excited to see me.

"That's the plan." I nodded, letting out a sigh. "I'm set up with a host family and already registered for classes. I'll be back for senior year, though. Will you save me a spot on the team?"

Jess was vying for captain of the cross-country team this fall, and competing was one experience in high school that I would miss.

"If I'm captain, honey, your spot is secure," she boasted animatedly, clearly drunk. Jess had always been nice to me despite the rumors that followed me year to year and the embarrassing pranks that reminded everyone why I was a joke.

"Thanks. I'll see you later?" I inched towards K.C.

"Yeah, but if I don't see you, good luck in France," Jess shouted as she danced her way out of the kitchen.

Watching her leave, my face quickly fell. Dread crawled its way through my chest and down to my stomach.

No, no, no . . .

Jared walked into the kitchen, and I froze. He was exactly the person I'd hoped not to see tonight. His eyes met mine with surprise followed by immediate displeasure.

Yep. I'm totally familiar with that look. The I-can't-stand-the-fucking-sight-of-you-so-get-off-my-planet look.

His jaw clenched, and I noticed how his chin lifted slightly as if he had just put on his "bully" mask. I couldn't seem to catch my breath.

The familiar pounding in my chest echoed in my ears, and a hundred miles away sounded like a really nice place to be right now.

Was it too much to ask that I had one night of normal teenage fun to myself?

There were so many times when we were kids, growing up next door to each other, that I thought Jared was the greatest. He was sweet, generous, and friendly. And the most beautiful boy I'd ever seen.

His rich brown hair still complimented his olive skin, and his stunning smile—when he smiled—demanded undivided attention. Girls were too busy watching him in the hallway at school that they ran into walls. Like *actually* ran into walls.

But that kid was long gone now.

Quickly turning away, I found K.C. at the bar and tried to fix myself a drink, despite my shaking hands. Actually, I just poured a Sprite, but the red cup would look like I was drinking. Now that I knew he was here, I needed to stay sober around the asshole.

He walked around to the bar and stood right behind me. A nervous heat ran through my body at his proximity. The muscles in his chest rubbed against the thin fabric of my tank top, and a shockwave burst from my chest to my stomach. *Calm down. Calm the hell down!*

Scooping up some ice and adding it to my drink, I forced my breathing in and out slowly. I maneuvered to the right to get out of his way, but his arm shot out to grab a cup and blocked my passage. As I tried to squeeze out to the left next to K.C., his other arm reached out to grab the Jack Daniels.

Ten different scenarios ran through my head of what I should do right now. What if I elbowed him in the gut? What if I threw my drink in his face? What if I took the sink hose and . . . ?

Oh, never mind. In my dreams, I was much braver. In my dreams, I might take an ice cube and do things God didn't intend a sixteen-year-old girl to do just to see if I could make his cool demeanor falter. *What if? What if?*

I had planned on keeping my distance from him tonight, and now he was positioned right at my back. Jared did things like this just to intimidate me. He wasn't scary, but he was cruel. He wanted me to know he was in control. Time after time, I let the jerk force me into hiding just so I wouldn't have to endure any embarrassment or upset. Enjoying at least one party had been my top priority all summer, and now here I was again, dreadful anticipation twisting me into knots. Why didn't he just leave me alone?

Turning around to face him, I noticed the corners of his mouth turned up. The smile was lost on his eyes, though, as he poured a hefty serving of alcohol into his cup.

"K.C.? Pour some Coke into here, please." Jared spoke to K.C. but his eyes were on me as he held up his cup for her.

"Um, yeah," K.C. stammered, finally looking up. She poured a small portion of the liquid for Jared and glanced nervously to me.

As usual, Jared never spoke to me unless it was to bite out a threat. His dark brow knitted before taking a swig of his drink and walking away.

Watching him leave the kitchen, I wiped away the cold sweat that broke out across my forehead. Nothing had happened, and he hadn't even said anything to me, but my stomach had hollowed all the same.

And now he knew that I was here tonight.

Shit.

"I can't do this, K.C." My weary whisper was a contradiction to the force with which I clenched my cup. It was a mistake to come tonight.

"Tate, no." K.C. shook her head, probably recognizing the look of surrender in my eyes. Tossing the cup into the sink and making my way out of the kitchen, I weaved through the throng of people as K.C. followed behind.

Grabbing the glass fishbowl, I began digging around for my keys.

"Tate, you are not leaving," K.C. ordered, every word dripping with disappointment. "Don't let him win. I'm here. Liam's here. You don't have to be afraid." She was bracing me by my upper arms while I continued my search.

"I'm not scared of him," I said defensively, not really believing it myself. "I'm just...done. You saw him in there. He was already messing with me. He's planning something. Every party we go to, or every time I relax at school, there's some prank or embarrassment to ruin it."

Still searching for my colorful DNA-shaped key chain, I relaxed the knit in my brow and offered a tight smile. "It's okay. I'm fine," I reassured her, my words coming out too quickly. "I just don't care to stay and see what he's cooked up this time. The dickhead can starve tonight."

"Tate, he wants you to leave. If you do, then he wins. He, or that jackass Madoc, might come up with something, but if you stay and stand your ground, then you will win."

"I'm just worn out, K.C. I'd rather go home mad now than in tears later." I returned my attention to the bowl. Every time I sifted through a pile of keys, though, my hands would bring up nothing resembling my set.

"Well," I shouted over the music and slammed the bowl back down on the stand, "it looks like I can't leave anyway. My keys aren't in there."

"What?" K.C. looked confused.

"They're not in there!" I repeated, looking around the room. My money and my phone were in my bag. Two lifelines safe and sound. My other escape plan was missing, and the walls felt like they were caving in. Curses ran through my head, and the weariness that got me running before turned to anger. I clenched my fists. Of course, I should've known this was going to happen.

"Someone could've grabbed them by accident, I guess," she

offered, but she must've known that the odds of that happening were slimmer than people leaving the party this early. Accidents didn't happen to me.

"No, I know exactly where they are." I locked eyes with Madoc, Jared's best friend and henchman, at the opposite end of the room by the patio doors. He smirked at me before redirecting his attention to some random redhead he had pressed to a wall.

Stalking over to him, K.C. followed in my wake as she viciously texted on her phone—Liam probably.

"Where are my keys?" I demanded, interrupting the pursuit of his next one-night stand.

He lifted his blue eyes slowly from the girl. He wasn't much taller than me, maybe a few inches, so I didn't feel as if he hovered over me like Jared did. Madoc didn't intimidate me. He just pissed me off. He worked hard to make a fool out of me, but I knew it was all at Jared's behest.

"They're about eight feet under right now. Feel like a swim, Tate?" He grinned wide, showing his dazzling smile that turned most girls into puppies on a leash. He obviously loved every moment of my predicament.

"You're a dick." My tone remained calm, but my eyes burned from the anger.

I walked out to the patio and peered into the pool. The weather was perfect for a swim, and people were carousing in the water, so I trekked around the pool looking for the silver glint of my keys through all of the bodies.

Jared sat casually at a table with a blonde on his lap. Frustration knotted in my stomach, but I tried to appear unaffected. I knew every ounce of my discomfort gave him pleasure.

Spying the shimmering silver of the keys, I looked around for a pole to grab them. When nothing could be found, I looked to some of the swimmers for help.

"Hey, would you mind grabbing my keys down there, please?" I asked. The guy turned his eyes on Jared, who sat quietly back, watching the scene, and retreated from me like a coward.

Great. No pole, no help. Jared wanted to see me get wet.

"Come on, Tate. Strip down, and go get your keys," Madoc shouted from Jared's table.

"Fuck off, Madoc. You threw them down there, no doubt, so why don't you go get them?" Liam, K.C.'s boyfriend, had joined her and was sticking up for me like he often did.

I slipped off my flip-flops and stepped to the edge of the pool.

"Tate, wait. I'll do it," Liam stepped up and offered.

"No." I shook my head. "Thanks, though." I gave him a grateful smile.

One whole year, I reminded myself, savoring the promise. I was going to have a whole year away from Jared.

I dove in hands first, and the water cooled my tense skin. My body immediately relaxed at the pleasure of the pool. No sound, no eyes on me. I savored the peace of it, the kind of peace I get when I run.

I continued downward using the breast stroke. Eight feet was nothing, and I reached my keys in seconds. Clutching them tight, I reluctantly ascended head first, releasing the air in my lungs.

That was the easy part.

"Whoo hoo!" An applause sounded from bystanders that weren't actually cheering *for* me.

I just had to get out of the pool and face the whole party dripping wet. They would laugh and joke. I'd endure a few comments, and then go home and eat my weight in Swedish Fish.

Swimming gently to the edge and climbing out, I wrung out my long hair and slipped on my sandals.

"Are you okay?" K.C. came to my side, the wind blowing her long, dark hair.

"Yeah, of course. It's just water." I couldn't meet her eyes. Here I was again. The laughing stock. The embarrassment.

But K.C. never blamed me. "Let's get out of here." She locked arms with me, and Liam followed behind.

"Just a minute." I paused and looked over at Jared, who still had his challenging brown eyes on me.

Walking over to him—something I knew was a bad idea—I crossed my arms and gave him a pointed stare.

"I leave in two days and that's the best you could come up with?" *What the hell am I doing?*

Jared fixed me with a hostile smile as he doled out the cards at the table. "You have a good time in France, Tatum. I'll be here when you get back." His threat made me want to hit him. I wanted to challenge him to deal with me now.

And I was none too comfortable with the thought of his impending wrath hanging over my head the whole year I was away.

"You're a coward. The only way you can feel like a man is to pick on me. But you're going to have to get your kicks somewhere else now." As I dropped my arms to my sides, my fists tightened as everyone around the table and in the general area witnessed our exchange.

"Are you still talking?" Jared snorted, and snickers erupted around me. "Go home. No one wants your stuck-up ass here." Jared barely spared me eye contact while he continued to deal cards. The girl on his lap giggled and leaned into him further. The crushing sensation in my chest hurt. *I hate him.*

"Hey, everyone, look!" Madoc shouted as I tried to hold back tears. "Her nipples are hard. You must be turning her on, Jared." Madoc's goading echoed through the backyard, and everyone began hooting and laughing.

My eyes closed with mortification as I remembered that I was wearing a white tank top and was definitely chilled from the water. My first instinct was to cross my arms over my chest, but then they'd know that they got to me. Hell, they already knew. My whole face stung with humiliation.

Son of a bitch.

I'd be going home in tears again. No doubt.

I opened my eyes, feeling flushed seeing everyone visibly entertained by the harassment I'd endured tonight. Jared stared at the table, nostrils flaring, ignoring me. His behavior still puzzled me after all this time. We used to be friends, and I still searched for that kid in his eyes somewhere. But what good did it do me to still hang on to a memory of him?

"Why is she still standing here?" the blonde sitting on Jared's lap asked. "Is she like 'special' or something? She can't take the hint?"

"Yeah, Tate. You heard Jared. No one wants you here." Madoc's words came out slow as if I really were too stupid to understand him.

My throat closed. I couldn't swallow, and it hurt to breathe. It was too much. Something inside me snapped. I pulled my fist back and popped Madoc right in the nose. He dropped to his knees, hands over his face, as the blood gushed through his hands.

Tears blurred my vision, and the sobs began erupting from my throat. Before I could let them get any more satisfaction out of me tonight, I walked as quickly as possible back through the house and out the front door without looking back.

I got in my car, K.C. climbed in the passenger side and Liam into the back. I hadn't even realized that they'd followed me. It was on the tip of my tongue to ask about Jared's reaction, but then I realized that I shouldn't care. *To hell with him.*

I looked out the front window, letting the tears dry on my cheeks. Liam and K.C. sat silently, probably not sure what to say or do.

I'd just hit Madoc. *I'd just hit Madoc!* The novelty of my action was overwhelming, and I let out a bitter laugh. That really just happened.

I took a deep breath and blew out slowly.

"Are you okay?" K.C. looked at me.

She knew I'd never done anything like that before, but I loved the rush of fright and power I felt.

Hell, the last thing I wanted to do was go home now. Maybe a tattoo or something else was in the cards tonight.

"Actually, yes." It was weird to say that, but it was true. Wiping the tears away, I looked to my friend. "I feel good."

I reached to put the key in the ignition but paused when Liam chimed in. "Yeah, well, don't let it go to your head, Tate. You'll have to come back to town eventually."

Yeah. There was that.

Chapter 2

Present Day

"So . . . how does it feel to be back home?" My dad and I video chatted on the laptop he bought for me before I left for Europe.

"It's great, Dad. I'm set." I counted off with my fingers. "There's food, money, no adults, and you still have beer in the 'frig downstairs. I smell a paaarty," I teased. But my dad could give it as good as he got.

"Well, I also have some condoms in my bathroom. Use them if you need."

"Dad!" I burst out, wide-eyed with shock. Fathers shouldn't use the word "condoms", at least not around their daughters. "That . . . just . . . crossed a line. Seriously." I started to laugh. He was the dad that all of my friends wished they had. He had a few simple rules: respect your elders, take care of your body, finish what you start, and solve your own problems. If I maintained good grades, demonstrated direction, and followed those four rules, he trusted me. If I lost his trust, I'd lose my freedom. That's a military parent. Simple.

"So what's the plan this week?" Dad asked, running his hand through his graying blond hair. I'd gotten my coloring from him but thankfully not the freckles. His once vibrant blue eyes were dull with fatigue, and his shirt and tie were wrinkled. He worked too hard.

I lounged cross-legged on my queen-sized bed, thankful to be back in my own room. "Well, there's about a week before school starts, so I have a meeting with the guidance counselor next Wednesday about my fall schedule. I'm hoping the extra classes I took last year will boost my Columbia application. She's helping with that, too. I also have some shopping to do and then catching up with K.C., of course."

I also wanted to start looking for a car, but he'd tell me to wait until he got home at Christmas. Not that I didn't know what I was doing. I just knew he'd want to share that experience with me, so I wasn't going to burst his bubble.

"I wish you were home to help me research projects for the science fair." I changed the subject. "I guess we should've done that while I visited you this summer."

My father retired from the military after my mom's death eight years ago and worked for a company in Chicago, about an hour away, that built aircraft and sold it around the world. Currently, he was on an extended trip to Germany, holding mechanical trainings. After my year ended in Paris, I'd joined him in Berlin for the summer. My mom would be happy to know I'd traveled and had plans to continue as often as possible after high school. I missed her so much, even more so in the past few years than when she first passed away.

At that moment, the French doors in my room blew open with a gust of sudden, cool wind.

"Hang on, Dad." I jumped off the bed and ran to the doors to peek outside.

A steady force of wind caressed my bare arms and legs. I leaned over the railing and took inventory of leaves flapping in the gust and garbage cans rolling away. The smell of lilacs wafted through

14

my doors from the trees that peppered our street, Fall Away Lane.

A storm was seconds away, and electricity filled the air with anticipation. Chills ran over my skin, not from cold, but from the thrill of a storm brewing. I loved summer rain.

"Hey, Dad," I interrupted him as he was speaking to someone in the background, "I need to let you go. I think a storm is on its way, and I should go check all of the windows. Talk to you tomorrow?" I rubbed my arms to erase the chill.

"Sure, honey. I have to run anyway. Just remember that the pistol is in the entryway table. Call if you need anything. Love you."

"Love you too, Dad. Talk to you tomorrow," I called out behind me.

Closing the laptop, I shrugged into my black Seether hoodie and opened the doors in my room again. Studying the tree outside, my brain snapped to unbidden memories of the many times I'd sat in that tree to enjoy the rain. I had shared many of those times with Jared . . . when we were still friends.

Quickly looking up, I took note that his window was closed, with no light to speak of coming from his house that sat less than ten yards away. With the tree acting as a ladder between our bedroom windows, it always seemed like the houses were connected in a way.

During my year away, I had fought the urge to ask K.C. about him. Even after everything he'd done, part of me still missed that boy that was my waking thought and constant companion as a kid. But that Jared was gone now. In his place was a sour, hateful douchebag that had no regard for me.

Shutting and locking the French doors, I pulled the sheer, black curtains closed. Moments later, the sky opened up with a *crack*, and the rain let loose.

*

Awakened later that night, my brain unable to ignore the thunder and thrashing of the tree against the house, I flipped on my bedside light and crept to the doors to check out the storm. I caught the sight of headlights speeding dangerously down the street. I tilted my head as far to the side as I could and caught the view of a black Boss 302 charging its way into Jared's driveway.

The car fishtailed slightly before jetting out of my sight into the garage. It was a new car model with a thick, red racing stripe running down the length of the car. I had never seen it before. Last I knew Jared had a motorcycle and a Mustang GT, so that car could've been anyone's.

Maybe I had a new neighbor?

I wasn't sure how I felt about that possibility.

On the other hand, that car would totally have been Jared's taste.

After a minute or so, a dim light fell across my floor with the illumination coming from Jared's room. I caught the sight of a dark figure moving behind his blinds. My fingers started to tingle, making them too weak to curl.

Trying to refocus my attention on the fantastical display of wind and curtains of rain, my heart jumped at the sound of Jared's blinds lifting up and the wash of light spilling between our two houses. I narrowed my eyes as I saw Jared lift up his window and lean out into the night storm.

Damn.

He appeared to be observing the spectacle, same as me. I could barely make out his face through the dense spatter of leaves, but I knew when he noticed me. His arms stiffened as he supported himself on the windowsill, and his head was bowed in my direction, unmoving. I could almost picture those chocolate-brown eyes piercing me.

He didn't wave or nod. Why would he? Absence wasn't going

to make his heart grow fonder—clearly. Dread and apprehension used to plague me when this guy was around, but now . . . I felt a strange mixture of nervousness and anticipation.

I slowly backed up to close and secure the doors. The last thing I wanted was to trip and give away the emotions boiling under my calm exterior. During my time away, I'd thought about Jared, but I hadn't dwelled on him, figuring that time and distance would cool him off.

Perhaps that prediction was too hopeful.

And maybe I wasn't as bothered by his shit anymore.

Chapter 3

"So, have you seen him yet?" K.C. leaned on the frame of my double doors looking over towards Jared's house. I didn't have to ask who she was referring to.

"No ... well, yes. Kind of. I saw a pretty severe-looking Boss charging into his garage late last night. Would that be him?" I didn't want to tell K.C. about seeing him at the window. Hoping to have a couple of days' reprieve before we came face to face, I was trying to hang on to the calm I'd achieved during my year away.

I continued to sort through the clothes in my suitcase, picking out what needed to be hung up and what needed to be washed.

"Yep. He traded in the GT shortly after you left and bought that. I guess he's been making a name for himself racing out at the Loop."

My fingers clenched the hanger tightly at her words. Disappointment coursed through me as I realized that things had changed in the year I'd been gone. When we were younger, Jared and I had dreamed of putting a car together for the Loop.

"It's a hot car." I hated to admit it.

Jared used to work with my dad and me in our garage fixing up my dad's old Chevy Nova. We were both eager students and appreciated the mastery it took to get a car in prime condition.

"In any case," I continued, "with racing and his job, I just hope he's too busy to get in my face this year." I circulated the room putting things away, but my brain throbbed with annoyance.

K.C. backed away from the door frame and belly-flopped onto my bed. "Well, I, for one, am pretty excited to see the look on his face when he sees you." She leaned her head on her hand, giving me a teasing grin.

"And why is that?" I muttered as I walked to my bedside table to reset my clock.

"Because you look great. I have no idea what happened between the two of you, but he won't be able to ignore you. No rumor or prank will keep the guys away, and Jared will probably be sulking that he treated you so badly." K.C. wiggled her eyebrows.

I don't know what she meant about me "looking great." As far as I knew, I looked the same as I always had. I stood at 5'7", blondish hair falling to the middle of my back, and dark blue eyes. Gym workouts made me want to gag, but I had continued my running to keep in shape for cross-country. The only difference was my skin tone. After traveling this summer and being in the sun so much, I was pretty tanned. In time, though, that would disappear, and I'd be pale again.

"Oh, he never had a problem ignoring me. I wish he would." I sucked in a breath through my teeth and smiled. "I had such an awesome year. The people I met and the places I saw. It all gave me a lot of perspective. I have a plan, and I'm not letting Jared Trent get in my way."

I sat down on the bed and let out a sigh.

K.C. grabbed my hand. "No worries, babe. This shit has to come to a head eventually. After all, we graduate in nine months."

"What are you talking about?"

"I'm talking about the foreplay between you and Jared," K. C. chirped, straight-faced as she hopped off the bed and into my closet. "It can't go on forever," she called out.

Foreplay?

"Excuse me?" Foreplay was a sex word, and my stomach flip-flopped at the thought of "Jared" and "sex" in the same sentence.

"Ms. Brandt, don't tell me this hasn't crossed your mind." K.C. poked her head out of the closet, using a Southern accent as she pinched her eyebrows together and placed her hand over her heart. She held one of my dresses up to her frame as she examined herself in the full-sized mirror that hung on the back of my closet door.

Foreplay? I spun the word around in my head trying to figure out what she was talking about until it finally clicked.

"You think his treatment of me is foreplay?!" I almost yelled at her. "Yes. It was foreplay when he told the whole school I had Irritable Bowel Syndrome and everyone made farting noises as I walked down the hall freshman year." My sarcastic tone failed to cover up my anger. How could she think all this was foreplay? "And yes, it was completely erotic the way he had the grocery store deliver a case of yeast infection cream to Math class sopho-more year. But what really got me hot and ready to bend over for him was when he plastered brochures for genital wart treatments on my locker, which is completely outrageous for someone to have an STD without having sex!"

All of the resentment I had let go of this year was now back with a vengeance. I hadn't forgiven or forgotten anything.

Blinking long and hard, I took a mental vacation back to France. *Port Salut cheese, French bread, bonbons . . .* I snorted when I realized that maybe it wasn't France but the food that I had really loved.

K.C. stared at me, wide-eyed. "Uh, no, Tate. I don't think he is engaging in *sexual* foreplay. I think he really does hate you. What I'm saying is, isn't it about time you fought back? Played the game? If he pushes you, push back. I tried to let her words sink in, but she continued, "Tate, guys aren't mean to attractive girls for no reason at all. In fact, most teenage guys' energy is for the sole purpose of getting laid. They don't want to diminish their options, so they are rarely mad at any girl ... unless she's betrayed him, of course," she mused.

I knew K.C. was right to an extent. There *had* to be a reason for why Jared acted the way he did. I'd wracked my brain a thousand times trying to figure it out. He was cold to most people, but he was downright cruel to me.

Why me?

I stood up and continued the task of hanging up clothes, my scarves draped over my shoulder. "Well, I haven't betrayed Jared. I've told you a hundred times, we were friends for years, he went away for a few weeks the summer before freshman year, and when he came back, he was different. He didn't want to have anything to do with me."

"Well, you won't know anything until you engage. Like before you left for France. You pushed back that night, and that's what you need to keep doing." K.C. shot out advice like I hadn't thought about it for the past year. My anger got away from me the night of Tori Beckman's party, but no good was going to come from me sinking to Jared's level again.

"Look." I evened out my voice in an effort to appear calm. *There was no way I was getting sucked into any more drama with this guy, damn it.* "We're going to have an amazing year. I'm hoping Jared has forgotten all about me. If he has, then we can both peacefully ignore each other until graduation. If he hasn't, then I'll do what I think is best. I've got bigger things on my mind anyway. He and that asshat Madoc can poke and prod all they want. I'm done giving them my attention. They are not taking my senior year." I stopped to look at her.

K.C. looked thoughtful. "Okay," she offered complacently.

"Okay?"

"Yes, I said 'okay'." She let the discussion go. My shoulders relaxed. She wanted me to be David to Jared's Goliath, and I just wanted to focus on getting into Columbia and winning the Science Fair in the spring.

"Okay," I mimicked and quickly changed the subject. "So my dad isn't due home for three more months. What trouble should I dare to stir up? Do you think I should actually break curfew while he's gone?" I continued to sort out my clothes.

"I still can't believe your dad is leaving you alone for three months."

"He knows that it's ridiculous to make me stay with my grandma, start a new school and then move back here when he gets home at Christmas. It's my senior year. It's important. He understands." My grandma always stayed with me while my dad was away, but her sister wasn't well and needed constant help. I was on my own this time.

"Yeah, well your grandma is only like two hours away anyway, so I'm sure she'll pop in here and there," K.C. pointed out. "Should we possibly risk having a party?"

She knew I was a worrywart, so her tone was cautious. My parents raised me to think for myself but to use common sense. Far too often had K.C. been disappointed by my lack of "devil may care" attitude. "That way, you wouldn't be breaking curfew! Because you'd ... be ... home," she quickly reasoned.

My chest tightened at the thought of an unauthorized party, but I had to admit, it was still something I wanted to do at some point.

"I guess it is a rite of passage for all teenagers, having a party while the parents are away," I admitted but swallowed hard when I remembered that I only had one parent. Although my mom had passed away so long ago, it still hurt every day. I glanced over to our last family picture sitting on my bedside table. We were at a

White Sox game, and my parents were each kissing one of my cheeks, my lips scrunched up like a fish.

K.C. patted me on the back. "We'll go slowly with you. We can start stretching the rules before we break them. How about having a guy over before you have a huge crowd?" She grabbed a black silk top I'd bought in Paris and held it up.

"Yeah, somehow I think my dad would find one guy more threatening that a houseful of teenage partiers. And I do break rules sometimes. I'm guilty of speeding and jaywalking and . . ." My voice trailed off as my lips pulled up into a grin. K.C. and I could be adventurous, but it was never of much interest to me to lose my father's trust. Normally, I didn't even bend rules. I respected him too much.

"Yeah, okay, Mother Theresa," K.C. muttered dismissively as she began flipping through some photos I'd taken during my year away. "So can you speak French fluently now?"

"I know some useful words for you," I deadpanned. She grabbed a pillow from my bed and flung it at me without looking away from the pictures in her hand. After three years of devoted friendship, we could exchange harmless insults as easily as clothes.

Walking into my private bathroom, I called out, "So, can you stay for dinner? We can do pizza."

"Tonight I have to be home, actually," she shouted back. "Liam is coming over for dinner. My mom is getting a little anxious about our relationship and wants to see him more." She enunciated "relationship" as if there was a double meaning.

Liam and K.C. had been dating for two years, and they'd been having sex for a while. Her mom no doubt suspected that their "relationship" had progressed.

"Uh oh, is Sergeant Carter on to you two?" I grunted while shoving my now empty suitcase under my bed. I called K.C.'s

23

mom 'Sergeant Carter' due to her authoritarian mothering. K.C. had little privacy and was expected to report on everything. However, it only made her want to keep her secrets more.

"I'm sure. She found my nightie and went ballistic." K.C. stood up and grabbed her purse off the bed.

"I would've loved to see you talk your way out of that one." I shut off my bedroom light and followed her down the stairs.

"If my parents were like your dad, then maybe I wouldn't be so nervous about telling them things," K.C. mumbled.

I was pretty sure I would never tell my dad about my first time, whenever it happened.

"Well, we can hook up tomorrow or whenever. As long as it's before school starts."

"Absolutely, tomorrow." She gave me a tight hug. "I need to go get myself cleaned up before dinner. I'll see you later." And she rushed out the door.

"Later."

Chapter 4

"Goddammit!" I bellowed up to my bedroom ceiling, now illuminated by the arrival of another partygoer.

Déjà vu struck me as the house next door roared with music and voices. I'd blissfully forgotten about Jared's raucous parties. The constant vibrations of engines revving and girls screaming—out of pleasure, I hoped—filled the air for the last two hours and was still going strong. My muscles tensed at every new noise.

I glanced, again, at the clock on my bedside table, willing it to stop ticking away the minutes. It was after midnight, and I had to wake up in five hours to meet up with my running club for their weekly workout. *I had to wake up*, I thought, and that was providing I could get to sleep in the first place.

And that wasn't going to happen without an intervention.

Isn't it about time you fought back? K.C.'s words buzzed through my head.

There was almost no chance that Jared would turn down the music if I asked, but the diplomat in me thought it was worth a shot. The "old Tate" would've lain in here awake all night, too intimidated by her bully to ask him to turn down his music. Now, bodily fatigue and weariness had chipped away my patience.

Maybe, just maybe, Jared had pulled the corn cob out of his ass and gotten over whatever problem he had with me. It didn't hurt to hope.

The evenings had turned chilly, so I was reluctant to step out of my warm bed. Throwing off the covers before I chickened out, I slipped on black Chucks and covered my white camisole with my black hoodie. My hair was hanging loose, I was wearing no make-up, and I sported my favorite pair of blue and white pin-striped linen sleep shorts. I could've looked better and probably should've put on some more modest bottoms, but I just didn't care. I was too tired, so I just stalked down the stairs and out the front door in all my disheveled glory.

It was either the warm, August evening or my nerves, but I had to roll up my sleeves to cool down as I left my yard and traipsed into his. The front lawn boasted random people, none of whom I recognized, and the beating of my heart relaxed a bit at the knowledge that there'd be few people I might know here. I knew Jared's list of friends included people from other schools, colleges, and even legal adults from questionable backgrounds. By now, the crowd was so wasted that I slipped by unnoticed.

Inside the house, the carousing was loud and obnoxious. People danced in the living room, or rather some slutty looking girls let themselves get dry-humped, while others sat or stood in various parts of the downstairs chatting, drinking, and smoking. My nose crinkled at the revolting den of underage debauchery and stench ... but, I admitted, everyone looked like they were having fun and being *normal*.

It was official. I was a stick-in-the-mud.

Chevelle started pumping through the speakers, which seemed to have an output located in every room. *Hats Off to the Bull* might make it worth my while coming over after all.

Entering the kitchen in my search for Jared, I immediately halted. While various people lingered around the keg and other, harder offerings located on the countertop, the sight of Madoc sitting at the kitchen table playing drinking games caught me off guard. He was with a few other guys and a couple of girls. It was too late to do an about-face.

"What the fuck are you doing here?" He popped out of his chair and stalked over to me. His sneer was plastic. For show purposes only. I knew Madoc relished any drama that spiced up his night.

And I was drama.

I decided to play it cocky. "Well, I'm not looking for you." Smirking, I continued to scan the room looking disinterested. "Where's Jared?"

"He's already got a girl for tonight. And I doubt he'd be interested in you anyway." He got in my face with the last.

More than a few girls wanted Madoc's attention, but I wasn't one of them. He was good-looking with his bright, blue eyes and styled blond hair. He had a great body, and his clothes complimented his form. However, I doubted he ever used girls for longer than one night.

I turned to leave and continue my search, but he grabbed me at the elbow. "Actually, I'm a glutton for punishment, but you do look fucking fantastic in your pajamas. If you're looking for some action, I can take care of you."

My stomach turned and my body stiffened. Was he joking? Didn't he have any pride? Freshman and sophomore year, he and Jared made my life hell. I was suffocated everywhere I went. Even at home. Now, he wanted to take me upstairs? Now, I was good enough?

"Hey, man, Jared says she's off limits." Sam Parker, one of Jared's nicer cronies, chimed in from the table.

Madoc's eyes glided down my body, lingering at my legs. "Jared's upstairs fucking Piper. He's got other things on his mind right now."

My mouth went dry. Unwanted images of the boy I used to share a tent with in my backyard flashed in my mind. Jared was upstairs, in bed right now, screwing some girl. Blowing out a breath, I turned to leave. I just needed to get out of here.

Madoc jerked me backwards into his body and wrapped his arms around me. I briefly registered Sam bolting out of his seat and out of the room. My body twisted and my muscles tensed, but I held off on any serious struggling for the time being. I wanted to see Jared, and hopefully that's where Sam went. If I could get out of here without major drama, I'd prefer it that way.

But Sam had better be quick, because Madoc's nose was about to meet the back of my skull.

"You don't learn, do you?" I stared straight ahead. A few feet away, some guys were playing pool, but paid us no attention. Clearly, the game was more important to them than a girl being assaulted.

"Oh, my nose? It's healed well, thanks. And I think I owe you for that one, by the way." His words were muffled as his lips glided down my neck. My shoulders wiggled from side to side as I tried to pry myself out of his grasp.

"You smell good," he whispered. "Keep fighting me, Tate. It turns me on." His snort was followed by his tongue darting out and licking my ear lobe before grabbing it between his teeth.

Motherfucker!

My pulse raced with anger, not fear. Fire surged in my arms and legs.

Play the game. I forgot if those were K.C.'s words or mine, and I didn't care.

Let's see how he likes being handled. I worked my hand behind me, in between our bodies, and grabbed Madoc by the crotch. I squeezed just enough to get his attention but not enough to hurt him . . . yet. Madoc didn't release me, but he stilled.

"Let. Me. Go," I gritted out. Onlookers were beginning to take more notice of the scene, but still stayed out of it, looking amused. No one made a move to help me.

I applied a little more pressure, and he finally released his hold. I quickly stepped away before turning to face him, forcing my anger down. Until I got Jared to turn down the damn music, I wasn't leaving.

Madoc raised an eyebrow. "You're probably still a virgin, aren't you?" He took me off guard. "Guys sure wanted to fuck you, but Jared and I took care of that."

Isn't it about time you fought back? K.C.'s voice egged me on.

"What the hell are you talking about?" Pulling my hoodie back into place, I stood my ground, my body a wall.

"What the hell is it between you and Jared anyway? I mean, when I first met him, and he wrangled me into sabotaging all of your dates freshman year, I assumed it was because he had a thing for you. Like, he was jealous or something. But then after a while, it was pretty clear he wasn't pursuing you ... for some reason. What did you do to him?" Madoc looked at me accusingly, cocking his head to the side.

My fingers curled into fists. "I didn't do anything to him."

Our confrontation was becoming a scene. My raised voice forced people to start clearing out. I circled around to the other side of the pool table to give myself distance.

"Think," Madoc goaded with a cocky smirk. "You're gorgeous, and speaking for myself, I'd have screwed you every which way by now. A lot of guys would've, if not for Jared."

My thighs tightened together. The idea of this asswipe thinking he could get into my pants reached a new level of grossness. "What do you mean 'if not for Jared?'" The hair on my arms stood on end as my breathing got heavier.

"It's simple. Every time we'd get word that someone was interested in you or had asked you out, we'd set out to make sure it ended as quickly as it'd started. We were pretty lame about it for the first few months. Todd Branch asked you to that bonfire freshman year, but he heard you were receiving lice treatments and never called you. You never wondered how he heard that?"

That particular rumor was one of the least hurtful ones over the years, but at the time, it was devastating. I had just started high school, was trying to make friends, and then I realized people were laughing behind my back.

"Daniel Stewart asked you out for the Halloween dance that year, too, but never picked you up because he heard you had lost your virginity to Stevie Stoddard." Madoc barely finished the last word, he started laughing so hard.

I grimaced uncontrollably as heat rose up my neck. Stevie Stoddard was an incredibly sweet kid, but he suffered from serious acne and ate his boogers. Every school had a Stevie Stoddard.

Madoc continued, "Yeah, we were pretty busy at first. A lot of guys wanted to get in your pants, but by sophomore year our rumors got more sophisticated. People had pretty much caught on that you were a social leper. Things got easier for Jared and me . . . finally."

And things had gotten harder for me.

Movement was impossible. What had I been thinking? Of course, it was *all* Jared!

I knew he was behind some of the pranks as well as all the parties I was shut out of, but I didn't think he'd been responsible for all of the rumors, too. I never knew why Daniel Stewart stood me up, and I'd never heard the Stevie Stoddard rumor. How much else escaped my notice? He pulled pranks on me, leaked some lies, and was an all-out dick throughout high school, but I never suspected he was so active in my unhappiness. Had he just gone ballistic for no fucking reason?

Think.

"What is she doing here?" Jolted out of my internal musing, I found Jared braced in the doorway between the pool room and

30

the stairs. His arms were above his head, hands secured to both sides of the door frame.

My breath caught. Seeing him face to face made me forget everything else. Madoc, his disclosures ... Shit! What the hell were he and I just talking about? I couldn't remember.

Even with my resentment towards Jared, I couldn't look away from the way the muscles in his smooth chest stretched with his arms. My body involuntarily reacted as heat gathered below my belly and steam moved up my neck. I'd been in France for a year, and seeing him again up close sent my stomach into a double back handspring.

His dark brown hair and eyes seemed to make his skin glow. The severe straight eyebrows enhanced his forbidding presence. Looking at him should be a sport. Whoever pulled their eyes away from him the soonest won.

He stood half naked, wearing only a pair of black pants featuring a wallet chain hanging from his pocket. His skin was tanned and his hair was shamelessly mussed. His two tattoos blazed, one on his upper arm and one on the side of his torso. His blue and white checkered boxers peeked out of the top of his pants, which hung loose due to the unfastened belt looped around his waist.

Unfastened. I closed my eyes.

Tears burned behind my lids, and the magnitude of his deeds came flooding back. Seeing this person that hated me enough to hurt me day after day made my heart ache.

He's not getting my senior year, I committed to myself. Blinking away the unshed tears, my breathing slowed. *Survival is the best revenge,* my mother would say.

Under one arm, I saw Sam peeking in, looking comically like Dobby cowering behind Lucius Malfoy. Under the other arm, a sexy brunette—whose name I assumed was Piper—squeezed through, looking like the cat that just ate the canary. I recognized her vaguely from school. She wore a skin-tight red halter-top dress with scary, black heels. Even with the six inches added to her height, she still fell below Jared's chin. She was pretty in a . . . well, in every way, I guess.

Jared, on the other hand, might've been about ready to eat a live baby with the scowl he wore. Making no eye contact with me, he made it clear that he spoke to Madoc and that I wasn't being addressed.

I stepped in before Madoc opened his mouth. "'*She*' wanted a brief word with you."

I crossed my arms over my chest and hooded my gaze, trying to look tougher than I was. Jared did the same, and while his lips were still, his eyes were amused.

"Make it quick. I have guests," he ordered.

He strolled into the room and took position on the other side of the pool table. Madoc and Sam took their cue and shuffled back into the kitchen. I caught Madoc out of the corner of my eye, swatting Sam over the head.

The control I was desperately trying to maintain threatened to rupture. After the epiphany brought on by Madoc's confession, I hated Jared more than ever. It was hard to look at him.

"I. Have. Guests," Jared repeated, fixing me with an annoyed stare.

"Yes, I can tell." I peered around him to the doorway where the brunette still stood. "You can get back to servicing them in just a minute."

Jared's expression fell to a slight scowl. The brunette finally took the hint, walked over to Jared whose eyes never left mine, and kissed him on the cheek. "Call me," she whispered.

His glare stayed on me as he continued to ignore her. After a few moments' hesitation, she backed out of the room, twisted on her heel and left. No wonder guys acted like jerks. Girls like that let them.

Pulling myself together, I held my head high. "I have to be up in about five hours for an appointment in Weston. I'm asking politely that you please turn down the music." *Please don't be an ass, please don't be an ass.*

"No."

So much for the power of prayer.

"Jared." I paused, already knowing that I wouldn't win. "I came here being neighborly. It's after midnight. I'm asking nicely." I was trying to keep my tone even.

"It's after midnight on a *Friday* night." He kept his arms crossed over his chest, giving the impression of being bored.

"You're being unreasonable. If I wanted the music off, I could file a noise complaint or call your mom. I'm coming to you out of respect." I looked around the empty room. "Where is your mother, by the way? I haven't seen her since I've been back."

"She's not around much anymore, and she won't be dragging her ass down here in the middle of the night to break up my party."

"I'm not saying to 'break it up'. I'm asking that you turn the music down," I clarified, as if I still had any chance that Jared would concede.

"Go sleep over at K.C.'s on the weekends." He started circling the pool table and rolling balls into pockets.

"It's after midnight! I'm *not* bothering her this late."

"You're bothering me this late."

"You are such a dick." The whisper left my lips before I could stop it.

"Careful, Tatum." He stopped and glared. "You've been gone for a while, so I'll cut you a break and remind you that my good-will doesn't go far with you."

"Oh, please. Don't act like it's such a burden to tolerate my presence. I've put up with more than a little from you over the years. What could you possibly do to me that you haven't done already?" I, again, crossed my arms over my chest and tried to look confident.

My past nervousness came from my inability to handle him. He was clever and quick-witted, and I always lost when we verbally sparred. But I was not afraid of him.

"I like my parties, Tatum." He shrugged his shoulders. "I like to be entertained. If you take my party, then you'll have to entertain me." His hooded gaze and husky voice were probably meant to be sexy, but it only came off as threatening.

"And what disgusting task, pray tell, would you like me to do?" I lavishly waved my hand through the air as if talking to a Duke or Lord. Maybe the jerkoff wanted his toilets cleaned or socks folded. Either way, he was only going to get my middle finger pointed in his face.

Sauntering over to me, Jared grabbed the hem of my hoodie and said, "Take this off and give me a lap dance."

My eyes widened. "Excuse me?" I choked out in a husky whisper. He stood so close to me, and my body hummed with energy. His head was level, but his dark eyes were downcast with a penetrating gaze. I was hyperaware of his body, his bare skin, and then the mental pictures of a lap dance started flowing. Oh, my. *I hate him, I hate him*, I reminded myself.

Jared flicked the Seether emblem on the left breast of my hoodie. "I'll put on 'Remedy.' Still your favorite song? You give me a quick lap dance, and the party's over." The corners of his mouth turned up, but the dead coldness was still in his eyes. He wanted to humiliate me again. The monster needed to be fed.

Isn't it time you fought back?

If I accepted his offer, Jared would only find some way to back out of the deal and embarrass me. If I didn't accept the offer, we'd be at an impasse. Either way, Jared was aware he didn't have to surrender anything. The jerk also assumed I was too flustered to think of a third choice.

Isn't it time you fought back?

In the brief moment it took me to make my decision, I took one final survey of him. It was such a shame. Jared was stunningly gorgeous, and once upon a time, he was a good guy. If things had been different, I could be his. Once upon a time, I thought I was his. But I wouldn't be sacrificing my pride to him. Ever. Again.

My legs started to shake, but I refused to let go of my resolve.

I backed away and screamed into the living room. "Cops!" Dancers looked around in confusion.

"Cops! Everyone get out of here! Cops coming in the backdoor! Run!" I was surprised by the amount of commitment I could summon to pull this off, but it worked. Damn, it worked!

Pandemonium ensued as the mob reacted with immediate panic. Partiers, the underage ones at least, started scattering to the four winds and seemed to pass the word to the people outside, too. Everyone else grabbed their weed and bottles before running off. They were too drunk to scan the area properly and actually look for the cops. They just ran.

Twisting around to meet Jared's eyes, I took notice that he hadn't reacted. He hadn't moved. As everyone bolted from his house in a flurry of screams and engines revving, Jared just stared at me with a mixture of anger and surprise.

Approaching me slowly, the huge smile that developed across his face forced my stomach to do a cartwheel. Letting out a fake pitiful sigh, he declared, "I'll have you in tears in no time." His tone was calm and decisive. I believed every word.

Taking a long breath, my eyes narrowed at him. "You've already made me cry countless times." I raised my middle finger to him slowly, and asked, "Do you know what this is?" I took my middle finger and patted the corner of my eye with it. "It's me, wiping away the last tear you'll ever get."

Chapter 5

The next few days passed in a flurry of activity as I prepared for school to begin. As much as I tried to talk myself into believing that Jared's silence was a good thing, it was only a matter of time before the other shoe dropped.

My actions at his party had been careless, but sometimes the worst ideas felt the best. Even now, after a week, my pulse sped up, and I couldn't help but grin at the thought of how I'd gotten him. The awareness I'd gained while living abroad made things that were once threatening seem more trivial now. Nervousness still surged in my chest at the thought of Jared, but I no longer felt the need to avoid him at all costs.

"So, are *you* in the fishbowl today!" It wasn't a question. K.C. bounced up next to me as I put my books away. Her hand gripped the top of the locker door as she peeked around it.

"I'm afraid to ask." I let out a small sigh without looking at her. It was the first day back, our first day of senior year. I'd had a full morning of Physics, Calculus, and P.E. I grabbed another notebook for French, which was my last class before lunch.

"So you haven't noticed everyone noticing you today? In a school of about two thousand people, I think you might've caught on that almost all of them were talking about you," she said with a giggle.

"Did I sit in chocolate pudding again? Or maybe a new rumor

is circulating that I spent the past year hiding a pregnancy and gave the baby up for adoption." I slammed my locker door shut then turned to head to French, knowing she'd follow me. I really didn't want to hear what people were saying, partly because I didn't care what bullshit they were circulating now and also because it was nothing new. France had been a peaceful respite, but Shelburne Falls was probably the same old, same old. Thanks to Jared, my high school experience had been one long succession of rumors, pranks, tears, and disappointments. I hoped for more this year, but I wasn't holding my breath either.

"Not even close. And actually, the talk is good. Really good."

"Oh, yeah?" I absent-mindedly responded, hoping she'd sense the disinterested tone and shut up.

"Apparently, your year in Europe has transformed you from ubergeek to ubercool!" K.C. broadcasted sarcastically, knowing that I had never been *ubergeek*. Not that I was ever considered *ubercool* either. My default identity had always been "of those on the outside", but only because the long arm of Jared Trent had deemed me less than acceptable in most social circles.

I jetted up the stairs to the third floor for class, sidestepping other students as they rushed down to their next destination.

"Tate, did you hear me?" K.C. jogged behind me, trying to catch up. "I mean, look around you! Would you stop for two seconds?" she whisper-yelled, eyes pleading when I glanced back at her.

"What?" Her urgency to pass on the latest gossip was amusing, but all I wanted was to walk into school without wearing my invisible body armor. "What's the big deal? So what? People think I look nice today. *Today!* What will they think tomorrow after Jared gets to them?" I hadn't told her about Jared's party and what I'd done. If she knew, she wouldn't be so optimistic about my chances.

"You know, he wasn't that bad after you left. Maybe we're worrying about nothing. All I'm saying is that—" K.C. was cut off.

"Hey, Tate." Ben Jamison came up behind K.C. and reached behind me. "Let me get the door for you."

I stepped aside, giving him room to swing the door open. Having no choice but to end our conversation, I pursed my lips and waved at an open-mouthed K.C.

"It's great having you back," Ben whispered as we walked into class, me first and him close behind. I widened my eyes and had to stifle a nervous laugh. The reality of Ben Jamison engaging me in small talk was too surreal.

He starred on the football and basketball teams and was one of the best looking guys in school. We had been in French I and II together, but he'd never spoken to me.

"Thank you," I muttered, keeping my eyes downcast. This was out of my comfort zone. I slipped stealthily into a front row seat.

It was great having me back? Like he ever cared before? This was probably one of Jared's tricks. I made a mental note to apologize to K.C. for trying to warn me about the unusual attention. Cute guys talking to me equaled unusual.

Madame Lyon, our actual *French* French teacher, started launching into a full-blown lecture right off the bat. Aware of Ben sitting right behind me, I tried to concentrate on the lesson, but even studying Madame's cute, bobbed haircut couldn't take my mind off the stares boring into the back of my head. Out of my peripheral vision, I noticed several students around the room glancing my way. I shifted in my seat. *What was everyone's problem?*

Thinking back to what K.C. had said when I first got back, I didn't really think I looked any different. After all, my year abroad hadn't consisted of any great makeovers or shopping trips. My skin was a little darker, my clothes were new, but my style hadn't changed.

I wore skinny jeans tucked into mid-calf-high black boots with no heels, and a white, flimsy boat neck T-shirt long enough to cover my butt. I loved my style, and no matter what anyone thought, I stuck to it.

After a painfully long fifty-minute class of smiles from unexpected people, I retrieved my phone from my black messenger bag.

See you outside for lunch? I texted K.C.

2 windy! She shot back. *Always about the hair.*

Fine. Heading in now, look for me.

As soon as I stepped in line in the cafeteria, goosebumps crept over my skin. I grabbed a tray and closed my eyes. *He* was in here somewhere. I didn't need to turn around or hear his voice. Maybe it was the climate of the room, the way others traveled or the polarity of his presence in relation to me. All I knew for sure was that he was definitely here.

In elementary school we played with magnets that clash together when you flip them to the positive side, but if you flip them to the negative side, then the magnets will repel each other. Jared was one side of a magnet, never flipping over to accommodate anyone. He was what he was. Everyone else either had a pull to him or was pushed away from him, and the flow of a room reflected this. There was a time when Jared and I were inseparable, like the positive sides of the magnets.

My lungs ached with a breath I didn't realize I'd been holding, and I exhaled. After choosing a salad with Ranch dressing and a water bottle, I handed the cashier my card to swipe and found a seat near the windows. The bustle of the room was an entertaining distraction from meeting his eyes. Several students nodded in passing and offered a "welcome back." My shoulders finally relaxed after the swirl of greetings.

Jess Cullen waved to me from a few tables over, and I reminded myself about practice this afternoon.

Where are you? K.C. shot a text.
By the north windows.
In line now!

K. I texted back. Twisting around in my seat, I spotted her in line. I gave her a little wave to signal my location and quickly turned back around before I gave in to the urge to scan the room for *him*.

Twisting the cap off my water bottle, I took a long swig, relishing the relief. It felt like my heart had been beating a mile a minute for the last hour. *Hydrate, hydrate, hydrate.*

My relaxation, however, was cut short by the voice of Madoc Caruthers.

"Hey, baby." Madoc placed his hand on the table to my side and leaned into my ear. As I replaced the cap on my water bottle, my shoulders slumped slightly. *Not again! Didn't the little fucker ever learn a lesson?* I stared straight ahead in an effort to ignore him.

"Tate?" He was trying to goad me into acknowledging him. Non-confrontational me was still not making eye contact.

"Tate? I know you can hear me. In fact, I know every part of you is *very* aware of me right now." Madoc ran the knuckles of his left hand down my arm. I sucked in a breath, and my body jerked at his touch.

"Mmmm, you've got goosebumps. You see?" He toyed with me.

Goosebumps? If I weren't so sickened, I would laugh. "Yes, you do make my skin crawl. But you knew that, right?" My disdain couldn't get any thicker.

"I really missed you last year, and I would actually like to call a truce. In fact, why don't we put everything behind us and you let me take you out this weekend?"

He had to be dreaming if he thought—

His hand glided down my back and quickly descended to my rear. I sucked in another breath.

Son of a bitch! Did he really just grab my ass? Without my permission? In public? *Oh, no.*

Then, he squeezed.

Everything after that point happened in a rush of reaction and adrenaline. I popped out of my seat like my legs had springs. The muscles in my thighs were taut with tension, and I clenched my fists.

As I faced Madoc, who had raised himself to meet my gaze, I grabbed him by the shoulders and lifted my knee into his groin. Hard. The amount of pressure must've been a lot, because he yelped and fell to his knees, moaning while holding his crotch.

I had been manhandled by Madoc enough. There was no way I was going to be able to turn the other cheek anymore. Breaking his nose a year ago clearly wasn't the end of my rope. It was the start of a new one.

With my heart pounding and a cool heat surging down my arms, I didn't stop to think about where this would put me tomorrow or next week. I just wanted him to stop.

Jared had been threatening for years, but he had never crossed *that* line. He had never touched me or made me feel physically violated. Madoc always crossed the line, and I wondered what the fuck was his problem! If what Sam had said was true, that I was off limits, then why did Madoc mess with me so much? And in plain sight of Jared?

"Don't touch me and don't talk to me." I hovered over him, sneering. Madoc's eyes were closed as he breathed hard. "Did you

41

really think I would go out with you? I hear the girls talk, and contrary to popular belief, good things do *not* come in small packages." The entire room erupted in laughter, and I crooked my pinky finger to the bystanders. I spotted K.C., tray in hand and an "oh, my God" expression on her face.

"Thanks for the offer anyway, Madoc," I sang with mock sweetness. Grabbing my tray, I headed through the ocean of eyes and threw away my food. The only thing that mattered was making it out of the lunchroom before I crumbled. Everything felt weak with tingles, and I was afraid my legs would give out. What had I just done?

But before I reached the doors, I threw caution to the wind. *Oh what the hell, I've developed a death wish lately. May as well drown in it.* I turned around and immediately locked eyes with the one person that made my blood boil more than Madoc.

Jared's full attention was focused on me, and the world in my peripheral vision stopped as we stared at each other.

He wore dark distressed jeans and a black T-shirt. No jewelry, no watch, only his tattoos as accessories. His lips were slightly parted but not smiling. Those eyes, however, seemed challenging and too damn interested. He looked like he was sizing me up.

Fuck. Shit.

Leaning back in his chair, he had one arm hooked behind him on the back of his seat and one arm resting on the table. He was staring at me, and unwanted heat rushed to my face.

There was a time when I had all of his attention and loved it. As much as I wanted him to leave me alone, I also liked how he seemed surprised. I liked the way he was looking at me right now.

And then I remembered that I hated him.

Chapter 6

The rest of the day unfolded as one surreal moment after another. I had to constantly tell myself that I was in a dream and this wasn't really the first day of school. I received mounds of admiration over my lunchtime rumble, and I felt like this couldn't really be my life.

After my high dissipated, it occurred me that I'd hit another student on school grounds. I could get in trouble—a lot of trouble—for that. Every announcement or knock at a classroom door had my hands shaking.

I texted K.C. after leaving the lunchroom and apologized for ditching her. Since I hid in the library for the rest of lunch, I had time to try to figure out what the hell was going on with me. Why hadn't I just walked away from Madoc? Had it been fun to knee him in the balls? Yes. But I was losing control lately, and perhaps I was taking K.C.'s advice of fighting back too literally.

"Hey, Jackie Chan!" Maci Feldman, a fellow senior in my Government class, sat down next to me. She immediately reached into her purse and pulled out a tube of glittery pink lip gloss, applying it while eyeing me happily.

"Jackie Chan?" Raising my eyebrows, I pulled a new notebook out of my messenger bag.

"That's one of your new nicknames. The others are Super Bitch and Ball Buster. I like Jackie Chan." She smacked her lips together and slipped the gloss back into her purse.

"I like Super Bitch," I mumbled as Mr. Brimeyer handed out the syllabus with a questionnaire attached.

Maci whispered, "You know, a lot of girls were happy about that scene in the lunchroom. Madoc's slept with half the senior class, not to mention some juniors, and he deserved what he got."

Not knowing how to respond, I just nodded. I wasn't used to people being on my side. My responses to Jared's and Madoc's antics might have changed, but my goal to keep my head focused on school remained the same. My first day had included too much drama already. If I'd kept my head down, I might've escaped notice for the most part. But it was almost as if I had no desire to be silent anymore, and my actions were inviting more trouble. *What was I doing? And why wasn't I stopping?*

Catching up with Madame Lyon after school, I was able to get my mind off the day's events. She expected me to speak to her entirely in French now, and it irked me that the German I learned during the summer was getting me flustered. I kept saying things like "*Ich bin bien*" instead of "*Je suis très bien*," and "*Danke*" instead of "*Merci*." But we laughed, and it wasn't long before I got my sea legs back.

Coach Robinson wanted us on the bleachers by 3:00, so I ran to get changed for cross-country practice. After a year away, my spot on the team didn't exist, but I had every intention of earning it back.

"Have you had any backlash from what happened at lunch?" Jess Cullen, our captain now, questioned me as we headed for the locker room after practice.

"Not yet. I'm sure it will come tomorrow, though. Hopefully the Dean will go easy on me. I've never been in trouble before," I replied hopefully.

"No, I mean from Madoc. You don't have to worry about the

Dean. Jared took care of that." She glanced back at me as we walked down the aisle to our gym lockers.

I froze. "What do you mean?"

She opened her locker door and stopped to smile at me. "Mr. Sweeney came by right after you left the lunchroom asking what happened. Jared walked over and said Madoc slipped and fell into a table or a chair . . . or something." Jess laughed.

I couldn't help myself either. It was too ridiculous.

"Slipped and fell into a table? And he believed him?"

"Well, probably not, but everyone backed him up, so there was little Mr. Sweeney could say about it." She started shaking her head in disbelief. "And when Madoc finally got back on his feet, he backed up the story, too."

No, no, no. They did not save my ass!

Caving, I took a seat on the bench in the middle of the aisle and planted my head into my hands.

"What's wrong? This is good news." She took a seat next to me and began removing her shoes and socks.

"No, I think I'd rather be in trouble with the Dean than indebted to those jerks." They wouldn't have covered for me unless they wanted to administer the punishment themselves.

"Aren't you applying to Columbia? I don't think they're interested in bright, young, scientific minds that have a penchant for assaulting guys. Just saying, anything is probably better than this winding up on your record."

She rose, finished stripping down, and headed to the shower with her towel. I stayed there a few moments, contemplating her final words. She was right. I had a lot going for me if I could keep my eyes on the ball. My grades were great, I was fluent in French, had a year abroad under my belt and a slew of note-worthy extra-curricular activities. I could survive whatever Jared had up his sleeve.

My first day back at Shelburne Falls High School was more eventful than I would have liked, but I was being noticed in a positive way. I might actually leave my senior year with a few good memories, like homecoming and prom.

Grabbing my towel, I headed for the showers.

The hot water cascaded down my back, giving me the kind of chills you get when you're cozy and enjoying something completely pleasurable. After the workout Coach gave us, I ended up lounging under the exhilarating pressure of the shower for longer than anyone else. My muscles were exhausted.

After coming out wrapped in my towel, I joined the other girls at the lockers, who were mostly dressed and going to dry their hair.

"Get out. Tatum stays."

I jerked my head up at the masculine voice and audible gasps. I zoned in on Jared. ...who was in the *girls'* locker room! I clutched my towel, which was still wrapped around my body, and pulled it tighter as I frantically looked around for Coach.

A chill ran over my body. His eyes were on me as he spoke to everyone else, and it made me disgusted with my sex to see how everyone scurried away, leaving me alone with a boy who had no right to be in here.

"Are you kidding me?!" I heaved at him as his advancing steps matched my retreating ones.

"Tatum"—he hadn't used my nickname *Tate* since we were kids—"I wanted to make sure I had your attention. Do I have it?" He looked relaxed, his beautiful eyes bore into mine making me feel like there was no one else in the entire world but us.

"Say what you have to say. I'm naked here, and I'm about to scream. This is going too far, even for you!" I stopped retreating, but my frustration was evident as my voice raised and my breathing quickened. Score one for Jared. He'd surprised me, and now I was completely vulnerable. No lifelines and . . . no clothes.

46

I clutched the towel at the top of my breasts with one hand and hugged myself with the other. All of my important parts were covered, but the towel rode up just under my butt, leaving most of my legs exposed. Jared narrowed his eyes at me before they began to fall downward ... and kept going. My mind swirled and my face flushed with heat as he continued checking me out. His intimidation tactics were stellar.

No smirk accompanied his violation. He didn't eye-fuck me like Madoc did. His roaming gaze was reluctant, as if it was involuntary. His chest heaved slightly, and his breathing got heavier. Tingles covered my body, and another sensation I was a little pissed off about settled between my legs.

After a few moments, his gaze met mine again. The corners of his mouth turned up.

"You sabotaged my party last week. And you assaulted my friend. Twice. Are you actually trying to assert some force in this school, Tatum?"

"I think it's about time, don't you?" Surprising myself, I didn't blink.

"On the contrary," he said, leaning his shoulder into the lockers and crossing his arms. "I've moved on to more interesting pastimes than punking you, believe it or not. It's been a very peaceful year without your smug, I'm-too-good-for-everyone-else fucking face around these halls."

His biting tone was old news, but the words cut me, and I clenched my teeth.

I mocked him with fake concern. "What—are you, big, bad Jared—feeling threatened?" *What the hell was I doing?* I had an out. He was confronting me. I should be trying to talk to him. Why wasn't I trying to reason with him?

In an instant, he pushed off the lockers and invaded my space. Walking up to me, he placed his hands against the locker doors on both sides of my head with his eyes glaring down at me. I suddenly forgot how to breathe.

"Don't touch me." I'd meant to yell, but it came out as a whisper. Even with my eyes to the floor, I could feel the heat of his stare mauling me as he hovered. Every nerve in my body was on alert at his proximity, and every little hair on my skin stood on end.

Jared moved his head from side to side trying to catch my eyes, his lips inches from my face. "If I ever lay my hands on you," he said low and husky, "you'll want it." He brought his lips in even closer. The heat of his breath covered my face. "Do you? Want it, I mean?"

I met his eyes and breathed him in. There was something I was going to say, but I completely forgot it as his scent invaded my brain. I liked it when men wore cologne, but Jared didn't wear any. Good. Awesome. The jerk just smelled like soap. Yummy, delicious, musky bodywash.

Shit, Tate! Get a grip.

His hooded stare faltered while I maintained eye contact. "I'm bored," I finally choked out. "Are you going to tell me what you want or what?"

"You know?" He looked at me curiously. "This new attitude you came back with? It surprised me. You used to be a pretty dull target. All you'd do was run away or cry. Now you've got some fight in you. I was prepared to leave you alone this year. But now . . ." he trailed off.

"What will you do? Trip me in class? Spill O.J. on my shirt? Spread rumors about me, so I don't get any dates? Or maybe you'll up your game to cyberbullying." Though that was no joke, and I immediately regretted giving him the idea. "Do you really think any of it bugs me anymore? You can't scare me."

I should shut up. Why wasn't I shutting up?

48

He studied me as I tried to control my temper. Why did he always appear so calm, so unaffected? He never yelled or flew off the handle. His temper was in check, whereas my blood boiled to the point that I felt like I could go another round with Madoc.

My eyes were level with his mouth as he leaned in slowly. One of his arms stretched over my head resting on the lockers to bring his face within an inch from mine. A sexy grin played on his lips, and I had a difficult time looking away from his full mouth.

"Do you think you're strong enough to take me on?" His slow, soothing whisper caressed my face. If it weren't for his formidable words, his tone might've calmed me . . . or something.

I should've moved away, but I wanted to appear confident by standing my ground. I could give back as good as I got. At least I thought I could.

"It's on." My stare met his as the raspy challenge left my throat.

"Tatum Brandt!" Shocked out of the strange trance Jared created, I looked up to see Coach and half the team at the end of the row staring at us.

"Coach!" I knew there was something for me to say, but words failed. Horror took root in my brain and held it hostage as I tried to search for an explanation. Jared was leaned into me, speaking intimately. It couldn't have looked good. A few of the girls had their phones out, and I cringed at the sound of pictures being taken. *No!*

Dammit!

"There are other places for you two to do this." Coach spoke to me but then looked to Jared. "Mr. Trent? Leave!" She spoke through her teeth, and the girls around her stood giggling behind their hands. No one looked away.

Jared assaulted me with a smug grin before walking out of the locker room, winking at some salivating girls as he left.

Realization dawned, and my eyes widened. He'd planned this!

"Coach—" I started and pulled the towel tighter around me.

"Ladies," Coach interrupted me, "get on home. We'll see you Wednesday. Tate? I'll see you in my office before you leave. Get dressed."

"Yes, ma'am." My pulse thumped in my ears. I'd never been in trouble before, not at school. I dressed quickly and tied my wet hair into a bun before hauling ass to Coach's office. Only a few minutes had passed, but I guessed those pictures were probably up on the Internet already. I wiped the sweat off my forehead and swallowed down the bile rising in my throat.

Jared had sunk low—really low—this time. I came back to town prepared for another year of aggravations and embarrassments, but it chilled my bones when I realized how our exchange must've looked. The rumors before had been just that, but now there were witnesses and evidence to our encounter.

Tomorrow, half the school would have some version of what was happening in those pictures. If I was lucky, the story would be that I'd thrown myself at him. If I was unlucky, the rumor would be more sordid.

Jess exited Coach's office as I made my way in that direction. "Hey." She stopped me. "I talked to Coach. She knows Jared ambushed you in there . . . that he wasn't invited. I'm sorry I abandoned you like that."

"Thanks." Relief flooded me. At least my butt was safe from Coach's wrath.

"No problem. Just please don't tell anyone I spoke up for you. If people knew I got Jared in trouble, it wouldn't be good," Jess explained.

"Are you scared of him?" Jared had a lot of power around school.

"No." She shook her head. "Jared's fine. He can be a jerk if he's provoked, but he's never concerned me. Honestly, it seems like you're the only one he wants to beat down—metaphorically speaking, of course." Jess's narrowed eyes made me think she was turning over something in her head.

"Yeah, well. Lucky me."

"Jared's important around here, so I don't want people getting on my case about ratting him out." Her eyebrows lifted as she waited for my understanding.

I nodded, wondering what the hell Jared did to deserve anyone's loyalty.

Chapter 7

The fishbowl got smaller over the next few days.

Some people heard that Jared and I were in the locker room having sex. Others believed that I'd invited him in an effort to seduce him. A few thought that he'd come in to threaten me after the episode with Madoc. Whatever story people latched on to, I was receiving more stares and hearing more whispers behind my back.

"Hey, Tate. Do you just screw in the locker room or do you do blowjobs as well?" Hannah Forrest, queen bee of the mean girls, shouted to my back while I walked to Calculus. Her drones laughed with her.

I spun around to face them and held my hand to my heart. "And steal all of your business?" I took the time to enjoy their dumbstruck looks before I twisted on my heel and headed to class.

As I disappeared around the corner, the echo of expletives from her and her crew brought a smile to my face. I'd been called a bitch before, and it didn't hurt the way being called a slut did. Being a bitch could be a survival technique. They get respect. There was no honor in people thinking you were a slut.

Jared must not have received much of a punishment for being in the girls' locker room, since he was at school every day. He didn't look at me or otherwise acknowledge me even though we shared a class together. I had transferred out of a Computer class in the afternoons, having already exceeded the senior syllabus in France, and transferred into Themes in Film and Literature without knowing he was in that class, too. The elective was supposed to be a cruise course, lots of movies and reading.

"Tate, do you have an extra pen I could borrow?" Ben Jamison asked when we sat down in Themes. He, thankfully, had continued to be friendly and respectful in French, despite the current talk, and I was relieved with the distraction from Jared in this class.

"Um . . ." I reached in my messenger bag, searching. "I think so. Here we go." Ben awarded me with a brilliant smile that accentuated his dark blond hair and green eyes. Our fingers touched, and I pulled away quickly, dropping the pen before he'd grasped it.

I don't know why I'd pulled away, but I felt Jared's eyes wash over the back of my head.

"No, I got it." He stopped me as I bent over to grab it. "Don't let me walk off with it at the end of class, though."

"Keep it." I waved my hand in the air. "I'm stocked. I mostly use pencils, anyway. With all of my Science and Math classes, it's a necessity. Especially with me . . . lots of erasing." I was trying at humility, but it came out as verbal diarrhea instead.

"Oh yeah, that's right. I forgot you were into that stuff." He probably didn't forget. He almost certainly had no idea. My nostrils flared with the reminder of all of the damage Jared had done. He was the reason more boys hadn't taken an interest in me.

"I'm trying to get into Columbia, pre-med. What about you?" I inquired. I hoped I didn't sound like I was bragging, but I didn't feel self-conscious with Ben. His family owned a newspaper, and his grandfather was a judge. He'd probably be applying to Ivy League schools, too.

"I'm applying to a few places. I have no head for Math or Science, though. It'll be Business for me."

"Well, I hope you like some Math. Business goes with

Economics, you know?" I pointed out. His eyes widened, and I realized he didn't know.

"Uh, yeah." He looked confused, but recovered quickly. "Absolutely. As long as it's not too much." He smiled nervously as I registered a snicker coming from behind me.

"So ... " I tried to change the subject. "You're on the Homecoming Committee, right?"

"Yeah. You coming?" Ben looked excited.

"We'll see. Have you booked a band, or is there a D.J.?" *Band. Band. Band.*

"A band would be nice, but they tend to play one genre of music, so it's hard to please everyone. We'll have a D.J. I think that's what everyone decided. He'll keep the party going with a good mix: pop, country ... " He cast a smile as he trailed off, while I struggled to keep a happy face.

"Oh ... pop and country? Can't go wrong there." I mentally cringed as I registered another snicker behind me, this time louder. Without the sense to let it go like the last time, I glanced back to Jared, whose eyes were downcast as he fiddled on his phone. But I saw his lips turned up and knew his pent-up amusement was provoked by my conversation with Ben.

Jackass.

Jared knew I hated country music and had little tolerance for pop. As did he.

"So, you like pop and country?" I redirected my attention to Ben. *Please say "no." Please say "no."*

"Mostly country."

Ugh, that's worse.

Math and Science? Negative. Musical tastes? Negative. Ok, last ditch effort to find something in common with the guy I would be sitting next to in two classes this semester. The teacher was going to be in soon.

"You know, I heard we get to watch *The Sixth Sense* in here this semester. Have you seen it?" My phone beeped with a text notification, but I silenced it and stuck it in my bag.

"Oh, yeah. A long time ago, though. I didn't get it. I'm not a big fan of those thriller-mystery type movies. I like comedies. Maybe she'll let us watch Borat." He wiggled his eyebrows teasingly.

"Hey, Jamison?" Jared piped up from behind us, his inflection overly polite. "If you like Bruce Willis, *Unbreakable* is a good one. You should give it a shot. . . .you know, if you're looking to change your mind about thrillers that is."

My desk had suddenly become the most interesting view. I refused to turn around and face Jared. Words failed me when I realized that he'd remembered.

Ben turned in his seat and responded, "Yeah, I'll remember that. Thanks." He turned back around and flashed me a smile.

Jared was bold. He wanted me to know he remembered that Bruce Willis was my favorite actor. We had watched *Die Hard* one day when my father was gone, because Dad wouldn't let me see it due to all of the swearing. Jared had a lot of knowledge about me, and I resented that. He didn't have the right to claim any part of me.

"Alright, class," Mrs. Penley called out with a stack of papers in her hands. "In addition to the packet I am handing out, Trevor is giving you a template of a compass. Please write your name at the top, but leave the areas surrounding North, East, South, and West blank."

We all took papers, stuffing the list from Mrs. Penley to the side and following the directions regarding the compass. Starting class with an activity relieved me. The tormenting pressure of the stare I could feel boring into the back of my head was distracting, to say the least.

"Ok." Mrs. Penley clapped her hands together. "The packets I gave you are lists of films where important monologues occurred. As we've already started discussing monologues and their importance in Film and Literature, I would like you to start looking up a few of these on the Internet for research. We'll discuss, during tomorrow's class, your first project for presenting a monologue to the class."

Solo presentation. Ugh! Acting out a monologue. Double ugh!

"Also," Mrs. Penley continued, "for various discussions this year, you'll be asked to pair up with a different person in class. You'll know who to pair up with based on this compass. You'll have five minutes to circulate the classroom finding partners for your North, South, East, and West. Whoever you pick to fill in on your North, for example, they will also put you as their North, and so on. Kind of elementary, I know, but it'll help mix things up."

Group work was fine occasionally, but I preferred to work on my own. My nose scrunched up at the thought of hearing "Buddy up!" constantly this year. Dreadful words.

"Go!" the teacher shouted. The screech of chairs scraping across the floor filled the room. Grabbing my paper and pencil, I started looking for someone not already paired up. As I looked around, others were jotting each other's names down, while I hadn't even started.

Ben grinned and nodded at me, so I filed over to him where we exchanged names on East. Catching sight of others' papers and their blanks, I was able to secure West and South from two girls.

I need a North. I mentally sang to myself as I looked around for another partner. Almost everyone scampered to their seats as the five minutes came to a close. I glanced to Jared, who I don't think even got out of his seat. Everyone probably rushed over to him.

This was the part of school I hated. The sinking feeling in my stomach reminded me of all the awkward times, before France, that I'd felt left out. Grade school was easy. I had friends and never had to feel lonely in these situations. High school had made me less confident and more introverted.

I was still down one partner and would be left odd man out again. Weary of this feeling after being accepted in France for a year, I grabbed the bull by the horns.

"Mrs. Penley, I'm missing a North. Is it alright if I make a threesome with two others?"

Snorts sounded around the room, while some whispered under their breath. I knew I'd walked into that one.

"Hey, Tate. I'll do a threesome with you. My compass always points North." Nate Dietrich fist-bumped his buddy as others laughed again.

Surprising myself, I threw back, "Thanks, but I think your right hand will get jealous." The class erupted in *Whoas* and *Burn!*

It was that easy. Due to the use of a couple of immature quips today, I was able to regain a little respect from my classmates. Who knew? Pride hit me, and I had to bite back a smile.

"Does anyone need a North?" Mrs. Penley interrupted the barbs before Nate could shoot back with something else.

Everyone else was seated, meaning they had all of their partners. I kept my attention on Mrs. Penley, waiting for her to just tell me to find a threesome.

"She can be my North." Jared's formidable voice hit me from behind, sending shivers down my spine.

The teacher looked expectantly to me. This couldn't be happening. Why hadn't he gotten off his ass and found a North like everyone else?

"Well, Tate. Go ahead then," Mrs. Penley urged me.

Spinning around, I practically huffed back to my seat without sparing a glanced at my North, and carved *"Jared"* on my paper . . . and I think accidentally on my desk, too.

Chapter 8

"So when do you come home exactly?" My Calculus homework was done, and my Government book was cradled in my lap as I video chatted with Dad.

"I'll be home by the twenty-second for sure."

Still more than three months away. My dad's arrival back home would be welcome. My days felt lonely without him to share things with, and after my mom passed away from cancer, our home was even emptier without him around. K.C. and I had spent time together, but she had a boyfriend. I was slowly making more friends at school, despite Jared's latest blow to my reputation, but I'd decided to stay in this weekend and focus on planning for the Science Fair. I'd yet to decide on my research topic.

"Well, I can't wait. We need a decent cook around here," I chirped, holding my steaming cup of tomato soup. As light as my supper was, the cascading warmth soothed my body. My limbs were still adjusting to the cross-country practices.

"That's not your supper, is it?"

"Yeah." I drew it out like *"duh."*

"And where are the vegetables, the grains, and the dairy?"

Oh, here we go. "The tomatoes in the soup are the vegetable, there's milk in the soup too, and I'll make a grilled cheese to go with it if that'll make you happy." My playful air told my dad *"see, I'm smarter than I look."*

"Actually, tomatoes are a fruit," Dad responded flatly, knocking me off my pedestal.

Laughing, I put the cup down and picked up a pencil to continue my outline for the essay we were assigned on Henry Kissinger. "No worries, Dad. I'm eating fine. Soup just sounded good tonight."

"Alright, I'll back off. I just worry. You inherited my eating habits. Your mom would freak if she saw the things I let you eat." Dad frowned, and I knew he still missed Mom like it was yesterday. We both did.

After a moment, he continued, "You've got August's bills all paid, right? And you have plenty of money in your account still?"

"I haven't blown my entire trust in a week. Everything's under control." He did this every time we talked. I had complete access to the life insurance my mom left me, and he still always asked if I had enough money. It was like I was going to go ballistic with my college fund without him looking, and he knew better. Maybe he thought he was doing his job as a parent the best he could from so far away.

My phone buzzed with a text, and I grabbed it off my bedside table.

Be there in 5.

"Oh, Dad? I forgot K.C. is stopping over. Can I let you go?"

"Sure, but I'll be leaving tomorrow for a day or so. Taking the train to Nuremberg for some sightseeing. I want to chat with you in the morning before I leave and hear about the Science Fair prep you're doing."

Ugh, shit. No prep had been organized, because I hadn't even come close to deciding my project.

"Okay, Dad," I mumbled, leaving that discussion for tomorrow. "Call me at seven?"

"Talk to you then, sweetie. Bye." And he was gone.

Closing my laptop and tossing my book onto the bed, I walked to the French doors and opened them wide. School had ended for the week three hours ago, but the sun still cast a radiant glow around the neighborhood. Leaves from the maple outside my doors rustled in the subtle breeze, and a few tiny clouds sprinkled the sky.

Turning around, I slipped out of my school clothes and into a pair of plaid pajama shorts with a white and gray fitted raglan T-shirt. I let out an overly dramatic sigh. *Of course, I would be in my pajamas at six p.m. on a Friday night.*

The doorbell echoed from downstairs, and I jogged to answer the door.

"Hey!" K.C. breathed, stepping into the house with her arms loaded down. *What the hell?* We were just doing my hair, not a makeover.

My eyes watered at her perfume. "What's that scent you're wearing?"

"Oh, it's new. It called *Secret*. You like?"

"Love it." Don't loan it to me.

"Let's go up to your room. I want to have access to your bathroom when we do this." K.C. insisted on coming over to give me a honey hair treatment she read about in *Women's Day*. It's supposed to soothe sun-damaged hair, which she says is a danger with all of the outdoor sightseeing I did this summer and with the cross-country practice.

Okay, so I didn't really care. I thought my hair looked fine, but I wanted to catch up with her after the busy first week.

"Can I take the chair to the window? There's a nice breeze coming in." The honey would be messy, but the room boasted dark hardwood floors, so it would be an easy cleanup.

"Yeah, sure. Just take your hair out of the ponytail and brush it out." She handed me a brush, and I positioned myself in front of the doors, enjoying the serene evening.

"I'm going to put some olive oil in, to thin it out, and a bit of egg yolk for protein."

"Whatever you say," I accepted.

As she mixed the ingredients and brought me a towel to protect my clothes, I caught sight of Jared backing up his car from the garage into the driveway. My stomach fluttered, and I realized my teeth were clenched together like glue.

His black T-shirt rode up as he got out and popped the hood. Grabbing a towel out of the back pocket of his jeans, he used it to unfasten something under the hood.

"So you like the view?" K.C.'s voice made me blink as she appeared at my side. I quickly looked down.

"Back off," I mumbled.

"It's fine. For an asshole, he's pretty." She began dampening my hair with a water bottle, while running her fingers through the wet strands.

"But he's still an asshole." I looked for a change of subject. "So, how bad is it? The talk at school, I mean?" I had stayed far away from Facebook, Twitter, and the cheer team's secret blog. Seeing pictures of myself in a towel, photos that everyone in town had probably seen, would only make me want to jump a plane back to France . . . or murder someone.

K.C. shrugged. "It's already dying down. People are still circulating this story or that, but it's lost its momentum. I told you, no prank or rumor will keep the guys away this year. And with this hair treatment, you'll be absolutely fabulous." I couldn't see her face, but I was sure she was kidding around with me. *Absolutely Fabulous* was a British television show we watched on Comedy Central a couple of summers ago.

I tossed around the idea of telling K.C. about the things Madoc told me at Jared's party—the date sabotaging and the rumors. But the drama that followed me every year was embarrassing. I had no interest in being one of those friends always caught up in trouble, so I tried to act like it all bothered me less than it really did.

As she started brushing the syrupy mixture onto my hair, my eyes darted to Jared, who was now pulling his shirt over his head. His amazingly toned arms were put to shame when he turned around, and I saw his chiseled torso. My mouth went dry, and chills shot out like needles over my body.

It was the breeze. It was totally the breeze.

"Oh, you get to look at that every day?"

I rolled my eyes. "No, I *have* to look at that every day. Whose side are you on, anyway?" My whine was meant as a joke, but I wasn't sure it came out that way.

"The boy doesn't have to talk for me to look. I'm appreciating from afar."

"You have Liam, remember?" It bugged me that she was drooling over Jared, even if it was jokingly. He was beautiful, but it didn't need to be pointed out like it actually mattered. His personality sucked.

"How's everything going with you and Liam?" I hadn't seen him, except in passing since being back to school.

"Oh, we're fine. He's gotten his Camaro ready for the Loop, and he's been hanging out down there a lot. I've gone once, but it's boring hanging on his arm while he discusses cars all night. He doesn't even race yet. Apparently, there's a waiting list, and even then you're behind proven cars that get first dibs, because that's who the audience wants to see."

I hated to ask, but it spilled out anyway. "How's Asshole performing out there?" *Why did I need to know that?*

"Jared? He's one of the ones that doesn't have to wait. He can usually just race whenever the mood suits him. According to Liam, he's out there either on Friday or Saturday nights but not usually both."

"Are you spending enough time with Liam?" I'd noticed a change in tone and demeanor when I'd brought him up.

She shrugged. "I feel bad, because I should take an interest in his hobbies, I guess. It's just that, if he's not going to race, I feel like I'm wallpaper standing at his side. I don't know many people or anything about the car scene."

"Well, maybe you could just go once in a while? Tough it out for him now and then?" I suggested as the weight of my head increased with the amount of honey she piled on.

"I don't know." K.C. walked around me to the doors and peered out. "I'm thinking of coming over to your house more instead."

I gave her a light kick on the leg.

"Mmm . . ." She devoured Jared with her eyes as she backed up to my hair. "I hate to say it, but I wonder what it'd be like to have him."

"K.C.! Stop it. You're my friend," I scolded.

"I'm sorry, okay? It's just that he wasn't that bad while you were gone. Honestly. He wasn't the hell raiser he was before you left."

"What do you mean?"

"I don't know. I don't even know if it had anything to do with you. He seemed moodier for a while but then got better. It's just that I got to see him with different eyes. Before it was always about how he treated you—which was horrible," she rushed to add. "But after you left, he seemed different. More human."

The idea of present-day Jared as human was incomprehensible to me. He was driven, confident, and severe. That's the only side of him I'd seen since we were fourteen. I hadn't seen him happy in years, and I thought for sure he'd be pleased as punch to be rid of me for a year.

But why had he acted moodier *after* I left? It didn't make sense.

Was he having a hard time entertaining himself without his favorite chew toy?

Aww, poor baby.

Chapter 9

"Ugh!" I let out a guttural moan into the darkness as I stared at my ceiling that night, which was lit up by the headlights of another arrival next door.

It was after one in the morning, and the bombardment of party noises coming from next door wouldn't relent. The pillow brought up to both of my ears to drown out the sounds hadn't helped. Texting K.C. to text Liam to text Jared hadn't helped. Calling the police and filing a complaint an hour ago hadn't helped.

If it wasn't the loud music or the constant arrival and departure of muscle cars with their sorry exhaust systems, then it was the shouting or laughing coming from Jared's yards. I liked loud music, but a party in the middle of the night that was keeping the whole neighborhood awake should be shut down.

Throwing the covers off, I stomped out of bed and stood at the French doors. His whole house was lit up and bustling with noise and activity. Some people stumbled around the front yard, which was littered with red Solo cups, and some gathered in the backyard either smoking or enjoying the hot tub.

He is such a dick! My hands were on my hips, gripping harder than usual. What kind of person had no regard for anyone else? The self-absorbed asswipe living next to me, I guess. I had a video chat with my dad in six hours, and I wasn't going to be up all night just because they wanted to get drunk and high.

Screw it. I slipped on my purple Chucks and black hoodie and headed downstairs.

I opened the door in the kitchen leading to the garage and went to my dad's workbench, still as organized as we'd left it. Grabbing the big bolt cutters from the bottom tool-box drawer, I maneuvered them up my right sleeve. With my free hand, I opened another drawer and picked a padlock out of the three extras. Sliding that into the front pocket of my hoodie, I headed out.

I rounded the corner of my house and strode to the rear, my heart beating faster with every step. Finding the hole I had made in the hedge years ago, I swiped the new growth aside and slipped through. As I took a right and continued to walk, I could hear the partygoers in his backyard on the other side of the hedge. I was about five feet away from them, but there was no way they could see me.

Jared's backyard, as well as mine, was encased by fences on the sides and tall hedges on the back. When I made it to the fence at the other side of his house, I poked my hand through the dense brush of leaves. I tried to push the branches aside as much as possible but still the needle-like sprigs scraped and stung my legs as I shimmied my way through.

The party was going hard, and there were tons of people here. What I was going to do needed to happen fast.

Taking several glances in all directions to make sure I had arrived unnoticed, I jogged up the side of Jared's house to the circuit breaker. I'd spent enough time at his house as a kid to be able to find it in the dark. I slid the bolt cutter out of my thin sleeve and clamped both handles down with all of my strength on the padlock securing the panel. As soon as I'd shoved the old padlock into my pocket, I opened the panel door and began flipping switches.

I tried not to register what was happening around the house, the sudden loss of music and light, and the cacophony of *What the fuck?* coming from everywhere. I finished flipping switches, took the new padlock out of my sweater, and secured it to the closed panel.

Jared wasn't stupid. Once he realized that no other houses had lost electricity, he'd be out here checking the circuit breaker. So I got out of there. Fast.

Running with JELL-O-like legs and sliding back through behind the hedge, I started panting instantly. A drop of sweat glided down my back, and I realized that I wanted to laugh, scream, and throw up all at the same time. I wasn't certain which law I'd just broken, but I was sure I'd get into some kind of trouble if anyone found out. My legs pumped with liquid heat, making my knees feeble.

The anxiety of being caught drove my tense muscles back through my side of the brush and into the garage. I couldn't help the ear-to-ear smile on my face. I was scared of being caught, but the feeling of giving him a metaphorical kick in the ass made my toes curl.

And after all of that, I wasn't tired anymore. *Just fucking awesome.*

I made sure the doors were locked, out of habit, and ran up the stairs, two steps at a time. I closed the door to my room and, keeping the lights off, went to the French doors and peered outside in hopes of seeing the party disperse. I scanned the front and back yards, and, thankfully, saw a few people heading to their cars. I grimaced as I thought that maybe putting drunken people on the road wasn't the smartest idea.

I saw more and more people heading to their cars and some starting to walk down the street to their homes. The only way Jared could get the electricity back on was by cutting the lock or calling the electric company.

As I glanced around, from the front to the back, my eyes quickly reverted to the one light I did see. Jared was standing at his bedroom window with a flashlight in one hand and both hands on either side of the window frame above his head.

And he was staring at me.

Shit!

My pulse sped up again, and a scorching heat washed over my body. My sheer, black curtains were drawn, but I was positive he could see me. His head was bowed in my direction, and he was still . . . too still.

Throwing off my hoodie and climbing into bed, I resolved to deny anything if he came to my door. *Or maybe I shouldn't,* I thought. It wasn't like he could do a damn thing about it, anyway. Maybe I wanted him to know.

I lay there for about two minutes resisting the urge to investigate what was going on outside. It wasn't hard to figure out that the party was dispersing, though, as the sound of engines fading away filled the neighborhood. Thrill surged through my body, giving me energy enough to want to hop out of bed and start dancing.

I'm awesome, I'm awesome, I sang to myself.

But I froze mid-song and damn near choked on a breath at the sound of a door slamming shut through the house.

My house!

68

Chapter 10

"What the . . . " Tremors shook my legs down to my bones. Was that the vibrations or me shaking?

Scrambling out of the covers, I grabbed my baseball bat from under the bed and ran out of the room. I had no intention of going downstairs, even though that's where I'd stupidly left the pistol. I just needed to peek over the railing to see if I'd actually heard someone entering my house.

My body instantly reacted at the sight of shirtless Jared rounding the corner into the foyer and flying up the stairs. He was definitely pissed and primed for murder with the way he charged up the staircase, taking two at a time. I darted back into my room, letting out a little yelp as I tried to run for the French doors and escape. I had no idea what Jared's plan was or if I should be afraid, but I was. He'd just broken into my house and that freaked me out.

"Oh no, you don't!" Jared burst through my bedroom door, and the doorknob slammed against the wall, probably denting it.

There was no way I'd make it out of the doors in time. I spun around to face him, raising the bat. Jared yanked it out of my hands before I even got primed for a swing.

"Get out! Are you crazy?" I started to veer around him, trying to get back to my bedroom door, but he cut me off. I was surprised he wasn't strangling me, judging by the look on his face. Lava was about to come out his nose, I was sure.

"You cut the electricity to my house." His nostrils flared as he got an inch from my face and stared me down.

"Prove it." A tap dance was happening in my chest. No, more like the Paso Doble.

He cocked his head to the side, lips curling dangerously.

"How'd you get in here? I'll call the police!" *Again*, I thought. Not that it did me any good when I called earlier about the noise. Maybe they'd show up if I was murdered?

"I have a key." Every word was slow and threatening.

"How do you have a key to *my* house?" If he had a key, I wasn't sure if I could call the police.

"You and your dad were in Europe all summer," he said with a sneer. "Who do you think got the mail?"

Jared collected our mail? I almost wanted to laugh. The irony of him doing something so mundane slowed my heartbeat a bit.

"Your dad trusts me," Jared continued. "He shouldn't have."

I clenched my jaws. My dad and grandma knew very little about the state of Jared's and my relationship. If they knew how bad it'd gotten, then they would've spoken to his mother. I wasn't a whiner, and I didn't want to be rescued. It hurt that Jared was pleasant with my dad but a monster to me.

"Get out," I gritted through my teeth.

He advanced on me until I was forced back against the French doors. "You're a nosy bitch, Tatum. Keep your fucking ass on your own side of the fence."

"Keeping the neighborhood awake makes people irritable," I spit back.

I crossed my arms over my chest as Jared braced against the wall with both hands positioned on either side of my head. I don't know if it was from the adrenaline or his proximity, but my nerves were shot. Something had to give.

I looked anywhere but in his eyes. The burning lantern tattoo on his arm was all in blacks and grays. I wondered what it meant. His abs were tight with tension—at least I hoped they weren't normally that rigid. The other tattoo on the side of his torso was in script lettering and impossible to read in this light. His skin looked smooth and . . .

The air left my lungs as I tried to ignore the tingling sensation in my core. *It's best to just look him in the eye.* We hadn't been this close to each other in a long time, and we'd been nose to nose a lot since my return.

Jared must have realized the same thing, because his eyes hardened on me and his breathing turned ragged. His gaze drifted down my neck to my camisole, and my skin burned everywhere he looked.

Refocusing and straightening his expression, he inhaled deeply. "No one else is complaining. So why don't you shut up and leave it alone?" Pushing off the wall, he started to walk away.

"Leave the key," I called out, getting used to this new boldness.

"You know." He laughed under his breath and turned around. "I underestimated you. You haven't cried yet, have you?"

"Because of the rumor you started this week? Not a chance." My voice was even, but a smug smile threatened to break out. I was getting off on our confrontation, and the realization that things between us were finally "coming to a head" as K.C. had said. Look at us already. Jared and I hadn't been alone in my room in over three years. This was progress. Of course, he was uninvited, but I wasn't going to nit-pick.

"Please, like I even have to resort to spreading rumors. Your cross-country pals did that. And their pictures," he added. "Everyone drew their own conclusions." He let out a sigh and inched towards me again. "But I'm boring you. I guess I have to step up my game." His eyes were spiteful, and my foot twitched with the urge to kick him.

Why did he keep this up? "What did I ever do to you?!" The question that coursed through me for years erupted out of my cracked voice.

"I don't know why you ever thought you did something. You were clingy, and I got sick of putting up with it is all."

"That's not true. I wasn't clingy." My defenses were crumbling. I remembered, very well, the history between the two of us, and his words made me want to fucking hit him! How could he forget? As kids, we'd spent every waking moment together when we weren't in school. We were best friends. He'd held me when I cried about my mom, and we'd learned how to swim together at Lake Geneva. "You were over at my house as much as I was at yours. We were friends."

"Yeah, keep livin' the dream." He pushed all of our history and friendship back at me like a slap in the face.

"I hate you!" I screamed at him and meant every word. An ache settled in my gut.

"Good!" he shouted in my face, boring down on me. "Finally. Because it's been a long time since I could stand the sight of you!" He slammed his palm against the wall near my head, causing me to jump.

Flinching, I screamed to myself. *What had happened to us?* He'd scared me, but I stood my ground, telling myself that he wasn't going to hurt me, not physically. I knew that, didn't I?

My brain shouted for me to run, to get away from him. No tears fell, thankfully, but the pain of his words made my breathing almost turn to dry heaving.

I had loved Jared once, but now I knew, without a doubt, that "my Jared" was gone.

As I took a deep breath, I met his eyes. He seemed to search mine, probably for tears. *Fuck him.*

Out of the corner of my eye, I noticed flashing lights coming from outside and turned to stare out the window. A small, insolent smile tugged at the corners of my mouth.

"Oh, look. It's the police. I wonder why they're here." Jared couldn't have missed my insinuation of why the cops were there and who'd called them. I guess they'd finally responded to my noise complaint. Turning my head to face him, I delighted in his fury. The poor guy's face looked like someone just pissed on his car.

He raised his chin and relaxed his brow. "I promise you will be in tears by next week." His vengeful whisper crowded the room.

"Leave the key," I called out to him as he left.

Chapter 11

On Sunday afternoon, I was laying out tanning in the backyard when K.C. arrived and plopped down in a chair at the patio table.

"Liam's been cheating on me," she cried. Her head was in her hands as she sniffled.

"What?" A shriek sprang out of my throat as I popped my head up. I pushed myself up off my stomach and walked over to sit next to her.

"I saw him last night wrapped around another girl. Apparently, he's been double dipping for a while! Can you believe it?" She wiped away tears but more fell. Her long, dark hair looked as if she hadn't brushed it today. K.C. was always dressed to impress and never left the house without hair and makeup done. Red splotches covered her face, so I knew she'd been crying for a while. Probably all night.

"What did you see exactly?" I asked, rubbing circles on her back.

"Well," she said, wiping her tears and taking a breath, "I was at the Loop, and he was there. Jared said he was racing last night, so I showed up to surprise ... "

"Wait, what? Jared?" Confused, I interrupted her. "What are you talking about? You've talked to him?" I hadn't seen Jared for two days. He and K.C. were hardly chummy. *What the hell?*

"Yeah ... no," she answered vaguely. "I just ran into him at work yesterday. I was at the theater, and he came in to see a movie. He mentioned that Liam was getting a shot at racing last night and that he'd be happy to give me a ride to surprise him."

Ugh! Was she seriously that stupid? "That didn't seem a little convenient to you?"

"Tate, what do you mean?" K.C. looked confused as she blew her nose with a tissue from her bag. I instantly felt guilty for taking the focus of the conversation off Liam and turning it to Jared. But I couldn't let it go.

"Jared, nice guy that he is, offers you a ride to *surprise* your boyfriend who you conveniently discover has been cheating on you. K.C., Jared knew what Liam was up to." I'm sure it's some code with guys that you don't get them in trouble with their girlfriends. So why would Jared do that?

Looking puzzled and flustered, K.C. threw her tissue on the table. "Okay, but it doesn't change the fact that Liam was being unfaithful. I mean honestly, Jared seemed just as shocked as me. He was really nice about the whole thing."

Of course he was. Jared broke up Liam and K.C., which was a good thing considering, but his actions didn't spring from the goodness of his heart. He definitely wasn't protecting K.C. So what was his angle?

"Alright," I offered, "so how do you know for sure that Liam was cheating regularly? Did you talk to him?"

"Yeah," she almost whispered. "I had gotten out of Jared's car. He picked me up since you can only enter by invitation, and we circulated, looking for Liam. I saw him leaning against his car with a really sexy-looking girl in super-slutty clothes. They were kissing, and he had his hands all over her. There was no mistake." Her chin started wobbling, and her eyes filled with tears again, so I dug in her bag for more tissues.

She continued, "We got into it, and that girl rubbed it in that they'd been hooking up for months! Months! I'm sick to my stomach. I gave that guy my virginity, and now I have to go get checked for STDs." She continued to cry, and I held her hand while she let it out.

Liam had always treated me respectfully, and I was a little heartbroken for K.C. What an ass! We'd all hung out for years, and there were few people in this town I could call a friend. Now he was just one more person that couldn't be trusted. I was jaded when it came to people, but K.C. wasn't, and I hated that she was being hurt. She was completely blindsided.

Two things could be safely assumed, though: Jared probably knew Liam was cheating for a while but didn't interfere until now, *and* K.C.'s breakup with Liam served a purpose in his trying to antagonize me.

"Well, I hate to ask a silly question, but how was the race? Did Liam win?" *He probably hadn't raced. Another ploy on Jared's part to get her to the Loop.*

"We stayed for a while, but Jared raced, not Liam."

Exactly. "How come? It might've been nice for you to see his ass left choking in the dust." I tried to sound like I was just lightening her mood, but I really wanted information.

"Oh, it turns out he wasn't racing last night. Jared misunderstood." She waved it off.

Complete. Set-up.

"But Jared did say he would make sure Liam is on the roster for next week, and he'll beat him for me." K.C. let out a small laugh, as if that would make her feel better.

"Are you going to be okay?" The end of a two-year relationship by the time you're seventeen was going to take time to get over.

"I'm sure . . . eventually. Jared was really attentive and brought me home early. I think he felt bad that I'd had such a horrible time. Really, Tate, even if he did know, he did me a favor." Leaning back in her chair, she pulled out another tissue.

K.C. stayed a while. We lay under the sun, trying to cheer each other up. She obviously needed to come to terms with the fact that she gave her virginity and two years to that Lothario, and I'd had a less-than-stellar first week of school.

Liam had cheated on K.C. I still couldn't wrap my brain around it. If ever there was a case for longevity in a high school romance, Liam and K.C. were it. So why was I preoccupied with Jared's role in all of this? K.C. clearly believed he was on the up-and-up, but I knew he had a plan. Would she listen if I tried to steer her away from him?

After K.C. left, I went back to the patio to clean up and water the plants. Decked out in my little red bikini I'd bought in Europe but was only brave enough to wear at home, I grabbed the hose and turned up the speakers on my iPod dock. "Chalk Outline" came through ear-splittingly loud as I turned the mist on the flowers and bushes.

My hips and shoulders swayed, while my head was lost to the music.

A couple of fruit trees decorated our small back patio area along with bushes and various plants and flowers. The cobblestone pavement and smell of roses made our oasis a great retreat. When the weather was pleasant, my dad and I ate most of our meals out here, and I often read in the hammock. Homework was a no-go, though, since the birds, wind, or barking dogs created too much sporadic distraction.

Speaking of dogs . . .

Excited barking pierced through the music, catching my interest. It was close, like *next door* close.

Madman!

Jared and I found this crazy little Boston Terrier when we were twelve. My dad was gone a lot, and my grandma was allergic, so Jared took him home. The dog was insane but completely adorable. We named him Madman. I swear he purposely waited for oncoming cars before he tried to cross a street. Picking fights with bigger dogs was child's play, and he would jump to amazing heights when he was excited ... which was a lot.

I switched off the water and walked to the fence separating Jared's backyard from mine. Squinting through the sliver of space offered between the wooden panels, I felt like I was glowing on the inside. My heart warmed at seeing Madman again.

He did the whole "bounce when you bark" thing that little dogs do and switched between racing the length of the backyard to jumping up and down. Even though he was technically Jared's dog now, in my heart, the little guy was still partly mine.

I found a small hole to peer—ok, snoop—through. Jared entered my vision, and I flinched, remembering our last encounter. He started tossing miniature chunks of meat for Madman to catch. The dog gobbled them up and wagged his tail anxiously for another morsel. The little animal seemed giddy and well-cared-for.

Jared knelt and offered the last piece of meat from his hand. Madman approached and licked his palm after scarfing down the treat. Jared smiled and closed his eyes while Madman stood on his hind legs to lick his master's face. Jared grinned, and I realized how long it'd been since I'd seen him genuinely happy. His smile hollowed my stomach, but I couldn't look away.

As my heart tugged at the rare scene of Jared actually looking human, my eyes snapped to his naked back and the faded scars marring his skin. Funny I didn't see that the other night when he was shirtless in my room, but the light was dim, so I guess I missed it.

Scattered in no particular pattern were welts, about five or so, covering his muscular and otherwise smooth back. He didn't have them when we were kids. I tried to remember if I'd heard about him getting injured. I came up with nothing.

At that moment, Apocalyptica's heavy cellos vibrated out of my speakers, and Madman's head twisted towards me. I momentarily froze before deciding to back away. He started barking again, and the sound of claws scratching the fence got my heart beating faster. Madman loved this heavy metal cello music that I'd been listening to for years. From the looks of it, he remembered.

Grabbing the hose off the ground, I dropped it again when I heard the fence panels shaking. Turning around, I laughed at seeing Madman climb through one of the loose boards and charge me at top speed.

"Hey, buddy!" I knelt down and caught the little dog in my arms as he squirmed with excitement. His panting breath warmed my face, and the slobber was pretty gross. But he was happy to see me, and I smiled with relief. He hadn't forgotten me.

I stopped dead at the sound of Jared's voice. "Well, if it isn't the party pooper disturbing the whole neighborhood with *her* noise."

My temper flared. He had no problem with my music, just me.

I looked up and met Jared's sardonic stare. He tried to look annoyed with his cocked eyebrow, but I knew he wouldn't engage me unless he got off on it. He hung over the top of the fence, his body perched on something giving him height.

Son of a bitch. Why did it always take me a second or two to remember why I hated him?

His shiny brown hair was a mess.

I loved that.

His chocolate eyes glowed with confidence and mischief.

I loved that.

His toned arms and chest just made me wonder what his skin felt like.

I loved that.

He made me forget how awful he was.

I hated that.

Blinking, I refocused my attention on Madman and petted his black and white fur in long, soothing strokes. "Shelburne Fall's noise ordinance doesn't go into effect until 10 p.m.," I clarified and looked at my invisible watch. "See? Plenty of time."

Madman started playfully gnawing on my fingers, and I shook my head, unable to believe how we could just pick up where we left off after so long. Since Jared's and my fallout, I hadn't pressed him about seeing the dog. The only contact Madman had with me over the past few years was accidents like today. But I hadn't seen him at all since my return, and, even after a year, he responded to me like we'd just been together yesterday.

Jared still stood on the other side of the fence, watching us silently. I couldn't tell what he was thinking, but part of me wondered why he didn't try to get the dog back immediately. It almost seemed *nice* of him to let us visit.

I couldn't help the huge ass smile on my face even though I tried. *What the hell?* The damn dog seemed so happy to see me that my chest shook with silent laughter. I never had a pet other than Madman, and after being alone the past couple of weeks, I guess I was hard up for a little love. If a dog's attention could do this to me, I couldn't imagine how glad I would be to see my dad when he came home.

"Madman, come," Jared barked, shocking me out of my little utopia. "Visitation's over." He whistled and pulled the board back, so Madman could slip through.

"You hear that?" I choked, my lips quivering. "Back to your cell, little guy." I let the dog lick my face, and then I patted his behind before gently pushing him away. Jared whistled again, and Madman ran back through the fence.

"Jared, are you out here?" a woman called out. Jared turned to the voice but didn't nod or respond.

"Tate, is that you, honey?" Katherine, Jared's mom, stepped up onto whatever he was standing on to see over the fence.

"Hey, Ms. Trent." I waved lazily. "It's good to see you." His mom looked great with her shoulder-length brown hair and stylish blouse. A lot better than the last time I'd seen her. She must've gotten herself sober in the past year.

Growing up, I often saw her hair in messy ponytails from being too hung-over to bother with a shower and dull-looking skin from lack of healthy sustenance.

"You, too." Her eyes flickered with genuine sweetness. "And it's good to see you two talking again."

Of course she had no idea we were still at each other's throats. It seemed Jared and I had that in common. We kept the parents out of the loop.

"Why don't you come over for a few? I'd love to catch up with you and see how your year went."

"Come on, not now." Jared's face was twisted up in displeasure, much to my delight.

"That's sounds great, Ms. Trent. Just let me throw on some clothes." Jared's eyes swept over me, as if just realizing I was in a bikini. His gaze lingered too long, and yet, not long enough, making my toes curl.

"Fine." Jared sighed and looked away. "I'm off, anyway." With that, he hopped off his step and disappeared inside the house. Before I had reached my room to change, I heard the thunder of his engine and the peel of tires.

Chapter 12

"So why haven't I seen you in the two weeks I've been home?" I asked Katherine after we'd discussed my trip and plans for senior year.

She poured more coffee for herself. "Well, I met someone a few months ago, and I stay with him a lot."

I raised my eyebrows in surprise, and she must've seen it. She shook her head and gave me a contrite smile.

"I guess it sounds bad," she offered. "Me leaving Jared alone so much. Between my job, his school and job, and then all of the things he's involved in, we just don't run into each other a lot. I figure he's happier on his own more and well . . ."

Her over-explanation and inability to finish her thought said more about her disappointment over her relationship with her son than anything else.

And why was he so busy that her being home was unnecessary?

"What do mean 'all the things he's involved in'?" I asked.

She knitted her brows. "Well, he works at the garage a few days a week, races, and then has other obligations. He's hardly ever home, and when he is, it's just to sleep usually. But, I do keep tabs on him. When I bought us both new phones for Christmas last year, I installed a GPS app on his so I always know where he is."

Okay, that's not weird.

"What other obligations did you mean?" I asked.

"Oh," she said with a nervous smile, "around the time you left last year, things got pretty bad here. Jared was out at all hours. Sometimes, he didn't even come home. My ... drinking ... got worse with the stress of Jared's behavior." She paused and shrugged her shoulders. "Or maybe his behavior got worse with my drinking. I don't know. But I entered rehab for about a month and got detoxed."

Since I'd lived on this street, eight years now, Jared's mom had had a drinking problem. Most of the time she'd been functional, able to go to work and handle Jared. After he came back from visiting his dad that summer three years ago, he'd changed, and Jared's mom had sought escape in the bottle more often.

"He got into some trouble, and then he got it together. But steps needed to be taken, for both of us."

I continued to listen, unfortunately too interested in this rare peek into Jared's life. She still hadn't explained the "other obligations", but I wasn't going to pry further.

"Anyway, a few months ago I started seeing someone, and I've been staying with him on the weekends in Chicago. Jared has a lot going on, and I just don't feel like he needs me. I stay here most school nights, but he knows to stay out of trouble on the weekends."

Yeah, instead of taking his debauchery elsewhere, he brought it home with him.

Some people might see her reasoning as logical, since Jared was almost an adult, but I let my judgment form. As much as I liked her, I blamed her for a lot of Jared's unhappiness growing up.

I didn't know the whole story, but I'd heard enough to figure out that Jared's father wasn't a good man. He had left when Jared was two, before I even lived in the neighborhood. Katherine raised her son almost completely alone, but she had developed a drinking problem during her marriage. When Jared was fourteen, his father called and asked if Jared could come and visit him for the summer. Happily, Jared agreed and left for eight weeks. After the visit, though, he returned cold and cruel. His mother's problem got worse, and he was utterly alone.

I'd always known, deep down, that Jared's problem with me was tied to that summer.

The truth was I resented Katherine. And even though I'd never met Jared's father, I resented him, too. I would take responsibility if I'd hurt Jared, but I had no idea what I could've done to deserve his hatred. His parents, on the other hand, had clearly abandoned him.

It was one the tip of my tongue to ask her about his scars, but I knew she wouldn't tell me.

Instead, I asked, "Does he see his father?"

She glanced at me, and I instantly felt like I'd invaded Top Secret territory. "No," was all she said.

The next day in first period, I sat taking notes about linear approximations when I got a text from K.C. Covertly sliding the screen to bring up the message, I completely lost my attention to Calculus.

Jared texted me last night.

I swallowed hard. Before I had a chance to respond, she'd sent another message.

He wanted to make sure I was o.k. See? He's not all bad.

What the hell did he want with her? K.C. was pretty. Definitely. She was also my best friend, and that had to factor in somewhere with him.

I texted back: **He's up to something!**

Maybe, maybe not. was her response.

That was the last I heard from K.C. until lunch. Physics, P.E. and French passed in a blur as I fought the urge to text her again.

"Hey," she said as we met in line to grab our lunch.

"Hey, so talk to me."

"Well, like I said, he texted to see how I was doing, and we exchanged a few more texts after that. I just thought it was nice that he checked up on me."

She thought he was nice? We exited the line after paying and made our way outside, while I tried to sift through how the hell K.C. went from agreeing that Jared was a dick to thinking he was "nice."

"Well?" I was trying hard to seem like I didn't care. "What could you two have talked about after that?"

"Oh, not much … other than *you* cut the electricity to his house?!" She laughed it off, but I could tell she wasn't as amused as I thought she'd be. Maybe she was pissed that I didn't tell her myself.

"Um, yeah." I was fighting for words. Jared complained about me to her? "The asshole's party was too loud, so I shut it down." I cleared my throat. It didn't sound as good saying it out loud.

We took our seats at a picnic table and began digging into our food. She stayed quiet, but I caught her glancing at me between bites.

"What?" I asked, annoyed. "You told me to play the game, remember?"

"Did you at least ask him to turn it down first?"

"No." It came out more like a squeaky question. "Well, yes. On a different occasion I did." It started to feel like I was on trial.

"And how'd that turn out?" She paused, water bottle in hand.

"Well, he wasn't cooperating. So . . . I incited a panic and yelled 'cops.' People kind of left after that." I tipped my head back and gulped some water to keep from meeting her eyes. I was still proud of that night, but K.C. clearly didn't find it funny.

Instead, she rolled her eyes. "Tate, when I said to play his game I meant—"

"You meant play *his* game!" I blurted out. "You didn't say to kill him with kindness. You're defending him?" What had happened here? It was like I was in the Twilight Zone, and K.C. had been body-snatched.

"All I'm saying is that Jared has talked to you." Her voice was calm, the opposite of mine. "That's it. You look like the bully now. You've broken up two of his parties, broken his friend's nose, and kneed that same friend in the balls."

Great! Fucking great! He's coming off looking like the victim?

"He's not telling the whole story," I sputtered. "He broke into the girls' locker room while I was getting dressed."

K.C. frowned, looking confused. "He just talked to you, though, right? He didn't touch you?" Thankfully, she showed some concern for me, finally. I was ready to rip her head off.

"Well, he didn't attack me, of course," I snapped defensively. For a moment, I considered telling her that he'd broken into my house, but that would just send her back to him with questions that he'd answer . . . *his* way.

"He has issues," K.C. conceded, "but I told you, there's something going on between you two that you haven't dealt with. I'm just not convinced that he's such a bad guy after all."

Sweat beaded my brow, and I took a deep breath. "K.C., Jared is bad news. You know this. I mean really, he's a jerk, and I don't want you making excuses for him. He's not worth it."

She shrugged, probably not wanting to argue but definitely not wanting to give in. The discussion was over, and for the first time, I wanted to throttle my best friend. My only friend, pretty much.

"So, have you talked to Liam at all since Saturday night?" I changed the subject before ripping a bite out of my chicken sandwich.

"No, and I couldn't care less," she snipped and concentrated on her phone.

"Uh huh," I muttered, not convinced. Liam and K.C. had been together longer than any other couple I knew. I had a difficult time wrapping my head around the idea that K.C. didn't care about his betrayal and losing him. If I were her, I probably wouldn't be able to forgive him, but that didn't mean it wouldn't hurt.

"Hey, Tate. How are you?" Ben Jamison plopped down on the bench next to me, looking as good as always. We had zilch in common, but he was cute and made me laugh.

"Hi. I'm good. You?" I had spoken to Ben a few times lately. He seemed not to notice the rumor about Jared and me in the locker room.

"I'm good . . . " He strung out the "good" like he was nervous and looking for what to say next. "There's this Mexican restaurant, Los Aztecas, that opened up while you were away, and I was wondering if you'd let me apologize for being a dick and not asking you out a lot sooner by taking you to dinner this week?" He raised his eyebrows and waited.

A surprised laugh jumped out of my throat. Well, he was refreshingly honest.

"Um, well . . . " I searched for words. "How do I know you won't be a dick on our date?" I challenged him. K.C. giggled beside me.

Ben's eyes smiled, and he bit his bottom lip, clearly turning over something in his head. He took out a piece of paper from his notebook and started writing. After about a minute, he handed the paper to me and walked off. Looking over his shoulder just once and offering a winning smile, he turned and disappeared into the cafeteria.

"What does it say?!" K.C. peered down at the note in my hand before taking a bite of her chicken wrap.

Opening it up, I immediately smiled. He had written a contract.

To Whom It May Concern,

I promise to take Tatum Brandt to dinner. She is pretty, smart, and lovely. I should consider myself lucky if she says yes.

If I act like a dick, then I am a stupid, brainless asshole. All who see this note have my permission to retaliate in any way necessary.

The Most Attractive, Humorous, Wealthy Superhero in School,
Ben Jamison

I passed the note to K.C. and watched as she tried not to spit out food during her laughter. Not three seconds later I got a text.

Tonight, pick u up at 7?

He wasn't giving me much time to think about it, was he? I had been using my dad's car since returning, so I texted him back and told him I would meet him there. I'd rather have the option to leave when I wanted.

Sounds good! he shot back right away.

I couldn't keep the smile off my face, and K.C. was looking at me curiously.

"Well?" she asked with her mouth full.

"He's taking me to dinner tonight." Even though I was excited to be on an actual date, my tone was cavalier. Ben seemed like nice guy, but I noticed that my heart didn't beat faster when he was around. Wasn't it supposed to? "I'm meeting him at seven."

There had been a few dates while I studied abroad, but none of them turned out to be more than friends. Ben and I had different interests, but it wasn't like guys had been pounding down my door lately. I could go on one date with him. Hey, maybe he'd surprise me.

"That's awesome. Call me tonight after you get home. I want to hear how it goes." K.C. probably knew I was still apprehensive about the attention I'd been getting. After so long of not trusting people and being ignored outside of my small circle, my head fogged at the idea of one of the best looking guys in my class asking me out.

Paranoid! I chastised myself.

After the latest rumor, things seemed to have calmed down, though. Apparently, Mr. Fitzpatrick, the Drama teacher, was caught in a rendezvous with senior Chelsea Berger, so I was old news . . . for now.

Dinner with Ben started off with him clearing the air, so to speak.

"I never believed that crap about you, Tate. I'll admit, I was one of the ones to laugh at first, but after a while all I had to do was look at you or see how you acted in class to know that something wasn't adding up." He took a sip of soda and added, "Plus, you look too clean to have lice."

I shook my head and smiled at those stupid rumors. "Well, you'd be one of the few to think differently of me, then. But be honest. It was the picture of me in my towel that got you, wasn't it?"

Ben nearly choked on his chip as he laughed. Blowing off all the shit of the past few years seemed like the best idea right now. Jared was drama. K.C. was drama. I wanted Ben to be easy. I just wanted to have fun tonight.

We ate enchiladas, and he joked that if they made a Mexican-Sushi restaurant, he would never eat anywhere else again. Even though I wasn't a fan of sushi, I snorted at the hilarious concept.

"So why did you ask me out?" I dipped one of the remaining chips from our meal in the salsa and took a bite.

"Honestly? I've been wanting to for a long time. I never had the guts, though. You're kind of on my bucket list."

I wasn't sure whether that was a compliment or an insult. "How do you mean?" This date might be ending sooner rather than later.

"You know, one of those 'I-simply-must-do-this-before-I-die' type lists? I needed to get to know you better. I was always interested. Then, when you came back from Europe, and I saw you the first day of school, I just couldn't get you out of my head."

I narrowed my eyes, listening to him. I'd kept my head down for most of high school, not knowing that Ben had a crush. I couldn't help but think how different school would have been if Jared had never turned on me.

"So you've been scared away by rumors all these years? What a coward," I chastised sarcastically. What surprised me was that the barb came out of my lips so easily. I wasn't nervous around him, and my shoulders relaxed. It nipped at the back of my mind that it also meant that I didn't care what he thought either.

He leaned in, his full lips turned up. "Well, I hope I'm remedying that tonight."

"So far, so good."

We left the restaurant and laughed as we walked around downtown, talking about plans for college. On the way back to our cars, I sucked in a breath as he leaned in to kiss me. Surprisingly, his lips were soft and gentle, and his warmth willed me to lean into him. I placed my hands on his chest as he wrapped his arms around me, and he didn't try to force his tongue into my mouth. It was safe ... comfortable.

Definitely not what it should be.

I hadn't experienced any of the thrill K.C. talked about when being close to a guy you're attracted to. Definitely not the kind of excitement I read about in the books about high school girls and fallen angels. And not the kind of pulsing heat I felt when I was around. . . *no, no!*

I stopped my train of thought dead in its tracks. *That's not attraction,* I told myself. It's just adrenaline brought on by confrontation. My body's reaction to *him* wasn't something I could control.

"Can I call you?" he whispered.

"Yes." I nodded, a little embarrassed that my mind was preoccupied by another guy.

I was interested in spending time with him again. Maybe the spark hadn't been there tonight, but I was stressed, and he deserved another chance. Maybe it just took time.

Ben waited for me to get into my car before he pulled out. Grabbing my phone, I hurried to text K.C. and share the details of my date. Even with the slight doubt about my attraction, I had a good time and was excited to share good news with her.

Can I come over?

Did you have fun? she asked.

Yes, but I wanted to talk ... in person. *I am not about to have a whole conversation over text messaging.*

Was he nice?

Yes! It was good. No worries. Just kind of excited and wanted to talk. My impatience almost made me start the car and head to her house without an answer.

I have to work late. See you tomorrow before class? My shoulders slumped slightly at her response. I was close to her work, but I wasn't going to bug her there.

Yeah, that's fine. 'Night. I shot back.

'Night! Glad you had fun.

Just then, I heard the rumble of a motorcycle engine cruise past my car and perform a U-turn ahead. It came to stop on the other side of the street, about fifty yards away, in front of Spotlight Cinemas—where K.C. worked. My fingers tingled at the sight of Jared, and everything else stopped. He left the engine running as he sat back, holding the bike in place with both jean-clad legs on either side of it. He took out his phone from his black hoodie and appeared to be texting . . . and waiting.

Not a minute later, K.C. came bouncing out of the theater, running up to him. She leaned in and touched his arm.

Holy mother son of a . . .

I was having trouble breathing. What the hell am I seeing right now?

I watched as she smiled up at him. He grinned back at her but didn't touch her. She was so intimate with him. Taking off his helmet, he offered it to her with a few words. She wasn't getting the smirks or threatening kinds of looks I received. She ran her fingers through his mussed hair before taking the helmet and putting it on her own head. He fastened the straps for her before she climbed on behind him and wrapped her arms around his stomach.

I instantly slouched in my seat as they sped past me. They both knew my dad's car, but I was hoping they wouldn't notice it. At any rate, it wasn't like they were going to stop and say "hi."

Needles dug under the surface of my skin, and my ears were ringing. My throat ached as I fought back tears.

He had won over K.C.

K.C. had lied about working late.

She had her arms around him.

I wasn't sure which one I was most upset about.

Chapter 13

After sitting in my car for more minutes than I cared to admit, I was calm enough to drive.

The entire time it took me to get home and stalk up to my front porch I had several versions of internal conversations with K.C. and choice monologues directed at Jared, including all of my favorite expletives. The more I talked to myself, the more pissed I got. Screaming, crying, stomping on some bubble wrap—they all sounded good right now.

What was she thinking? Even if Jared had smooth-talked her, was it worth hurting her best friend over?

I now guessed what Jared's move was. He was trying to turn my friend against me. K.C. was very aware of what Jared had done to me, but he had gotten to her. He brought it to her attention that her boyfriend was cheating and then swooped in to pick up the pieces. How else could she be so weak-minded?

She needed to know Jared was using her. But how the hell could I tell her that?

Keeping myself busy so I wouldn't do anything stupid, I finished my Calculus homework, completed the assigned reading for Government, and cleaned out the refrigerator and cabinets of expired food. After I'd exhausted myself with enough chores so that I'd finally stopped talking to myself, I walked upstairs to take a bath.

About an hour after I'd gotten out of the tub, the whir of Jared's motorcycle sounded down our street. I leapt out of bed to spy through the window. Noticing that the clock read midnight, I calculated that it'd been three hours since I'd seen him with K.C.

Three fucking hours! What'd they been doing?

He arrived home alone. That was good, at least.

As he pulled into his driveway, I noticed the headlights of another vehicle coming to an abrupt stop in front of his house. Jared hopped off his bike and removed his helmet but kept it secured in his hand. He raced to the curb to meet the car's occupants. The driver and his passenger had already vacated the car and met up with Jared toe to toe.

What's this?

Jared towered over them, not only in height but in build. He had been tall at fourteen, and by now he had to exceed six feet. Judging by the way he got in their faces, these guys were not his friends.

I opened the double doors to get a better view. Jared waved the helmet in the space between them, and the other guys were yelling and trying to advance in his face. I caught the words "fuck you" and "get over it." They continued to bark at each other, loudly and intrusively.

It was hard to catch my breath all of a sudden. Their argument seemed to be getting out of control. *Should I call the cops?*

As much as they pushed into his space, Jared didn't retreat. The odds were against him, though. *Shit, Jared. Just get out of there.*

One of the men pushed him, and I flinched. Reacting, Jared got in the guy's face and pushed into him with his body until the guy was forced to back up.

At that moment, Madoc's GTO sped down the street to a screeching halt. As soon as the strangers saw him hop out of his car and run in their direction, they started throwing punches at Jared. He lost hold of his helmet, and it slammed to the ground.

Jared charged one of the guys, and they dropped to ground level looking like an MMA fight. Each boy rolled on the lawn, jabbing and belting.

Snatching my phone off the bed, I raced out of my room and down the stairs. Pulling open the drawer to the entryway table, I grabbed the Glock-17 my father instructed I keep there when I was home alone.

I clutched the doorknob. *Call the cops or go outside?* This would be over before the cops got here. *Screw it.*

I swung open the door and stepped onto the porch. The boys were all on Jared's front lawn, with Madoc and Jared straddling their opponents, punching them into oblivion. My heart pounded at the display, but I couldn't look away. The sense of urgency that made me run outside lessened when I realized Jared was winning.

Mesmerized by the fight happening in front of me, I blinked when I heard Jared's disgusted howl. His opponent, an older, tattooed guy, had pulled out a knife and sliced his arm. I ran down the stairs, gun in hand, in time to see Jared dive for his helmet and hit the guy over the head with it. The other guy crumpled to the ground, moaning and blood dripping off his forehead. The knife lay on the grass at his side. Jared stood up, hovering over the nearly-unconscious guy.

Madoc pounded his fist one more time into his opponent's gut, and swinging him over his shoulder, he dumped him onto the ground near his Honda.

Jared left his opponent bloody and barely moving on the ground, while he squeezed his left bicep. The arm of his black hoodie was blood-soaked and glistened where he'd been cut. My worried eyes shot to the hand on that arm. A steady red stream dripped off his fingertips. I had a brief impulse to go and help him but resisted. The kindness would only be thrown back in my face. He and Madoc would need trips to the ER, but as it was a school night, Jared's mom *should* be home.

Walking over to the Honda, Jared raised his helmet above his head and brought it down with a deafening crash on the windshield. Again, he repeated the action, smashing the windshield again and again until it was shattered beyond usefulness.

Heading back towards the house, Jared stopped by the man on the ground. "You're not welcome at the Loop anymore." His voice was low and strained. His tone was eerily calm.

I could do nothing but stand there, paralyzed with shock at the scene I'd just witnessed.

As Madoc bent to pick up the second guy, his attention snapped to me. "Jared," he warned. Jared, following his gaze, turned his eyes on me.

A little too late, I realized I was standing with a gun ... in the open ... in my underwear. My Three Days Grace T-shirt and red boy shorts covered me, but they were tight. My feet were bare, and my hair hung loose down my back. The Glock secured tightly in my right hand hung at my side with the safety on. *Was the safety on? Yes, the safety was on ... I think.*

Madoc was bleeding from the nose, no doubt broken again, but he grinned at me.

Jared looked ... dangerous. He studied me, his dark eyes and severe brow making me feel more exposed than I already felt. His hands clenched into fists, while his gaze traveled warily down my body and then to the gun in my hand. I could feel the energy coming off him in heat waves.

Ugh, I'm a stupid girl! Had I really wanted to help him?

I cocked my eyebrow and pursed my lips in an effort to look annoyed. What an asshole to bring this drama to our street!

Turning, I walked quickly up my porch steps and slammed the front door behind me.

Taking the gun to my bedroom that night, I wasn't sure what I was protecting myself from. A damn gun wasn't going to keep those brown eyes out of my dreams.

Chapter 14

The bubble-popping sound of my computer sounded early the next morning, notifying me that I had an incoming call.

"Hey, Dad," I drawled out sleepily after clicking on the call.

"Good Morning, Pumpkin. Looks like I woke you. Sleeping in today?" He sounded concerned.

Glancing at the clock on my laptop, I saw that the time read six thirty. "Damn!" Throwing off the covers, I ran into my closet. "Dad, can I talk to you after I get home tonight? I'm supposed to be in the lab in thirty minutes."

Tuesdays and Thursdays worked best for Dr. Porter, my mentor and Chemistry teacher from sophmore year, so I opted to make it to the lab those mornings for some extra work time on my Science Fair research.

"Yeah, sure, but it will be pretty late for me ... or early, actually. Listen, I just needed to tell you that Grandma is coming in tonight."

I poked my head around the closet door and suppressed a groan. "Dad, do you think you can't trust me? I've been just fine here by myself." It almost felt like I was lying. Everything from the night before, K.C. and then the fight, hit me so hard that I wanted nothing more than to punch something.

"I trust you completely ... but your grandma doesn't." He laughed. "She's just worried about you being on your own, so she said she'd come by for a few days, possibly a week, and lend a hand. You are still a minor after all, and she keeps watching those news shows like *Sex Slaves in the Suburbs*. She worries."

My dad and his mom hated the idea of me practically living alone for three months, but my desire to be in my own school for my senior year won out.

I shimmied into some skinny jeans, slipped a long-sleeved, fitted violet tee over my head, and walked out of the closet.

"If it will put her mind at ease, but as you can see, I'm fine," I sighed.

"I'm not even sure what the law says about this, actually. You are staying out of trouble, right?" His eyes narrowed at me as I slipped on some black ballet flats. Dad was calm about most things, but trying to parent me from Germany was driving him up the wall. This was the seventh time we'd talked in the past two weeks. With the time difference, that was an accomplishment.

"Of course." I almost choked on my words. If you could call running out of the house to possibly shoot a couple of street thugs "staying out of trouble ..." "And I'll be eighteen in a couple of weeks. I'm barely a minor anymore."

"I know." My dad exhaled wearily. "Alright, I'll let you go. Just be home for dinner for your grandma tonight."

"Yes, sir. I'll call you tomorrow morning. Sound good?"

"Talk to you then. Have a great day, Pumpkin." And he clicked off.

The breakfast bar and juice box I grabbed before leaving the house held me over during the lab work, but by first bell, the hunger pangs started. Coupled with the fact that K.C. hadn't shown up or texted back this morning, I rushed in aggravation down the hall to the cafeteria for a vending machine run before class.

My concentration was flying in five different directions this morning. I'd forgotten to run to the hardware store for supplies last night, so the research I'd wanted to accomplish this morning turned out to be very little. After I broke a beaker and damn near burned my hand with the Bunsen burner, I'd cleared out of the lab before I killed myself.

My jaw ached from clenching my teeth all morning. Images of K.C.'s legs hugging Jared's hips on the motorcycle kept assaulting me. "What if's" of what would have happened last night if that knife had sliced Jared's neck or stomach instead of his arm flashed through my mind.

Rounding the corner, I immediately halted.

What? WHAT!

K.C. leaned against the yellow wall next to the cafeteria doors, while Jared leaned into her. His arm was posted to the wall above her head, and his head was dipped, bringing his lips within inches of hers. The white top she wore rode up to reveal a sliver of skin as Jared's thumb caressed her softly while holding her hip.

He said something against her lips, and K.C.'s chest rose and fell in deep breaths.

No.

My heart pounded, and heat rushed through my body. I watched him finally catch her lips with his. He slowly pulled her body to his, and she wrapped her arms around his neck. Nausea rose in my throat, and my eyes burned. K.C. looked like she was at a buffet, savoring all of the desserts one bite at a time.

That bitch!

Wait, what? I should be mad at him, if not more so than K.C., then at least equally. Jared had pursued her, and I knew, with all certainty, that it was to hurt me. Why did I want her off of him instead of him off of her?

Luckily, nearly everyone was already in class. Otherwise, they'd be putting on quite a show. I was their only audience.

100

As I glanced to them again, Jared's lips were still devouring her. He nibbled at her mouth before moving on to her neck, achieving a groan of pleasure from her. Her eyes were closed, and she bit her bottom lip, showing that she was putty in his hands. He did look like a good kisser, and I was breathless with the ache in my chest. I flinched when I saw the delicate way he buried his lips behind her ear.

Oh, Christ.

The second bell sounded. We had one minute to get to class. K.C. jumped and giggled at the interruption. Jared gave her a smirk before tapping her on the tip of the nose. As she turned to run to class, he gave her a light slap on the ass.

I dashed back around the corner. If he didn't follow her, then he was coming this way. I definitely didn't want him to know I'd witnessed their display. My anger fed his hunger, and I didn't want to lose my cool around him.

"Hey, man." I heard Madoc's voice as he barged through the cafeteria doors. "Was that K.C. that ran off? You haven't tapped that yet?"

Jared exhaled a small laugh as their footsteps came closer. "Who's saying I haven't?"

I swallowed hard.

"Uh, because you've never been seen with a girl after you've fucked her. I doubt you even wait until the condom's off before forgetting their names."

Jared stopped just in front of the stairs across from the darkened doorway where I'd hidden. He knit his brows together in surprise. "And you do?" he asked defensively, shoving his hands into the pockets of his jeans. His white T-shirt and black thermal hung loose over his torso.

"Yeah, yeah. I know." Madoc rolled his eyes, bruised from the night before. His nose wasn't bandaged, but it was cut. "I'm just saying, *you* never had to work this hard to get a girl into bed."

"I'm in no hurry. I might want to play around with this one for a while." Jared shrugged as he started to climb the stairs but stopped and turned to face Madoc, looking like he was about to say something before Madoc cut him off.

"Tate's going to be pissed." Madoc's voice sounded amused, and I wanted to run at hearing my name.

"The whole point," Jared stated flatly.

"Oh ... so that's the plan." Madoc nodded, finally understanding the end game.

My throat tightened, and my mouth went dry. He knew she was my best friend, my only friend pretty much, and losing her would make me miserable. The tightness spread to my jaw, and I shook my head in disgust. He hated me that much?

"Thanks again for backing me up last night." Jared jerked his chin at Madoc before turning to the stairs.

Madoc spoke. "This thing, with Tate ... " Jared stopped and turned again. Madoc continued, "Why do we do it? I know I've asked before, but you don't tell me shit. I just don't get it."

Jared's eyes narrowed. "I think you go above and beyond. You mess with her without me telling you, so why do you care?"

Madoc let out a nervous laugh. "This isn't about me. I never wanted to make an enemy of that girl. She came outside last night like she was ready to back us up. She's hot, athletic, tough, and she can handle a gun. What's not to like?"

Jared descended the stairs to stand one above Madoc. His dark brow pulled together in a scowl as he stared his friend down. "Stay away from her."

Madoc held up his hands. "Hey, man, no worries. She broke my nose and kicked me in the balls. I think that ship's sailed. But if you don't want her, why can't anyone else have a shot?"

Jared paused as if searching for words. Then he let out an exasperated sigh. "I'm not standing in her way anymore. If she wants to date and screw every guy in school, she can have a ball. I'm done."

"Well good, because word is she went out with Ben Jamison last night." Madoc's tone sounded a little too pleased to deliver that news. Jared's eyebrows pinched closer together, if that was possible. His grim expression accompanied by his dark looks made him appear formidable.

"That's fine," he said, but his jaws remained clenched. "I couldn't care less. They can all have her."

My breath caught in my throat.

He finished climbing the stairs and disappeared. Madoc stared after Jared for a moment before continuing down the hall and disappearing himself.

The stabbing sensation in my throat surrendered to the tears wanting their release. I raced to the nearest ladies room and locked myself in a stall. My back collapsed against the wall, and I slid down until my rear landed on the floor. Hugging my knees, I gave myself over to the tears. My breakdown was quiet, the misery uprooted from my gut and not my throat. The worst part was I didn't know if I was angry, sad, desperate or miserable. The deep wailing came from my body silently, but the tears streamed down my cheeks like a river.

Jared indulged in my misery like it was candy. He had fed me to the wolves time and again, reveling in the unhappiness he caused. Jared, my friend, was completely gone, leaving a cold monster in his place.

His last words also irked me. He was setting me free, *allowing* me to date. *The nerve!* In my sick, twisted attachment to the boy who used to be my friend, I still took *some* comfort in the attention he showed me. Even if it was negative attention, at least he acknowledged my existence in some way. Maybe, if he still took the trouble to cross my path, then he might be holding a piece of me with him, too. *But he was done,* as he'd said.

As I stood, I remembered that Jared had promised to have me in tears this week. Job well done, and it was only Tuesday. Wiping my eyes, I had to admit that the dick had skill.

"Sorry I left you hanging this morning," K.C. apologized while sliding her leg over the picnic table bench. She was late to lunch, too. "So, tell me everything about last night!" She sounded plastic, like her excitement took effort. Her head was elsewhere.

Last night, I thought. The first image that hit me was her and Jared on his motorcycle, and then the kiss this morning. The second thing that came to mind was the fight I'd witnessed. The super scary figure Jared presented last night as he pounded his opponent was why people at this school fell in line around him. Some wanted to be in his orbit while others kept a respectful distance. Some people wanted to be recognized by him, while others considered themselves lucky to be unnoticed.

"Last night? Why don't you go first?" I looked at her out of the corner of my eye while I sipped my water. I tossed around the idea of acting like I knew nothing, but she and Jared weren't going to be in control of my emotions. This needed to be settled.

"What do you mean?" K.C. was wide-eyed.

Gotchya.

"You're going to lie to me then? I saw you. I saw you and him on the motorcycle last night and then again this morning by the cafeteria." I pursed my lips and threw my wadded up napkin on the table.

"Tate, this is why I didn't tell you . . . "

"Tell me what? That you're screwing the guy that hurts me? That you two are laughing behind my back?" My voice cracked, but I was grateful that I hadn't started yelling.

"It's not like that."

I knew she didn't want to hurt me, but I just couldn't listen to it. There was no excuse. The heat of anger clouded my reason. I was fucking mad, and I wanted her to feel as bad as me.

This is how bullies are made, I thought, but it still felt good to lash out, and I didn't want to stop.

I let out a small, spiteful laugh. "You know, I think I might have to thank Jared for saving me from all of this drama over the years. Friends I can't trust and boys that would only piss me off. What are you doing with him?"

She ignored my question. "Jared saving you from what? What do you mean?"

Bloody hell. What did she care, anyway? I should just walk away, but I didn't.

"Madoc told me all about how they both sunk every potential date I had freshman and sophomore year. They started *all* of the rumors and ruined any hope I had of making friends or getting a boyfriend."

"You're listening to Madoc now?" She slammed me with an accusatory tone.

"Seems reasonable, doesn't it? Madoc wouldn't lie about his best friend. And he wouldn't tell me if he thought Jared would be mad. I think they're both proud of themselves."

Jared's pleasure would come from me starting a fight with my best friend over my hatred of him or her involvement with him. The painful lump in my throat got bigger. I wanted to calm down and fix this, but it took every ounce of reason I had to not walk away. She'd betrayed me, but she'd also stuck by me through everything. I owed it to her to not run away at the first sign of trouble.

"K.C.," I continued after a couple of breaths, "I'm not okay with this. If you're going to date Jared ..." I guess I shouldn't worry about running into Jared at K.C.'s house or trying to double date. If he succeeded, I'd lose my friend, anyway. I should tell her that he was using her, but that'd just piss her off. "I don't trust him, and that's not going to change."

K.C. looked me in the eye. "And we're friends. That will never change."

Still mad as hell at her, I exhaled the breath I'd been holding. "Is it worth it?" I asked. "Dating him when you know I hate him?" Why was this so important? Did he really mean anything to her?

She offered a tight smile, eyes downcast. "He deserves how you feel about him, but what good has it done you to carry around this hatred?"

Annoyed, I shook my head. Believe me, if I could get rid of it, I would.

Last ditch effort to get her to use her head. "You know Jared is a major player, right? Like he's had a lot of girls in this school and a few other schools, too."

"Yes, *Mom*, I'm aware of his history. I'm not an easy target, you know?"

"No, but Jared is a good shot," I deadpanned.

We both looked at each other and laughed. The tension in my chest eased as I realized our friendship was safe . . . for today.

"Come over for dinner. We need a girls' night," K.C. asked while peeling an orange.

"No, I can't." I was exhausted, and to be honest, I didn't want to act like everything was okay. "My grandma is coming in today. I'd invite you over, but I'm sure she'll want to do a lot of catching up. It's been over a year since I've seen her."

"Yeah, right." At that moment, she got a text. Opening it up, she grinned from ear to ear as if enjoying a private joke.

Noticing me watching her, she gave me an apologetic smile and continued eating. Glancing at the windows to the cafeteria, I spied Jared inside, leisurely sitting at his table with his phone in his hand. He smirked at me, and I knew he'd been watching us.

And I wiped a fake tear with my middle finger. Again.

Chapter 15

By early afternoon, yawns were erupting from my body every five minutes. After the wake-up call, the lab, the episodes between Jared, K.C. and Madoc, the sob session in the bathroom, and the heart-to-heart at lunch, my body needed to shut down for a while. One more class and I could head home to crash. If I was lucky, we'd be watching a movie in Themes. When I remembered that Jared shared this class with me, though, a renewed tension spit fire through my shoulder and neck muscles.

After I sat down, Nate Dietrich walked up to my desk and leaned in. "Hey, Tate, how about you come out with me this weekend?"

I couldn't help but laugh to myself. This guy passed me in the hall last week and grabbed his crotch in my direction. "No thanks, Nate." With his curly brown hair and hazel eyes, he was somewhat cute, but too stupid to tolerate. If he wasn't cracking some immature joke, then he *was* the immature joke.

"Oh, come on. Give me a chance." His long, sing-song tone sounded like he was speaking to a toddler.

"Not. Interested." I made deliberate eye contact, shooting him a warning with my eyes. It was definitely no secret now that I could handle myself. He should take the warning. Opening my notebook and looking at my notes, I hoped he'd take the hint that this conversation was over.

"I don't get you." *Nope. As I said, too stupid.* "You give it to Trent in the locker room last week, and then you let Jamison take you out. You probably gave it up for him, too." He leaned in further and ran his hand up my arm.

Every nerve in my body was electrified. I wanted to bring this guy's head down on my knee hard enough to sprout blood flow that would rival Niagara Falls.

"Leave," I gritted out, still trying to study my notes. "That's your last warning." I couldn't even look at him, as gross as the encounter had made me feel. The idea of everyone thinking I was some sleazy throw-away made the walls cave in on me. As much as I tried to act like this was normal for me and that I was used to it, it still felt like shit. What people thought of me mattered.

"Jared's right. You're not worth it," Nate whispered with a snarl.

"Sit down, Nate." The deep, commanding voice startled us both.

Looking up, I saw Jared standing behind Nate, giving him his death glare. My heart skipped a beat when I realized that, for once, Jared's scowl was not directed at me.

As usual, Jared gave the impression that he could take on an army all by himself.

Nate twisted around slowly. "Hey, man, no offense. If you're not done with her . . . " Nate shrugged, backing off out of Jared's way.

"Don't talk to her again." Jared's voice was even, but his eyes were threatening.

What the hell?

"Go." Jared jerked his chin, and Nate left as if he was just dismissed.

I let out a bitter sigh. How dare he try to troubleshoot a problem he created! They all, at one time or another, had thought I was a slut because of him. Isn't this what he wanted? Isn't me being harassed and uncomfortable the goal of his bullying? Sick of his torment and games, I forced down the urge in my twitching fists to hit him. It was then that I realized I wanted to hurt Jared. Really hurt him.

I hate you.

My emotions fell into a relaxed lividness. "Don't do me any favors," I bit out, meeting his eyes. The satisfaction of hurting *him* for once would feel fucking great. "You're a miserable piece of shit, Jared. But then, I guess I'd be miserable, too, if my parents hated me. Your dad left you, and your mom avoids you. But who can blame them, right?"

Jared flinched, and I immediately felt my insides shake. What was I doing? This wasn't me! Bile rose in my throat. *What did I just say to him?* I waited for the satisfaction to come, but it never did.

He remained silent, and his eyes narrowed on me with a hint rage and despair. There was no way I could erase what I'd just done to him. Even though he hid his emotions, I'd seen the cringe.

This is how bullies are made.

I'd just purposely made him feel unloved and unwanted. I'd told him he was alone. Even with everything he'd pulled on me, I'd never felt abandoned or isolated. There was always someone that loved me, someone I could count on.

"Okay, class." Mrs. Penley walked through the door, startling me. Jared said nothing and continued down the aisle to his seat. "Please take out your compasses and look up your East. When I say 'go', please take your materials and sit next to that person for today's discussion. Feel free to move desks side by side or face to face. Go."

Blinking away the tears that'd pooled, I barely had time to catch my breath before my East walked up to me.

110

"Hey, pretty girl." I looked up to see Ben already at my side, looking for a vacant desk.

Not today. I tucked my hair behind my ears and took a deep breath. Ben and I hadn't talked since our date last night, and I hadn't realized that until now. "Hi, Ben." *Hold on for one more hour,* I chanted to myself. I needed my music, my bed, and definitely my grandma.

"I'm good. Now." He flashed a bright smile, and I couldn't help but exhale a weak laugh. He was a happy guy and easy to be with. I'd give him that.

"Alright, everyone, as you did with your South last class, please introduce yourself to your East," Mrs. Penley instructed the class. Everyone moaned, just like last class, because we all pretty much knew each other anyway.

"I know, I know." The teacher waved her hands to shut everyone up. "It's good practice for all of those college interviews you'll be doing. As well as introducing yourself, I want you, this time, to share your favorite memory to get to know each other. Go ahead."

Mrs. Penley started circulating the classroom that already buzzed with conversation. I looked to Ben, and we both snorted like this was the last thing we wanted to spend our time doing.

"Hi." He held out his hand, which I took, rolling my eyes and nodding. "My name is Benjamin Jamison. My favorite memory is making my first touchdown in high school. Knowing I was varsity, and the crowd was so much more intense, the feeling was incredible."

It was hard not to sympathize with a memory like that. With all of the spectators cheering him on, I bet it'd been heart pounding.

"Hi, my name is Tatum Brandt." I waved and felt like I was in a movie during an AA scene where I would tell him "I'm an alcoholic" next. "And my favorite memory is when . . . " My eyes immediately flashed to Jared and then my desktop. This particular memory was priceless to me, but I had a hard time admitting it to myself. Maybe I should just lie, but then why should I be the one to hide? "Uh, I guess it won't seem like as big of a deal as yours, but . . . I had a picnic in a cemetery once."

Ben's eyes widened. "Really?" He looked at me curiously. "So what was that about?"

"Well." I swallowed hard. "My mom passed away when I was ten, and I was afraid to visit her at the cemetery. It really freaked me out. For two years, I refused to go. I hated the idea of her being under the ground like that. So, this boy I was friends with . . . at the time, he packed a lunch for us and took me to the cemetery one day. I was pretty mad when I realized where he was taking me, but he told me that I should be happy that my mom was there. He said it's the prettiest, quietest place in town. He was really understanding and patient. We sat near my mom's grave and ate our lunch, listened to a radio he brought. He had me laughing in no time. We stayed a while, even after the rain started. Now, it's one of my favorite places to go. Because of him." My face hurt, and I realized I had a grin plastered to it during the entire story.

As awful as Jared had become, and now how terrible I'd become, I still treasured that memory. I smiled every time I thought of what he'd done for me that day. He gave me a little of my mom back.

"Wow. My touchdown story seems kind of shallow now." Ben actually looked interested in what I'd told him.

"I like your touchdown story. I wish I'd had more touchdowns, so to speak."

"So, are you and this kid still friends then?" Ben asked.

As I looked over at Jared across the room, his gaze caught mine, and the hair on my neck stood on end. His frosty stare drifted to

Ben, and then back to me. No hint of emotion resembling anything human.

"No, we're practically strangers now."

Walking to my car after school, I noticed K.C.'s ex-boyfriend leaning against it. "Liam?" I asked, momentarily curious as to why he was waiting for me but more annoyed, because I just wanted to get home.

"Hey, Tate. How have you been?" His hands were stuffed in his pockets, and he looked between me and the ground.

"I'm hanging in there. What can I do for you?" I asked abruptly. It was unlike me not to ask someone how they were when they had asked me, but I was upset with Liam. He could rot in his own tears for all I cared.

He smiled nervously. "Um, listen. I feel really bad about what happened between K.C. and me. I've tried calling her, and I stopped at the house, but she won't see me."

This was news to me. When I'd asked K.C. if she'd heard from Liam, she'd told me "no." My friend wasn't as honest as she used to be.

"And?" I opened the door to my dad's Bronco and tossed my bag inside.

"Tate, I just need to see her." His eyes were red, and he was fidgeting. "I fucked up. I know that."

"That's your excuse?" It was none of my business, but I liked Liam. At least I did before he cheated on my best friend. I wanted to understand. "Why did you cheat?"

Running his hands through his dark hair, he leaned back against the truck. "Because I could. Because I got caught up in the scene at the Loop. There were always girls around, and I let it go to my head. K.C. would only come with me every so often, and even then she wasn't interested."

My head hurt just trying to think of what to say to him. I couldn't do this right now.

"Liam, I need to go home. I'll tell K.C. that you'd like to talk to her, but I can't be on your side about this. If you deserve it, she'll forgive you." Personally, I wasn't sure if I'd ever forgive him if I were her.

"I'm sorry. I didn't mean to wrangle you into this."

"Yes, you did," I joked reluctantly. At heart, I didn't believe Liam was a bad guy. He messed up, though, and I wasn't sure if it was worth the risk to forgive him. Luckily, I didn't have to make that decision.

"Yeah, I know. I'm sorry. You were my last hope. Take care of yourself, and . . . for what it's worth, I am sorry about this mess." He backed away and walked to his Camaro.

Letting out a sigh, I climbed into the truck and drove off before this soap opera of a day turned into *Gone with the Wind*.

Chapter 16

"Mmmm ... what's cookin', Good Lookin'?" I yelled as I opened the front door. My body was screaming for my bed, but I decided to put on a happy face for my grandma. I'd missed her.

And I selfishly needed her to remind me that I was a good person. After what I'd said to Jared today, I didn't even want to face myself in the mirror.

Her arrival could be smelled from the driveway. The rich aroma of sauce and meat danced through my nostrils enveloping me in a warm blanket even before I closed the front door.

"Hi, Peaches!" Grandma seemed to dance from the kitchen to the foyer, taking me into her arms. In the year I'd been gone, I'd missed her scent-filled hugs. The hairspray from her hair mixed with the lotion and perfume she used, and the leather from her belts and shoes created this aroma of home in my mind. After Mom died, I'd needed my grandma a lot.

"Oh, I forgot about 'Peaches.' Dad still calls me 'Pumpkin.' What is it with you Brandts naming me after fruit?" I teased, knowing their endearments were out of love.

"Oh, now. Don't deny an old lady the pleasure of her pet names." She plastered a kiss on my cheek with a *mwah*.

"Grandma, you're younger at heart than me." I dropped my bag by the wall and crossed my arms over my chest. "The only thing old about you is your music." I cocked an eyebrow.

"The Beetles are timeless. Unlike that 'screaming' you call music." I rolled my eyes, and she hooked my arm, leading me into the kitchen.

My grandma is a product of Fifties' parenting—overbearing, every hair in the right place—but she also blossomed during her teens and the rebellion of the Sixties. The desire to be active in her environment and experience the world led her to travel a lot as a young adult. When she found out about me going to France for a year, she couldn't have been more thrilled. *Experience is the best teacher.* Her echo followed me everywhere.

While she was just over sixty, she looked much younger. Her hair was light brown with some gray, which she usually wore down around her shoulders. Healthy eating and exercise kept her fit, happy, and energetic. Her style was eclectic. I'd seen her in pants suits and Rolling Stones T-shirts.

"So tell me how school's been going?" She grabbed come lettuce off the island and began rinsing it in the sink.

"It's fine." My bed wasn't far off now, and my body was too listless to even entertain the idea of actually telling her the truth.

Her eyes shot up at me, though, and she turned off the water. "What's wrong?" She was breathing through her nose. That's never good. This woman knew me too well.

"Nothing's wrong. I said everything was fine." *Please just leave it alone.*

Her eyes narrowed. "When you're happy, you tell me everything: homework, Science Club, France, Cross Country—"

"I'm totally fine," I interrupted, running my hand across my forehead. "It's been a rough day is all. I woke up late and got off on the wrong foot. So what time did you get in?"

She raised a perfectly plucked eyebrow at my change of subject but let it go. "About noon, I guess. I thought I'd get in a little early to clean up and start some laundry . . . " Her words trailed off as she waved a hand through the air. "But you seem to have it all under control."

"Well, I was taught by the best. Not that I'm not glad you're here, but you really don't need to worry. I've been doing great."

"That's good." Frowning a little, she continued, "Actually, it's great. Knowing you'll be going off to New York next year worries me, and seeing how well you've taken care of yourself and the house helps. I guess you don't need me or your dad so much anymore."

"I don't know about that. My cooking stinks, so having you around means I'll eat better!" I giggled as she shook the leafy lettuce at me and droplets of water flew across my face.

"Hey!" I laughed, taking a paper towel from the stand on the island and patting my face.

Already feeling a bit lighter, I bounced off my chair to help out with dinner. My grandma put together a salad, pasta, and sautéed mushrooms. I made my mouth-watering garlic bread, which was about the only thing I actually baked in the oven. The rest of my diet usually included whatever could be cooked in the microwave. She set up the table in the back patio, and I put on some ambient music, which was common ground for both of us.

"So you think I'll get into Columbia?" I asked as we served each other.

"I have a feeling about these things."

"Yeah, you also had a feeling my first kiss was going to be epic. We both know how that turned out," I joked with her, completely content with this moment. The food looked succulent, while the weightless breeze brought the trees to life and the smell of roses to our table.

She started laughing, almost choking on her sip of wine. "You know"—my grandma held up a finger— "in all fairness, I didn't know your first kiss was going to be with someone you barely knew. I thought it would've been that kid next door."

Jared.

My face instantly fell with the reminder of him. Distant memories of the now-ancient dreams I once had for Jared danced through my head. There were so many times growing up that I wanted to kiss him.

"Just because we hung out when I was a tween doesn't mean we were into each other like that. We were just friends," I mumbled, my brow now creased with aggravation. The conversation was pleasant until the subject of him came up.

"No, but it was other things too." My grandma's pensive expression made me want to change the subject again. "There were things I'd pick up on. The way you two always had your heads together, the way he would look at you when you didn't know it . . . and the way he would sneak over for sleepovers."

She drug out the last part slowly, her knowing eyes mocking my wide-eyed expression. *Oh, crap!*

"You didn't think I knew about that, did you?" she asked.

Of course I had no idea my grandmother knew about that! From as early in our friendship as I could remember, Jared would climb through the tree between our bedrooms and sneak through my French doors. It wasn't a lot, just when his mom had been drinking and he needed to get away. Since I always had a queen-sized bed, we were very comfortable and maintained our own spaces, even though his hand would eventually find mine during the night.

"Well, you don't have to worry about that anymore. We're not close." Twirling some pasta around my fork, I stuffed my mouth hoping this subject would end.

"How has he been treating you since you got back?"

Mouth still full, I rolled my eyes and shook my head to indicate that things still weren't good, and I didn't care to talk about it.

"Have you ever talked to him like I suggested?" she inquired before starting her salad.

"Grandma, I don't even care to try. We were friends once; now we're not. My heart's not breaking over it," I lied.

"Tate, I know it hurts. He's been an ass to you."

"Really, I couldn't care less. And even if it did hurt, I certainly wouldn't let him see it. He's done horrible things to me, and if my tears are what he needs to get off, then he can suffer. He doesn't deserve my attention."

My grandma put her fork down, uneaten salad dipping into the pasta, "Tatum, that's your mother talking."

My eyes darted up to her, shocked by her annoyed tone.

"Honey, I loved your mom. We all did. And I know she meant well, trying to teach you to be strong, since she knew she wouldn't be here to guide you through tough times. But honey, letting yourself be vulnerable isn't always a weakness. Sometimes, it can be a conscious decision to draw the other person out."

Even though what my grandma was saying sounded sensible, the idea of approaching Jared for a heart-to-heart triggered my gag reflex. I felt horrible about what I'd said to him today, but it didn't erase all of the crap he'd done from my memory. Seeking him out would make him peel with laughter. That was an image that reeked.

"I don't care about drawing Jared out. Whatever he's got up his ass can't be bad enough to treat people how he does. I don't care." His brown eyes flashed in my mind.

"Yes, you do," my grandma stated flatly. "I know how your mother's death affected you. I know you want to be a doctor, so you can help people that are hurting the way she was with cancer. I know you take her advice to heart and think everything will be better once you go off to college. But Jared's faults aren't the only ones hurting you."

119

Throwing my fork down on my plate, I wiped the thin layer of sweat off my brow. How did this get turned around on me? "Now, wait a minute. I'm getting pretty tired of everyone being on his side. *He* walked away from *me*." Huffing back in my chair, I crossed my arms over my chest.

"And you let him, Tate."

"What the hell was I supposed to do?! He wouldn't talk to me. I tried."

Bed. Sleep. Escape.

"Calm down. I'm not saying you weren't a good friend. Of course you were. His issues started this. But it's easy to say you've tried and *then* just walk away. It's easy to say that you can't force help on someone that doesn't want help and *then* walk away. You think you're being noble and strong by turning the other cheek or biding your time until school's over. But that baggage that you aren't letting out is weakening you. Sometimes it's the best medicine to be vulnerable, to let it all out and let him see how he's hurt you. Then you can say that you've tried."

My eyes closed, and I cupped my forehead once again. I had so much on my plate right now with the Science Fair, cross country and K.C. Why was I even wasting my time having this conversation?

Exasperated, I waved my hand in the air and let it plop down to my lap. "Why do you care? You threatened to go talk to his mom when this started." As far as I knew, my grandma wasn't Jared's biggest fan. While she always encouraged me to talk to him, she was also disgusted over his behavior. I'd stopped telling her and my dad every nasty detail of his treatment of me, because I didn't want this resolved unless Jared initiated it. When that happened, I figured he'd seek me out. He never had.

"Because you've never been the same. And because when you do go off to college, I want your heart to be free."

Free. What did that even feel like anymore?

"I've let it go. I am free." I didn't know what she wanted from me.

"Acting like you don't care is not letting it go." She pinned me with her challenging stare.

My body slumped. There wasn't anything in my arsenal after that.

Feeling mentally and physically drained, I was pretty delighted when Grandma let me head up to bed without helping with the cleanup. Once in my bathroom, I stripped down and stepped into the warmth and quiet of my shower. This pulsating hideaway was the one place I could escape without leaving my house. I could think and just be quiet whenever I needed, and no one was the wiser, and no one disturbed me.

It was only six o'clock, and I had some chapters for *Catcher in the Rye* due tomorrow as well as some questions for Physics, but it was no use fighting the drowsiness. I set my alarm for four a.m., giving me enough time to get up and do my school work, and went to the French doors to draw the curtains.

I noticed the wind picking up and the sky overshadowed with ashen clouds. The neighborhood trees were still a vibrant green, and the voltage that suddenly coursed through the sky made a tiny, grateful smile flash across my face. Knowing a storm was on its way calmed me, so I left the doors open.

Stunned awake by a piercing crash, I sat up in bed trying to get my bearings. I wiped the grogginess from my eyes while yawning. Looking around the room, I noticed that the French doors were still open, and the rain was falling steadily outside. Glancing at my clock, I saw that I'd been asleep for about six hours.

Peeling off the covers and stepping out of bed, I went to the railing outside my French doors and took in the spectacle of thunder

121

and lightning around the midnight sky. *That must've been what had woken me.* The chilly air gave me goose bumps, and droplets of rain fell on my skin. Thankfully, it wasn't falling in buckets. Otherwise, my floor would've been soaked.

I studied the tree next to my doors, taking into consideration that the rain coming through the canopy of leaves was light. With my heartbeat surging through my chest, I grabbed on to the crown molding around my door, put my foot on the railing and hoisted myself up. I held on to one of the branches above my head and touched my foot to another branch jutting into the railing. Delicious fear heated up my muscles and reminded me that I'd been a lot braver as a child. I inched out until the branches got thicker and then teetered until I reached the trunk.

Sitting down in my old space, the familiar pitter-patter of raindrops hitting leaves welcomed me home. Propped with my back against the trunk and my legs resting on the thick branch from where I'd come, I gloried in how easy it was to reclaim this simple part of myself. I hadn't been out here in years.

Out of the corner of my eye, I saw a light, possibly from the front porch, in Jared's house pop on. Seconds later, a girl came running down the front pathway with a black sweatshirt over her head. I couldn't see her face, but I knew who it was when I saw the car she was running towards.

K.C.

At Jared's house.

At midnight.

There was no sign of him, and the porch light flickered off as soon as she was in her car. The uncontrollable pounding in my chest started, so I closed my eyes for several minutes trying to get back the peace I was enjoying just a minute ago.

"Sitting in a tree during a thunderstorm? You're some kind of genius." The deep voice almost shocked me right out of the tree.

My eyes popped open, and I twisted around to see Jared leaning out his window. He was clothed, at least. That made me feel better after seeing K.C. leave his house.

"I like to think so, yes," I mumbled, turning back to the storm. My anger with Jared had lessened. Considerably. After my hateful words to him today, I just felt embarrassed and ashamed now.

"Tree? Lightning? Ring any bells?"

Of course I knew it was dangerous. That's what made it so fun.

"It never mattered to you before," I pointed out, keeping my eyes focused on the glistening road shining under the streetlights.

"What? You sitting in a tree during a storm?"

"No, me getting hurt." The urge to look at him was strong. I wanted to see his eyes so badly that it felt like an invisible hand was forcing my face to turn to him. I wanted him to see me. I wanted him to see us.

There was no response for several seconds, but I knew he was still there. My body reacted to his presence, and I could feel his eyes on me.

"Tatum?" His voice sounded soft and gentle, and I instantly felt warm all over. But then he spoke again. "I wouldn't care if you were alive or dead."

All the air left my body, and I sat on the tree branch feeling completely defeated.

No more. I couldn't do this anymore. There was no life in feeling like this. It was all a game to him, but I didn't have the heart to play it anymore. I'm not strong. I'm not a bully. I'm not happy. I knew what I needed to do.

I'm letting you go.

"Jared?" I said, still staring out to the rain-soaked street. "I'm sorry about what I said to you today."

I looked over to him, but he was gone.

Chapter 17

"Hey, did you get my text?" Ben rested his hand on my shoulder as he came around to face me.

"Yeah." I vaguely remembered some sweet words about being anxious to see me again. "But not until much later. I went to bed early."

I'd finally fallen back asleep last night at about two o'clock and woke up at four with a stomach full of knots. After my disgusting behavior yesterday in class and the way I'd gotten sidetracked from my goals, I decided to give up the tough-girl act. His game was too hard, and I was turning into a person I didn't like.

I needed to talk to K.C., but I wasn't sure how to handle her. My temper still flared over the idea of her and Jared dating, but one thing she said made sense. This anger wasn't getting me anywhere, and I wanted to move on. I just didn't know if I could without holding a grudge.

"So would you like to go out this weekend? There's a bonfire at Tyler Hitchen's place on Friday night after the race."

"I'd love to, but I'm so swamped right now. I'll have to see how my week goes." I closed the locker door and began inching away.

"Can I help with anything?" Ben's knit his eyebrows together in concern. It was sweet and made me smile.

"Well, you can't run my laps for me, or do my Math or Science, or take my tests, so you're pretty useless."

"Yes, yes, I am. I see you've been talking to my mom." His eyes shined with amusement, and his grin was teasing. "Try to make yourself free. It'll be fun."

Hannah the Bitch walked by us with her crew, and they threw Ben some sultry looks of the you-don't-even-need-to-buy-me-dinner variety. Their antics were so transparent. Flipping hair and biting your bottom lip? Really? Who does that? She slapped me with an "L" for loser, and I flipped her off behind Ben's back as they walked past.

I guess I should be delighted that a guy like Ben wanted to date me. Hannah, and probably most of the other girls in this school, would be grateful to have his attention. He was attentive and behaved like a gentleman. I enjoyed spending time with him. It was just taking longer than I thought it would to develop a spark.

"Fine," I answered. "I'll try."

He took my bag and walked me to Physics. "Meet you at lunch?" He looked at me expectantly.

"Sure. I'll be sitting outside today." His presence would be welcome. I might need a buffer between K.C. and myself if I lost my temper again.

"See you there." His voice was low and warm. Arriving at class, he handed me my bag and backed away, heading off down the hall.

I wished I was more into Ben. Maybe I just needed to get to know him better.

The surprise Physics quiz burned panic right through my bones. Luckily, it was enough to take my mind off my personal life. I'd done the reading and completed the questions this morning in my haze, but I still felt unprepared.

The running we did in P.E. afterwards let off the steam of the morning. Even though Coach was testing us on our mile run time, and I completed that in six minutes flat, she let me keep running. The burn in my muscles singed off the frustration and hurt of Jared's words last night that had been floating through my head all morning.

I wouldn't care if you were alive or dead. My heels dug into the dirt as I envisioned digging his grave.

"Hey, you guys." K.C. came up behind Ben and me where we sat at a picnic table outside, eating our lunch.

"Hi," I said through a mouthful of pasta salad, unable to meet her eyes.

"So how are you doing, Ben? Ready for the game Friday?"

"I'm not as worried about the game as I am the race later that night. I've got some money riding on Wonderboy in there." He jerked his thumb towards the cafeteria, referring to Jared, I would assume.

"Oh, well he's a safe bet." She smirked and waved her hand in the air. "I'll be at the race, too. Are you bringing Tate?" Her gaze slid to me.

"I didn't think she'd enjoy the race, but I'm trying to get her to the bonfire afterwards."

K.C. narrowed her eyes at me as she mixed a flavored powder into her water. "Tate knows a lot about cars. She would love it," she pointed out.

"Guys, I'm sitting right here. Talk to me, morons," I barked sarcastically at the both of them, feeling like they were the parents discussing what to do with the child.

Ben tucked my hair behind my ear, and I jerked a little with the intimate gesture.

"Sorry, Tate. As I was saying, you love cars. Did you know that, Ben?"

"I didn't. Well, she has to come with me then." He grinned while popping a Cheetoh in his mouth, and I felt squeezed like the cream in an Oreo cookie. They were pushing me.

Like every other time we'd been in a social setting in the past, Jared had done something to ruin it. Why bother?

Looking at K.C., I geared up for verbal sparring. "You expect me to come to the Loop and cheer for Jared?"

"No, but I'd love you to be there with me since I won't know anyone. You can see the race, check out the cars, and explain to me the difference between a battery and an engine. I never understood that. If you have a battery, then why do you need an engine?"

Ben and I burst out laughing. She was being purposely dimwitted to get me to be agreeable. I wanted to go, but I knew K.C. would be all over Jared. If I wanted to spend time with her, then I'd have to be around him. I couldn't hang pathetically on Ben all night.

"I told Ben I'd see how my week went. I have a lot to do right now." While I was caught up on my homework, I wanted to get ahead on some reading and get to the library to research the Science topics so I could make my final decision. Not to mention, I needed to be at school by seven on Saturday morning to catch the bus for a cross country meet in Farley. It's not like I was trying to avoid Jared.

"And I know what that means." K.C. picked up her phone and started scrolling, clearly pissed.

She's pissed at me? Screw that.

"K.C.!" My mood turned as black as my fingernails. "I said I would try. Jesus."

"I'm just saying—" her eyes never leaving her phone— "that I think if it weren't for Jared, then you would go. You have to try, Tate. He said he wouldn't have any problem with you being there."

My face flushed with embarrassment, I glanced at Ben. I never aired my dirty laundry for others to witness. "Oh, *he* wouldn't have any problem with me being there? I guess since I have the dickhead's permission, then I should fall on my knees with gratitude."

"Well, Jared isn't the race master, and doesn't say who's in or out. I can invite who I like," Ben assured as he got up. "I need a Gatorade. Do either of you need anything?" he asked, probably looking for an escape while K.C. and I settled our little argument.

"I'll take a water." I reached into my pocket to dig out some money.

"No, no. I got it." He walked off inside the cafeteria. My gaze followed him as I appreciated how nice he looked in his jeans. Well, there was that at least.

K.C.'s voice broke my trance. "So if Jared's a dickhead, then what am I for seeing him?" K.C.'s voice was calm, but I could tell by her point-blank stare and pursed lips that anger boiled underneath.

Jared was a dickhead. It wasn't an assumption but a proven fact. My frustration with her spending time with that asshole started to escape me. I was trying to grab my anger before it got out of control, but the damn thing kept slipping away.

"You tell me. He's a prick. You know it, and I know it." *What the hell was I doing?* "But what you don't realize is that he's using you. He's using you to get under my skin. He cares about you as much as Liam did when he cheated."

Shit! Too far.

I was done for. The look on her face punctured my chest. I'd hurt her, and I hoped she would huff and puff and eventually see reason. But the look in her eyes left me with only doubt.

After a few moments' hesitation, she started packing up her things and grabbing her tray. "You know, Jared asked me to sit with him today, and right now I want his company a lot more than I do yours." She spat out her words before leaving. And I let her leave, because I understood her disappointment. Right now, I didn't even like myself.

As much as I tried to take part in a conversation when Ben returned, my mind was too focused on rewriting the argument with K.C. My dad always told me that I could say what I need to say as long as I said it nicely.

And fuck me for snarling out my words like a five-year-old.

I could've handled it so much better. You know what they say about best laid plans? My emotions got away from me, and she probably went to cry on Jared's shoulder. I'll bet he was lapping this up.

As I pushed through AP English and Government, I was already yawning with exhaustion and was in no way energized for practice or the dinner out that my grandmother had planned.

"Sit down everyone, please!" Mrs. Penley shouted over the clatter of moving desks and laughter. We had just finished our discussion on the assigned chapters in *Catcher in the Rye* and were moving our desks back to normal position. The class was energized about the story. Half of them, I think, were thankful that it wasn't a farming story like they thought, and everyone liked the idea of the rebellious teenager who smoked too many cigarettes.

The discussion had sucked for me. We'd been forced to move our desks into a circle, so that we could make eye contact with anyone that spoke. Jared kept flashing me smirks, no doubt fully informed of his progress on Operation Kill Tate and K.C.

The silvery feeling coursing down my arms and legs made me want to scream until the force of my upset made him magically disappear.

I wouldn't care if you were alive or dead.

I hated admitting to myself that I did care whether *he* was alive or dead. I'd been stung every day he didn't want me near him.

129

But that baggage that you aren't letting out is weakening you. Grandma was right. I was in no better position now than I was before I decided to fight back.

"Now, class," Mrs. Penley instructed from the front of the classroom. "Before we copy down assignments for homework, I want to touch base about your monologues. Remember, these are due in two weeks. I'll have a sign-up sheet outside the door, and you can pick your day. Your monologue can be from the list I gave you or you can choose another one with my approval. Now, I'm not looking for Oscar-worthy performances," she reassured, "so don't get scared. This isn't theater after all. Just perform the monologue and turn in the essay using the rubric I gave you explaining how that monologue reinforces the theme of the book or film." Mrs. Penley drifted off as people started to get out notebooks and copy down the assignment from the board.

Acting like you don't care is not letting it go.

Isn't it about time you fought back?

I want your heart to be free.

Weariness wadded my heart. I turned around to look at Jared. His eyes lifted from his notebook, and his eyes sharpened on me.

I wanted to walk down the hall and know there was no pain around the next corner. I wanted him to stop. And yes, I admitted, I wanted to know him again.

But that baggage that you aren't letting out is weakening you.

Before I could stop myself, I turned back around and thrust my hand in the air. Tightness knotted my stomach as I felt like I'd stepped into someone else's dream. "Mrs. Penley?"

"Yes, Tate?" Mrs. Penley was standing at her desk, writing something on a Post-it.

"We have five minutes left of class. May I perform my monologue now?" I sensed eyes and ears shifting my way, the whole class focusing its attention on me.

130

"Um, well, I wasn't expecting to grade anything yet? Do you have your essay ready?" Mrs. Penley stuck the pen in her hand into her tight bun.

"No, I'll have that by the due date, but I would really love to perform it now. Please."

I watched the wheels turn in her head as she probably worried if I was prepared, but I flashed my pleading eyes on her to hopefully make her see that I wanted to get this over with.

"Okay," she exhaled, "if you're sure you're ready." She motioned for me to come up front, while she moved aside to lean against the wall.

I rose from my chair and walked to the front of class, feeling the burn of looks on my back. Turning to face everyone, my heart pounded like a jackhammer in my chest. I swept my eyes across the room before beginning. If I didn't meet his eyes, I could do this.

"I like storms," I started. "Thunder, torrential rain, puddles, wet shoes. When the clouds roll in, I get filled with this giddy expectation."

Just keep going, Tate. I tried to envision that I was speaking to my dad or grandma. *Keep it natural.*

"Everything is more beautiful in the rain. Don't ask me why." My shoulders shrugged. "But it's like this whole other realm of opportunity. I used to feel like a superhero, riding my bike over the dangerously slick roads, or maybe an Olympic athlete enduring rough trials to make it to the finish line."

My smile spread with the memories. Memories of Jared and me.

"On sunny days, as a girl, I could still wake up to that thrilled feeling. You made me giddy with expectation, just like a symphonic rainstorm. You were a tempest in the sun, the thunder in a boring, cloudless sky.

131

"I remember I'd shovel in my breakfast as fast as I could, so I could go knock on your door. We'd play all day, only coming home for food and sleep. We played hide and seek, you'd push me on the swing, or we'd climb trees. Being your sidekick gave me a sense of home again."

I exhaled, finally relaxing, and my eyes drifted over to meet his. I saw him watching me, breathing hard, almost as if he was frozen. *Stay with me, Jared.*

"You see"—my eyes stayed on him—"when I was ten, my mom died. She had cancer, and I lost her before I really knew her. My world felt so insecure, and I was scared. You were the person that turned things right again. With you, I became courageous and free. It was like the part of me that died with my mom came back when I met you, and I didn't hurt anymore. Nothing hurt if I knew I had you." Pools of tears filled my eyes as the class leaned in to listen to me.

"Then one day, out of the blue, I lost you, too. The hurt returned, and I felt sick when I saw you hating me. My rainstorm was gone, and you became cruel. There was no explanation. You were just gone. And my heart was ripped open. I missed you. I missed my mom." My voice cracked, and I didn't wipe away the tear that fell.

"What was worse than losing you was when you started to hurt me. Your words and actions made me hate coming to school. They made me uncomfortable in my own home." I swallowed, and the knot in my chest lessened.

"Everything still hurts, but I know none of it is my fault. There are a lot of words that I could use to describe you, but the only one that includes sad, angry, miserable, and pitiful is 'coward.' In a year, I'll be gone, and you'll be nothing but some washout whose height of existence was in high school." My eyes were still on Jared, and my voice got strong again. The ache in my face from trying to hold back tears eased. "You were my tempest, my thunder cloud, my tree in the downpour. I loved all of those things, and I loved you. But now? You're a fucking drought. I thought that all the assholes drove German cars, but it turns out that pricks in Mustangs can still leave scars."

Looking around the class, I noticed everyone leaned in and quiet. One girl was tearing up. I finished wiping a tear from my cheeks and grinned. "And I'd like to thank the Academy ... "

Everyone started laughing, coming out of their trance from my serious and sad story, and began clapping and cheering. My head fell back to look up at the ceiling before I took a dramatic and sarcastic bow making my classmates giggle more. The deafening applause distracted me from the wobbliness in my legs.

This was it. Jared could push me, hurt me, take what he wanted, but showing him that he had hurt, but not broken me, was how I won. Euphoria settled in my stomach as waves of contentment washed over me.

Free.

"What was that monologue from? Mrs. Penley, she made people cry! How is anyone going to live up to that? And we're allowed to swear?" One of the girls from my compass jokingly complained.

"I'm sure you'll do fine, and Tate, that was wonderful. You really set the bar. I don't remember that one on the list, though, so I trust everything will be in your essay?"

I nodded as I headed back to my seat, figuring I'd deal with that part later. The bell rung and people started for the door, ready to be done with the day.

"Great job, Tate!"

"Wow!"

People I'd never spoken to patted me on the back and offered compliments. Jared drifted out of class, like the fuse on a stick of

133

dynamite. Only this time, I was free from the explosion. I let him go, not even sparing any effort to make it *look* like I didn't care.

I'd bared my soul up there, and now the ball was in his court.

"Tate." Ben walked up to my desk as I grabbed my bag. "That was great. Are you sure you want to waste your time on medicine and not go into theater or something?" He took my bag off my shoulder and hung it over his own.

I headed for the door as he followed behind.

"Are you okay? You were crying." He sounded genuinely concerned.

I turned to face him and plastered a no-effort grin on my face. "I'm great. And I would love to go to the race with you this weekend."

He looked surprised by my change of subject, but his eyes lit up as he grabbed my hand. "Okay! But . . . you know you have to wear a really short skirt, right? It's kind of a uniform for the girls." He teased, and I could tell he was being flirty.

"Well, I'm a rebel, or didn't you know?"

We pushed through the door, hand in hand. My eyes shot to Jared, who had his forehead leaned into the wall.

"See ya, Jared," Ben called out as we passed, oblivious to what had just passed between Jared and me in the classroom.

He turned around but didn't reply. I noticed that the whites of his eyes were red. Hands tucked into the front pocket of his black hoodie, he was breathing like he'd just run a mile. Other than that, there was no emotion. He didn't look upset or happy. Nothing.

What was happening in his head?

And would I ever find out?

Chapter 18

"Tate!"

I twirled around, stunned out of my celebration, and met my grandma's expectant stare.

Whoops. I wondered how long she'd been standing there.

I ran over to the iPod dock and switched off AFI's "Miss Murder." "Sorry. Just getting my groove on." I smiled sheepishly. After a practice where I could've run at least another hour, I returned home with energy to spare. A weight had lifted off of me, and I felt like celebrating.

I'd decided to shelve my homework—since nothing was due this week, anyway—and forge a hole in my carpet with some horrendous dance moves.

"Well, you left your phone downstairs. K.C. called." She tossed me my cell, which I caught. "And it's almost seven. Are you ready to go eat?" Grandma waved her hand towards the door.

"Absolutely." I grabbed my black cardigan and black Chucks. I'd changed into jeans and a T-shirt after I'd come home to clean up following practice. Since Jared's locker room intrusion, I'd opted to shower at home now.

"I'll be down in a minute. I want to call K.C. back."

Grandma nodded and walked out.

The idea of apologizing to K.C. caused my stomach to roll. She was dating a guy that treated me badly, and it hurt that she could turn a blind eye to that. But, I also realized the she and Jared were using each other. In time, probably sooner rather than later, this fling of theirs would be over. As long as she wasn't teaming up with him to treat me like shit, then I'd decided not to give him what he wanted.

"Hey," I greeted K.C. timidly when she picked up.

"Hey." Her voice sounded curt.

I took a deep breath and let out a sigh. "So, I hope I can cash in a Get Out of Jail Free card. I'm sorry I said what I said today."

She was silent for few moments as I nervously drifted around my room.

"You acted like a dick," she mumbled.

I almost laughed. Well, she was talking to me at least.

"I know. He has nothing to do with me anymore. If he's what you want, then I can grow up and get over it."

"Apology accepted." I could hear the smile in her voice.

"Alright. I'll see you tomorrow. I'm off to dinner with Grandma." I could hear her mother calling her in the background anyway.

"Have fun. And I love you, Tate," she said sweetly.

"Love ya, too. Later."

We hung up, and I already felt better. Thank goodness that was done. Now, if I was lucky, I'd only have to endure minimal meetings with Jared. If I was really unlucky, though, he'd make all of K.C.'s and my outings into threesomes.

I also still felt like slapping my friend a little. But, at least, I'd let go of my bitterness about Jared. If she wanted to rebound with him, then that was on her. I was tired of making a problem where there wasn't one, and to save myself some stress, I decided to mind my own business. She knew how I felt, and I knew she wouldn't betray my trust. That's all I needed.

I practically danced down the stairs, feeling like the hippo that'd been sitting on my chest decided to finally move on.

"Well, you seem like you're in a good mood." Grandma's eyes followed my movements. "School was good today?"

"Yeah, actually. It was great." Letting Jared know how much I'd been hurt by him let the frustration out. I no longer felt buried under his actions and my struggle to maintain a façade.

"Good. What are you in the mood for? Judging from your jeans, I guess O'Shea's is out." Her flat tone showed disappointment. O'Shea's was her favorite restaurant in our less than diverse town.

"How about Mario's?" I asked as I sat down to tie my shoes. I loved their pasta with basil and olive oil. The old couple that ran the restaurant was sweet and inviting, and my parents went on their first date there.

"Sure. Sounds good." She grabbed her purse, and I snatched her keys. I always had to drive unless the situation didn't allow it. Everywhere felt like forever to get to unless I was in control of the vehicle. Luckily, the adults in my life were indulgent.

As she stopped to fluff her hair and button her blazer in front of the mirror by the door, I slipped my arms through my cardigan and hooked my purse strap over my head.

"Gram? While we're out, do you mind if we circle some lots, so I can check out some cars after dinner?" Finding a car hadn't been on my mind in weeks, but the idea spilled out of my mouth like it had been on the tip of my tongue all day.

I couldn't pretend that I needed the car to get around. After all, I had my dad's Bronco. The control I'd asserted today was like slipping into new skin. Everything felt warm, delicious, and possible. Getting a car of my own was another dose of control, straight to the vein.

Grandma narrowed her blue eyes at me through the mirror. "Does your dad know you want to get a car?"

"Yeah, but I'm just looking right now, anyway."

"You won't want a car in New York City, honey," she asserted, turning around to open the door.

"Is it okay if we just look? After all, I might still like a car when I come home for vacations." I followed her out.

Turning to lock up the house, she nodded. "Sure, I don't see any harm in *looking*."

After a much-needed night out and light-hearted conversation with my grandma, I'd come home feeling calmer than I had in weeks.

I sat back on my bed, reading one of Chelsea Cain's thrillers, when I heard yelping coming from outside.

My French doors had been open a crack, so I could hear the rain. The light drizzle that started when Grandma and I got home was coming down in buckets now. Swinging one of the doors open, I leaned outside and listened.

The barking was consistent, distressed . . . and close.

Madman.

As I peered down into Jared's yards, I didn't see any lights or sign of the little dog. The whole house looked quiet and dark. It was after nine, so he and his mom must still be gone for the night.

Slipping on my Chucks, I walked down the stairs, taking a moment to check that my grandma's bedroom light was off. Once at the front door, I switched on my porch light and walked outside.

Shit! It was raining.

How had I forgotten that in the three seconds it took me to get downstairs? Thank goodness for the covered porch. Hugging myself, I walked to the edge nearest Jared's house and took another look. I put my hand to my mouth to stifle a small gasp at the sight of Madman whining and clawing at the front door. He was soaking wet, and I could tell from here that he was shivering. Luckily, he had a small awning protecting him from the thunderous downpour.

Without a second thought, I dived out into the storm and ran across our yards to Jared's small front stoop. I only wore my sleep shorts and a tank top, so, like Madman, I was now shaking with the cold rain splattered on my bare legs and arms.

"Hey, buddy. How'd you get out here?" I bent down to pet his head, and he licked my hand excitedly. "Where's Jared, huh?"

A shiver shot down my body, making my shoulders twitch.

The last thing I wanted to do was knock on the dickhead's door, but there's no telling what bullshit I'd wake up to if I took Madman home with me. Jared would probably accuse me of trying to steal *his* pet.

Madman had been collateral damage in Jared's and my fallout. As much as I loved the dog, it just seemed like he should be with Jared. A few things had been like that after he came back from that summer away. One of our favorite hangouts was a fish pond at Eagle Point Park. When Jared and I stopped being friends, he stopped going there.

I got the pond. He got the dog.

"Jared? Ms. Trent?" I called while ringing the doorbell. The rain pounded to the ground, giving a flood-feel to our street. The howling wind forced the rain sideways, which soaked my shoes and calves, even under the awning.

I doubted anyone could hear someone scream in this ruckus, so I pounded on the door and rang the bell two more times. The house remained dark and silent. "Well, Madman. You may be coming home with me." The little guy yelped again, clearly unhappy being outside.

Before I walked away, I gripped the door handle and turned. To my surprise, the door opened.

Not locked? Weird.

Madman darted inside, pushing the door completely open like he was running from a fire. His claws against the hard wood floors echoed down the hall. He'd gone to the kitchen, probably to his food dish.

I took a hesitant step into the foyer. "Hello?" The house was nearly pitch black except for the streetlights that cast a dull glow through the windows. "Ms. Trent? Jared?" I looked around and felt a chill shoot down my arms.

Something's not right.

The house seemed almost dead. No ticking clocks, no hum of a fish tank. I wasn't even sure if they had fish, but an occupied house makes some kind of noise, even in the middle of the night.

Madman barked, and I took a step towards the kitchen, but I stopped when I heard a crackle under my shoe. Taking a closer look, my eyes having adjusted to the dark, I noticed broken glass or . . . maybe it was pottery, on the floor. I surveyed the area and took in more disarray that I hadn't noticed when I'd entered.

Chairs were overturned, a lamp was broken, and couch cushions lay about the living room. Even the framed pictures of Jared on the wall by the stairs were shattered and hanging by a corner.

Jared?! My heart pounded in my ears. What had happened here?

Madman continued to bark, more persistently this time. I ran down the hall and into the kitchen. The dog sat looking out of the open backdoor, whining and wagging his tail.

As I looked through the door, I could see Jared sitting on the top step leading down to the backyard. I let out a breath.

His back was to me, and he was drenched. Water poured down his bare back, and the hair on his head stuck to his scalp.

"Jared?" I called out, stepping up to the doorframe.

He turned his head enough to see me out of the corner of his eye, which was almost completely covered by his soaked hair.

Without acknowledging me otherwise, he turned back around and lifted a liquor bottle to his lips.

Jack Daniels. Straight.

My first thought was to leave. He was safe. The dog was safe. Whatever he was doing wasn't my business.

But my feet wouldn't move. The house had been vandalized, and Jared was drinking alone.

"Jared?" I stepped outside, thankful for the covering over the backdoor as well. "The dog was barking outside. I rang the doorbell. Didn't you hear it?" I guess I felt a need to explain my presence in his house.

When he didn't answer, I walked down the stairs to face him. Rain cascaded down my face, drenching my hair and clothes. My muscles tensed with the urgency to get back inside, but, for some reason, I stayed put.

Jared's head was level, but his eyes were downcast. His arms rested on his knees, and the half-empty bottle was secured in his left hand where he swung it back and forth between his fingers.

"Jared? Would you answer me?" I yelled. "The house is trashed."

None of my business. Just leave.

Jared licked his lips, and the raindrops on his face looked like tears. I watched him as he raised his eyes lazily and blinked away the water.

"The dog ran away," he mumbled, matter-of-factly. His voice was calm.

Stunned by such a cryptic reply, I almost laughed. "So you threw a temper tantrum? Does your mom know you did that to the house?"

His brow narrowed as he looked me dead in the eyes. "What do you care? I'm nothing, right? A loser? My parents hate me. Weren't those your words?"

For a moment, I closed my eyes, feeling guilty all over again. "Jared, I should never have said those things. No matter what you've—"

"Don't apologize," he interrupted. Swaying as he stood up, he adopted his usual sadistic tone. "Groveling makes you look pathetic."

Asshole!

"I'm not groveling!" I snapped as I followed him into the house. "I can just admit when I fucked up."

I stood inside the doorway while he put his bottle on the kitchen table and grabbed a dish towel off the counter. Walking over to Madman, who was huddled underneath a chair, he wrapped the cloth around the dog and slowly dried him off. He continued to ignore me, but I couldn't leave until I'd said what I needed to say.

"I'm sorry if I hurt you, and it won't happen again." There, I'd said it. No need for me to be here anymore.

But I didn't stop there. My gaze fell on the not-yet-empty bottle of Jack, and I was worried. His mom was a recovering alcoholic, and hard liquor could be dangerous in large quantities. By the looks of the house, he was not in control of his faculties.

Snatching the bottle off the table, I walked to the sink and started dumping its contents down the drain. "And I'm not letting you hurt yourself, either."

"Son of a bitch!" Jared heaved at my back, and I shook the bottle nervously when I heard his quick footsteps behind me.

Jared snatched at the container, which was still a few sips from being empty, but I spun around to face him, keeping hold.

"This is none of your business. Just leave," he growled. His breath fell on my face, smelling of whiskey and rain, and his wild eyes made my arms go weak. I almost released the bottle, overwhelmed by the force he used to get it away. As he yanked, my whole body jerked.

Well, this is new.

The Jared I'd gotten used to walked around calm and collected, but this Jared was desperate and reckless. I should be scared, but, for some reason, I was intoxicated with the face-off.

I wanted this confrontation with Jared. I hungered for it.

We both breathed hard as we tried to get the bottle away from each other, but no one was giving up. His arms flexed with the struggle, and I felt the bottle start to slip out of my fingers. I knew I was going to lose.

"Stop it!" I cried. Was the fucking bottle that important?!

Get a grip, jerk! He'd obviously lost control, and I needed to snap him out of this.

I let the bottle go and slapped him across the face. His head twisted to the side with the impact, and my hand stung. I'd never hit Jared. Not even when we were kids and playing around.

Stunned and furious, Jared dropped the bottle to the floor, forgotten, and turned his vicious eyes on me. I gasped when he hoisted me off of my feet by my waist and slammed me down on the hard edge of the sink. Before I knew it, he had locked my wrists in a hold behind my back and positioned his body between my legs. He pulled me to him, roughly, and I was trapped. My chest rose and fell quickly, desperate for air.

Oh, God. "Let me go!" I screamed.

My body was constricted between his arms at the back of me and his torso in front. His grip was tight, enough to keep me still but not enough to hurt. I tried to twist and wiggle my way free, but he only jerked me harder against him and tightened his hold.

"Jared, let me go." I tried to make my voice sound forceful, but with the struggle, my strength had dwindled.

His eyes met mine, our faces less than an inch away from each other. Several moments passed as he held me, trying to stare me down.

143

But it didn't work.

Once my gaze met his, it was impossible to look away. His eyes were like the cover of a book—giving you hints but not the whole story. And I wanted to know the story. If I searched his eyes long and hard enough, maybe what I craved would seep out.

Damn it!

Even with the liquor on his breath, he smelled incredible. Like some kind of bodywash. My thighs were cold where his wet pants rubbed, but the rest of me was on fire. Heat spilled from the pores on my neck, and a drop of sweat glided between my breasts where my chest touched his. Dizziness fogged my head with the pressure he was putting between my legs.

Our breathing matched up, and his expression was no longer angry.

He spoke shakily, almost sadly. "You fucked me up today."

I assumed he was talking about the monologue. "Good," I bit out.

He jerked me again. "You wanted to hurt me? Did you get off on it? It felt good, didn't it?"

Was he talking about me or him?

I tried to keep my face even, but my body tingled everywhere. His scent was all around me as he leaned in. Our bodies were melting together, our lips were so close. When I felt him harden between my legs, I squeezed my eyes shut, too afraid of why I wasn't struggling anymore.

Taking a deep breath, I opened my eyes and stared boldly at him, my pulse throbbing in my ears.

He's nothing to me. Nothing.

"No, I didn't get off on it," I answered calmly. "I feel nothing. *You* are nothing to me."

He flinched. "Don't say that."

144

The heat from his mouth wafted around me as I leaned in. "Nothing," I repeated, barely a whisper. "Now, get off—"

His mouth crashed down on mine, drowning out my protest.

His lips devoured me, hard and fast, like I was being eaten alive. His tongue dived into my mouth, and I let it, needing to feel all of him. The pulsing sensation in my core quickened, and I wrapped my legs around his waist before I closed my eyes, savoring the release.

I tried to think, but I couldn't. I didn't want to. All the years that we'd been apart filled this one moment.

He released my arms, threading one hand roughly through my hair and the other gripping my ass. Pulling my hips harder against his, he assaulted my mouth like he was starving. He sucked on my bottom lip and then turned his attention to my jaw and neck in hot, frenzied kisses. A legion of butterflies took flight in my stomach, and I moaned with the pleasure.

And I kissed him back.

Oh, my God! I was kissing him back!

"Jared," I gasped out. He should stop. *We* should stop. But I forgot why.

I was lost.

I tightened my legs around his waist and grasped his wet hair, holding him to me, while he sucked on my neck. His left hand ran down my thigh, and I brought his lips back up to mine again, needing more. Pressure was building as he pressed our centers together. He groaned, and I didn't want him to stop. Ever.

When he bent his head to nibble under my ear, images of him and K.C. in the hall yesterday flashed through my mind.

This is what she felt.

Everything came flooding back. My eyes popped open as realization dawned.

He hurt me.

He hated me.

"Jared, stop." My tone was meant to be stronger, but it only sounded desperate. He ignored me as he kissed and lightly bit my shoulder, while his hand moved underneath my shirt.

"Jared! I said 'stop!'" Putting my hands on his chest, I pushed him away. He stumbled back a few steps, breathing hard and eyeing me like an animal.

Too far.

Jumping off the sink ledge, I nearly ran out of the kitchen and the house. It felt like steam coming off my skin as the cool rain hit my arms and legs outside. My heart was nearly beating out of my chest as I made it to my front porch.

What are you doing?! I screamed to myself.

A hollow ache settled in my stomach, and a horrible void filled my arms where he'd just been. I'd let him kiss me. And feel me.

And I'd done the same to him.

I tried to catch my breath. How could I have let that happen? It was like I hadn't even been in control! I knew what we were doing was crazy, but the feel of him made me forget everything. Even now, my body still craved him, and I hated that. Shame burned my skin where he'd touched me.

Jared always calculated his moves. Did he plan this? This was lower than I thought he'd ever go. He was probably in there laughing at me right now, knowing that he'd gotten my pride.

A thousand questions filled my head, but I pushed them away. *No.* One thing was certain: Jared couldn't be trusted. He hadn't even begun to make amends, and I was nauseous with humiliation.

That wouldn't happen again.

Chapter 19

I rushed from one class to another the next day. My heart was in my throat—knowing that at any minute I could run into Jared—so I kept my eyes focused straight ahead. Literally.

All through French class it had been almost impossible to keep my mind off last night. His hands, his lips, his . . .

Nope. Not going there.

I had liked it. That much I was willing to admit. But why did he kiss me if not to prove that he could? And why the hell did I let him?!

I'd decided to treat it as a drunken move on his part, and an emotional breakdown on mine.

As I headed to lunch, I hurriedly stuffed my crap into my locker and jetted around the corner to the cafeteria, trying to keep my eyes from wandering.

"Oomph." The air was knocked out of my lungs, and I stumbled to the ground.

What the . . . ?

I winced with the ache in my ass from the collapse to the cold tile floor, and I tried to blink away the disturbance to my equilibrium.

Looking up, I sucked in a breath and felt a warm fluttering to my belly at the sight of Jared hovering over me.

Shit. I'd crashed right into him. And here I was, trying to avoid him like the plague. So much for best laid plans.

I couldn't get over how just the presence of him undid me. I gawked stupidly, unable to tear my eyes away from how awesomely his T-shirt hung below his narrow waist or how sexy his rich dark hair was styled today.

Seeing me flat on my bum, he should've given me a smug smile or scowl. I flushed with embarrassment, knowing how stupid I must've looked.

But I got nothing from him. Nothing bad, anyway.

He reached out to me, and I looked at him wide-eyed, wondering what the hell he was doing.

Was he . . . helping me up?

He held his smooth, long-fingered hand, palm up, to me, and my toes curled with the gesture.

Wow. Maybe the kiss wasn't such a bad thing. Maybe he'd start behaving himself now.

And then he quirked an eyebrow at me, as if annoyed that he was waiting.

I scowled at his same old haughty attitude.

Oh, no. Don't do me any favors, buddy!

Pushing myself roughly off the ground, I dusted off my jeans and stalked past him, around the corner.

While my body definitely reacted positively to him, my brain practiced a zero tolerance policy . . . from now on.

Ben and I met up Friday night after the game. I wanted to keep our date, even though I had spent the better part of the last two days trying not to think of someone else. There was nothing between Jared and me. There was no reason to call off a date with a not-yet-boyfriend just because I kissed another guy, even if I did feel a little guilty about it.

Ben was easy. And I needed easy. I deserved it. I just needed to get my body under control.

Fucking hormones.

"So I've been meaning to ask you something." Ben seemed amused but timid as we finished our pizza.

"Let me see." I put my index finger to my lips. "Yes, I do all of my own stunts, and no, I don't normally eat that much," I joked and took a sip of my Coke.

"No, not exactly." He wagged his finger at me and took out his credit card for the waitress as she came by.

"I'm listening."

"You mentioned this boy that your character was friends with in the monologue. They were close, and then he turned against her. You said he drove a Mustang?"

I nodded, wondering where he was going with this.

"Jared Trent drives a Boss 302. A Mustang Boss 302," he pointed out.

Sweat broke out across my brow, but I nodded again. I knew what he was getting at, but there wouldn't be any answers if that was what he was hoping for. It was bad enough that I'd kissed Jared, behind K.C.'s back, but Jared and I only had one kiss. And that's all there would be. I wasn't about to explain something I didn't even understand to Ben.

"And?" He placed his elbows on the table and crossed his arms, leaning in.

"And what was your question?" I hoped being evasive would come off cute, and then he'd surrender his line of questioning.

Looking to the side and then back to me, he laughed under his breath. "I noticed him giving you his undivided attention during that monologue. Were you and Jared Trent friends?" His wide green eyes were interested.

"How do you mean?" Playing hard to get was turning out to be easy. I could do this all night.

He looked like he was trying to contain a smile, but he pressed further. "Was the monologue about him?"

I cocked my head at him. "I thought the monologues were supposed to be from a book or film?"

"What book or film did yours come from?" he shot back.

The continued play had my stomach shaking from pent-up laughter.

"It'll all be in my essay," I whispered when the waitress brought Ben's card and receipt back. "But . . . Jared is nothing to me, just so you know."

His lips curled up at the corner, hopefully satisfied with what I gave him. Taking my hand, he led me out of the restaurant and to his car. Unfortunately, he was driving, so he opened the door for me to slide in.

"You've never been to the Loop, right?"

"Nope." I fastened my seatbelt and pulled my black pinstripe skirt as far down my thighs as it would go. The three thin buckles over the right thigh caught the streetlight shining through the window.

"Well, you'll love it. And they'll love you." His gaze slid to my chest before he quickly averted his eyes. I suddenly wished I had worn a T-shirt instead. My white tank was slightly less revealing, thankfully, under my short gray military jacket, but I still felt exposed. The need to cover myself irked me. I wanted to look nice for Ben tonight, didn't I?

Or maybe it wasn't Ben I was thinking about so much when I got dressed.

"They'll love *me*? Why is that?" I asked.

"Because you look like candy." He shook his head and started the engine.

K.C.'s words came back to haunt me. Well, I, for one, am pretty excited to see the look on his face when he sees you!

My hands clenched into fists, and I bit my bottom lip to stifle a smile.

Yep, I bit my bottom lip. *Shit*.

The Loop was located on Mr. Benson's farm outside the town limits. His son, Dirk, who graduated two decades ago, started a weekly racing scene around the pond on the premises. Over time, Dirk took control of the farm and still allowed races to take place on the property even though he rarely attended. As long as he received the fee charged to get through the gate, everyone else could make their bets and have fun without any intrusion.

We travelled down the long, dirt road leading to the farm. Normally, the farm would be pitch black this time of night, but with the traffic coming down the lane, it was lit up like a Saturday night cruise.

"I'll just park here. You don't mind walking a little, do you?" Ben asked. Cars lined the sides of the road, and since we were pushing race time, parking was scarce.

"Here's fine." My fingers tingled with the anticipation in the air. I hopped out of his Escalade, immediately thankful for the Chucks I'd worn. Not very stylish with the skirt, but I wasn't a heels kind of girl. The dirt road featured dips and puddles, along with tiny gravel.

"Here, take my hand." Ben reached out as he came around the front of the car to meet me. He pulled me to a stop and gestured to the car. "Do you want to leave your bag in the car?"

"No, I might need my cell. I'm fine." I hooked my thumb behind the strap of my purse, which held two of my three life-lines. "Let's go," I chirped and started walking at a brisk pace.

Ahead of us, the track split to the left and to the right. Directly in front was the pond. The smell of exhaust already filled my nostrils, and I couldn't help the bounce in my step. My eyes hungrily swept the scene, and I saw headlights from cars parked along the sides, facing inward, illuminating the track.

Fortunately for Dirk's family, the pond wasn't even within eye sight of the main house. Most of the time, people came and went without any disturbance to the family. Since most of the town's current police force graduated around the same time as Dirk, the Loop was seen as a local treasure instead of a nuisance. Since racing was just as illegal as allowing people to use your property for it, anyone injured couldn't throw the Bensons under the bus without themselves as well. It was all very convenient and tidy.

As we headed onto the Loop, Ben guided me to the right towards what looked like the starting line. There were two cars already parked side by side, and people crushed around the scene like tightly packed molecules. One of the cars was Madoc's 2006 GTO and the other was a late model Camaro.

Liam.

"Tate!"

I spun around to meet the scream and noticed K.C. charging towards me. She fell into me in an attempt at a hug, and I stumbled to keep my balance.

"Whoa!" I burst out. "It hasn't been that long since we've seen each other, has it?" Laughing at her obvious beer-induced love, I straightened us up.

We'd made amends, but now I felt uneasy about making out with Jared, and their relationship still bugged me. I aimed to keep my promise to mind my own business, but there was a distance between us that wasn't there before, and I wasn't sure how to get back what we used to have. Maybe I looked at her differently, or maybe our conversation wasn't as easy, but I knew something had changed.

Ben held up his finger and mouthed "one minute" before he walked off to talk to a guy from our class.

"Is that Liam's Camaro?" I jerked my head towards the starting line where the tenacious, red machine idled. The symmetry of his vehicle fit in any crowd or on any road. It was tough business not to respect a Camaro. And the tires were so wide that they looked like they could keep the car afloat.

"Yeah," she said, scrunching up her nose in disgust.

"He's racing Madoc?" What Madoc would do to Liam's car would be considered a Shakespearean tragedy. Although I'd never seen Madoc race, I'd heard about it. He wasn't dirty so much as he was reckless and scared the shit out of the other driver.

"Apparently," she answered.

"I thought you said Jared was going to avenge you." I placed my hand over my chest and batted my eyelashes.

"Oh, shut up," K.C. said with fake irritability and took a sip of her beer. "That was actually the plan, but Roman is back from college for the weekend and wanted to race Jared. So ya know . . ." she trailed off.

The best had to race the best, I guess.

I started to fidget at the mention of Derek Roman. He was a world-class jerk and treated everyone the same. Like shit. It didn't matter if you were a man, woman, or child. Young, old, rich, or poor. Roman behaved like everyone was beneath him, and had no regard for ethics. He was dirty.

"Where is Jared?" Suddenly uneasy at the thought of him racing Roman, I scanned the crowd for his wispy brown hair.

"Up with Madoc, giving him a talk." K.C. gulped down her beer, and by the way she rocked her feet, I could tell she was restless.

"I'm sure Madoc won't do anything stupid. He won't want to mess up his car. Liam will be fine," I assured.

"I couldn't care less." Her eyes looked anywhere but at me.

Yeah, right.

Startled by the thundering roar of an engine, I jerked my head towards the starting line and stood on my tiptoes to peer through a gap in the crowd. Jared was leaning on Madoc's doorframe, talking to the concealed driver. His hair fell in his eyes, and an easy grin spread across his lips. The way his face lifted with the radiant smile . . .

Oh, someone was playing the steel drums on my stomach.

I hated myself for going gooey at the knees. It was unacceptable to be affected by Jared, of all people. I was here with Ben, and he was very good looking, too, I told myself.

"Hey." Ben walked back up and put an arm around me. His body next to mine warmed me, and he smelled like cologne.

I almost begged for the flutters or whatever to take root in my stomach, but they never came. Having him close or having his eyes on me just didn't affect me like it should.

Damn.

"Hey," I replied. "Should we move to get a better view?"

"You're really into this, aren't you?" Ben looked down at me, an amused expression playing on his face.

"Cars? Hot chicks? Yeah." I narrowed my eyebrows in a "duh" expression.

"Come this way." K.C. motioned to the right. "Jared's parked right off the track. We can watch from over there."

She was here with Jared. I'd almost forgotten. Of course she'd want to watch the action with him.

And why not? I was over our bullshit, and if he could ignore me for the past two days, then I could do the same.

We fought our way through the crowd as everyone took their viewing positions. Jared was already leaning on the hood of his mean, black car. With one leg propped up on the bumper, he fiddled with something in his hand. His black button-down was open to reveal a white T-shirt, and he and the car both looked angry.

"Hi, ya." K.C. strolled up to him and leaned in.

"Hi, yourself." He gave her a closed mouth smile, before looking to me. His smile faded before his eyes narrowed on Ben.

"Hey, man," Ben greeted Jared.

"Hey, how's it going?" Jared asked pleasantly but looked away too soon.

Ben must've realized the rhetorical question, because he didn't answer.

I stood there, trying to seem disinterested, as I looked anywhere but at Jared. Breaking out in a sweat as the images of us wrapped around each other the other night flashed through my head, I fanned myself slightly with the lapel of my jacket. The awkward vibe in the air made me contemplate who needed to be deleted from this equation to make it more comfortable: Jared, K.C., Ben, or me.

K.C. broke the silence. "And Jared, this is Tatum Brandt. Say 'hi,'" she joked as Jared slid an arm around her waist. My breathing hitched.

He glanced over at me through hooded eyes, and took in my outfit, only jerking his chin at me before returning his focus to the starting line.

I rolled my eyes and turned toward the action.

"And we're ready!" A young guy I assumed was the Race Master called out for people to clear the track. My eyes darted to all of the money changing hands as people placed their bets.

The roar of the engines vibrated under my feet and sent shivers up my legs. My toes curled. *Damn, I wish I was racing.* I hated being a spectator, but I still fidgeted with anticipation.

A girl in a short plaid skirt and tiny red camisole took position in front of the cars and raised her hands in the air.

"Ready?" she called out.

The engines revved, sending shouts of enthusiasm through the crowd.

"Set?" She raised her arms higher.

"Go!"

I jerked up to my tiptoes again to see the peel of the tires kicking up dust as they struggled to get going. I bobbed up and down a little with the excitement, and I couldn't contain my ear-to-ear smile. The cars shot past, sending a gust of wind in my face and a thunderous pounding in my chest.

"Shit!" I heard behind me and turned to see K.C. wiping her shirt.

"I spilled beer," she mumbled.

I saw Jared a few feet behind her, still leaning on his car, not even watching the race. His focus was entirely on me, something familiar in his expression. In that moment, the race, Ben, and K.C. didn't even exist.

A tiny moan barely made it out of my throat as my heart sped up and my stomach flip-flopped.

He was giving me the same look I got Wednesday night right before he kissed me, and I knew I hadn't imagined anything. It was anger and desire mixed together to make something hot enough for my knees to go weak. From the way he'd been ignoring me yesterday and today, barely sparing me eye contact, I had begun to wonder if it'd all been a wet dream on my part.

But, nope.

Taking a deep breath and tearing my eyes away, I tore off my jacket and tossed it to K.C. "Put this on."

"Thanks." She held the cup in one hand and slipped on the jacket with the other.

Sparing Jared another glance, I noticed that his chest rose and fell hard as his eyes spit fire. The desire was gone. His gaze was on Ben now, who I realized had also been looking at me but turned away as if he'd been caught eyeballing something he shouldn't have.

Again, I immediately wanted to cover myself.

I was here for the race. I reminded myself and turned back to the track.

Madoc and Liam were never head to head. Either Madoc was drastically behind Liam, or Liam was a ridiculous distance behind Madoc. After a minute, the crowd started laughing when they realized that Madoc was just toying with his opponent. No wonder Jared wasn't watching. He knew it would be an easy win. Not that Liam's Camaro wasn't worthy, but Madoc was more experienced and had done a hell of a lot of work to his car.

On the last turn, Madoc surged ahead one last time and crossed the finish line to the sounds of cheers and whistles. People rushed his car, and Madoc emerged with an idiotic grin on his smug face. Some girl grabbed his gray T-shirt and stuck her tongue in his mouth. *Eww*.

Liam slowly climbed out of his car and immediately looked to K.C. who, I noticed, was blatantly wrapped around Jared again. My leg spasmed with an urge to kick something when I saw him bury his head in her neck. She giggled with pleasure, obviously for show.

"Jared's up next." Ben rubbed his jaw. "Roman's awesome. I hope I didn't bet on the wrong guy."

I honestly didn't know who I would bet on if I cared to place money on either dickhead.

"Everyone clear the road!"

I jumped.

The Race Master was starting the next event. "Trent and Roman, get your asses on the starting line."

And suddenly I was nervous about this match-up.

Chapter 20

Ben and I parted with the crowd so Jared could pull his car out. K.C. came up to stand beside us, but for some reason, I couldn't look at her.

As Jared climbed in and started his engine, the girls around us started jumping and squealing. Papa Roach blared at a deafening level from his speakers. He revved the engine a few times to get the crowd going, a playful grin on his lips.

The Boss 302 pulled up onto the track, and I realized I almost felt like leaving. Jared and I had dreamed about being here together to race, and now I was on the outside looking in. He was living this without me, and I hated that I was being left out.

Roman had just pulled up in his Pontiac Trans Am. Even though his 2002 car was considered ancient compared to Jared's, it stood an outstanding chance of winning. The amount of work and options Roman had added to his vehicle made it a formidable machine. Unfortunately, Derek Roman didn't rely simply on his skills as a mechanic to win. There had been many injuries out here when he'd raced in high school.

"All right!" the Race Master announced. "Clear the track for the main event of the evening."

According to K.C., the Loop only has a few races per week during the school year as the college kids have gone back to school, so this was a light night with only two races.

Jared's music filled the air, and I saw him take something from his hand to hang it on the rearview mirror. I couldn't make out what it was, only that it was bulky and looked like a necklace.

The same girl who set off Madoc and Liam came to stand in front of the cars, shaking her ass as she walked in front of their headlights.

The smell of fuel and tires permeated the air, while the engines' rumble coursed through my legs. Jared stared ahead, wearing a stone face, waiting for the call.

"Ready?" Little Miss Look-At-Me called.

"Set?" The engines roared.

"Go!" Her arms fell hard to her sides, and the cars zoomed past her, kicking up dust and rocks in their wake. I darted onto the track with the flood of people to watch from behind, more afraid than excited this time.

As much as I hated to admit it, I was worried Roman would do something shady and hurt Jared. Even after everything, I didn't want to see him hurt.

The cars' taillights got smaller the closer they reached the first turn. It was four lefts, and the race would be over. The turns were sharp, and this was where a drift racer might be better for the Loop. The track was small, these cars were big, and the turns were hell. For this reason, no cars were allowed to park on the perimeter of the turns.

Jared took the gentleman's route by slowing down to make the turn after Roman, while the latter plowed ahead. Roman would either win or kill them both. Both cars skidded around the turn, sending a cloud of dust into the air, much to the delight of the onlookers, who screamed relentlessly. Forging ahead, Jared caught up to Roman and they proceeded head to head.

Come on, come on. I clasped my palms together to my chest, fingers entwined so tight that my skin felt stretched. I rotated my body to follow their progress, seeing Jared pull back patiently each time to let Roman take the turns first.

My heart pounded, and my stomach felt tight from the nervousness.

Coming up on the last turn, Jared pulled back behind Roman, but he wasn't slowing down. As Roman rounded the last corner, he skidded further to the edge while Jared took the inside. Both cars recovered and were neck to neck as they neared the finish line.

The crowd cleared the track in a mad rush, and watched as both engines thundered past. The cars were so close that I couldn't figure out who'd won.

As both cars slowed to a stop, everyone rushed them in a clustered mess of pushing and yelling. No one seemed to know who'd won.

I twisted my neck around, searching for the Race Master guy. He appeared to be deliberating with a couple of other people, probably trying to come to a decision.

"So did you see who won?" K.C. asked, looking confused as we walked up to the cars.

"No. You?"

She shook her head.

"There you are!" Ben sidled up next to me and grabbed my hand. "I guess they're not sure who won. Awesome race, huh?"

I let out a laugh. "My nails have been chewed into oblivion."

"Come on. Let's go see Jared." K.C. grabbed my wrist, and the three of us trekked up the track.

Approaching the cars, I noticed that the drivers were nose to nose between the vehicles. Their mouths were tight, and they were too close. They looked like they were about to turn the event into a fight.

As we pushed closer, I heard what they were saying.

"You were pushing into my lane!" Roman gritted through his

teeth. "Or maybe you just don't know how to handle your car." His black hair was slicked back, and his jeans and white T-shirt made him look like a 1950s' reject.

"There are no lanes on the track," Jared snickered. "And let's not talk about who can't handle their muscle."

Roman pointed his finger near Jared's face as he spoke. "I'll tell you what, Princess. Come back after you've grown some balls and taken off your training wheels. Then you'll be man enough to race me."

"Man enough?" Jared pinched his eyebrows together like that was the most ridiculous thing he'd ever heard. Turning to the crowd, Jared held his hands out to his sides, palms up. "Man enough?" he asked sarcastically.

The trampy brunette from Jared's party, Piper, walked up and plastered herself to him like a snake. She cupped his cheek with one hand and grabbed his ass with the other. Plunging her tongue into his mouth, she kissed him slow and deep, putting her entire body into it.

The fucking crowd couldn't scream any louder.

Heat shot out of my nose, ears, and eyes before I looked away.

He'd kissed me like that only two days ago.

Fuck him.

I peered over at K.C., whose eyebrows were raised in surprise.

"Are you okay?" I asked. Did I really care? Probably not, but at least it took my mind off the ache in *my* chest.

"Fan-fucking-tastic," she snarled. "Liam just saw that. Awesome."

I almost laughed, realizing that the only thing she was pissed about was Liam's reaction. If Liam didn't think that Jared was serious about K.C., then he wouldn't feel threatened.

She didn't give a damn about Jared. That was for sure. And that made me feel a little better about kissing him behind her back.

"Okay!" The Race Master cut through the crowd. "Out of the way, out of the way."

His eyes swept the crowd, waiting for them to quiet down. Piper peeled herself off Jared and retreated back to her friends, wiping him off her lips as she stumbled.

"Listen up. We have some good news and bad news. The bad news is that we're calling a tie." Moans and expletives sounded around the crowd. Bets had been placed, and people were upset. "But, the good news is," he continued, "we have a way to solve the stalemate."

His smirk scared me. I let go of Ben's hand to inch closer, now standing at the inside of the crowd. Jared and Roman were both frowning.

"A rematch?" Jared asked.

"Kind of." The Race Master looked a little too amused. "If you boys want to settle this, then your cars will race again, but . . . you won't be the drivers."

Murmurs could be heard around the crowd, and my eyes darted to Jared to see his stunned expression.

"Excuse me?" Roman inched closer and questioned.

"We know you're exceptional drivers. The race was close enough to prove that. Let's see who has the better machine."

"So who's going to drive the cars?" Jared all but shouted, his face gone pale.

The Race Master's face puffed out as he grinned. "Your girl-friends."

Chapter 21

I was sure the laughter at the Loop could be heard all the way to the Benson house. Some people cheered at the Race Master's innovative solution, while others bitched about their bets. But everyone seemed to agree that a race by two dimwitted teenage girls in high performance machines would be hilarious.

"Dude! That's not happening!" Roman glanced over to his girlfriend, a petite Mexican girl with more weight in her chest than the rest of her body. Knowing Roman, they could've been dating for two months or two minutes. Who knew?

"Zack, I don't have a girlfriend. I never have a girlfriend," Jared stated point blank to the Race Master, emphasizing the word "never."

"What about the pretty little thing you arrived with?" Zack asked.

Jared's stare flipped over to K.C., and her eyes bulged.

Swallowing hard, K.C. yelled, "He's just my rebound." The crowd let out a loud "ohhhh," to which K.C. smiled at her own tenacity. Jared raised his eyebrows to Zack in a "you see?" kind of look.

"No one drives my car," Jared clarified to Zack.

"I agree with the Princess here." Roman jerked his head at Jared. "This is stupid."

Zack shrugged. "The crowd's already seen you two race. They

want to be entertained. If you two have any interest in settling this score so people can get paid, then you'll play it my way. Be on the starting line in five minutes or leave." He started walking away, but stopped and turned. "Oh, and you can ride shotgun if you like. . . .you know, for moral support." He couldn't get the last words out without cracking up. He probably expected the poor girls to wind up in tears before finishing the race.

Zack walked off, and whispers broke around the crowd. Roman stalked away, while Jared walked over to us.

"This is bullshit." He ran his fingers through his hair.

"Hey, man. I could drive for you," Madoc chimed in. "We'd just have to tell them about our secret relationship." He hooked his arms over my and Ben's shoulders playfully, but I shrugged him off.

Jared ignored him. The wheels in his brain were turning as he paced the ground in front of us. He was probably trying to think of a way out of this, but when he stopped and let out a defeated sigh, I knew he was cornered.

I looked over at Roman, who was leading his girlfriend to his car, apparently giving her instructions on a manual transmission.

Oh, boy. My cheeks sucked in as I tried not to laugh.

"Jared, I can't race for you," K.C. laughed out. "There's got to be someone else."

He looked up to the sky and shook his head. Even though I didn't want to see his car get trashed, I found the situation amusing. *Serves him right.*

"There's only one other person who I'd even slightly trust driving my car." He raised an eyebrow and turned to lock eyes with me.

All the air left my body. "Me?"

"Her?" Madoc burst out, and Ben and K.C. echoed.

Jared crossed his arms over his chest and approached me like a cop in an interrogation room. "Yeah, you."

164

"Me?" I peered up at him like he was crazy. If he thought I'd do him any favors, he *was* crazy.

"I'm looking at you, aren't I?" Jared's snotty tone and condescending stare made me want to say "yes" and then crash the damn car in the hopes he'd be the one to break into tears.

I blew him off and looked at my date. "Ben, can we get an early start to that bonfire? I'm bored here." Turning around, ignoring Ben's dumbfounded look, I headed for the edge of the crowd.

A hand hooked me at the crook of my elbow and gently pulled me to a stop. I looked up to see Jared struggling to meet my eyes.

"Can I talk to you?" His voice was hushed, and his demeanor gentle. It had been so long, I'd forgotten how human he could be. Though, it wasn't enough for me to forget how horrible he'd been, either.

"No." I spat out the same flat response he'd given to me weeks ago when I'd asked him to turn down his music.

He took a breath. "You know how hard this is for me." He looked away and then back again. "I need you," he sighed, sounding defeated.

I sucked in a breath at those words. *He needed me?* By the way he breathed through his nose and wouldn't make eye contact, I knew he was uncomfortable saying those words. Part of me wanted to help him, but the other part of me just wanted to walk away. Where was he when I'd needed him in the past?

I hated myself for, even a moment, considering that I could forgive him for everything after uttering those three simple words. Too little, too late.

"And tomorrow when you don't need me? Will I be shit under your boot again?" My response was angrier than I'd planned. I resented how easily I found myself caving to him.

"She'll do it," K.C. called out over Jared's shoulder. I hadn't realized she was standing near us, but when I looked up I noticed Ben and Madoc crashing our conversation, too. My heart sped up again.

"K.C.!" I chastised. "You don't speak for me. And I'm not doing it!" I directed the last to Jared.

"You want to," she retorted.

And she was right.

I wanted to drive his car badly. I wanted to show all of these people what I was made of. I wanted to show Jared that I was worth something.

And it was that thought that made me want to walk away. I didn't have to prove anything to him. I knew my worth, and I didn't need his approval.

"Perhaps," I conceded. "But I do have pride. He's not getting a damn thing from me."

"Thank you." Jared cut off K.C. before she had a chance to respond.

"For what?" I shot back.

"For reminding me of what a disappointing, self-serving bitch you are," Jared gritted through his teeth as he got in my face. Heat rose to my head as I started to feel like words weren't enough anymore.

My arms went stiff, my fingers curling into fists. I was fantasizing about having Jared handcuffed while I punched the hell out of him.

Before I could respond with a snarky comeback, Madoc snapped, "That's enough. Both of you." He stepped between us, switching his glare from Jared to me. "Right now, I don't give a fuck what the history is between you two, but we need asses in that car. People will lose a hell of a lot of money."

He rolled up his sleeves as if he was going to personally throw us into the car. "Jared? You're going to lose a lot of money. And

Tate? You think everyone treated you badly before? Two-thirds of the people here tonight bet on Jared. When they hear that his first choice turned him down, the rest of your school year will be hell without Jared or me having to lift a finger. Now, the both of you, get in the goddamn car!"

Everyone stood there, shocked. Madoc never made sense, but he succeeded in making me feel immature and childish. A lot of people were counting on Jared's win, and as much as I hated admitting Madoc was right, he made a valid point.

"He has to ask to me nicely." I crossed my arms, keeping my expression impassive.

"What?" Jared blurted out.

"He has to say 'please,'" I repeated for K.C., Madoc and Ben, not willing to address Jared after he'd just insulted me.

The others stood staring at Jared and me as if they were waiting to see which bomb would go off first. Jared shook his head with a bitter smile on his face and finally took a deep breath before responding.

"Tatum." His voice was calm, but the underlying bitterness was there. "Would you ride with me, please?"

I eyed him for a moment, appreciating this rare show of humbleness, even if it was forced, before I held out my hand. "Keys?"

Jared dropped them in my hand.

As I bit the corner of my mouth to stifle a smile, I ran up onto the track with Jared following behind. I saw Roman hopping out of his car, having backed it into place behind the starting line for his girlfriend. I jogged up to Jared's car, and the clusters of people around the track erupted in whispers and whistles at seeing me head for the driver's side.

Jared climbed into the passenger's seat, and I slammed my door shut after sinking into the cool leather. The impressive car was almost entirely black on the inside, and I immediately felt chills on my arms. Jared's car sang of its power with its cave-like feel: cool, dark, and animalistic.

Hot damn.

Turning the key, I backed into position as the crowd departed to the sidelines. The vibration through my thighs made my center tingle, and I immediately looked over to Jared, who was watching me.

His elbow propped next to his window, he leaned his head on his hand and peered at me with a mixture of curiosity and amusement. I wondered what he thought of me behind his wheel.

"You're smiling," he pointed out, almost as an accusation.

I stroked the steering wheel without meeting his eyes. "Don't ruin this for me by talking, please."

Jared cleared his throat and continued anyway. "So, your dad taught us both how to drive sticks, and the Bronco is a manual, so I'm assuming you don't have any questions about that part, right?"

"None." My pulse was hammering through my fingertips.

"Good. The turns are tight. Tighter than they look. The idea is to get there first, or fall behind to go after. Don't try to make a left with Roman's car, got it?"

I nodded. My eyes stared straight ahead, ready to get going as my foot anxiously tapped.

"At each left, let off the gas before you turn, and then accelerate after you've straightened out. If you feel like you need apply the brake on the turn then do it but as minimally as possible. Don't accelerate until you've rounded the turn. You'll spin out."

I nodded again.

"Hit the gas in between turns. On the last leg, hit it hard." His voice was commanding.

"Jared, I got it." I looked over to him. "I can do this."

He didn't look like he believed me, but he stopped anyway. "Buckle up."

Following his order, I glanced over to my left and saw Roman barking orders at his girlfriend while she nodded nervously. Zack walked between the two cars to take his position up front. Thankfully, it appeared he would send us on our way instead of the slutty jailbait from before.

As I looked out the front windshield, keeping my eye on Zack, I noticed what Jared had hung on his rearview mirror. I reached out and grabbed the oval-shaped piece of clay, secured by a light green ribbon. Heat crept up on my neck, and my throat tightened.

It was the Mother's Day necklace I'd made for my mom after she'd died.

Jared and I had made fossils of our fingerprints one year to give to our moms. Using air dry clay, we made a thumbprint and hung the small oval piece from a ribbon, making a necklace. He gave his to his mom, and I had put mine on my mom's grave. The next time I'd visited her, the necklace was gone. I figured it was lost or the weather had worn it away.

Turns out it was stolen. I looked to Jared, partly puzzled and partly angry.

"Good luck charm," he offered, not meeting my eyes. "I took it a couple of days after you left it there. I thought it would be stolen or ruined. Kind of had it with me ever since."

Letting it go, I looked out the window and tried to even out my breathing. I guess I was glad it still existed. But it was my mom's, and he had no right to take it.

But he still had it? Even after everything. Why?

I made a mental note to get it back after the race.

"Are. We. Ready?" Zack's voice startled me as he shouted to the crowd. They screamed through their beer drenched excitement.

Jared tuned the iPod to Bullet for My Valentine's "Waking the Demon." I gripped the steering wheel, using the music to clear my head and zone in.

"Ready?" Zack called out and I revved my engine, seeing Roman's girl jump to rev her engine immediately after.

"Set?" Jared put one hand on the dash while turning up the music with the other.

"Go!" Zack dropped his arms.

Slamming on the gas, I peeled over the dirt road and took off. As the music filled the moment, my hands pushed against the steering wheel, so that my back dug into the seat. With my arms full of tension, I focused on the road ahead.

Shit! The car had a lot of power.

"The first turn comes up fast," Jared warned. I didn't know if the other car was next to me or behind me. All I knew was that it wasn't in front of me, and I didn't care about anything else. I would race this car without any opponent.

My thighs, dampened with sweat, grated across the seat as I lifted my leg to push in the clutch. I lightly applied the brakes in preparation for rounding the corner. As I let off the brake and made the first turn, the rear started to slide. I quickly steered to the right as the car slid left, to keep from skidding out. Dust clouded the track, and my heart was pounding. I stepped down on the clutch and shifted back into third gear. As my speed picked up and I shifted immediately into fourth, I caught sight of the other car in my rearview mirror.

"Hit the gas!" Jared shouted. "And don't turn so hard. You're losing time correcting yourself."

Whatever.

"Who's in first place?" I reminded him.

"Don't get cocky." Jared alternated between scoping the road and looking behind us to the Trans Am.

Sweat dripped from my brow and my fingers were exhausted from clenching the wheel so hard. Relaxing, I turned up the music and kicked us into sixth gear, bypassing fifth altogether.

This is awesome! The easy way the gas propelled the car forward felt like a space shuttle. Or so I assumed.

"Next turn is coming. You need to slow down."

Yap, yap, yap.

"Tatum, you need to slow down." Jared's voice echoed somewhere in the back of my mind.

The turn was three seconds away, and the vibrations shooting through my legs prevented me from laying off the gas. Gripping the steering wheel tighter, I charged ahead.

Taking my foot off the gas, but not braking, I made a sharp left, and then skidded right, and then forced the wheel left again until I was straightened out. More dust flew around us, but I recovered quickly and slammed on the gas again. Looking behind us, I saw that the Trans Am had spun out around that turn and was now trying to recover. They were more than thirty yards behind us.

Yes!

"Don't do that again," Jared grumbled, now holding the dash with both hands as I stared down the road ready for more. The next turn came and went successfully no matter how much Jared wailed about slowing down.

For an asshole and a rule-breaker, he really played it safe. And for someone who always played it safe, I'd turned out to be quite the rule-breaker.

As we advanced on the last turn with a significant gain, I slowed down to about thirty miles an hour and shifted down to third. Cruising around the bend at a comfortable speed without any skidding or dust, I looked over at Jared with a wide-eyed, innocent expression.

"Is this okay, Ms. Daisy?" Biting the corner of my mouth to keep from laughing, I noticed his eyes flash to my lips. Heat rose in his gaze, and tingles blossomed through my stomach and down to the sensitive area between my legs.

"Tatum?" His eyes narrowed to slits. "Stop toying with your opponent and win the damn race already."

"Yes'm, Ms. Daisy," I retorted with my best Southern accent.

I cruised over the finish line at a safe and hilarious thirty-five miles an hour as I caught the Trans Am in my rearview mirror stuttering around the last turn. Clusters of people swarmed the car, but Jared and I stayed inside for a few moments.

Putting the car into neutral and lifting the e-brake, I leaned my head against the headrest and massaged the steering wheel. My pulse was still going a mile a minute, and I felt alive. That was the most exciting thing I'd ever done. Every nerve in my body felt like it was on a sugar high.

"Thank you, Jared," I whispered, not looking at him. "Thank you for asking me to do this."

I reached over and grabbed my mom's necklace off the mirror and slipped it over my head.

When I looked over at him, he was leaning against his fist with a finger across his lips. What was he trying to hide? A smile?

Raking a hand through his hair, he opened his door, and the sounds of cheers and screaming rushed in like water into a sinking boat. Looking down at his boots, he shook his head. "Waking the demon . . . " he mumbled to himself, and I wasn't sure what he meant.

Before he climbed out, he looked over at me again through hooded lids. "Thank you, Tate," he whispered.

The hair on my neck stood up, and my hands shook.

He hadn't called me "Tate" since we were fourteen. Not since we were friends.

Chapter 22

Maci Feldman charged me once Ben and I had arrived at the bonfire. "That was awesome! My brother is like so unbelievably happy he won that bet."

Bonfires were held on Marcus Hitchens's property, on the banks of Swansea Lake, practically every week, especially following races and football games. The bitter cold of January and February was the only time when little happened, both at the lake and the Benson farm track.

"I'm glad I could help," I responded. And it was true. Racing tonight had been the best time I'd ever had. "But I only won because the other girl had no idea how to drive a manual."

Why did I say that? I rocked that race whether or not the twit knew what she was doing.

She hooked my arm, while Ben had his hand around my waist. Others came up to greet us, either to say "hi" to Ben or to congratulate me.

"Well, I for one would love to see you race again. How about you, Ben?" Maci addressed my date as he turned his attention away from his football buddies.

"I think I'm a lucky guy." He peered down at me, and it didn't escape my notice how he evaded the question. I wondered if it embarrassed him to have his date doing something the guys typically only took part in.

As it was already ten-thirty, I committed to staying for an hour before having Ben take me home. With the meet in the morning, I'd have to get home and rest whether I liked it or not.

"Great race tonight, Tate." Jess Cullen patted me on the shoulder as she passed by.

"Thanks," I exhaled, feeling unsettled with the attention.

"You alright?" Ben pulled me close.

"Absolutely," I choked out before inching towards the refreshments. "Can we get something to drink?"

He held up his hand to keep me put. "Stay here, I'll be back." And he walked off to the keg.

Clusters of people stood around the fire or sat on boulders, while others circulated. K.C. hadn't arrived yet, that I could see, and I assumed she drove with Jared. I stood there, feeling uneasy about my place. I guess I could thank Jared for me being more comfortable around a small group than lots of people. Because of him, I'd never been invited to these things.

I shook my head slightly to clear my thoughts. I needed to stop blaming him. It was his fault that I'd been blacklisted in the past, but it wasn't his fault that I'd accepted it. This was on me now.

Looking over to the group of girls giggling near the water, I recognized one from my cross-country team.

"Screw it." I shrugged my shoulders and decided to dive in. I took a step towards the group when a voice stopped me.

"Screw what?"

Goosebumps spread over my body as I turned around to face Jared. He held a cup in one hand and his phone in the other. He appeared to be sending a text while waiting for my reply. He slipped the phone into his back pocket and raised his eyes to me.

The hair on my arms felt electrified with static as if it were drawn to Jared. Rubbing my hands up and down my arms, I turned my head back to the fire, trying to ignore him. I still wasn't sure where we stood. We weren't friends, but we weren't enemies anymore either. And having a normal conversation was still out of the question.

"You're cold." Jared pulled up beside me. "Does K.C. still have your jacket?"

I sighed, unsure about what was causing my annoyance this time. Maybe it was because every time Jared was around me, the nerves in my body became springs pulsating heat, whereas Ben made me feel like curling up on the couch to watch *American Idol*.

Jared probably never watched T.V. Too mundane of an activity.

Also, I found it ridiculous that Jared acted concerned about me being cold when earlier this week he'd said he didn't care whether I lived or died. He'd apologized for nothing, and I couldn't forget that.

"Well, she was wearing my jacket when you brought her here, wasn't she?" My snippy remark was greeted with a smirk.

"She didn't come with me. I don't know if she's even here yet." His head turned and his eyes looked down to me.

"What do you mean? You left the race with her, didn't you?"

"No, she caught a ride with Liam. I came here alone." Jared's low, husky tone washed over me, and I fought back a smile hearing his last words.

It looked like K.C. and Liam were on the road to recovery.

I cleared my throat. "And that was okay with you?" I asked.

"Why wouldn't it be?" he asked me point-blank, a confused expression on his face.

Of course. What was I thinking? Jared didn't date, and there was no way he was invested in K.C. I dug into the small bag resting on my hip and searched for my phone.

"If I see her, I'll tell her to find you." Jared started to walk away but stopped after a few steps and turned back to me. "I'm going to need the fossil back." He gestured towards the necklace around my neck.

I realized he was talking about his good luck charm. "Not going to happen." And I directed my attention back to my phone.

"Oh, Tate. I always get what I want." His low, flirty tone made me freeze. My fingers were paused above my cell screen as if I'd suddenly forgotten how to send a text. I looked up in time to see him smile and walk away.

Watching him head to Madoc and others in his crew, I was more puzzled now that I was earlier this week. I'd wanted Jared to become more human, and I'd wanted him to treat me well. Now that he's showing signs of both, I was sick with unanswered questions. Old feelings seeped through the cracks of the wall I'd built to keep him out.

"Hey, here you go." Ben walked up with two beers, handing me one.

"Thanks." I licked my lips and took a sip, letting the bitter taste wet my tongue and throat.

Ben ran his fingers down my hair and combed it behind my ear. My muscles tensed. My invisible three feet of personal space had been breached, and I wanted to step away.

Why? Why couldn't I just like this guy? I was frustrated with myself. He seemed decent and goal-oriented. Why wasn't he turning my insides to goo or making me daydream?

I felt the certainty creep up on me, and I was powerless to stop it. I didn't want Ben. Plain and simple. I wasn't going to be one of those silly girls in a love triangle romance novel who couldn't choose. Not that I was in a love triangle, but I never understood how a girl can't *know* whether or not she wants a guy. We can be confused about what is good for us but not about what we truly want.

And I didn't want Ben. That much I knew.

"Was that Jared you were talking to?" He gestured with his beer to the other side of the fire where Jared laughed with a couple of guys from school.

"Yeah." I took another sip.

Ben exhaled a chuckle and took a gulp of his beer. "Still not big on giving up information, are you?"

"Oh, it was nothing. I was looking for K.C., and I thought they came together."

"She gets around, huh?" Ben commented more than asked.

"How do you mean?" I said defensively. K.C. and I had been stressed lately, but she was my best friend.

"Moving from Liam to Jared, and back to Liam. I saw them after your race. They looked pretty close."

"Two guys means she gets around?" I was actually relieved that she'd moved past Jared, but I didn't like Ben or anyone else drawing conclusions about her.

Ben gave me a contrite look and changed the subject. Clearly, he was smart enough to know that he shouldn't go there. "Well, you did great tonight. The school is going to be talking about it for a while. Looks like I scored the jackpot." Ben hooked an arm around me and led me around the bonfire.

The jackpot? What was that supposed to mean?

Ben and I circulated to different clusters of his friends, in between him running back and forth to the keg. I'd had two sips of my beer and put it down. Despite my best hints to Ben that I needed to be home soon, he was on his fourth beer, and I knew he wasn't going to be able to drive. I was starting to wonder how I'd be getting home.

I'd spotted K.C. and Liam a half an hour ago, sitting on a boulder talking. Or rather, Liam talked while K.C. listened and cried a little. Their conversation looked intense and important by the way their heads were together, so I'd opted to leave them alone.

While I tried to ignore the vibe of Jared's presence, I found myself unable to keep from looking for him. I'd seen him chatting with his friends, and the last time I looked, Piper had her face buried in his neck. She looked trashy in her short, tight black dress and heels. Who wore heals to the beach? Not even a real beach, either, but a rocky and muddy lakeshore.

To my delight, he looked about as interested in her as he would a plate of parsnips. I stole enough glances to see him try to throw her off a few times. She finally took the hint and stalked off in a pout.

Jared caught my eyes more than once, but I broke contact immediately every time. The images of the other night mixed with his penetrating, smoky stare created a throbbing need deep inside of me.

I let out a rough sigh. *It's definitely time to get out of here.*

Glancing at my watch, I met Ben on his way back from the keg. "Hey, I really need to go now. I have that race tomorrow," I reminded him.

Ben's eyebrows raised in surprise. "Oh, come on. It's only eleven-thirty."

The whining was a shock, and I was definitely turned off.

"We can stay for a little while longer," he said.

"Sorry, Ben. That's why I offered to drive myself instead. I really do have to go." With my best apologetic smile, I stood my ground. I wasn't afraid of what he thought, because I knew that this was probably our last date. The spark wasn't there, and aside from the racing, I would've been happier staying at home with a book tonight.

"Let's just stay for another half an hour." He tried shoving his beer at me as if getting me drunk was the answer, but he ended up swaying to the side and had to latch on to my arm for support.

"You're not okay to drive," I pointed out. "I can drop you at home, and you can pick up your car at my house tomorrow."

"No, no." Ben held up his hands. "I'll cut myself off now and sober up. We'll be on our way soon."

"Well, you shouldn't drive. Not at all." I averted my eyes, my aggravation building

"I can take care of myself, Tate," Ben asserted. "If you want to leave now, then you'll have to find another ride. If you want to leave with me, I'll be ready in a while."

What?! How long is "a while?"

This was getting ridiculous, and my patience was spent. He'd said we could leave by 11:30, and I'd taken him at his word.

Ben pulled at my arm to lead me back to the bonfire, but I yanked it free and stalked away. He didn't say another word, so I assumed he kept going without me.

I needed to get home, and Ben was no longer my ride. Was this the scene I'd been itching to be a part of? Ben and his friends were about as interesting as cornflakes, the girls had no other interests beside shopping and makeup, and the guys here gave me the urge to sanitize my eyeballs after seeing the way they looked at me.

After a quick sweep of the area, I ascertained that K.C. was already gone. I dug my phone out of my purse and dialed her anyway. No answer.

Looking around for the cross-country teammate I'd spotted earlier, I noticed that she, too, was nowhere in sight. The only other option was to call my grandma, who I dreaded waking up at this hour, but she'd at least be happy to know I'd called for a safe ride.

I twisted my lips up in disappointment when my Grandma didn't answer her phone, either. That wasn't unusual, since she often forgot to take her phone to bed. And thanks to the convenience of cell phones, we'd disconnected our hard line years ago.

Awesome.

My only options at this point were to wait for Ben and convince him to let me drive or hike it to the parking lot and ask someone I knew for a ride.

Ben could go piss up a tree.

I trekked over the rocks and into the woods for the short traipse to the clearing near the road where everyone parked.

With no flashlight available, I used my cell phone screen as a light to guide my way. It was a straight shot, but the path was littered with sticks and stumps. Trees had already begun losing their leaves, but the rain we'd received this fall kept everything moist and pliable. Droplets splattered my ankles as I stomped on wet foliage, and a few bare branches poked at my skin, stinging me.

"Well, look what I found."

I jumped, startled out of the quiet that had just surrounded me. Looking up, I cringed at the sight of Nate Dietrich . . . who was eye-fucking me as usual.

It looked like he was coming from where I was trying to go, and now he blocked my way. "It's fate, Tate," his sing-song voice rhymed.

"Get out of my way, Nate." I approached him slowly, but he didn't budge. I tried to go around him, but his hands shot out to grab my waist, and he pulled me to him. My muscles tightened, and my hands curled into fists.

"Shh," Nate implored as I tried to push myself away. His breathing echoed in my ear, and he reeked of alcohol. "Tate, I've wanted you for so long. You know that. How about you put me out of my misery, and let me to take you home?" His nose was in my hair, and his hands dropped to my ass. I stiffened.

"Stop it," I ordered and tried to bring my knee up between his legs. But it seemed he already anticipated that move, because his legs were too close together.

Nate shook with laughter. Kneading my ass, he whispered,

"Oh, I know your tricks, Tate. Stop fighting it. I could take you on the ground right now if I wanted to."

His lips crushed down on mine, and the acidic taste of vomit rose in my throat.

I bit down on his bottom lip, hard enough for my bottom teeth to feel my top teeth through the skin. He growled and released me, pawing at his mouth to check for blood.

Grabbing the pepper spray out of my purse that my dad insisted I keep there, I shot for his eyes. He screamed and stumbled backwards as his hands covered his face. I finally brought my knee up between his legs, and watched him crumple to the ground, grabbing the strap of my tank top as he fell.

Run! Just run! I screamed to myself.

But no. I leaned over him as he let out wails of pain. "Why are the guys at our school such dicks?!"

One hand covering his eyes and the other hand clutching his crotch.

"Shit! You fucking bitch!" Nate groaned as he tried to open his eyes.

"Tatum!" Jared's voice boomed behind me, and my shoulders jerked before spinning around. Eyes furiously jetting between Nate and me, Jared looked as rigid as a lion before the pounce. He let out shallow breaths between his lips, and his hands were tight fists. I saw his eyes dart to my shoulder where the strap of my top lay flopped forward where it had ripped.

"Did he hurt you?" Jared asked evenly, but his lips were tight, and his eyes were murderous.

"He tried." I covered my shoulder where my skin was exposed. "I'm fine." My voice was curt. The last thing I wanted tonight was to play the damsel in distress for Jared.

Peeling off his black button-down, Jared tossed it to me as he headed my way. "Put this on. Now."

Catching the shirt as it hit me in the face, part of me wanted to throw it right back at him. Although Jared and I had found common ground during the race, it didn't mean that I wanted or needed his help.

However, I was exposed, cold, and in no mood to draw attention to myself. Slipping on the shirt, the heat from Jared's body warmed my arms and chest. The cuffs fell below my hands, and when I brought them up to let the warmth cover my cold cheeks, I could smell his man scent. The hybrid musk and tire smell almost made my lungs burst as I tried to take deeper breaths of the aroma.

"You have a poor, fucking memory, Dietrich. What did I tell you?" Jared bent down to growl in Nate's face. He grabbed a handful of Nate's shirt at his chest and hauled him upright before delivering a strong blow to Nate's stomach.

My eyes damn-near bulged at Jared's attack. The guttural punch reminded me of molding clay. Nate's figure bent with the hit, and he wouldn't be the same for a while. His wheezing, as he tried to catch his breath, sounded like a cross between a smoker and a zombie's gurgling.

Jared used his left hand to clamp Nate around the neck as he backed him up to a tree. With his right fist he delivered blow after blow to Nate's face. My knees started to cave as I watched Jared squeeze Nate's neck until his knuckles were white.

Stop, Jared.

He kept punching until blood dripped from Nate's eye and nose.

When he didn't show any signs of stopping, I stepped forward. "Stop. Jared, stop!" I called out, my firm voice carrying over Nate's grunts and gasps.

Jared ceased his assault but immediately yanked Nate by the crook of his elbow and threw him to the ground. "This isn't over," he assured the bloodied, crumpled mess on the ground.

What was he doing?

Turning to face me, Jared's chest rose and fell heavily with his breathing. The exertion made his body seem weighed down as his shoulders slumped, but his eyes were still vicious. He looked at me with a mixture of weariness and fury.

"I'm taking you home." He turned to walk for the lot, not even seeing if I'd follow.

Take me home?! Yeah, so he could feel like the big hero?

Letting Jared feel like he'd dug me out of a situation I had control of cut my pride. *Screw that.*

"No thanks. I have a ride." I spit out the lie before I let him do me any favors.

"Your ride," Jared turned to look at me with disgust, "is drunk. Now, unless you'd like to wake up your poor grandmother to come out into the middle of nowhere to get you after your date gets drunk, and you almost get raped—which I'm sure will do wonders for your father trusting you to be alone, by the way—then you'll get in the goddamn car, Tate."

And he turned to walk away, knowing I'd follow him.

Chapter 23

The click signaling that the car doors had been unlocked sounded, and I climbed into Jared's warm car, the passenger side this time. My hands were shaking from my encounter with Nate, so I struggled as I tried to take off Jared's shirt.

"Leave it on." He didn't even spare me a glance before turning the ignition.

I hesitated. His anger was visible as the muscles in his jaw clenched. "But I'm not cold anymore."

"And I can't look at your ripped shirt right now."

I shrugged the shirt back over my shoulders, put my belt on, and slammed into the back of the seat as he peeled out of the parking lot.

What the hell was his problem?

Was he mad at me or Nate? Obviously, Jared didn't want to see me hurt—not physically, anyway. But why was he being so curt with *me*?

The car fishtailed slightly as it left the gravel lot and pulled onto the paved road of the highway. Jared weighed down on the gas and shifted forcefully as we picked up speed. No music played, and he didn't speak.

The highway was deserted except for the haunting trees that loomed over us on the sides. Judging by how quickly everything flew past my window, Jared was way over the speed limit.

Peeking at him through the corner of my eye, I saw that he was seething. He licked his lips and took several heavy breaths, while he tightened and retightened his grip on the steering wheel.

"What's your problem?" I grabbed the bull by the horns and asked.

"*My* problem?" He raised his eyebrows as if I'd just asked the dumbest question. "You come to the bonfire with that idiot Ben Jamison, who can't stay sober enough to drive you home, and then you traipse off into the woods, in the dark, and get groped by Dietrich. Maybe you're the one with the problem." His voice was low but bitter and spiteful.

He was mad at me? Oh, hell no.

I turned in my seat and looked straight at him. "If you recall, I had the situation under control." I tried to keep my voice calm. "Whatever favor you think you were doing me only satisfied your own anger. Leave me out of it."

He sucked in his cheeks and continued down the highway.

As I glanced at the speedometer, my eyes bulged when I noticed that Jared was driving over eighty miles per hour.

"Slow down," I ordered.

He ignored my plea and gripped the steering wheel harder. "There's going to be situations you can't handle, Tate. Nate Dietrich wasn't going to take too kindly to what you did to him tonight. Did you think that was going to be the end of it? He would've come after you again. Do you know how badly Madoc wanted to do something after you broke his nose? He didn't want to hurt you, but he wanted to retaliate."

Why didn't he then?

Madoc had been humiliated, no doubt, at that party more than a year ago when I broke his nose. But he'd just let it roll off him, or so I thought, and hadn't sought any payback. Thanks to Jared.

I guess Nate Dietrich wouldn't be seeking retribution, either. Not with Jared involved.

I felt gravity pull my body towards the other side of the car, and my heart thumped wildly when I saw that Jared wasn't slowing down as we rounded the soft turn.

"You need to slow down."

Jared snorted. "No, I don't think so, Tate. You wanted the full high school experience, didn't you? Football player boyfriend, casual sex, reckless behavior?" He goaded me with his sarcasm.

What was he talking about? I never wanted that stuff. I just wanted to be normal.

And then he switched off his headlights.

Oh, God.

The road was black, and I couldn't see more than a foot in front of us. Thankfully, there were reflectors that separated our lane from the oncoming traffic, but the country roads were busy with deer and other animals, not just traffic.

What the hell was he doing?

"Jared, stop it! Turn on the lights!" I braced one hand on the dash as I turned to confront him. We were zooming down the road at a frightening speed, and a lump formed in my throat.

The tattoo on his arm peeked out of his T-shirt, and it stretched with his tensing muscles while he gripped the stick shift. My legs were weak, and for the first time in a long time, I was too scared to think.

"Jared, stop the car now!" I yelled. "Please!"

"Why? This isn't fun?" Jared's voice was disturbingly calm. None of this scared him, or even excited him. "Do you know how many squealing airheads I've had sitting in that seat? *They* loved it." His eyebrows pinched together as he looked at me with mock puzzlement. He was pushing me.

"Stop. The. Car!" I screamed, my heart pounding with dread. He was going to kill us.

Jared twisted his head to face me. "You know why you don't

like this? Because you're not like them, Tate. You never were. Why do you think I kept everyone away from you?" His voice sounded angry, but clear. He wasn't drunk, at least I didn't think he was, and this was more emotion than I'd experienced from him in years, except for the night of the kiss.

He kept everyone away from me? What did that mean? Why?

The tires screeched as he rounded another turn, and we drifted into the other lane. I was breathing as fast as the car was speeding now, I was sure. We were going to hit something or flip over!

"Stop the fucking car!" I bellowed with the full force of my lungs, pounding my fists on my thighs before hitting him on the arm.

The last thing I wanted to do was distract him, driving at a speed like that, but it worked. Jared slammed on the brakes, using some choice words directed at me and down-shifted as he veered to the side of the road and stopped.

I scrambled out of the car, and Jared hopped out at the same time. We both leaned over the roof, eye to eye.

"Get back in the car." Jared's teeth were bared as he growled.

"You could've killed us!" My throat tightened, and I noticed his furious eyes graze over my ripped shirt that had poked out of the button-down I was still wearing.

"Get back in the damn car!" He slammed his palm down on the roof, his eyes on fire.

"Why?" I asked, tears threatening.

"Because you need to go home," he spat out like "duh."

"No." I shook my head. "Why did you keep everyone away from me?" He'd started this conversation, and I had every intention of finishing it.

"Because you didn't belong with the rest of us. You still don't." Jared's eyes narrowed in disgust, and my heart sunk. He was being deplorable as usual.

I hate him.

Without another thought, I ducked inside and grabbed Jared's keys out of the ignition. Rounding the car door, I ran a few yards ahead and unfastened the twist oval key ring. Slipping one of his keys off, I held it in a fist near my face.

"What are you doing?" He approached slowly, annoyance evident in his eyes.

"One more step, and you're losing one of your keys. Not sure if it's the car key, but eventually I'll get to that one." I loaded my arm behind my head, ready to toss it at any second. He halted.

"I'm not getting in your car. And I'm not letting you leave. We're not moving from this spot until you've told me the truth."

Sweat beaded my brow, even with the temperature down to the mid-sixties. Lips pursed, I waited for him to start.

But he didn't. He looked to be working something out in his head, but I wasn't about to give him to time to think of some lie to distract me.

When I raised my arm to toss the first key, his eyes shot helplessly between me and my fist, while he raised his hand motioning for me to stop.

After only a moment's more hesitation, he finally let out a defeated sigh and met my eyes.

"Tate, don't do this."

"Not the answer I was looking for." And I flung one of his keys into the brush off to the side of the road.

"Dammit, Tate!" he snapped, looking nervously between me and the dark forest where his key had disappeared.

I quickly unhooked another key and stuck my hand behind my head ready to catapult it at any second. "Now, talk. Why do you hate me?"

"Hate you?" Jared breathed heavily and shook his head. "I never hated you."

What?

I was stunned. "Then why? Why did you do all the things you've done?"

He let out a bitter laugh, knowing he was cornered. "Freshman year, I overheard Danny Stewart saying he was going to ask you to the Halloween dance. I made sure he never did, because he also told his buddies that he couldn't wait to find out if your tits were more than a handful each."

I cringed in disgust.

"I didn't even think twice about my actions. I spread that rumor about Stevie Stoddard, because you didn't belong with Danny. He was a dick. They all were."

"So you thought you were protecting me? But why would you do that? You already hated me by that point. That was after you'd returned from your dad's for the summer." My confusion sprang forth with every syllable. If our friendship had ended by that point, and he didn't care for me, then why did he care to protect me anymore?

"I wasn't protecting you," Jared said matter-of-factly, pinning me with a heated stare. "I was jealous."

Flutters attacked my belly. It felt like something was circling a drain in my stomach, the tingles going further and further down.

I barely registered him inching forward, stalking closer as I tried to catch my breath. "We got to high school, and all of a sudden, you've got all of these guys liking you. I handled it the only way I knew how."

"By bullying me? That makes no sense. Why didn't you talk to me?"

"I couldn't." He wiped his brow before stuffing his hand into his pocket. "I can't."

"You're doing fine so far. I want to know why all of this started in the first place. Why did you want to hurt me? The pranks, the blacklisting from parties? That wasn't about other guys. What was your problem with *me*?" I accused him.

His cheeks puffed out as he sighed. "Because you were there. Because I couldn't hurt who I wanted to hurt, so I hurt you."

That can't be it. There has to be more.

"I was your best friend." Frustration pushed my patience further away from me. "All these years ..." My voice broke off, barely containing the tears that pooled in my eyes.

"Tate, I had a shitty summer with my dad that year." His voice sounded closer. "When I came back, I wasn't the same kid. Not even close. I wanted to hate everybody. But with you, I still needed you in a way. I needed you to not forget me." Jared's voice never cracked, but I could tell there was remorse in his tone.

What had happened to him?

"Jared, I've turned it over and over in my head wondering what I could've done to make you act the way you did. And now you tell me that it was all for no reason?" I looked up to meet his eyes.

His body inched closer, but I didn't care. I wanted to hear more. "You were never clingy or a nuisance, Tate. The day you moved in next door I thought you were the most beautiful thing I'd ever seen. I fucking loved you." The last was barely a whisper as his eyes dropped to the ground. "Your dad was unloading the moving truck, and I looked out my living-room window to see what the noise was. There you were, riding your bike in the street. You were wearing overalls with a red baseball cap. Your hair was spilling down your back." Jared didn't meet my eyes with his confession.

We'd moved to a new house in town after my mom passed. I remembered seeing Jared for the first time that day. He remembered what I was wearing?

I loved you. A tear spilled over as I closed my eyes.

"When you recited your monologue this week, I ..." He drifted off with a sigh. "I knew then that I'd really gotten to you, and instead of feeling any satisfaction, I was angry with myself. I wanted to hate you all these years; I wanted to hate someone. But I didn't want to hurt you, and I didn't really realize that until the monologue."

Suddenly, he was in front of me. Cocking his head to the side, his glistening eyes searched mine. I didn't know what he looked for, and I didn't know what I wanted to reveal. I hated him for the years of torment. He threw away everything we had because he was angry at someone else. Needles pierced my throat as I struggled to hold back more tears.

"You're not telling me everything." My voice cracked, as he reached up to cup my cheek and wipe the tear away with his thumb. His long, muscular fingers were warm on my skin.

"No, I'm not." His husky whisper caused tingles to spread over my body, or maybe it was his thumb caressing circles on my cheek. I was becoming light-headed with everything that had happened tonight.

"The scars on your back," I choked out, my eyes fluttering with the sensation of his touch. "You said you had a bad summer, and that when you came back you wanted to hate everybody, but you haven't treated anyone else as badly as . . . "

"Tate?" His lips were inches from mine, and his body radiated heat. "I don't want to talk any more tonight."

I blinked and noticed how his body had drawn me in. Or maybe I'd drawn him in. We were like the positive sides of twin magnets again. He was so close now, and he'd eaten the distance between us without me noticing.

You're not getting off that easy.

"You don't want to talk anymore?" I spit out, not quite believing what I heard. "Well, I do." And I twisted around to launch another key into the air, but Jared's arms darted out and circled around my body, trapping me from behind.

I gasped for breath, while I tried to squirm free. Thoughts

swirled in my head, and it was hard to latch on to just one. He'd never hated me. I'd done absolutely nothing! Even though I knew that, part of me always thought there had to be a reason. And now he didn't want to finish his story? I needed to know!

His solid arms secured me, his breath was hot against my hair as I struggled to move out of his arms. "Shhh, Tate. I won't hurt you. I'll never hurt you again. I'm sorry."

Like that was going to erase everything!

"I don't care about you being sorry! I hate you." My hands gripped his forearms, which were braced over my chest as I tried to yank them loose. My anger turned to rage with his mind games and bullshit, and I was sick of the sight of him.

His hold on me lessened as he used his hands to peel the keys out of my fist. He let go of me, and I stepped forward before turning to face him.

"You don't hate me," he asserted. "If you did, you wouldn't be this upset." The cocky twist to his tone made my body stiffen, but I eased up when I felt the sting of my nails dig into my skin.

"Go screw yourself," I snapped and began walking away.

Like hell was he going to get the upper hand! He wanted to me to forgive him in one night for years of embarrassment and unhappiness, and then he assumed that I cared about him. He thought he was coming out of this unscathed.

What a colossal douchebag!

The next thing I knew, my feet were being swept off the ground, and I was upside down. Jared had tossed me over his shoulder, and all the air left my body as his shoulder bone dug into my stomach.

"Put me down!" The heat of anger was like a blazing fire covering my skin. I kicked my feet and punched his back, but he simply held me tightly by the backs of my knees as he walked back the way we'd come. I knew my skirt covered nothing in this position, but we were alone out here, and I didn't really care anyway, in my mood.

"Jared! Now!" I barked.

As if following orders, Jared swung me back upright where I landed in a sitting position on the hood of his car. It was still warm under my thighs from when it'd been driven, but the heat was not a welcome comfort, since I was already burning with fury.

Jared leaned in slowly, probably afraid I'd hit him, and placed his hands on either side of me. His legs stood between mine, and I immediately flushed with the memory of the last time we were in this position.

"Don't try to get away," he warned. "As you remember, I can keep you here."

I sucked in a breath. Yes, I did remember.

My toes curled at the thought of that kiss, but I knew it couldn't happen again.

"And I know how to use pepper spray and break noses." My voice sounded like a pathetic little mouse, squeaky and barely audible. I leaned back on my hands to maintain as much distance as possible, but my heart was pounding like the Rakes of Mallow.

"I'm not Nate or Madoc," he threatened. "Or Ben."

And his meaning wasn't lost on me. I wasn't attracted to them, and he knew it.

He leaned in closer, his black-brown eyes making my body want to do things my brain knew it shouldn't. His lips were an inch from mine, and I could smell his cinnamon breath.

I hate him. I hate him.

"Don't," I whispered.

His eyes searched mine. "I promise. Not unless you ask."

His mouth dipped to the side and lightly grazed my cheek. Unwanted pleasure escaped my throat, and I let out a little moan.

Dammit!

193

He never kissed me. He never put his lips together or tasted me. His mouth only glided along my skin leaving a delicious trail of desire and need. Down my cheek, his velvety lips caressed my skin before moving across my jaw bone and then descending to my neck. I closed my eyes, savoring the new sensations.

I'd never made love before, and I'd definitely never made out with anyone that made me feel like this. Hell, he wasn't even kissing me, and I was struggling not to surrender.

As his lips moved over my ear, he asked, "Can I kiss you now?"

Oh, God. No. No. No.

But I wasn't saying that. I said nothing. Giving in felt like letting him win. And telling him to stop was out of the question, too. I didn't want him to stop. He felt too good. Like a roller coaster multiplied times one hundred.

His lips moved back over my cheek, inching closer to my mouth.

"I want to touch you." His words were against my lips now. "I want to feel what's mine. What's always been mine."

Oh, sweet Jesus.

Those words shouldn't turn me on. But holy hell, they did. My mouth quivered with wanting to take him in. I tasted his breath and wanted to capture and taste all of him. I wanted to fulfill my need.

But my eyes snapped open when I realized that it would fulfill his need, too.

Shit.

I bit down on the corner of my mouth to stifle the ache between my legs, and used my weak muscles to shove him away.

I could barely meet his eyes. He knew he'd gotten to me. He had to know.

"Stay away from me." I hopped off the car and walked to the passenger side.

I heard his chuckle behind me. "You first."

Chapter 24

My eyes flutter open with the sudden chill. I am in bed, but a draft caresses my body. Are my French doors open?

Looking around me, I widen my eyes with shock when I notice Jared standing at the foot of my bed with my blanket in his hand.

"Jared?" I wipe my eyes and look at him questioningly. My arms go up to cover my chest, which is hardly modest under a white camisole.

"Don't," his husky voice commands me. "Don't cover yourself."

I don't know why I obey. I let my arms fall beside me to the bed. Jared's intense gaze scours every inch of my body as he drops the blanket to the floor. My skin is seared by his hungry observation, and I can't seem to get enough air.

His naked chest shimmers in the moonlight coming through my window. He wears black pants, which hang low from his strong, narrow hips.

Leaning down, he wraps his fingers around my ankles and gently eases them apart.

My legs, which are slightly bent at the knee, are now spread and hiding nothing except what is covered by my pink boy shorts.

Bending one knee onto the bed, he lowers himself until each of his hands falls beside my hips. While my knees shake with excited nerves, I watch as his head dips and kisses the top of my thigh. I gasp at the feel of his lips, soft and warm, against my skin. The flip-flop of my stomach is nothing compared to the throbbing at my core.

Why aren't I stopping him?

I am scared to let him continue but completely in awe of the sensations pouring over my body. I watch him quietly as he trails more kisses, leading inward. The hair on the top of his head brushes my sex, and I grip the bed sheet to keep from wrapping my legs around his body and pressing him into me. His tongue touches my thigh with the next kiss, and the scorching heat of his mouth almost sends me jerking off the bed. I thread my hands through his hair, unable to control myself.

"Jared," I plead.

He comes to hover over me, looking down into my eyes with fire and need. While his head remains high above, never breaking eye contact, his hips meet mine, and we start moving against each other. I feel him harden through his pants, and I like that I do that to him. My eyes close with the pleasure boiling my blood, and my need for him builds with the friction of his hard-on rubbing between my legs.

"Don't stop," I gasp out, the throbbing growing intense deep inside, and I know exactly where I need him to be. I need more of him.

"You're mine, Tate." Jared's right hand holds the side of my chest under my arm, and his thumb strokes my breast.

"Please." Between his finger on my nipple and the pulsing between my thighs growing faster with our increasing pace, I squeeze my eyes shut, delirious with craving. Our bodies move in a frenzy, and I suck in breath after breath to keep up. I don't know how long this can go on, but I know we are building to something sweet.

"Say you're mine," Jared commands as he grinds into me, harder. Damn, he feels good. He lowers his lips to mine as we breathe each other in. He smells like wind and rain, and fire.

"I . . . " My voice is lost. I just need a few more seconds.

Oh, God.

"Say it," Jared pleads against my lips, our bodies flush with each other now. I grab him by the hips and pull him into me as much as

our clothes will allow. My body begins to spasm, and I hold my breath waiting for it to come.

"Say it," Jared whispers into my ear.

I jerk my hips against him and gasp out, "I'm yours." Shivers shoot through my center and trail through my belly and down my body. A wave of pleasure pours over my body like vibrations under my skin. I've never felt anything like this before.

And I want more of it.

As the sweet pulse between my legs throbbed, my eyes fluttered open. I looked to my left and right before I shot up in my bed. Sunlight shined through my bedroom window, and I realized I was all alone.

What the hell?!

I twisted around, sure that I'd find Jared there. But no. Nothing. No Jared. No moonlight. I had gone to sleep in my pajama shorts and black T-shirt. My blankets rested on my body. Jared had never been here.

But the orgasm had been real. I still felt my body shuddering on the inside with the arousal he, or rather the dream of him, caused. My muscles, weak from the tension, barely kept me sitting up in bed. I crashed back onto my pillow and let out an exasperated sigh. That had been amazing, but I couldn't believe that had actually happened! I'd heard about guys having wet dreams but not girls.

Tate, you're psychotic. Fantasizing about that jerk was sick. I took deep, long breaths to calm myself down. It was all because he'd been on my mind so much. Nothing more.

I hadn't been properly kissed in months, not since the few dates I'd had in France. Jared had gotten under my skin last night, but no matter how turned on he got me, I had to remember that he was off limits. Apologizing for treating me like dirt wasn't enough. I didn't trust him, and I never would.

Not without the whole story.

He also had too much control over my body, and that had to change.

Last night, after the non-kiss, Jared had driven me home without another word. He drove off afterwards, and now I was exhausted from lying awake until two a.m. wondering about his last words to me.

You first. Did he mean that I couldn't stay away from him?

Bold son of a bitch.

"Are you up, Tate?" My grandma poked her head through my doorway. I shuffled with the covers as she came into the room, and I grimaced internally, wondering if I'd made any suspicious noises out loud during my dream.

"Uh, yeah. Just woke up." Sitting up, I plastered an innocent smile on my face.

"Good. You better get dressed. I have breakfast downstairs. You need to hurry if we're going to make it to your meet on time." She nodded her head and waved her hand in a get-out-of-bed motion as I tried to remember what she was talking about.

Meet?

"Come on. Up and at 'em." She clapped her hands before turning and leaving.

Glancing at the clock, I realized I'd forgotten to set the alarm last night. My meet! The whole reason I'd let Jared give me a ride in the first place. I should've been up a half hour ago!

Thankfully, Grandma was giving me a ride and would stay to watch before she drove back to her own house today. Tomorrow, I'd be on my own again.

Throwing off the covers, I sprinted to my closet and threw on my shorts, sports bra and tank top. I'd put on my team shirt when I got there, so I stuffed that in my duffle bag with my socks. Grabbing my shoes and a hair tie, I hopped down the stairs and filled a paper plate with some toast and sliced up fruit.

"Sit down and eat." Grandma pointed to the chair.

"I'll eat in the car. I hate being late." I crammed a couple of snack bars and water bottles in my bag before heading to the door. "Come on," I said, ignoring her stare.

The last thing I wanted to do this morning was sit across from my grandma and try to eat breakfast, knowing she'd walked into my bedroom minutes after I'd had an orgasm.

Even with as little sleep as I'd had, the opportunity to pound out some energy and frustration proved useful at the meet. My team took part in a competition in which we placed second, and I also competed in an individual race spanning a few miles through a nearby recreational area. The high walls of the quarry around us, and the dense population of trees, made the trail space feel cramped. And that was how I liked it today. I couldn't imagine that I was alone, so it was hard to let my mind wander off the race.

Coming in second again, I smiled as my grandma snapped picture after picture. I was glad she was here to see me race, probably for the last time in my high school career. Although, my dad missed it, and now I missed him even more. It'd been hard dealing with my mom not being around for the important events, but I really wanted my dad today.

After chilidogs at Mulgrew's, she drove us home.

"I'm going to miss you. I told your dad I'd be back at Christmas, though." Grandma packed up the last of her belongings and set everything by the front door.

"Looking forward to it. And I will miss you too."

"So, do you want to tell me about last night?" She peered up from her purse as she checked to make sure she had everything.

My heart skipped a beat. "Last night?" I could come clean with her, but instead, I chose to play ignorant. I had no idea where to start about last night.

"Yes. A dangerous looking black car, similar to the boy's next door, dropped you home after curfew?" she questioned with laughing eyes. Clearly, she wasn't too concerned.

"Yesss." I drew it out dramatically. "Jared gave me a lift home. We were at the same party. No big deal." My eyes averted to my shoes as my omissions had me feeling guilty. There was more to tell her, a lot more, but as always, I chose to keep my Jared issues quiet.

And now there was a whole new can of worms to sort out—his kissing and my dirty dreams.

She stood there for a few moments studying me as I continued to act oblivious. "Okay, if you say so." She hooked her purse over her shoulder. "You remember the rules about locking up?"

I nodded.

"Good. Well, give me a hug."

She held out her arms, and I wrapped myself around her, inhaling her perfume-lotion scent one more time. I picked up one of her bags and led the way to her car.

"See you in no time," I assured her as I saw her bring a tissue to her eye.

"In no time," she sniffled. "Put up some Halloween decorations. It'll cheer you up if you get lonely."

"Already?"

"It's October," she laughed. "That's the time for Halloween, Tate."

October? I hadn't realized. My birthday was coming up.

After my grandma left, I texted K.C. After everything that happened last night, I hadn't had a chance to talk to her.

How's it going?

Fine. Sorry I couldn't make the meet. Busy. She shot back a minute later.

So . . . you and Liam? I queried. Part of me hoped that she and

Liam were back on. I felt guilty. Only a lousy person would kiss the guy her best friend was dating, and I worried about how I would tell her. If she and Liam were back together, then maybe I wouldn't need to come clean?

Don't judge. She texted back.

Relief flooded me. There *were* back together.

Never. If you're happy . . .

I am. Just hope I can trust him. She still had doubts, and rightly so. I don't think I could take back a guy that cheated on me, but then again, I'd never been in love. I guess I wouldn't know anything until I'd experienced it.

You may never know for sure, but as long as he's worth it, I wrote.

I think so . . . So Jared's all yours.

What?! The thumping in my chest actually hurt.

Apparently, I took too long drowning in my own sweat, because she texted again.

No worries, Tate. He was never mine anyway.

I couldn't text back. What would I say? *Thanks?*

Jared wasn't hers, and he definitely wasn't mine. He made it abundantly clear that he belonged to no one. Was Jared holding back with her because of me? Is that why she said what she said?

I spent the rest of the weekend doing anything to keep my mind off Jared. Saturday and Sunday I spent cleaning the house, washing the Bronco, completing homework, typing up procedures for my experiment, and avoiding texts from Ben and K.C.

I needed to be alone, and I wasn't sure I could keep what happened between Jared and me a secret. K.C. deserved to know that I kissed him, but I didn't want anyone to know, so I chose to avoid everyone. Even my dad when he called.

Ben deserved my silence, even if he had called and texted several times to apologize. If he'd just taken me home like he'd promised, then I wouldn't have gotten into that mess with Nate.

Honestly, Ben was probably a very decent guy, despite his behavior at the bonfire. But the problem remained—I didn't feel firecrackers going off in my stomach when he kissed me. I didn't feel anything.

Jared was like the Fourth of July . . . all over my body.

As I stepped out of French class Monday morning, I immediately halted. Madoc stood across the hall, leaned up against the lockers, eyeballing me with a goofy grin.

"Hey, Little Speed Racer." He sauntered over as kids behind me bumped into my back trying to get out of class.

I rolled my eyes, not ready for another irritation. Already this morning, I'd been late to school after coming out of the house to find that the Bronco had a flat. Dr. Porter had emailed to tell me the lab was off limits tomorrow afternoon. And people had been talking to me all day about the race Friday night.

As positive as that attention was, it was like someone scraping their teeth across their fork. I didn't want to be reminded of how Friday night had gone from good to bad, and then good again, and then to worse. The week was starting off rough, and I wasn't in the mood for asshole Madoc.

"What do you want?" I mumbled, walking past him down the hall.

"Well, it's nice to see you, too." He seemed to hold back his usual sinister self. He wasn't making innuendoes or trying to grope me. He just stared down at me, almost timidly, with his ridiculously playful smile.

Ignoring him and making a beeline for my locker, I felt an urge to kick something when Madoc only increased his speed to keep up. "Listen, I want you to know that I was really impressed with your driving Friday night. And I heard you placed second in the three mile. Sounds like you had a great weekend."

No, actually, I'm completely in knots. I hadn't seen Jared at all since Friday. His house seemed abandoned until late last night when I heard the roar of his engine crawl up the driveway. I hadn't seen him today either.

And I was looking for him. I was more irritated about that than anything.

"Spit it out, Madoc. What disgusting, demeaning prank are you pulling on me today?" Reaching my locker, I didn't even spare him a glance as I dumped my bag and books.

"I have absolutely nothing up my sleeve, Tate. I've actually come to beg your forgiveness." Madoc took my hand, and I turned to look at him.

He placed his hand over his heart and made a low bow.

Oh, what now?

Looking around to see the flood of students in the hall, all gawking at Madoc Caruthers making his grand gesture, I swatted him on the back.

"Get up!" I whisper-yelled as people around us laughed and murmured to each other.

What was he up to?! Dread tightened my stomach.

"I am truly sorry for everything I've done to you." Madoc raised his body again to face me. "I have no excuse. It's not my thing to make an enemy out of beautiful girls."

So you've said.

"Whatever." I crossed my arms, ready to go get lunch. "Is that it?"

"Actually, no." He waggled his eyebrows. "I was hoping you would go to the Homecoming dance with me?"

Chapter 25

My muscles tensed. I immediately started scanning the hallway to see if anyone was laughing, a sign that this was all a joke.

But none of Madoc's pals were around to witness the prank, and Jared was nowhere in sight.

Turning back to Madoc, I fixed him with a glare. "Did you really expect me to fall for that?"

"Fall for what? My charm and amazing body? Absolutely."

His sarcasm did nothing to ease my distrust. I rolled my eyes, already wondering why the hell I'd stood here listening to him. "Enough. I'm going to lunch. Tell Jared that I'm not that stupid."

I turned around and headed for the cafeteria.

"Wait." Madoc jogged up beside me. "You think this is a set-up?"

Ignoring him, I kept walking. *Of course, this was a set-up.* Why would Madoc want to go to Homecoming with me? And why would he think that I'd say "yes?" We'd been at each other's throats for years.

"Tate, Jared would probably set fire to my hair if he knew I was talking to you, let alone asking you out. I'm being serious here. No pranks. No jokes. I really want to take you to the dance."

I pushed on towards the cafeteria hoping he'd get the hint. I started to feel like I was suffocating. He needed to get away from me. Now.

"Tate, please stop." Madoc touched my arm.

I whirled around to face him, hot with anger. "Even if you are being serious, did you really think I'd ever trust you? You've groped me, and I've broken your nose. You're asking me out? Really?"

This was the dumbest turn of events I'd never anticipated, and what's more? It was a waste of my time.

"I realize we have an interesting history," Madoc started, holding up his hands, "and I want to assure you that I'm not asking you out in a romantic way. Jared will have my balls as it is. I've been a jerk, and I want to make amends. If you don't already have a date, I'd love to take you and show you that I can be a good guy."

Aww, what a nice little speech.

"No," I replied.

His charm didn't work on me the way it worked on others, but the shocked look on his face gave me a little pause. Part of me wanted to laugh, because he actually looked disappointed. And part of me was troubled, because he *actually* looked disappointed.

I owed Madoc nothing, I told myself.

After everything, I shouldn't even be speaking to him. But then again, after overhearing his talk with Jared last week in the hall, it seemed like he never was fully on board when it came to trying to hurt me. Maybe he really did want to make amends.

Doesn't matter. It's not going to happen.

Twisting around, I headed for the cafeteria again when I really just wanted to run out the front door. It was only Monday morning, and I was already climbing the walls to get out of here.

It was true that I wanted to go to the dance, and I didn't yet have a date. And going with Madoc would make Jared jealous. Maybe I wanted to see him twisted up in knots over me.

I shook the thoughts from my mind. *Don't go there, Tate.*

*

"Are you thinking of trying for an athletic scholarship?" Jess asked me as we threw away the remains of our lunches.

"Not really. I like running, but I'm not sure if I want to make that kind of commitment while I'm in college," I answered.

K.C. and Liam had joined us for lunch but had disappeared a while ago, probably underneath the bleachers near the football field to *talk*. She seemed happy, and Liam had been even sweeter than usual. It would be a long time before I could look at him without thinking about his betrayal, but I was glad they were together again.

After they'd left, I barely ate any of my chicken burrito. Madoc kept smiling at me from across the cafeteria.

Ben kept texting me, too. He wanted to talk before lunch was over, but thanks to my friends, I had an excuse not to be alone with him. He'd been stupid, and while I was aggravated, I knew I'd have to talk to him some time. Even if it was just to say "let's be friends."

"Well, you were awesome on Saturday." Jess finished off her juice before tossing the bottle. "Oh, and Friday, too. I didn't see the race, but the school's been buzzing about it. You made people a lot of money. Derek Roman was pretty pissed, I hear."

"I'm sure he was." I swept my long hair up into a ponytail and felt a flash of heat bore into the back of my neck.

It was crazy how my awareness of Jared worked, but I was pretty sure he was in here somewhere.

He'd been AWOL all morning, no sign of his car or him. I kept my attention on Jess, even though the pull to turn around vibrated all over my body. After the two kisses and the dream, not to mention his apology, I'd thought about him a lot this weekend.

Before I could give in and search for him, I made my way to the doors with Jess. A moment later, I halted when I heard someone calling my name.

"Tatum Brandt!"

I jumped, instantly embarrassed that the person yelling made me the focus of the entire lunchroom.

"Will you please go to the Homecoming dance with me?" the idiot's voice asked behind me.

I closed my eyes. I. Am. Going. To. Kill. Him.

I spun around slowly to see that Madoc was kneeling a few feet away. He stared up at me with big, blue, puppy dog eyes, and I noticed that the lunchroom had gotten very quiet as people hushed others and looked at us wide-eyed and breathless.

"You've got to be kidding me," I mumbled and offered an apologetic smile to Jess. Walking on his knees in short, hilarious steps, he came flush with my shoes and cocked his head all the way back to peer up at me. He took my hand in his.

Girls were giggling, and everyone was staring at us. Only Madoc could get away with this flamboyant display and still be considered manly.

"Please, please! Don't say no. I need you." His dramatic tone caused an uproar of laughter and chants encouraging him further.

My heart was pounding. Any second now I was going to go ballistic on him, and I probably wouldn't be lucky enough to stay out of the Dean's office a second time.

"Get up," I snapped, pulling on my hand. My head swam with ideas of how I was going to hurt this kid. They'd never find the body.

"Please, let's make this work. I'm sorry for everything." He was deliberately speaking above the laughter so that everyone knew our business.

"I said no."

"But the baby needs a father!" he implored.

My heart sunk at his words. Oh, my God. No, no, no . . .

Hoots and hollers erupted from every corner of the room, and heat rose up my neck and face. I felt like I was having an out of body experience. This could not be happening. Is this how he was making amends? By embarrassing me more?

He grabbed my hips and pressed his face into my stomach. "I promise I'll love our kid," he whispered for only me to hear. "I can say it louder if you want."

"Fine, I'll go. For now," I said through clenched teeth. "But if you pull any more shit, I'll break your arm."

He popped up, wrapped his arms around me and pulled me off my feet into a hug. Swinging me around, everyone clapped and whistled, and I felt like throwing up. Once I was back on my feet, I slapped him on the arm and stalked out of the cafeteria, knowing I did not want to catch the expressions on Jess's or Jared's faces.

Chapter 26

Thankfully, by the time school ended, everyone knew Madoc's joke was just that ... a joke. At least the douchebag proved honorable in correcting the rumor. I still hadn't come to terms with the fact that I'd said yes. Homecoming was still two weeks away, so hopefully I'd find a way out of it. As proven in the last month, a lot could happen in a short time.

Jared wasn't in Themes class, so instead of fighting to not look at him, I had to fight to avoid Ben looking at me. Life could be a bitch. I was going to Homecoming with the one person in this school who made my skin crawl, I was getting attention from a gorgeous, star football player that I couldn't care less about, and I was having wet dreams about a potential sociopath who acted like he hated me most of the time.

Eight more months.

"Hi, Dr. Porter." I smiled tiredly as I walked into the lab after school. Since the room wasn't available tomorrow as we'd scheduled, I'd opted to take him up on the offer to work today. Coach had given us the afternoon off, so it all worked out.

"Hi, Tate." Dr. Porter was a middle-aged ex-hippy who often left his long, rust-colored hair flowing free and drops of coffee dangling from his scraggly mustache and beard. My first few classes with him sophomore year were irritating. I kept wanting to take a napkin to his face.

"How long can I stay today?" Dropping my bag on the floor underneath my usual table, I looked to Dr. Porter.

"I'll be around for at least an hour, probably more." He gathered some folders and papers, trying to find a way to grab his coffee cup, too. "Do you need anything?"

"I'll go get my crate from the closet, and I know where everything is that I need."

"Good. I have a planning meeting with the Science department, but it's in another classroom. Feel free to come and get me if you need anything. I mean it. Room 136B." He headed for the door.

"Okay, thanks." Grabbing a heavy vinyl apron off the coat rack, I slid it over my head and tied it around my waist. The tie scratched at my back in the small sliver of space where my jeans and top failed to cover my skin.

Digging my supplies out of the closet, I nearly dropped the heavy load as soon as I walked back into the classroom. Jared sat at the teacher's table up front.

Hell.

He leaned back in the chair with his hands behind his head and one foot propped up on the edge of the table. His eyes gave nothing away, but his stare was focused entirely on me. That alone made the heat rise to my face and a cool sweat seep out of my pores.

Damn him. Why did he have to look like that?

The softness of his lips, and his tongue hot and heavenly on my neck flashed through my memory. An anxious twitch started between my legs, and I really wanted to straddle him on that chair.

Shit. I was a walking time bomb of nerves.

I shook my head and averted my eyes as I carried my crate to my table. "Not now, Jared. I'm busy." Honestly, that was the truth. I needed to focus, and as much as part of me wanted to indulge in this drama, I needed to be left alone.

"I know." His smooth voice was strangely calm. "I came to help you."

I stopped unloading the crate and stared at him wide-eyed. "Help me?" My tone dripped with sarcasm as I was sure this was either a joke on his part or an effort to sabotage my experiment. "I don't need help."

Dropping his arms, he stuffed his hands into the front pocket of his black hoodie. "I wasn't asking if you did," he replied, quickly and assertively.

"No, you're just assuming." Continuing to unload my materials, I avoided his eyes. That damn dream kept coursing through my mind, and I was scared that I'd give something away if I looked at him.

"Not at all. I know what you can do." There was laughter in his voice, and I didn't miss the double meaning in that remark. "I thought that if we're going to be friends, this might be a good place to start."

Getting off the chair, he walked towards me. I breathed in and out slowly.

Just take the beaker and flask and set them down slowly. Nice and slow.

"I mean, it's not like we're going to be able to go back to climbing trees and having sleepovers, is it?" he asked suggestively as his fingers grazed the lab table.

Sleepovers? My core started pulsing harder, and I knew my body was ready for what it needed. I felt it.

The idea of having Jared for a sleepover, even though he was joking, thrilled me. Damn, I'd love to let him keep me up all night doing things that we sure didn't do as kids. I wanted his hands on me, bringing me close, and his mouth all over.

But I wanted him to care, too. And I didn't trust him.

Blinking, I narrowed my eyebrows at him. "Like I said, I don't need help."

"Like I said, I wasn't asking. Did you think that Porter was going to let you conduct experiments with fire by yourself?" He laughed bitterly and came to stand next to me.

"How do you know about my experiment? And who said we're going to be friends?" I asked before bending down to grab my binder from my bag. "You know, maybe too much damage has been done. I know you've apologized, but it's not so easy for me."

"You're not getting girly on me, are you?" he sneered.

Sifting through my binder, I pulled out notes and procedures I'd researched. I tried to read over the material, but having Jared so close made it hard to concentrate.

Turning to my left, I fixed him with my best bored expression. I didn't want him thinking I was the least bit intrigued by his presence.

"Jared, I appreciate the effort you're putting in here, but it's unnecessary. Contrary to what your ego is blowing you up with, I've been surviving just fine without you for the last three years. I work better alone, and I would not appreciate your help today or any other day. We're not friends."

His cool façade faltered, and he blinked. His dark eyes searched mine. Or maybe he searched for something to say.

Feeling slightly guilty, I turned back to my binder but ended up knocking it to the floor in the process. Its contents, not secured by the three rings, floated to the floor. A wave of embarrassment spread over my body as my tough girl speech ended in a clumsy mess.

Jared jetted to my other side and bent with me to pick up the binder and its contents. "You're looking at cars?" He eyed the printouts I'd taken from the internet to be prepared when my dad got home.

"Yeah," I replied curtly. "I'm getting myself a birthday present."

He held the information in his hand, not really looking at anything, but he seemed to be thinking about something.

"Jared?" I held out my hand to get the information back from him.

"I forgot your birthday was coming up," he said almost to himself as I took back the papers and stuffed everything in my binder.

I wondered if that was true. Our birthdays were a big deal when we were friends, but in recent years he could've forgotten, I guess. I hadn't forgotten his. It was October second.

Yesterday!

Ugh, should I say something? I hadn't done anything for Jared's birthday the past few years, but now that the subject was up, I had no idea what to do.

Screw it. He would've forgotten mine, too.

"Does your dad know you're looking to buy a car so soon?" Jared interrupted my thoughts.

"Does your mom know you provide alcohol to minors and sleep around on the weekends?" My remark came out way snippier than I wanted it to.

"'Does my mom care' would be a better question." His sarcasm was a cover for the annoyed look I saw boiling underneath.

I frowned as I thought about Jared's life. He grew up without a father and an absentee mother. He had no healthy role models or love in his life—that I knew of, anyway. Having no comeback to that, I remained silent as he slowly started helping me unload my crate.

Beakers, flasks, test tubes, and an assortment of liquids and dry materials covered the tabletop. I wouldn't need all of this stuff, but had gathered it anyway when I was still trying to decide my project. Three different store-bought flame retardants and some ingredients for a homemade one cluttered the counter, along with different cotton fabrics. My experiment would consist of testing how cotton reacted to different resistant sprays. I had already put together my purpose, hypothesis, the constants and variables, and my materials. Today, I'd be putting together my procedures and getting started on one round of tests.

On top of all that, my nerves were now firing at both ends.

There was a time when Jared's presence calmed me and made me feel safe. Now, his proximity had me hyper-aware of every time his arm came close to brushing mine or whenever I thought his eyes flashed to me. My head felt cloudy, and my hands clenched.

Annoyed, I twisted to grab my notes out of my binder and bumped a flask off the counter. Heat covered my face as I turned around to try to catch the flask, but instead, watched it shatter all over the floor. With my back to the counter, I stared down at the mess and inhaled deeply. At this point, I didn't care if he thought I was crazy or overreacting. I needed him gone.

Jared moved in front of me and stared down at the broken glass. "I make you nervous," he said without looking up at me. His assessment was dead-on. I knew it, and so did he.

"Just go." My desperate whisper pleaded with him as I refused to meet his stare, which I was sure was now on me.

"Look at me." Jared cupped my cheek with his hand, his fingers reaching my hair. "I'm sorry." My eyes shot up to his at the sound of his repeat apology. "I should never have treated you the way I did." Eyes burning, I searched his face for any sarcasm or insincerity, but came up short. His expression was all seriousness, and his breathing was deep as he waited for my response.

Jared brought his other hand up to cup my other cheek and moved in closer. His hands slid around the back of my neck, and his thumbs grazed my ears. My breathing became shallow as his body pressed gently against mine. His eyes were now concentrated on my lips as his face inched closer. Jared was barely an inch from my lips, but I could still taste him.

He had started so slowly, but I groaned in surprise when he dived in and caught my lips with his. Fireworks started in my mouth and filtered up through the top of my head and down my neck. I was lost as his arm wrapped around my waist and his other hand stayed buried in my hair. He clutched me tighter, pulling me up to my toes. I inhaled him, smelling the wind and rain from his skin, and for a brief moment, I was home.

This is everything I needed. Everything I wanted—on me, around me, inside of me. My hormones were out of control. I wanted to rip his clothes off and feel his naked chest against mine. I wanted to kiss him until I was too hot and delirious with need. Who was I kidding? I was already aching with desire. It pooled in my abdomen and shot downward to my sex like a damn tornado.

His tongue flicked under my top lip, sending shivers down my arms. I snaked my arms tightly around his neck and pressed into him. His hands rubbed down my sides and grabbed my ass. My body loved every touch. I molded into him like a piece of clay. Where he caressed, I melted. Where he pulled, I followed.

His mouth was so hot, and I couldn't help but wonder how good the rest of him would feel, too.

"I've wanted you for so long," he whispered, his breath on my lips like a drug drawing me in. "All the times I'd see you next door . . . it drove me crazy."

My toes curled at his words. He wanted me the whole time. I liked knowing that. I liked that he desired me.

He took my lips again in a deep kiss, my back pressed against the lab table. As he bit my bottom lip, my head reeled with what was happening. I loved finding out that he never hated me, that he always wanted me. But what was happening between us? Were we getting together? Or was Jared scratching an itch?

"Don't . . . " I gasped out and pulled myself back. I didn't want to move, and I didn't want to be anywhere else but with him. But I knew why I stopped.

He can't win. He can't treat me like shit and then have me.

Jared was breathing hard and stared at my swollen lips like he was far from done. His eyes drifted up to mine, and I saw the intense need, as if he was either really pissed I'd stopped him or turned on to the point of tying me down.

Releasing his hold and dropping me back to my feet, his expression became indifferent as he backed away.

"Then I won't," he said coldly. I guess I didn't expect him to argue or pursue me more. Jared wasn't a beggar. But I was thrown off balance by how quickly he could go from blazing hot to bitterly cold.

I studied him for a few moments, wondering if I'd ever get around this prideful indifference of his. "What are you up to?" I questioned, narrowing my eyes at him.

He let out a dry laugh. "I want us to be friends," he admitted somewhat sincerely.

"Why now?"

"Why so many questions?" he countered.

Was he serious? He had some explaining to do. "You didn't think it was going to be this easy, did you?"

"Yes, I was hoping we could move forward without looking back." His annoyed tone fit perfectly with the scowl forming around his eyes.

"We can't," I said flatly. "You go from threatening me one day to kissing me the next. I don't switch gears that fast."

"Kissing you? You kissed me back . . . both times. And now you're off to the school dance with Madoc. You might say I'm the one with whiplash here." He stuck his hands into the pockets of his hoodie and leaned against the window sill. His eyes were challenging me, and I barely had a response for his comeback. He was right. I dated Ben, was going to a dance with Madoc, and kissing Jared.

"I don't have to explain myself to you." My response was pathetic.

"You shouldn't go."

"I want to," I lied. "And he asked me." Dismissing him, I turned to my work.

Jared came up behind me as I tried to look busy sorting my papers. "Has *he* been on your mind, Tate?" His breath fanned my hair. Placing both hands on either side of me, locking me in, he taunted me. "Do you want him? Or is it me you dream of?"

I closed my eyes, remembering my dream the other morning. What the thought of him did to me, and now he was right behind me.

"I said that when I put my hands on you, you'd want it. Remember?"

I turned to look at him. He moved his head up to meet my eyes. "I don't think it's any secret that I like it when you touch me. When you're ready to tell me everything you're holding back, then maybe I'll trust you again. Until then . . . "

His eyes narrowed and anger descended like a black cloud on his face as he backed away.

His back straightened and his fists clenched. Knowing I'd said exactly what I needed to say, I turned back around to my work. My heart was caving to him, and I couldn't look at him anymore without the fear of giving in. If he wanted me as a friend or for more, then he'd have to give me more. As enticing as his offer of moving on without looking back sounded, I knew that Jared's story made him the man he was now. I needed to know him.

"Jared?" a female voice whined from the doorway. "There you are."

I looked up to see Piper with her cheerleading skirt pulled down to show off her hip bones and flat stomach. I think I just vomited a little in my mouth.

"Weren't you giving me a ride home today?" She brushed her long, dark hair over her shoulder and bit her bottom lip. *Oh, please.*

"I've got my bike today, Piper." Jared sounded bitter from behind me. He was pissed. With who? I wasn't sure, but I could guess.

"I can handle it," she asserted. "Let's go. It doesn't look like you're busy here anyway." Her gaze fell on me, and anger heated up my cheeks.

Jared was quiet for a few moments, and I felt his eyes on my back as I continued to sort materials for today. Every move was slow and methodical as I struggled not to drop anything else. But pretending not to pay attention was as impossible as not paying attention.

"Yeah, I'm not busy," Jared finally replied coolly as he walked past me towards the door.

"So, Terrance . . . " The idiot girl acted like she didn't know my name. "You didn't go and give your Homecoming date a black eye, did you? He can barely see. You should really stop beating up on guys or people will start thinking you're a dyke."

She was trying to bait me, but I was at a loss. I had no idea what she was talking about. Someone had given Madoc a black eye since I'd see him at lunch?

"She didn't give Madoc a black eye. I did." Jared walked past her and opened the door, now not sparing either of us eye contact.

"Why?" Piper's nose scrunched up as she turned around to exit the door he held open. Jared raised an eyebrow at me and swung the door shut with enough force for the vibrations to travel up my legs.

Staring at the closed door for several moments, I finally realized that Jared had punched Madoc over me.

What the hell?

Well, this definitely wasn't some joke between the two of them, then. Madoc was interested in spending a little time with me, and that drove Jared crazy.

I let out a hard laugh. I wasn't interested in Madoc. But, if it bugged Jared, I might be interested in having a little fun, after all.

Slipping in my ear buds, I spent the rest of the afternoon in a great mood.

Chapter 27

"Hey, Dad," I chirped after clicking the *Accept Call* button on my laptop. "What are doing up so late ... or early?" Germany was nine hours ahead of us. I had just returned from a run and beating thoughts of Jared, Madoc, and everyone else out of my head. It was after six, and I'd heated up a ham and cheese Lean Pocket for dinner.

"Hi, Pumpkin, I just got off a flight from Munich and am heading to bed now. Thought I'd check in to make sure you're doing alright without Grandma."

He looked weary and disheveled. His gray hair stood in half a dozen different directions as if he'd spent the last twenty-four hours running his hands through it, and bags hung under his blue eyes. His white collared shirt was unbuttoned at the top with his tan and blue tie loosened.

"Munich? I didn't know you were going there," I said with my mouth full.

"Just a spontaneous daytrip for a meeting. I took the red eye back to Berlin. I have today free, so I'll sleep late."

My dad's idea of sleeping in was seven o'clock in the morning. If he didn't emerge from his room by then, something was wrong. "Okay, well make sure you actually sleep late. You work too hard, and it's showing. How will you get a date looking like you do?"

He laughed it off, but there was sadness in his smile. I immediately felt guilty for bringing up dating. Since my mom died, my dad had kept as busy as possible. He worked a lot, and when he wasn't working, we were both on the go. We never stayed home on vacations, and he rarely spent any free time at the house. We were always off to one event or another: basketball games, dinners, camping trips, and concerts. My dad never wanted to have too much time to think. I was sure there had been casual "girlfriends" over the years on his travels, but he never considered anyone seriously.

"Hey, Mr. Brandt," K.C. called out as she came out of my bathroom and plopped down in my chair next to the double doors.

She'd come over right when I got home, begging for details about Madoc asking me to Homecoming today, but I got saved by the call from Dad.

"K.C.?" Dad questioned me, since he was unable to see her.

"Yep," I slurred, taking another bite of my dinner. I still wore my black compression shorts with a white tank top and blue jacket. The smell coming off of me would definitely repel any guy. I should go visit Madoc right now and throw my arms around him, but even I wasn't that cruel. The fatigue in my muscles filled me with relief, though. I couldn't think or worry about anything right now even if I wanted to.

"Tatum Brandt. That is not your dinner." The shock in my dad's eyes made me roll mine.

"It's food. Now be quiet," I commanded comically. I looked over to see K.C. smile and shake her head.

"I'll be home in two and a half months. Do you think you can keep yourself alive until then?" Dad said sarcastically.

"People can survive on water alone for weeks." I tried to keep serious, but I started laughing when his eyes widened.

We chatted for a few more minutes. I told him about my experiments, but left out how preoccupied I'd been lately. He listened while I gave him a rundown of my upcoming meets, and he reminded me to get all of my college applications ready by Thanksgiving. Even though I couldn't entertain the idea of *not* getting into Columbia, we both agreed applying to other schools was smart. I suggested a few places, and he suggested Tulane, my mom's school. I agreed to add it to the list.

"So," K.C. taunted as soon as I'd hung up with my dad, "Madoc, huh?" I knew she'd been itching to ask as soon as she'd knocked on my door. She dug into me with her stare as she pulled her long, dark brown hair into a ponytail.

I climbed off my bed and took off my jacket. "Oh, it's not like that, and you know it. You should've seen how he ambushed me in the cafeteria." I walked into my newly redecorated bathroom.

Grandma had done it for me last week. The once off-white bathroom walls now boasted a calming deep gray. A black shower curtain was accented with matching accessories throughout the room. Black and white pictures of bare trees adorned the wall opposite the mirror, and a radio with an iPod dock sat on the sink counter. My Scentsy warmer contained *My Dear Watson*, my favorite scent.

This was my oasis. As silly as it sounded, the bathroom should be revered more. It's the one place where absolute privacy is respected.

For the most part.

"You said 'yes?'" K.C. shouted from my bedroom.

"I think I said 'fine,' actually. Believe me, I don't want to go anywhere with Madoc. I'll get out of it."

But maybe not. Now that I knew his asking wasn't orchestrated by Jared and that Jared was upset by it, I was considering a devious move by actually going.

"You could've just kicked him in the balls again." K.C. peeked around the corner of the bathroom.

"Maybe, maybe not." I raised my eyebrows, and K.C. let it go and came to stand beside me at the sink.

Taking one of my lipsticks off the counter, she began to apply it and spoke while looking at me through the mirror. "We can go shopping for dresses," she suggested.

"Are you going with Liam then?" I asked, tugging my hair out of my ponytail.

"He's asked, but I haven't agreed." She waved her hand at my questioning look. "Oh, I'll agree eventually, I just want him to suffer a bit."

"Are you sure you don't just want to space yourself from him for a while? I mean, he did cheat on you."

K.C. was smart, and even though I liked Liam, I didn't want her to get hurt again. If he cheated once, he might do it again.

"You don't have to worry, Tate. You're not saying anything I haven't told myself a hundred times already." She sighed and fixed me with a pensive expression. "I love him. And I believe he's sorry. Do I trust him? Of course not. And he knows it." She walked back into the bedroom, and I leaned on the bathroom doorframe.

So she and Jared were over then. How far had it gone? I wondered.

"And Jared?" I couldn't help myself. "You two . . ." Drifting off, not sure how to ask what I wanted to ask.

She gave me a look that made me embarrassed to ask, but she answered. "It wasn't like that. He took my mind off Liam, is all."

"So you two didn't . . . " I stared down to my dark hardwood floors, feeling incredibly awkward.

"No! What do you think I am?" She was shocked. That was a good sign.

I exhaled, my body suddenly feeling more relaxed until the next thought occurred to me. "Could you have?" Maybe she and Jared hadn't done the deed, but maybe it was just because she'd resisted. If *he'd* wanted to, it would be like they had done it in my book.

"You mean was he interested in having sex with me?" She smirked, trying to figure out how to carry this out and toy with me. "Maaaaybe. Why do you care?"

"I don't. Of course." I looked around the room, anywhere but at her. Why did I care?

"So you were hot for Ben, now you're hot for Madoc, and secretly hot for Jared?" I could tell by her pursed lips that she was trying to contain laughter.

"You're baiting me. Knock it off," I warned playfully and changed the subject. "Alright, dress shopping this weekend. Preferably Saturday after the meet."

Grinning and looking at me out of the corner of her eye, she walked to the door and grabbed her jacket off my bed. "See ya later, Hot Mama."

I grabbed my running shoe off the floor and hurled it at the door as she left. She squealed as she ran down the stairs laughing.

"I think you should know . . ." A snippy female voice came up beside me the next day at my locker. I turned to see Piper, whose last name I had yet to discover, giving me the stink-eye right before she slammed my locker door shut, missing my nose by centimeters. ". . . that Jared is not interested in you. Back off." Her warning came with a raised eye brow and laughable duckface lips.

Really? She was making this too easy.

"So are you naturally insecure or just with Jared?" I innocently inquired, enjoying a weaker opponent a little too much.

"I'm not insecure. I just protect what's mine." I could see up her nostrils with how high she held her sharp nose. She stuck her hands in the back pockets of her jeans, pushing her D cup chest further in my face.

Taking in her look, I felt insecure. She was sexy in her skin-tight jeans and red halter-top shirt. My look screamed goodie-goodie in my tight but not too tight jeans and black peasant blouse. She was stylishly adorned with silver bracelets and high-heeled sandals. *Really? Sandals in October?* My wrists were covered in rubber bracelets.

I wouldn't change for any guy, but I could see why guys found girls like her attractive. My skin burned to think that she had slept with Jared. He'd been on her body, inside of her.

My head started to ache. I fought the urge to give in to my jealous rage when I really just wanted to rip her hair out.

I picked up my bag from the floor and stuffed my Physics and French books inside. I opted to spend lunch in the library today, since I wanted to avoid Madoc and let K.C. have some time with Liam.

When I didn't say anything, she continued, "Every time I turn around, there you are making a spectacle of yourself, getting his attention."

"He's yours?" I asked calmly, remembering Jared's and my two-almost-three kisses. "Does he know that?"

Her expression faltered, but she quickly recovered. "Jared's a bad boy. He is what he is, and I can handle that. But if you come after him, you'll have to deal with me."

"He is what he is, huh?" For once, I felt no nervousness. My attack matched hers, and I wanted to see it out. "What's his favorite color? What's his mother's name? His favorite food? When's his birthday? Why does he hate the smell of bleach? Which band could he listen to every day for the rest of his life?"

Piper narrowed her eyes at me. Clearly, she was at a loss. Moreover, she was annoyed, because I was insinuating that I had the answers to these questions while she didn't. And I did.

I put my hand up before she retorted. "Rest easy, kitty cat. I'm not after him. But don't ever threaten me again, or I'll make a real big spectacle of myself. Got it?" Without waiting for her come-back, I twisted on my red ballet flat and headed toward the library.

"I do know where he goes on the weekends," she called behind me. "Do you?"

I turned around, the hairs on my neck prickling with interest. Piper seemed satisfied with my puzzled expression and gave me a smug smile before turning around and walking away.

That's right. He was gone most weekends. But where?

As far as I knew, he spent most Friday nights at the Benson farm, but the rest of his weekend was a mystery. There was usu-ally a party at his place on either Friday or Saturday nights, so it's not like he'd disappear all weekend. But she was right. I had no idea where he was during the days. I assumed at work.

Damn, Piper!

The rest of the school day I was a shadow in my classes as my mind was consistently preoccupied with ideas about Jared's where-abouts on the weekends, his scars, and that summer three years ago.

His constant stare on me during Themes was my only dis-traction as I tried to form a mental list of what I knew and what I didn't. And what I truly knew about Jared wasn't much any-more.

An idea popped in my head, sending a thrilling heat through my chest. It was Tuesday, and I had my lab after school today. But some afternoon this week I needed to do a little recon work. Hopefully, he still kept his window unlocked.

226

Chapter 28

"Are we heading into Chicago to dress-shop this weekend? We're already behind. The selection probably sucks by now," K.C. pointed out as I drove her home from school Friday afternoon. She was heading to the races tonight, and although Madoc had invited me to be his "co-pilot," I had other plans.

"I have that meet tomorrow morning, but it's local. Can you come? We can get a late breakfast afterwards and head into the city." Downshifting to second as I slowed and rounded the corner to her house, I noticed Liam's car parked in front of her two-story red brick colonial.

"Yeah, that sounds good. Text me the time later, and I'll be there. And you're getting a red dress, Tate." She pointed her electric blue finger nail at me and smirked. This was an old argument. She thought blondes rocked it in red, whereas I thought I looked best in black.

"Oh, yeah?" I challenged.

"You'll see," she chirped as if she'd already won our impending argument.

Shifting into neutral and pulling up the e-brake, I turned down Five Finger Death Punch on the radio and asked, "Did you know Liam was going to be here?"

She looked ahead of her outside the window at his Camaro. "Yeah. He's invited for dinner tonight before we head to the race.

My parents don't really know what went down between us. Just that we had an argument and split up for a while. If they knew—"

"Yeah." I cut her off. I could only imagine Sgt. Carter's reaction.

"Alright." She opened the door and climbed out. "Text me later, okay?"

"Sure. See you later," I called out as she slammed the door of my dad's Bronco.

The drive home took less than two minutes. A few twists and turns, and I was in my own driveway pulling into the garage. I took note that Jared's car was parked inside his garage before I noticed him and two other guys crowded under the hood.

Ignoring the tingling that started in my belly and drifted downward, I stomped into the house with a heavy sigh.

Spending the rest of the evening tied up in any menial activity I could think of, I passed the time waiting to hear the rumble of Jared's engine as it left for the Benson farm. I'd already swept and vacuumed, finished the laundry, and eaten dinner. I was about to go defrag my hard drive when the vibrations of Jared's Boss caused me to jump.

Finally!

My bare feet got rug-burned as I leapt up my stairs. I looked out my French doors to see his car peeling out of the driveway. The black machine raced down the street, and my heart started thumping with what I was about to do.

His house was dark, so I assumed his mother was already at her boyfriend's for the weekend.

I climbed out of the doors and through the tree, using my bare feet to clutch the branches. I swayed with the déjà vu flooding me. It'd been a long time since I'd made this trip.

My body weight had increased over the past three years. Branches creaked, and I hurried to his window, since there was no longer much density with the leaves. Most of them had already fallen for the upcoming winter, and I was sure to be seen from the street if I lingered too long.

Clutching his window sill with my fingers, my nails chipped the white paint as my muscles strained to work the window up.

Yes! It's unlocked.

Pushing myself over the edge, I swung a leg over and crawled through the window. Rising to my feet, I let my eyes adjust to the near pitch darkness of the room. My pulse pounded so hard in my ears that I thought they'd bleed, and I was shaking with nervousness. I left the window open just in case I needed a quick escape.

Taking a survey of the room, I noticed he'd changed the furniture around since I'd last been in here. The room seemed clean, but it was messy. Clothes were strewn across the floor and on the bed. The top of his dresser was two inches deep in random junk, money, and receipts. The walls were still painted a midnight blue, though.

When he was younger, his mom had decorated the room in a nautical theme. From the looks of it, he'd tossed all the boat and lighthouse décor. Now, the walls boasted some posters of bands and flyers for events coming up in the area.

I started tiptoeing around, but stopped short. *Why am being quiet? No one's home.* Perhaps I was feeling guilty. The little angel in my head whispered its disapproval at my dishonest snooping. But the little devil screamed its urgency.

Keep going!

I walked to his closet, and threw open the wooden doors. Anything of interest would probably be hidden in here. I still wasn't sure what I was looking for, but at this point, I was interested in anything that would give me insight into his life now.

I closed my eyes at the sudden rush of Jared's scent. Wind, rain, and man. I briefly ran my fingers over his shirt sleeves and sweat-shirts before bending down to look for anything of consequence on the floor.

Shoes cluttered the bottom of the closest and a couple of shoe boxes filled with pictures. As I sifted through the boxes, running into pictures of Jared as a child, I realized not a single picture of me was among them. *That's not right.* Jared and I were joined at the hip for four years before our fallout, and there had been pictures. Lots of them. I still had some. Had he gotten rid of his?

Placing everything back the way I found it, I closed the closet with more force than needed and spun around. Jared's chest of drawers sat across the room, so I walked over and started sifting through the gas station receipts crumpled up on top. I noticed several were from Crest Hill, about an hour from our suburb of Chicago. *Crest Hill?* What would he be doing there?

A search of the drawers revealed nothing, so I walked to his bed and knelt down to peer underneath.

Jackpot! I drew out a shallow box with no lid that was stuffed with file folders and papers. Heaving it into my arms, I placed it on my lap as I sat down on his bed.

His bed.

Once upon a time, it wasn't at all weird to be in Jared's room, but now it was like being inside a theme park after hours: wrong, but fascinating.

Inside the box, I picked through several things, each more intriguing than the last. There was a legal document from Jared's grandfather. He'd left Jared a lake house in Wisconsin, a piece of shit from the looks of the pictures, too. But the land was beautiful. Several more receipts revealed months of trips to Crest Hill spanning the past year. A court order for Jared to appear in municipal court for assault was dated shortly after I'd left for France. More receipts for meals and hotel rooms were thrown

230

haphazardly in the box, and as I dug deeper, my hand grasped a thick, smooth folder at the bottom of the box.

But I released it and stopped breathing when I heard a door open from the hallway.

Oh, shit!

I stuffed the box of papers back under the bed and leapt to a small hiding space between the closet and Jared's bed. I couldn't hear anything now with the way my heartbeat blasted through my ears, but I got out of sight in just enough time. Jared walked into the room wearing one towel around his waist and drying his hair with another.

Why is he home?! I saw his car leave, and I hadn't heard it return. So what was going on?

He switched on a table lamp, which created a soft glow in the room, and continued drying his hair. His long body moved to the window, where he placed a hand against the frame and gazed out. I watched him, wondering what the hell I was going to do. Any minute he'd turn around, and I'd be discovered.

His towel was wrapped around his waist and covered him down to his knees. My stomach felt like it was on a roller coaster, and my mouth went as dry as the Mojave Desert. The gentle light washing over his skin seemed to make the sporadic droplets of water on his chest glow. I had to blink away the desire to just sit here and wait for him to drop the towel.

There was no way I was getting out of here without him noticing. It was either let him catch me and be cornered or come up with some story. Before he turned around, I stood up from the corner and took a deep, painful breath.

"Jared." My voice was low.

His head whipped around, and his gaze narrowed on me. "Tate?" He paused for a moment. "What the hell are you doing in my room?"

My hands were shaking, so I locked them behind my back as I inched towards him. "Well, I thought about what you said about trying to be friends, and I wanted to start by wishing you a happy birthday."

Smooth, Tate. Really smooth.

His eyes shifted to the right as he turned over what I said, and I knew he didn't believe me. I wouldn't believe me either. It was a lame excuse.

"So you broke into my room to tell me 'Happy Birthday' a week after my birthday?" His sarcasm couldn't be missed. I was drowning in it and fighting for air.

Shit.

"I climbed through the tree, just like we used to do," I pointed out, but my face was on fire. I could only imagine how red it was.

"And your birthday's tomorrow. Can I climb over to your bedroom?" he asked condescendingly. "What are you really doing in here?" I held my ground as he approached, his stern eyes boring a hole into me.

Shit, shit, shit.

"I ... um ..." I fought for words but held his stare. *What would get him to shut up?*

His freshly washed hair stood up all over the place, and the challenge in his eyes made him look incredibly sexy. I was in his room. He was half-naked. And he was asking questions I couldn't answer. I needed to use the two things I had that would throw him off: the element of surprise and my body.

"I have something for you, actually. Consider it your present to me as well."

He watched me with wariness as I leaned in and kissed him. Tingling began with the touch of his soft lips and spread across my cheeks. I pressed into him, and when I felt his mouth move with mine, I wrapped my arms around his neck. My lips parted, and I teased him with my tongue, sending it out to lick his top lip. When I caught his bottom lip between my teeth, he took me in his arms, too.

For once, we were going slowly. The other times we'd kissed, it'd been more like an attack. But now, every touch was like kindling to a fire.

He held me to him, his strong arms wrapped around my back, and our lips consumed with hungry kisses. The need to get out of his room without him finding out why I was really here was forgotten. All that I saw and felt was Jared now. He smelled overwhelmingly good, and I craved to see if he smelled this good everywhere. I clutched him to me as I buried my head in his neck, kissing and biting.

"Jesus, Tate," Jared gasped out.

The campfire in my belly had turned into a bonfire in my core. My hands glided down his back, registering the dips in his skin from his scars, and I slid my hand inside the towel. My fingers prickled at the feel of his smooth skin, and my stomach ached with hunger. I trailed kisses from his ear to his collarbone, my tongue darting out every so often to taste him.

He sucked in a breath through his teeth and tightened his hold on me, while I gently rubbed my hips against his.

More.

His arms still encircled me, but my hands ran down his back and up his rigid stomach. I couldn't get enough of him, and I no longer cared why I was here. I needed him beyond reason.

"I'm not stopping," I whispered in his ear and then claimed his mouth again.

He took that as his cue and lifted me off the ground. I wrapped my legs around his waist as he carried me to the bed. Lowering us down, I pulled him with me.

I should stop. In just one more minute I would stop.

He lifted my tank top to just under my bra, and his fingers grazed my skin while he stared down at me.

"You're so beautiful." One corner of his mouth turned up with a small, thoughtful smile. My heart beat faster when his lips dipped to my stomach.

I let out a moan and arched up to him. "Jared," I choked out.

His mouth scorched my skin from my rib cage down to my hip bone, and I felt a throbbing at my center. He kept kissing me while unbuttoning my jeans. I could feel through his towel that he was ready.

Was I? I wanted Jared so much. I just wanted to give in and let it happen.

I gasped at the touch of his mouth right above my panties. His tongue skimmed over my skin as I felt my underwear come off. I barely registered it, because his mouth was all over my stomach and thighs. The pulsing between my legs started to hurt, and I needed relief.

"Jared," I breathed out, trying to get control of myself.

"Don't stop me, Tate. Please, baby, don't stop me."

I closed my eyes. I'd tried to put up a fight, didn't I? It was okay to surrender now. I yanked my shirt over my head, and Jared pulled my bra straps down to release my breasts.

His lips cascaded over my body, and the moist trail from his mouth was like a fuse on a stick of dynamite. And the dynamite was between my thighs.

"Oh!" My eyes snapped open, and my body jerked when I felt his tongue run the length of my sex. "What are you doing?" Oh, my God. That felt awesome. If I weren't so embarrassed, I would grab him by the hair to keep him there.

He cocked his head to the side, figuring out something in his head. "You're a virgin," he stated quietly.

Yep, I guess I made it kind of obvious now.

But before I could feel self-conscious about my lack of experience, he kissed my inner thighs, sending me reeling again. "You have no idea how happy that makes me." And he moved his mouth back on my clit.

Oh. My. God. Everything felt so good. I almost couldn't stand it. His tongue licked the length of me, and he sucked on my clit. Every ounce of energy and desire in my body pooled between my legs, and I knew that something was building inside of me. My nipples were hard, and Jared kneaded one breast at a time while he worked between my legs.

"Jesus Christ, if you could see yourself from my view. Fucking beautiful." He breathed against my core.

He swirled his tongue around me, and I felt a sudden need to hold my breath. It felt like depriving myself of air would increase the urgency down below. And I was right. It allowed me to concentrate on everything he was doing. The throbbing sensations pounded inside of me, and I was incredibly wet.

Jared plunged his tongue inside, and I threw my head back, arching into him for more. I came, holding my breath while the waves of ecstasy heated up my body and made me cry out for him. Jared continued to work me until the final shudders left my body.

"Damn, Tate." Jared inched back up to meet my eyes, his arousal poking me. "Your beauty is nothing compared to how you look when you come."

"That was ... " I couldn't think. My body had never felt anything that wonderful, and I wanted him to feel the same.

He came up to meet me eye to eye and pressed his hips into mine. My muscles tensed, and I was in agony with his slow grinding. He was ready.

He cupped my cheek. "I've wanted you for so long."

I pushed myself up and captured his mouth in mine. My hand

traveled down between his legs and grasped him, hard in my hand. The size of his tongue and what it had just done to me was nothing compared to his erection. It both scared and thrilled me.

Unfastening my bra strap, he shed my last piece of clothing and brought his lips down on one of my nipples. Shivers spread over my skin with the pleasure shooting out of my pores, and I held his head to me, savoring his hot mouth. He switched from one breast to the other, and I wrapped my legs around him, needing him as close as possible. I wanted more.

Jared and I both jumped at the sound of knocking on his bedroom door.

"Jared, you ready yet?" a male voice asked.

What? Who was that?

"I'm going to kill him," Jared growled quietly. "Go downstairs!" he shouted at the door, but stayed on me.

"We're already late, man. The car's gassed up. Let's go!"

And then it hit me. I hadn't seen Jared leaving before. One of the friends he had over took the car to get gas, and Jared stayed behind to get cleaned up.

"I said wait downstairs, Sam!" Jared bellowed, tightening the towel around his waist as he got up off the bed.

"Alright!" Sam must've taken the hint, because I heard his footsteps fade away.

I grabbed my tank top and covered myself, the buzz of desire slowly disintegrating.

"No, don't get dressed," Jared commanded. "I'm going to go get rid of him, and we're finishing this." He bent down to kiss me and heat rushed to my face again.

"You're racing tonight?"

"Not anymore." He slipped on some jeans underneath his towel.

I slipped the top over my head and stood up to slip on my

underwear and jeans. "Jared, go. It's fine." My detective work tonight took an unexpected turn, and his "birthday kiss" turned into much more than I'd bargained for. I needed to regroup, although I did feel guilty about leaving him hanging.

Jared wasn't taking "no" for an answer, though. He lifted me off my feet again and set me on the edge of his dresser taking my mouth in his. His body was positioned between my legs, and he pulled me to him with a slow, deep kiss.

"Races aren't important, Tate," he said against my lips. "There's nowhere else I want to be other than with you."

I think my heart skipped a beat, and a lump formed in my throat. I felt the exact same way.

But I needed to cool down. Things moved too fast, and I still didn't trust him.

"Take me with you then," I suggested. I loved the thrill of the races, and we could be together in a public setting, sure to keep us from pawing each other. The only downside was I wouldn't be able to search his room if I was with him, but I didn't feel so right about that anymore.

"Take you with me?" He looked at me skeptically but then turned thoughtful. "Alright, go get something warmer on, and I'll come get you when we're ready." He moved towards the door, but stopped. "And after the race, we'll come back here and finish this." His promise made me smile despite myself.

I hopped off the dresser after he walked out, deciding it would be easier to climb back through the tree than face the walk of shame in front of his friend, but I stopped short when I noticed something on the floor. I bent to pick up a photograph near the bed, and my heart sped up when I realized that I must have dropped it when I went through that box.

Shit!

As I took a quick look at it, bile rose in my throat. The picture was of the torso of a boy or a young man, but the skin was blood-ied and bruised. Blue and purple marks covered the chest and ribs, while cuts spanned the entire area from his stomach to his neck.

Oh, my God.

Someone didn't just hurt this kid. They tried to kill him.

Chapter 29

The farm was packed. By the looks of everyone excitedly clearing the road for Jared's car, we'd arrived just in time for his race. People stepped off the track slowly, eyeing Jared and me with curiosity. Most people probably thought Jared hated me, so they must be pretty confused. I didn't care.

The car vibrated under me, and I tapped my feet on the floor with uncontrollable energy and a little residual nervousness.

I'd stuffed the picture I found in Jared's room into the front pocket of my hoodie. I didn't want to take the chance of him catching me trying to put it back in the box under his bed. I wasn't sure if it was Jared in the picture, but I guessed it was. Why else would he have it? Unless . . . unless he did that to a kid.

My teeth clenched together. I didn't like that thought one bit.

"Hey!" People, mostly female, shouted at the car. I took a deep breath and didn't even try to hide my annoyance. Luckily, he didn't greet them back, and my shoulders relaxed. His face was stone as "Sick" by Adelita's Way pounded out of the speakers.

As Jared pulled into position next to an '80s Camaro I didn't recognize, I unfastened my seatbelt to hop out of the car, but Jared grabbed my hand.

"Hey." He spoke softly, and I turned to look at him. "I like to keep my head in the game here. If I don't act very friendly, it has nothing to do with you, okay?"

Translation: *I don't do the girlfriend thing, especially in public.* Not that Jared and I were together, but I knew what he was trying to say.

I shrugged my shoulders. "You don't have to hold my hand." And I stepped out of the car.

It bugged me that Jared kept up an image, or maybe he just didn't feel comfortable around people, but I'd be damned if I was going to stand on the sidelines feeling out of place all night.

Walking to the front of the crowd, I picked up whispers and sideways glances directed at me. "What's Jared doing with her?" and "Maybe she's racing" were some of what I heard. I watched Jared get out of the car, his eyes on me as he walked around to the front to meet with Zack and the other driver.

"Tate, how's it going?" Ben stepped up next to me. I let out a sigh. Even though I didn't see anyone else I really knew here tonight, I still didn't want to chat with him. I wasn't sure what Jared and I were, but I was interested in finding out.

"Hey, Ben."

"You're here with Jared?" he inquired.

"Yep," I snipped, not meeting his eyes.

"And you're going to Homecoming with Madoc?" Even though I wasn't looking at him, I could hear the smile.

What a douche.

"And I might go to prom with Channing Tatum. That's the kind of girl I am. Haven't you heard?" I met his eyes, boldly challenging him.

His shoulders scrunched up, and he let out a nervous laugh. "Alright, if you say so. But I'd opt out of taking Channing Tatum to prom. It's the names. 'Channing Tatum accompanying Tatum Brandt?' It doesn't work."

It took me a minute to figure it out, but his playful tone sealed the deal. He was joking. He wasn't trying to apologize, and I wasn't trying to avoid him. We were just enjoying some friendly banter, and I felt a little more comfortable that I could handle this. He wasn't pressing for information about my dating status—which was questionable—and I sensed that he wasn't pursuing me anymore.

Grinning at his joke and looking at him like he'd just put pencils up his nose, I knew the tension had finally dissipated. We might never be friends, but were back to the beginning of the year and the simplicity.

Until I saw Jared spitting fire at us. Zack was speaking to both of the drivers, but Jared's cold eyes were locked on Ben and me. His gaze narrowed, and I could tell by the way he breathed through his nose that he was pissed.

Whatever. I rolled my eyes.

"Clear the track!" Zack shouted, and we all herded to the side of the road, kicking up cold dust in our wake.

Jared climbed into his car without sparing me another glance and revved the engine, the bass vibrating under my feet. I cringed when girls started screaming excitedly. It felt like someone stuck a toothpick in my ear.

But that was nothing to the sinking feeling in my stomach when Piper stepped onto the track to send the racers off. She sauntered in front of Jared's car wearing a blue school-girl skirt and black halter-top.

I groaned under my breath.

Her gleaming eyes zeroed in on Jared. I couldn't see his face from my angle, but I knew she was eyeing him. She rocked back and forth, poking out her chest, or maybe that's just how it looked. In the headlights of the cars, I'm sure she was quite a sight. The men in the audience whistled and hooted, and I ran my fingers through my hair to get it off my hot neck.

My fingers curled into fists when I saw her approach his driver's side window. He had it rolled down, and she leaned in, giving him a perfect view of her chest and the other driver a view of her ass. My eyes burned with fire as they almost bugged out of my head.

"Excuse me," I mumbled to Ben before I walked onto the track.

Rounding Jared's car, I came up to Piper and grabbed her by the hair. I forced her away from his window and pushed her ahead of me.

Too extreme, I told myself. But I wasn't thinking.

And I liked how not thinking felt.

"What the hell?" she shouted and turned to look at me.

"Tate," Jared called, but I ignored him.

The crowd was abuzz in the background, and their chanting for a fight made my heart race. I could barely hear anything else with their unintelligible noise filling the air.

"You bitch!" she snarled. "What the fuck is your problem?" But she didn't wait for my answer. Instead, she charged me in high heels, and I almost laughed. As she stomped up to me, I swept her foot out from underneath her, and she fell to the ground.

As she lay on her ass, I clapped my hands twice in her face and shouted. "Hey! Now that I have your attention, I just want you to know—he's not interested in you." I tossed her words back at her like a pie in the face.

Taking a deep breath, I looked up to Jared, who had gotten out of his car and looked at me with a mixture of shock and amusement.

"I'm not wallpaper," I clarified, walking up to him.

Pulling the fossil that I'd made for my mom out of the pocket of my hoodie, I pooled the necklace into his palm. "Don't hide from me, and don't ask me to hide," I said for only him to hear.

He nodded and tipped my chin up, running his thumb along

my jawbone. I sunk into him, and he caressed my lips with a light kiss. I instantly felt relief. More taunts and whistles came from the crowd, but I only cared about the warmth of his body close to mine.

"Ahem!" The guy in the next car signaled us loudly. "Jared, if it's okay with you, I'd like to get this done some time tonight."

I shook my head and sighed happily. "Good luck," I wished to Jared as I pushed away and walked to the crowd.

"Are you tired?" Jared asked as we headed home, to which I shook my head.

He had won the race, of course, and without a scratch to either car. There was another bonfire afterwards, but Jared hadn't even considered it or asked me if I wanted to go. I didn't mind, though, and a giddy tingle spread over my body when I thought he probably just wanted to get home to finish what we started before.

Part of me was scared. We'd almost had sex earlier, and if Sam hadn't interrupted us, we probably would have. Did I want to be with Jared? I only had to think about it for a second before I knew the answer was yes. But was he ready to be with me?

I wasn't so sure.

I still hated the memories he left me with the past few years, and I wasn't sure if I'd forgiven him. Did I know for sure he wouldn't hurt me again? Did he deserve me?

No. Not yet. Without a doubt, he hadn't earned my trust yet.

"Jared?" I broke the silence. "Where do you go on the weekends?"

His fingers tightened around the steering wheel, and he wouldn't look at me.

"Just out of town," he mumbled.

"But where?" I pressed. If he cared about me, then it was time to come clean, about everything.

His eyebrows creased with annoyance. "What does it matter?" He turned onto our street and hit the gas way harder than he needed to. My head nearly hit the roof with how roughly he drove over the dip leading to his driveway.

Steadying myself, I grabbed the handle above the window. "Why can Piper know, and I can't?"

"Fuck, Tate." He threw off his seatbelt, and hopped out of the car. "I don't want to talk about it." The edge in his tone was angrier and louder.

I climbed out of the car after him. "You don't want to talk about anything! What do you think's going to happen?"

He stayed on his side of the car, so distant, and he looked at me like I was the enemy. I saw the wall go up behind his eyes. The wall that said we were done.

"What I do with my free time is my business. Trust me or not."

Ugh!

"Trust?" I spat out. "You lost mine a long time ago. But if you try trusting me, then maybe we can be friends again." *Or more*, I hoped.

He pinned me with disdain. "I think we've moved beyond friends, Tate, but if you want to play that game, then fine. We can have a sleepover, but there will be fucking involved." His sour words cut me, and I sucked in a breath.

Was I nothing to him? My vision blurred with the tears pooling in my eyes.

He must've seen the pain on my face, because his hard expression faltered, and his eyes dropped.

"Tate . . ." He started walking towards me, his voice softer, but I plucked out the photo I'd stuffed in my pocket and shoved it in his chest. I darted around him and ran home. I barely made it inside the house before I broke down.

No more.

I slid down the door after I'd locked it and cried at his cruelty and my stupidity. Had I really been ready to give him my virginity a couple of hours ago? I banged my head once lightly against the door, but it didn't help erase the blow to my pride.

Jared didn't deserve me, but with little effort, he'd almost gotten me.

No more.

Chapter 30

"I love birthdays. It's the only time I let myself eat cake," K.C. mumbled through a mouthful of the Mint Chocolate Chip ice cream cake she'd bought me.

"I can't live like that." My fork dug into the icy sweetness. "I'd go nuts counting calories."

"*You* don't have to count calories, Tate. Maybe if I started running . . ." She drifted off as if she couldn't finish the thought. K.C. enjoyed exercise classes but hated the idea of motivating herself in her own time.

She'd taken me to Mario's for my birthday dinner and just had the server bring out the surprise cake. The distant sound of Rosemary Clooney's "Mambo Italiano" played from the speakers, and my nerves finally relaxed.

I'd been on edge all day from the fight with Jared last night. He'd peeled out of his driveway after I'd run into my house and, as far as I knew, hadn't been home all day. It was the weekend. I guess he was off doing whatever it was that he did.

Ideas had been popping into my head all day. Maybe he sold drugs in Chicago? Worked for a crime family? Or maybe he volunteered at an elderly home? But every stupid thought drove me crazier than the last.

"Tate?" K.C. stopped chewing and looked at me. "Are you going to tell me about last night?"

I felt like the thumping in my chest shifted my body. Was she talking about me breaking into his room? The near-sex? But how would she know any of that?

"Last night?"

"The race. I heard you showed up with Jared and ... staked your claim, so to speak." Her grin made me smile.

"Oh, yeah," I answered hesitantly. After the fight with Jared, I was more confused than ever about where we stood. I couldn't explain it to her if I didn't understand it myself.

"Well?" She moved her finger in a circle to keep me going.

"Not much to tell, K.C. Jared and I have called a truce, I guess. Other than that, I'm not sure what's going on." I stuffed more cake into my mouth.

"Do you care about him? More than a friend?" Her fork was paused in midair, and she stared at me expectantly.

I cared about Jared. A lot. But what good did it do me?

"Yes," I sighed. "But he doesn't care about me, K.C. Just leave it alone."

She gave me a sad smile and did what good friends do—gave me a second slice of cake.

After Mario's, she drove me home instead of going to the movies like we planned. I was more interested in catching up on missed episodes of *Sons of Anarchy* than seeing the romantic comedy she wanted.

"What is that?!" she exclaimed, looking at something out the front windshield.

I followed her gaze and sucked in a breath at the sight of my yard, full of neighbors. They were eyeing a hugely bright spectacle by my house.

What?

My pulse started to race. Was my house on fire?

I quickly shot out of the car and raced up my front yard. I gasped at what I saw.

The tree between Jared's and my house was lit up with lights. Hundreds. Of. Lights.

Oh, my God. Who did this?!

I couldn't control the smile that spread across my face. The tree was decorated with an assortment of radiant lighting. White lights, small and big bulbs, as well as lanterns of different styles and sizes adorned the tree. The awe-inspiring magical quality of the world within the branches was too intense for words. I was sure I would never enjoy looking at this tree without lights again.

Jared.

My lips began to quiver. As I walked closer to the tree, I understood why so many people were hanging around outside now. The sight was beautiful.

I'd spent a lot of time climbing this tree, reading in it, and talking with Jared in it until the stars faded with morning's light.

He'd done this for me. I didn't know who else it could've been. This was our special place—one of many—and he'd lit it up with magic and wonder.

The quake in my chest grew stronger, and a few tears cascaded down my cheeks as I silently took in the spectacle.

"Do you know what this is about?" K.C. asked beside me.

"I have an idea." My voice was hoarse from the lump in my throat.

Noticing something stuck to the tree trunk, I walked away from my dispersing neighbors and ripped the sheet of paper from its staple.

Yesterday lasts forever.
Tomorrow comes never.
Until you.

Breathless, I looked over to Jared's house, but it was pitch black. Where was he?

"Why's your bedroom light on?" K.C. piped up, and my eyes shot to the second floor of my house where, indeed, my light was shining. I never kept any lights on when I left the house, except for the one on the porch.

"I must've forgotten to turn it off," I muttered distractedly as I hurried to the house. "I'll see you later. Thanks for dinner," I called out behind me, racing up the stairs.

"Uh ... okay. Happy Birthday!" K.C. stuttered before I slammed the door. I was being most definitely rude, but my head was elsewhere now.

I dropped my jacket and purse on the floor. I could see my bedroom light shining from my open doorway, and I slowly climbed the stairs. I wasn't scared, but my heart pounded, and my hands shook.

As I walked into the room, Jared sat on the rail outside my French doors. He looked beautifully disheveled, jeans hanging from his narrow hips and sexy-messy hair. My arms ached to hold him.

I wanted to forgive him and forget about everything right now, but my pride held me back.

Luckily, he didn't give me a chance to make a decision.

"Is that what you were looking for in my room last night?" He gestured to a thick manila file folder on my bed.

I must've been fire-engine red at that moment. All day, I'd been thinking about his behavior and what he was so afraid to tell me, and I'd forgotten about the fact that I'd let him know I was snooping in his room by shoving that picture at him last night. I guess I'd just wanted him to know that I knew something was up.

"Go ahead," he urged gently. "Take a look."

Debating for only a moment if he was serious or not, I walked to the bed and leaned down to open the folder. I nearly choked on my own air.

There were pictures, just like the one I'd found, of a boy—no, scratch that—of Jared bruised and bloodied. Scanning the pile of thirty or so photos, I caught Jared's fourteen-year-old face in some of them. Others were of parts of his body.

I spread the photos out, carefully scanning each one.

The pictures detailed different injuries to his body: legs, arms, but mainly his torso and back. In one of them, I saw the fresh mutilations of the faded scars he now had on his back.

I held my fist to my mouth to stifle a groan of disgust. "Jared, what is this? What happened to you?"

He looked down to his feet, and I could tell he was searching for words. Jared didn't enjoy pity parties, especially his own.

So I waited.

"My father . . . he did that to me." He spoke low as if he didn't even want to admit to himself. "And to my brother."

I snapped my eyes up to his. *What?! A brother?*

Jared, like me, didn't have any siblings.

He continued, "The summer before freshman year, I was hyped up to spend my whole summer hanging out with you, but as you remember, my dad called out of the blue and wanted to see me. So I went. I hadn't seen him in more than ten years, and I wanted to know him."

I nodded and sat down on the bed. My mind was reeling from wondering how a parent could do this to their child—or children—but I wanted to hear about everything, including this brother.

"When I got there, I found out that my dad had another son. A kid from another relationship. His name is Jaxon, and he's only about a year younger than me."

Jared paused, looking thoughtful. His eyes had lit up when he'd said Jaxon's name.

I couldn't believe he had a brother. I'd known him so well growing up, and even though he didn't find out about this secret brother until he'd been fourteen, it still felt wrong that I didn't know this about him.

"Go on," I prodded softly.

"Jaxon and I got along really well. Even though it was a shock to find out I'd had a brother that long without knowing, I was thankful to have a family. We were close in age, both into cars, and he wanted to be around me all the time. Hell, I wanted to be around him, too."

I wondered if Jared still saw Jaxon, but I decided to shut up and ask questions later.

He continued, "My dad's house was a real dump. It was dirty, and there was never a lot of food in the place, but I was enjoying my brother. It was just the three of us. The first couple of weeks weren't that bad."

Not that bad?

"Then I started to notice that something was off. Our dad drank a lot. He'd wake up with hangovers—which was nothing new for me with my mom—but then I started seeing drugs, too. *That* was new to me. His house parties were filled with these horrible fucking people who talked to us like you shouldn't talk to kids." Jared's eyes started to pool with unshed tears, and his voice was barely a whisper. I started to get scared.

What the hell had happened?

After a few seconds of pause, he let out a huge sigh. "I kind of got the feeling that Jaxon might've been messed with by these people. Like 'messed with' other than just roughed up."

Messed with? I closed my eyes as realization dawned.

No. Please, not that.

He sat down next to me on the bed, still not making eye contact. "One night, about three weeks into my visit, I heard Jax

251

crying in his room. I went in, and he was hunched over the bed holding his stomach. Once I got him to turn over I saw the bruises all over his abdomen. My dad had kicked him—more than once—and he was in a shitload of pain."

I tried not to picture the young boy, but it was impossible.

Jared continued, "I didn't know what to do. I was so fucking scared. My mother never hit me. I had no idea that people did these things to kids. I was sorry that I'd come but also glad, for Jax's sake. If my father did this to him while I was here, I couldn't even imagine what he did when I wasn't around. Jax insisted that he was fine, and that he didn't need a doctor." Jared's shoulders slumped, and I could feel the tension roll off his body as he spoke slowly and quietly.

"My dad targeted Jax. He was the bastard and worthy of less respect in my father's eyes, apparently. He didn't hit me until later."

"Tell me." I needed to know this. I wanted to know everything.

"One day—not long after I found out how he really treated Jax— my father asked us to go to a house and pretend to be selling something. He wanted to break inside and rob the place."

"What?" I blurted out suddenly.

"From things they would say, I knew money was tight, especially with his expensive habits. Jax would tell me that this was normal, that he did this for my dad a lot. He never refused. My father abused him for anything and everything: burning dinner, making messes . . . Jax knew that saying no wouldn't do any good. We'd still have to do the job but just with bruises. But I refused anyway. And my dad started hitting me."

Nausea burned my stomach. While I was wasting away my summer resenting him for not calling or writing, he was being hurt. "Did you try to call your mom?" I choked out.

"Once." He nodded. "It was before my father started abusing

252

me. She was drunk, of course. She didn't see it as a bad situation, so she didn't come to get me. I tried to tell her about Jax, but she didn't consider him her problem. I thought about just getting out of there, running away. But Jax wouldn't leave, and I couldn't leave him."

Thank God she'd cleaned herself up otherwise I'd have to hurt her.

"So I gave in to my father," Jared admitted flatly, his eyes waiting for my reaction. "I helped him and Jax do jobs. I broke into houses, delivered drugs for him." He walked back to the window and peered out at the tree. "One day, after weeks of hell, I refused to listen to him and demanded to go home. And I was taking Jax with me." He pulled his T-shirt over his head and showed me his back. "He took a belt to me, the end with the buckle."

I ran my fingers across his scars. The edges were rigid, but the dip of the welts was smooth. There weren't very many, and the rest of his skin was unmarred.

He paused for a moment and turned to meet my gaze, the ghost of his pain still deep in his eyes. "So I finally just ran away. I stole fifty bucks and jumped a bus home. Without Jax."

Chapter 31

I could see the agony in his eyes. What had happened to his brother? Jared had thought that life with Katherine was bad, but his father turned out to be a horror. And he had to make the decision to abandon ship without his brother.

"Did you go to the police?" I asked.

He shook his head. "Not at first. There was no way I wanted to deal with that. I just wanted to forget about it. But when my mom saw what happened to me, she forced me to go. I never told them what happened to me, but I did report what happened to my brother. She insisted on taking pictures of me just in case, though. The police took my brother away from my dad and put him into foster care. I wanted him with me, but my mom's drinking didn't inspire any confidence with the state."

"Have you seen your dad since?" I wanted to gag using the word "dad" for a man like that.

"I saw him today." Jared stunned me. "I see him every weekend."

"What?! Why?" So that's where he went, but how could he put himself in the same room as a monster like that?

"Because life's a bitch, that's why." He gave me a bitter smile and looked away. "Last year, after you left for France, I went a little crazy. I drank and got into a lot of fights. Madoc and I both had a ball for a while. I hated that you were gone, but I'd also

254

found out that Jax had been transferred to another foster home after the last family had hit him. It was a bad time."

He got up to go stand at the window, and I noticed he was clenching his fists. He wasn't teary anymore. He was pissed.

"So I tracked down his old foster dad, and I fucked him up. Like, really bad." His eyebrows lifted, but there was no regret in his tone. "He was in the hospital for a week. The judge decided that, while my feelings were understandable, my reaction was not. He thought it would be poetic to sentence me to forced visits with my father in prison, since he was still in jail for abusing my brother as well as the drugs that the cops found at his house. It looked like I was on the same path, so the judge ordered one visit a week for a year."

"So that's where you go. To Stateville Prison in Crest Hill." It wasn't a question, just a clarification. I remembered the receipts in his room.

"Yeah, every Saturday. Today was my last visit, though."

I nodded gratefully. "Where is your brother now?"

The first hint of a smile played on Jared's lips. "He's in Weston. Safe and sound with a good family. I've been seeing him on Sundays. But my mom and I are trying to get the state to agree to let him live with us. She's been sober for a while. He's almost seventeen, so it's not like he's a kid."

This was a lot to absorb. I was elated that he'd finally confided in me. He'd been hurt, which had probably made him feel abandoned by the people that should've protected him. But I was still puzzled about one thing.

I walked over to him. "Why didn't you tell me all of this years ago? I could've been there for you." I got up from the bed, and walked over to him.

He ran a hand through his hair and inched away from me to lean on the railing. "When I finally got home that summer, you were my first thought. Well, other than doing what I could to help Jax. I had to see you. My mom could go to hell. All I wanted was you. I loved you." He gripped the railing at his sides, and his body went rigid. "I went to your house, but your grandma said you were out. She tried to get me to stay. I think she saw that I didn't look right. But I ran off to find you, anyway. After a while, I found myself at the fish pond in the park." He raised his eyes to meet mine. "And there you were . . . with your dad and my mom, playing the little family."

The little family?

"Jared—" I started.

"Tate, you didn't do anything wrong. I know that now. You just have to understand my mindset. I had been through hell. I was weak and hurting from the abuse. I was hungry. I'd been betrayed by the people I was supposed to be able to count on: my mom who didn't help when I needed her, my dad who hurt me and my helpless brother. And then I saw you with *our* parents, looking like the happy, sweet family. While Jaxon and I were in pain and struggling to make it through every day in one piece, you got to see the mother that I never had. Your dad took you on picnics and for ice cream while mine was whipping me. I felt like no one wanted me and that life moved on without me. No one cared."

Jared's mom had gone on a couple of outings with us that summer. My dad was always trying to help her get straight. He loved Jared and knew Katherine was a good person at heart. He was only trying to get her out of the house and show her, in a humble way, what she was missing out on with her own son.

"You became a target, Tate. I hated my parents, I was worried about my brother, and I sure as hell couldn't rely on anyone but myself. When I hated you, it made me feel better. A lot better. Even after I realized that nothing was your fault, I still couldn't stop trying to hate you. It felt good, because I couldn't hurt who I wanted to hurt."

Silent tears streamed down my face, and Jared walked up to me and cupped my cheeks with his hands. "I'm sorry," he whispered. "I know I can make this up to you. Don't hate me."

I shook my head. "I don't hate you. I mean, I'm a little pissed, but mostly I just hate the wasted time."

He wrapped his arms around my waist and pulled me close.

"You said you loved me. I hate that we lost that," I said sadly.

Bending down, he grabbed the backs of my thighs and lifted me up. My breath caught, and I held on to his neck. His warm body only made me want to curl up into him. I wrapped my legs around him as he walked us to the bed and sat down.

He put a hand to my face and guided my eyes to his. "We never lost that. As much as I tried, I could never erase you from my heart. That's why I was such an asshole and kept guys away from you. You were always mine."

"Are *you* mine?" I asked as I wiped my tears.

He kissed the corners of my mouth softly, and I felt heat rise up my neck. "Always have been," he whispered against my mouth.

I wrapped my arms around him, and he held me tight as I buried my face in his neck. My body relaxed into him, knowing without a doubt that we had crossed over. He wouldn't hurt me again, and I knew that I needed him like water.

"Are you okay?" I asked. It seemed pretty late for such a dumb question, but I wanted to know.

"Are you?" he responded.

And I loved that about him. He'd been abused, abandoned, and helpless to protect his brother. My embarrassment at his hands seemed like small potatoes compared to that. But I also knew that his trauma wasn't an excuse to treat me badly all those years.

"I will be," I promised. If he could take the step to trust me with all of this, then I could try to move forward, too.

"I love you, Tate."

He lay back on the bed, and I fell with him, clutching him tight. We stayed there, just holding each other, until I felt the steady rise and fall of his chest telling me he was asleep.

It was after midnight when I awoke. I'd fallen asleep half on and half off of Jared's chest. My legs were entwined with his, my head tucked in his neck, and my arm draped over his chest. His musk and wind scent filled my world, and I closed my eyes as my fingers slowly threaded through his hair. My lips glided up the side of his smooth neck, tasting his salty skin with an uncontrollable need to touch him with more than just my hands.

Damn. He's asleep. And he looked peaceful, too. Not one worry creased his brow, and no scowl marred his face.

Shaking my head and deciding to leave him alone, I gently crawled off the bed. Heading to the double doors to pull the curtains, I noticed a light rain splattering my window panes.

Perfect. I had Jared and a rainstorm. I couldn't help but smile.

I tore off my socks and tiptoed out of the bedroom, letting him sleep.

Heading out the backdoor from the kitchen, I stepped onto the porch with my bare feet. My fingers tingled, and I clenched them into fists with the renewed energy coursing through my body already. The air smelled like autumn. Like apples and burnt leaves.

The awning protected me from getting wet, so I walked down the steps and onto the brick patio. Drops of water fell on my feet, spilling between my toes, and the familiar hum of electricity charged my skin. Crossing my arms over my chest to help keep warm, I felt a surge of goosebumps fall over my arms and legs as

I listened to the peaceful pitter-patter of rain dotting the trees and ground.

Tilting my head back to let the sprinkles cover my face, I already felt years younger than I'd been feeling lately, and the wind chimes clinking from Ms. Trent's backyard lulled me into a peaceful meditation.

The rain was getting slightly heavier, and I closed my eyes as the light wind caressed my face. Thoughts drifted through my mind like clouds, and nothing existed but the distant rumble of thunder and my hair floating on the wind around my face.

As the sprinkle started to turn into a downpour, I opened my eyes and twisted around to head back inside. A semblance of calm had fallen over me, but I nearly screamed when I saw Jared leaning against the house by the backdoor.

"Jared! You scared me. I thought you were asleep."

I held my hand to my chest, since my heart felt like it was trying to push through my ribs.

But Jared wasn't saying anything, and I straightened up when he started to approach me. His eyes were scary intense. He didn't look mad, but he still looked about ready to explode.

If only I could move, then I'd meet him halfway. But I was stuck. His piercing eyes were burning me, and he looked … hungry.

When he reached me, his hands rested on my hips, and he just stared into my eyes for a minute. Normally, anyone making direct eye contact with me for too long of a time was uncomfortable, but Jared looked at me like I was his last meal.

And damn if I didn't love it.

His teeth were slightly bared as he breathed, and his eyes cut right through me. I knew what he wanted. And when I remembered how good his skin had tasted earlier, I couldn't keep myself from touching him.

As my arms went around his neck, I pushed up on my toes and took his mouth.

And that's about where my control of the situation ended.

He was like an animal sinking his teeth into a juicy kill. One of his arms wrapped around me, while the other held my face. He guided our every movement. When he pushed, I surrendered.

His tongue made my whole world slide on its ass. It was so hot, and when he used his teeth to nibble my lips, I knew what I wanted, too.

My pulse was racing, and I had a desperate ache between my legs. I needed him. I needed him inside of me.

"You're cold," he said as the rain drenched our clothes.

"Warm me up," I begged.

I left a trail of soft kisses along his neck and jaw, and I heard him suck in a breath when my tongue darted out to taste his skin again. "I love you, Jared," I murmured in his ear.

He took my head in his hands and captured my mouth in a deep kiss. His breath was hot, and he tasted like rain. Like a memory that I wanted to wrap myself up in forever.

"We can wait," he suggested, but it was more of a question.

I shook my head slowly, desire spreading through my belly like a fire. We were not wasting time anymore.

I lifted the hem of his shirt over his head and let my hands trail across his skin. My fingertips drifted down his back, and he tensed when I deliberately stroked one of his scars. I craved him. All of him. I wanted him to know that I wasn't scared, that I loved every part of him.

Holding his gaze, I pulled my black, silk blouse over my head and unclasped my bra, letting both fall to the ground. Jared's breathing grew harder, and I moaned when his fingers glided down my breasts. His touch sent heat shooting through my veins, and my fists clenched with anticipation.

He swept my soaked hair behind my shoulders and drank me in with his eyes. Normally, I was self-conscious about everything. I never walked around naked in the locker room. But I loved his eyes on me.

Jared pulled me flush with him, and the pulsing at my core throbbed harder when I felt his skin against my bare breasts. Our lips melted together in a rush, and when I felt him through his jeans, I moaned, thinking for sure that I was going to lose it.

I need you.

I peeled off my jeans and let out a little whimper when he lifted me up unexpectedly. My legs wrapped around his waist, and he carried me across the patio to the chaise lounge that had a canopy.

Laying me down, he hovered over me looking at every inch of my body that his eyes could cover. He bent his head and kissed my chest over my heart. My body jerked up when he took a nipple in his mouth, and I held him to me feeling anything but chilled now.

"Jared . . . " My chest shook with the overwhelming pleasure.

As he sucked, his hand skimmed down my body, caressing my hip and leg. The pressure at my core was agonizing, and I knew what I needed.

"Jared, please."

He left my breast and continued kissing down my stomach; his tongue made me jerk every time it touched my skin. "Be patient," he ordered. "If you keep begging like that, I'm going to lose it right now."

As he trailed kisses, he pulled my panties down my legs and dropped them to the ground. Standing up, he fished a condom out of his wallet and unbuttoned his jeans, taking everything off in one smooth motion.

Oh, my God. He was definitely as ready as I was.

Coming down on top of me, he positioned himself between

my thighs, and I throbbed with his hardness rubbing against me. I closed my eyes; the twitch of my clit where his skin grinded on my sex sent thrilling waves of excitement through my body. This was it. I needed him inside of me. Right. Now.

He looked down at me as I wrapped my legs around him. Arching my body into his, I felt him glide against my opening.

He groaned with need . . . or maybe agony, and I couldn't help but love the sound. Everything was perfect. Having him. In the rain. And he loved me.

He ripped the condom from its wrapper. Slipping it on, he leaned down to kiss me.

"I love you," he said before he slipped inside of me.

"Ahhh . . . " I gasped loudly, and my body went rigid and still.

Jared stopped and leaned back to look at me. He was breathless and flushed as he gazed at me with care and love.

I knew there would be pain, but that hurt! I took deep breaths, trying to let my body adjust.

"Are you okay?" he asked.

I nodded, slowly feeling the ache fade away. "I'm good. Don't stop but go slow."

When Jared saw me relax, he slowly went deeper until he was all the way in.

"Damn," he breathed out. "You feel so good. Perfect."

He kept his weight off of me, and I held his hips, feeling his slow thrusts against me. I started moving with him, feeling the quiver of what his body was doing to mine. With each meeting, I pulled him harder into me. It didn't hurt anymore.

My body had to stretch to take him, but now I was feeling the familiar burn in my belly and pulsing between my thighs.

We weren't making love long and slow. Not tonight. I grabbed for his face to bring his lips down on mine. I needed every inch of his body on or inside me. I whispered against his mouth, "I feel you everywhere."

He let out a raspy moan. "Don't talk like that, baby. I'll be done too soon."

Our bodies moved in sync, my hips rising up to meet his. He was coming undone. His eyes were glazed over, and he was breathing hard.

I ran my fingers down his back, which was damp with sweat and rain, feeling the power of his thrusts into me. Our foreheads met, and his teeth clenched as he looked down at my body moving with his.

My orgasm came quickly as his hips grinded into mine, and I cried out in pleasure as Jared went harder. After a few more seconds, his body tensed, and he closed his eyes as he came, too. We lay there, unmoving, trying to catch our breaths for several minutes.

There was nothing in the world better than what we'd just done. I wanted him forever. I could still feel where we were connected, and there was no happiness greater than knowing he was sweating and shivering because of me.

He leaned down and kissed my lips after our bodies had calmed down. "You were really a virgin." He wasn't asking.

"Yeah," I replied weakly. "I haven't had much of a dating life, you know?"

Rising up to hover over me, Jared kissed me on the cheeks and forehead. "So you're truly mine." His voice was husky.

Always. I told myself but opted for my usual sarcasm when I responded. "Only so long as you can keep me happy."

He pinned me with a knowing smile, because we both knew that he just made me *very* happy. Rolling us over, so I lay on top of him, he ran his hand up and down my back. "Don't fall asleep," he commanded. "I can make you happy again in about five minutes."

Chapter 32

"Yeah, Dad, I promise to be careful." I laughed, trying not to move too much to mess up my hair or makeup. "Anyway, K.C. and Liam will be there, so I'll be able to find a ride if I get too wasted."

My laptop speakers vibrated with the loud sigh my dad let out. "Tate."

"Oh, relax. You know you can trust me."

I guess I could still say that, but somehow I felt like it was less true than before.

My fingers fidgeted. I needed to get off this call, so I could get into my dress. Jared and Madoc had compromised about Homecoming. I'd be going with both of them. As much as I just wanted to spend every second with Jared, I'd decided to give Madoc an opportunity to make amends. If he was Jared's best friend, then it was no skin off my nose to give him another chance.

Just one more chance.

"It's not you I'm worried about," my dad grumbled.

I narrowed my eyes. "But you like Jared, Dad."

"He's a teenage guy, honey. I trust him, just not with my daughter."

Heat rose to my cheeks, and I hoped my dad didn't see a blush. His suspicions were too close to home.

If he only knew. Guilt sullied the otherwise exciting night I was about to have.

Jared and I had made love twice on my birthday a week ago and again the next morning. Keeping him off me since then so I could get some school work done had become a full-time job. A delightful and fun full-time job. I enjoyed the effect I had on him and how easily I could get him worked up only to say no. He called me a bully for it last night, and I'd laughed, because I did kind of get off on the power.

But if my dad knew that Jared spent all of his nights here now, he'd jump a plane home immediately. I would do the same thing if it were my daughter, but I just didn't want Jared anywhere without me, and he seemed to feel the same way. We couldn't control ourselves. Or maybe we just didn't care to try.

"Well, how do I look so far?" I asked, meaning my look from the neck up.

He gave me a sad smile, and I knew he was sorry he couldn't be here with me. "Beautiful. So much like your mom."

My eyes welled up. "Thanks," I barely whispered. My mom and I didn't look a lot alike. She had red hair and was more petite, but it made me feel proud that my dad thought I was just as beautiful. I wanted her here tonight fluffing my hair or helping me zip my dress.

My honey-colored hair was parted in the middle, and wide curls cascaded down my back. The makeup I'd bought when I purchased the dress turned out to be less overwhelming than I originally thought. Whereas I usually applied minimal color to my face and eyes, I'd decided to go all out tonight and the result had been shocking. My eyes popped, and my lips looked like candy.

"Alright, go get dressed, and text me when you get in tonight." He rubbed the stubble on his jaw.

"I love you. Talk to you later," I replied.

"Love you too. Have a great time." And we clicked off.

Casting off the white button-down, I slipped my dress off the hanger. Stepping into the nude and silver sequined material, I felt shivers down my arms and legs as giddiness overtook me. The slim-fitting, short, strapless dress featured a sweetheart neckline. My legs, arms, and cleavage were the main attractions, since the dress covered none of them. I took a deep breath while I worked the zipper up and adjusted my body inside the dress as it hugged all the right places. The sheer overlay featured a pattern of sequins that made me look like I glowed. My toes dug into the floor when I saw myself in the mirror.

Wow. I'd never looked like this before.

After a few makeup touch-ups and adding some bracelets and earrings, I headed downstairs to grab my heels out of the Bronco. Waiting until this afternoon to purchase the finishing touch on my outfit had been playing with fire, but shoes had been the last thing on my mind this week.

Taking the box from the passenger side of the truck, I spun around to see Jared frozen in his driveway, staring at me. I swallowed with the sudden shock of seeing him dressed up. He wore a black suit, of course, with a black shirt and shoes. The jacket didn't hang on him limply but was tailored in at the waist before it fell past his hips. His hair was trimmed and styled to perfection and out of his eyes, making them seem brighter. I just wanted to take him inside and forget about the dance.

His deep stare travelled down my body, and his breathing got heavier by the second.

Yes. Exactly the reaction I was hoping for.

Taking the top of the box and fitting it underneath the bottom, I slipped both high heels onto my bare feet one at a time. Jared kept his eyes on me, following every movement.

"So, is the dress for him? Or me?" he teased, crossing to my yard.

"For you?" I arched an eyebrow. "Why would this dress be for you?" My snarky attitude was meant to play with him. Something I'd gotten very good at.

Jared wrapped his arms around my lower back and picked me up, bringing his lips to mine in a hard "take that" kiss.

"You taste like a Starburst," he groaned against my lips. "And you look like the sun."

Elation swept over me at his words. "You look great, too."

The distant hum of Madoc's GTO echoed through the neighborhood, and I squirmed out of Jared's arms. I was sure my dress had ridden up a little when he grabbed me and that was not a sight for his friend.

Madoc pulled up alongside my house and climbed out of the car in nearly the same black suit and shirt as Jared's, but Madoc had added a purple tie. With his blond hair and handsome face, he looked cavalier and gorgeous. The bruises from his fight a couple of weeks ago were pretty much gone.

Whereas Jared had the movie star look, Madoc was pretty like a model. Too pretty for my taste but pretty all the same. Walking in with these two tonight, I'd be the talk of the town tomorrow.

Great.

Madoc slowed when he looked up and noticed Jared in front of me. Whatever Madoc saw in Jared's eyes gave him pause. Any trace of a grin he was wearing had now vanished.

"I'm not going to get hit again, am I?" Madoc asked, half-timid and half-joking.

"Go fuck yourself. You're lucky you're getting her at all tonight." Jared sighed and walked back over to his house. "I'll get my keys. We're taking my car."

Madoc smiled after Jared as he watched his friend disappear inside his house and slam the front door.

I registered a low whistle and brought my eyes back to Madoc. "You look . . . edible." He shook his head as if he couldn't believe I could clean up nice. I rolled my eyes and fixed him with an impatient stare.

"Relax." He smiled and held up his hands. "I'll mind my manners . . . tonight." He added the last with a threatening smirk.

Shaking my head, I turned towards the house. "I'll grab my bag."

After I slid my clutch purse off the entry-way table, checked myself in the mirror, and locked up the house, I twisted to see Madoc holding a corsage in his hand.

Feeling slightly uneasy, since I thought Jared would be the one getting me a flower, I looked at him suspiciously.

He approached me, a thoughtful expression on his face. "If you don't mind, I asked Jared if I could get this for you." He widened the wristlet, and I slipped my hand through. "I'm sorry for being an asshole all these years. I did have a plan, though."

Puzzled, I asked, "Which was?"

He smiled to himself. "Jared's my best friend. I've known for a while that he cared about you. The first time I came over to his house freshman year, I found a stash of pictures of the two of you. He keeps them in his nightstand."

My heart beat faster, but I was relieved. I hated that I didn't see any pictures of us among his box of photos the night I snooped. Now I know that he kept them somewhere else. Somewhere close to him.

"Anyway," Madoc continued, "I never understood why he treated you the way he did, and Jared is about as revealing as a hermit crab. He's like one of those piggy banks that you have to break to get anything out of. You can't just shake him and he'll give up the goods. You have to get the hammer." He looked straight at me. "You were the hammer."

"I still don't follow."

He pursed his lips like he was annoyed he had to explain it further. "I messed with you more than he asked me to, because I wanted him to react. He's never been a particularly happy guy, and I was sick of his brooding. He went ballistic after you left for France, and I figured out that his destructive behavior had something to do with you. Like he was lost without you or something. So, I decided to try to make him jealous when you got back and see what happened."

"And you think that makes you a good friend?" Why would Madoc want to rile Jared up? Why not just talk to him?

"I don't know," he said sarcastically. "You two seem pretty damn happy."

We were very happy. But I doubt it was Madoc asking me to Homecoming that got Jared to act. I guess it didn't matter, though. Jared and I had come together again, stronger I hope, and Madoc got to entertain himself.

"So you wanted to see him happy. Why do you care about Jared so much?" I asked.

Madoc stuck his hands in his pockets and tried to hide a grin. "Did you ever hear about the time freshman year that I got stuffed naked into my locker by some Seniors?"

Madoc got bullied? "Uh, no," I laughed, not believing a word of it.

"No one knows. And that's why Jared is my best friend." His voice was even, and I could tell he was serious. Jared had helped him.

I didn't know what to say, but we both turned our attention to Jared as he came walking out of his house. Taking my hand, he kissed me under my ear.

"Sorry that took so long. My mom was giving me a talk."

Madoc came to my other side and held out his arm for me to take, which I did.

"About?" I pressed, a little nervous about what kind of parenting Katherine was doing today.

"About not getting you pregnant," he whispered without looking at me.

I cleared my throat. *Pregnant?*

We both exchanged wary grins, not sure what to say to that. Jared and I had been using protection, but I guess I should get on the pill, too.

"Are we ready?" Madoc piped up from my side.

I held Madoc by the inside of his elbow and held Jared closer to me by the bicep. While a month ago I never would've thought I'd be here with these two, I felt at ease. "Totally. This is the start of a great friendship." I jostled Madoc's arm playfully.

"It could be the start of a great porno, too," Madoc deadpanned, breaking into laughter.

"Son of a bitch! You're going to get it tonight," Jared threatened, and I shook my head laughing.

Chapter 33

The dance was more enjoyable than we anticipated, even with the watered down music and trying to juggle two dates. New York, New York was the Homecoming theme, and the gym was awesomely decorated with cut-outs of the New York City skyline and twinkle lights.

Madoc and Jared were like yin and yang. Madoc loved everyone and everything. Jared—I love him—barely tolerated anything. Madoc got great pictures of himself and me leaning up against a retro New York City cab for our Homecoming photo. I played along, even though he kept trying to pose like a Goodfella. Jared had to be coerced in front of the camera, but I'm sure he just did it for me.

After the initial weirdness of trying to be together on an actual date, Jared and I loosened up and had a little fun. I met some of his friends, and we got over the awkwardness of being around K.C. I think she was more comfortable with Jared than Liam was. But after a while, it was all good.

"Alright, let's get fucked up." Madoc led the way into the Beckman house in search of liquor. We arrived at Tori's after-party just as most people were getting there, and I stopped as soon as I stepped inside. The memory of the last time I was here over a year ago got my heart racing.

Damn it.

Jared halted in front of me, probably because I hesitated. My breathing quickened, and I clenched his hand. Even in my head, I couldn't piece together why I was reacting this way. I wasn't scared. I knew nothing was going to happen tonight.

"Tate, are you okay?" Jared's eyes looked concerned.

"Yeah, I need a drink." I'd be damned if I was going to be trapped by my past. My body was at DEFCON 1 right now, and I just wanted to enjoy this party.

Once we made it to the kitchen, complete with a makeshift bar just like last time, Madoc set to work making us drinks. Jared declined, since he was driving, and I was proud of him for being responsible. Madoc was simply happy he had a DD.

Snatching the red cup out of Madoc's hand, I swallowed the burning liquid mixed with Coke as fast as I could. With each gulp, the alcohol stung worse and the bitter taste had me wishing for a cookie or a Jolly Rancher or anything sweet. Successfully consuming every last drop, I swung the cup into the sink and coughed into my hand as Madoc laughed at me.

"Aw, she's about as red as a tomato," he joked to Jared.

"Piss off," I mumbled.

Jared wrapped a hand around my waist and pulled me close, kissing my hair. Closing my eyes, I let the alcohol heat up my blood, relaxing my muscles.

"Hey, guys." K.C. bounced into the kitchen, pulling Liam behind her. He nodded to Madoc and Jared, clearly not happy with Jared and K.C. briefly dating. Liam cheated, but he was acting upset because K.C. spent a couple of dates with another guy.

Get over it.

"What are we drinking?" she asked.

"Well, I just had a little liquid courage, so I'm good for now." My voice was still raspy from the rush of liquor.

While she and the others set to work making their concoctions, Jared bent down to my ear. "Come with me."

Goosebumps spread across my arms as his breath tickled my ear. He took my hand, and I let him guide me out of the kitchen and up the stairs to the second floor of the house.

The Beckman place was huge, which was why parties here were so popular. Jared's and my house were happy mediums, but Tori and Bryan Beckman enjoyed a lush and spacious two-level home with a finished basement and fully landscaped backyard that was big enough for a modest golf course. This house probably boasted seven or eight bedrooms.

And it looked like Jared was taking me to one.

Oh, my.

He knocked on a door to make sure the room was empty and then led us inside.

As soon as the door was closed behind us, he backed me up against it, causing me to grab his upper arms for support. I gasped from the surprise and met his kiss when his lips crushed down on mine. His hand went down to my ass, and he pulled me up to meet his hips. I ripped my mouth away from him to catch my breath as he dipped his head to my neck.

"God, Tate. Your dress should be burned." His mouth was hot on my ear as he started sucking the lobe.

"Why?" I asked, the desire burning down below making it almost too hard to concentrate.

He laughed against my neck. "Every fucking guy has been looking at you tonight. I'm going to get arrested."

Taking his head in my hands, I forced his eyes to meet mine as our noses touched. "I'm yours. It's always been you." My promise hung in the air while he gazed down at me, his chocolate eyes full of desire.

"Come here." He led me to the center of the large bedroom,

which looked to be a guest room by the absence of photographs or other personal paraphernalia.

Jared took out his phone and pushed a few buttons before Seether's "Broken" started playing. Setting the phone on the chest of drawers, propped up by its kickstand, he walked back over and took me in his arms as I wrapped mine around his neck. Slowly, we started moving together to the music in our very first slow dance.

"I'm sorry I didn't dance with you tonight." His eyes wouldn't meet mine, and there was regret in his voice. "I don't like doing things like that in public. It feels too personal, I guess."

"I don't want you to change who you are," I told him. "But I might like to dance with you some time or hold your hand."

He pulled me closer in a hug and wrapped his arms around my back like a steel band. "I'll try, Tate. Yesterday is gone. I know that. I want that comfort we used to have back."

I tipped my head up further to meet his eyes as we continued to sway to the music. "Your tattoo—Yesterday lasts forever, Tomorrow comes never—that's what it says. What does it mean?" I'd finally been able to read the script on the side of his torso one morning this week while he'd been sleeping.

His hand skimmed down my hair. "Just that I was living in the past. What happened with my father, what happened with you, I could never get over the anger. Yesterday kept following me. And tomorrow, the new day, never seemed to come."

Until you, he'd written on the note.

"And the lantern on your arm?"

"Oh, you ask too many questions," Jared complained playfully, and I could tell he was embarrassed.

But I waited, not letting him off the hook.

He pinned me with a resigned smile. "The lantern is you, Tate. The light. I got it after I got in trouble last year. I needed to clean up my act, and my mom decided to do the same thing with her drinking. We both picked one thought that would get us through the day. A dream or a desire . . . " He shook his head and trailed off.

His confession made me breathless. He had thought of me every day?

"Me?" I asked.

He gazed down at me and stroked my cheek with his thumb. "It's always been you." He used my words, and I couldn't swallow for the lump in my throat.

"I love you, Tate." Jared looked at me like I was the most important thing in his world.

I closed my eyes and touched his lips to mine. "I love you, too," I whispered against his mouth before sealing it with a kiss.

Our bodies melted together, and his fingers threaded through my hair as we devoured each other. His lips were soft but strong against mine, and my fingers dug into his back as his hands claimed my body. I wanted him everywhere.

I was insatiable, and guilt reared its ugly head at me. I wanted him here and now, but sex in someone else's room while a party happened downstairs was not something a nice girl did.

I pressed my hips into his, and we were both breathless in between kisses.

I trailed a path to his jaw, and my teeth lightly grazed his chin. "Unzip me," I panted.

He groaned. "Let's just get out of here. I'm in the mood for more than a quickie."

"Well, I've never had a quickie," I pointed out. "Unzip me."

He complied, but the corners of his mouth lifted in a sexy smile. "Where'd my good girl go?" The question was rhetorical. I knew he loved the way I wanted him.

I felt the draft when Jared's hand reached behind me to unzip my dress, and I moaned when his hands slipped down and caressed my back. His hands were like a drug, almost as addictive as his mouth. I peeled off his jacket, while he let my dress fall down to my waist.

Jared's mouth seared my neck in soft kisses, and I worked the buttons of his shirt. I sucked in a breath when his hands went to my breasts. Tingles spread across my skin, craving more of him.

"Jared," I whispered and wrapped an arm around his neck, placing my lips to his. "I really am a good girl. But tonight I want to be really, really bad."

His breath shook against my mouth, and he captured my lips in a fierce kiss. God, he wanted me. And I was thrilled, because I didn't want to wait until we got home.

Jared tore open the rest of his shirt, sending buttons scattering to the hardwood floor. I let my dress spill to my feet and then peeled off my panties, leaving my high heels on.

"Fuck, Tate." Jared clenched his jaw, taking in the sight in front of him. And he pulled my lips to his again, devouring almost every part of me with his mouth and hands. "I'm sorry. I want to go slow with you. It's just so hard. Do you think in ten years I'll finally get to where I'll actually need foreplay to get hard with you?"

His eyes questioned me, but I could only smile. There was just something about the way he wanted me, the way his eyes drowned out any doubts, that made me feel powerful.

Jared, from what I'd seen, was a one-nighter kind of guy. He didn't do sleepovers, and he didn't take phone numbers. I worried that he'd lose interest or consider it a mission accomplished when we'd first slept together, but instead, he'd become even more hungry.

Every touch this past week, every kiss, every time we'd loved, he acted like everything we were doing was new. Ridiculous, I know. He had more experience than me, so why would anything be different than what he'd experienced before?

Unless he loved me. That was something I was sure he hadn't had with any other girl. I hoped, anyway.

I wanted to be bold, even though my nerves wanted me to run for the hills. I wanted to experience everything with Jared. No hiding, no fear. I was going to ask for everything I wanted, and be brave about it. Forever or never.

His shirt dropped the floor, followed by his pants.

Be bold.

I put my hand on the swollen proof that he wanted me. He jerked and sucked in a breath while I wrapped my hand around him and stroked. I expected him to close his eyes. Wasn't he supposed to do that? To concentrate on the feeling more? But instead, he just watched me touching him. He got harder in my hand, and I clenched my thighs, turned on by the smooth length that had been inside of me and would be inside of me again.

He watched me with dark, heated eyes. He watched me touch him, and I thought I would come just from what I was doing to him. The way his hands clenched into fists and his erection jerked when I rubbed a certain way, and the way his breathing got heavier all got me throbbing to the point where I couldn't take anymore.

He tore open the wrapper of the condom he'd put on the nightstand when he took his pants off and slipped it on.

Thank God!

Melting my body into his, my breasts rubbing against the smooth skin of his chest, I kissed him long and deep, running my hands all over his back.

Be brave.

"My turn," I whispered in his ear.

Jared's eyes widened when he realized what I meant.

I lightly pushed him back on the bed and slid on top of him. Perfect. A shot of adrenaline coursed through me when I felt his hands on my hips and his sex pressed against me.

"You're perfect. Perfect for me." He ran his hands up and down my thighs.

I moved, gliding his tip along my slit, teasing him. When I came down on him, putting him inside me, my toes curled with the unbelievable feeling. It was so much deeper like this, and I leaned backward a little to be able to absorb every inch. I was filled and stretched, and I wanted him to feel as complete as I did.

Jared put a hand on my breast and used his other hand to guide my hips as I worked him slowly. "Tell me you like it, Tate."

"I . . ." I clenched my thighs tighter at his sides and moved in a front-back motion against him rather than the up-down I'd been doing.

Oh. My. God.

He hit the spot deep inside of me, and my head flipped back as I moaned. Damn! There was nothing better than having him inside of me.

I loved that I could still feel where he was the next day. And I wanted to feel him tomorrow, too.

He pushed his hips up hard against me, sending shudders through my body. "Say it."

"I love it." My body had lost control. The ripple inside of me turned into a wave, and I grinded against him faster and harder. "I love it with you."

Afterwards, we lay collapsed on the bed, too tired to move, and I just wanted to crawl under the covers with him. I couldn't believe I'd just done that in a strange house. We needed to get out of here before everyone figured out what we were up to. I had to start being more careful. My dad trusted me, but that wouldn't last if I kept making irresponsible decisions.

Of course, he liked Jared. I was eighteen. My dad knew me having a sex life was bound to happen sooner or later. However, this school year had been full of behavioral mishaps on my part, and having sex in a strange house at a party wasn't on my list of great ideas. It was fun once, but I reminded myself to not try this again.

I kissed Jared, and we both smiled and laughed as we helped each other get dressed.

"I have a question." I finally broke the blissful silence as I smoothed over his hair. It was the same question I'd tried to ask him before. There was only one more piece of the Jared-puzzle that I needed.

"Shoot."

"You didn't want to tell me about your dad or your brother. But Piper knew where you went on the weekends. Why could she know and not me?" The idea of Jared close enough to that girl to confide in her pissed me off.

"Tate, I didn't tell Piper anything. Her dad is a cop. The cop that arrested me last year for attacking Jax's foster dad. She found out through him." He circled his arms around my waist and held me close.

"So you just happened to be dating the daughter of the cop that arrested you?" I knew it was more than a coincidence without him saying anything. He'd sought out Piper for some silly revenge. Bagging the cop's daughter was a "screw you" to her father.

He shrugged. "Yeah, I'm not proud of that, but would it make you feel better if I actually liked her?"

I looked away. No. No, it wouldn't.

Chapter 34

You know that expression—walking on cloud nine? Well, that was me as I strolled down the halls on Monday. Everything was going so great—K.C. and Liam, Jared and me, and school—that I felt like I was on a happy drug and never wanted to come down.

Jared had kissed me goodbye Sunday morning after Homecoming, having to leave for a daytrip to Weston to visit his brother. I hinted that I'd love to join him some weekend and meet Jax, but I didn't want to push it either. I got the impression that Jared really enjoyed his alone time with his brother, so I'd wait until the time was right.

He hadn't called or texted all day yesterday, so I started to worry when I hadn't heard from him. But, at about ten o'clock last night, he'd finally crawled through my window and slid into bed next to me. As he spooned me, we both fell into a deliciously deep sleep.

Between the tickle torture he woke me up with this morning and the rush to school, I had barely talked to him about his visit with his brother.

"So, get your ass out to the parking lot right after school today." Madoc sauntered up to me as I headed to French class. He was grinning from ear to ear. "We're going to practice racing out on Route Five. Lots of dirt road and hills."

I pushed up the sleeves of my thin, black cardigan that I wore over my Avenged Sevenfold T-shirt. I was hot as hell as I battled the crowd in the hallway. "Why would I want to practice racing? And with you?"

"Because Jared said you were looking at a G8 to buy. We could spend the winter getting it ready to race in the spring. Jared says he's got work after school, so that means you're free, and we can bond." He nodded his filthy-flirtatious head like I should be so excited.

I couldn't lie and say that I wasn't interested in buying a car. Jared had seen my internet printouts. A guy in Chicago was selling a Pontiac G8 that had me drooling, but I hadn't decided to buy it yet.

Madoc raised his eyebrows. His light blue oxford hung open over a dark gray T-shirt, and with his boyish demeanor, it was hard to stay agitated with him. He was trying to be friendly, after all.

But I forced a stern voice. "I have labs twice a week, including today. I have cross country. Not to mention, I have papers due in Themes and French early next week, and a Math and Chemistry test right before Halloween next Friday. Some other time ... maybe." I breathed out the last part as I opened the door to French class.

"Don't be such a party pooper!" Madoc followed me in and shouted loud enough for the whole classroom to hear. "Those naked pictures of us skinny dipping were for my eyes only."

I halted, and closed my eyes as I sensed every student in the room turn to stare at me. *Was he seriously doing this to me again?!*

Snickers and not-so-subtle laughs erupted, while I took a moment to straighten my shoulders and proceed to my desk. I caught Ben out of the corner of my eye, his long legs crossed at the ankles and one hand tapping a pen on his notebook. His eyes were downcast, but he was clearly trying to hold back a laugh.

"Mr. Caruthers." Madame Lyon stepped out from behind her desk and addressed Madoc in English, crossing her arms over her chest. "I assume you have somewhere you need to be right now."

Madoc placed one hand over his chest, while the other hand gestured to me. "Nowhere but by her side until the end of time," he answered.

I cleared my throat as I took my seat. "Piss off," I mouthed to him.

With a fake pout puckering his lips, Madoc backed out of the door and disappeared.

As soon as the door closed, I heard some cell phones ringers go off around me including some vibrating from other phones, including mine. Weird. Why were we all getting notifications at the same time?

"*Mettez vos telephones off, s'il vous plaît!*" Madame told us to turn our phones off. It was a school rule to keep them silenced during instructional time, but everyone carried theirs on them.

I quickly reached into my bag to completely silence mine as a few others were bold enough to actually check their notifications covertly.

As I went to lower my volume, I saw that it was a text from Jared. A little shot of heat surged through my chest, and I hid my phone under the desk so I could check the message.

When I opened up the video he'd sent, I nearly choked on my own air.

I couldn't move. I couldn't breathe. My hands shook as I watched a video on my phone of Jared and I having sex Saturday night. I could tell it was Saturday night from the way my hair was styled for Homecoming.

What the . . . ?

My stomach rolled and putrid bile rose up in the back of my mouth. I think I would've vomited if not for my throat closing off the oxygen trying to get in.

Us. Having sex. We were recorded.

And there I was, perfectly visible and extremely naked as I straddled Jared.

Oh, my God. I wanted to scream. This could not be real!

What was going on?

Snickers, snorts, and whispers popped up around me, and I jerked my head when the girl sitting next to me laughed out loud. She smirked, with her phone in her hand, and I could only stare in horror as she flashed me her screen. *No, no, no.* The same sordid video played on her phone.

As I looked around, my eyes wide, I knew others in the class were seeing the same video message.

This can't be happening! I struggled to take in breath after breath as my brain worked to figure out what the hell was going on. My eyes burned with tears that didn't fall, and I felt like I was on another planet.

No, this is not real. It's not . . . I shook my head, trying to wake up from this nightmare.

I couldn't stop the tremors rocking through my fingers. I glanced back down to my phone and backed out of the video. The text accompanying the message read: "She was a great fuck. Who wants her next?"

My chest shook with dry sobs.

Jared.

The message came from his phone. It was sent to everyone.

Madame called out, trying to get the class focused, "*Écoutez, s'il vous plaît.*"

I stood up shakily, pulled my bag over my head and hurried out of the room. The laughs and taunts behind me were like white noise. They were there. They were always fucking there. Fuck me for getting comfortable.

Why didn't I listen to my instincts? I knew I couldn't trust him. Why was I so weak?

I held my stomach, trying to hold back the cries, wails, and screams that I wanted to let loose. My lungs felt stretched from the deep, fast breaths I'd been taking.

That video was everywhere! And by tonight, there wouldn't be one person in Shelburne Falls who hadn't seen or heard of it.

Jared. My head was splitting trying to take in the betrayal of what he'd done. He'd been patient and clever and waited for his revenge. He'd ruined me. Not just in high school but forever. I'd always be looking over my shoulder now, wondering who would discover that video on some sordid website and when it would happen.

And I loved him. How could he do something like this? My heart felt like it was tearing in two.

Oh, God. My stomach hollowed out, and I couldn't hold back the sobs anymore.

"Tate," a voice panted.

I stopped and looked up, my tear-filled eyes meeting Madoc's. He'd just come up the stairs, and I saw his phone in his hand.

"Tate, Jesus." He reached for me.

"Stay away from me!" I hurled at him angrily. I should've known better. Madoc would be just like Jared. He'd fooled me, too. And I couldn't trust either of them. I knew that now.

"Tate." He reached for me again, slower, like he was approaching an animal.

I wanted him away from me. I couldn't listen to any more painful insults or degrading innuendos. No—scratch that—I *wouldn't* listen to any more.

"Just let me get you out of here, okay?" Madoc inched towards me.

284

"No!" I cried, the tears blurring my vision. I slapped his hands away and caught him in the face with my palm.

He quickly stepped in front of me and wrapped his arms around my body, holding me tight as I struggled and cried.

"Stop it." He jerked me a couple of times. "Just calm down." His voice was strong and sincere. "I'm not going to hurt you."

And I wanted to believe him.

"They saw everything," I sobbed, my chest heaving from the heavy breaths. "Why did he do that to me?"

"I don't know. For once, I don't know what the hell's going on. We need to talk to him."

Talking. I was fucking done with the talking. Nothing I tried to do with Jared this year helped me. Nothing made my life better. In the end, his bullying had ended any hopes I had for happiness.

Somehow I'd been wrong when I thought he really cared. When I thought he really loved me. I believed every stupid lie he spewed. Maybe he was never abused. He probably didn't even have a brother.

He'd finally pushed me so far down that I only wanted to escape now. Escape into something other than hope, love, and all that other bullshit.

My anger and pain were molding into something else, something harder.

Numbness.

Indifference.

Coldness.

Whatever it was, it felt better than what I felt a minute ago.

I took a deep breath and sniffled. "Let me go. I'm going home." My voice was hoarse but steady when I pulled away from Madoc.

He released me, and I walked away slowly.

"I don't think you should drive," Madoc called out behind me.

I just wiped my eyes and kept walking. Down the stairs, through the empty hallways, and out the front doors.

I'd parked next to Jared that morning, and when I saw his car I let out a hard laugh. Not from amusement but from the look on his face when he came outside to see what I'd done.

I grabbed the crowbar out of the back of my truck and ran the sharp-cornered end along the side of his car as I walked to the front of the vehicle. The shrill screeching of metal on metal sent a warming high right to my veins, and I smiled.

And brought the crowbar down dead center on his windshield.

The impact splintered the glass into a hundred different cracks. It sounded like a fat roll of bubble wrap popping all at once.

After that, I went crazy. I pounded dents into his hood, doors, and trunk. My hands hummed from the vibrations of the blows, but I didn't stop. I couldn't. With each wallop, I got higher and higher. Hitting him where it hurt made me feel safe. No one could really hurt me if I could hurt them, right?

This is how bullies are made. A voice in my head whispered. I shook it off.

I wasn't becoming a bully, I told myself. A bully has power. I didn't wield any power here.

I slammed the crowbar across his driver's side window, shattering it. Bits of glass rained all over his seat.

Before I could get the crowbar raised to bust one of his quarter panel windows, I was grabbed from behind and turned away from the car.

"Tate, stop it!"

Jared.

I twisted out of his grasp and whirled around to face him. He held up his hands as if to calm me, but I was already calm. Didn't he see that? I was in control, and I didn't care what any of these people thought.

Madoc stood behind Jared with his hands on his head, sur-veying the damage to Jared's car. His eyes were so wide that I thought they would pop out of his head. The school's windows were nearly spilling with bodies anxious to get a glimpse of the display.

Fuck them.

"Tate. . . . " Jared said timidly, eyeing the weapon in my hand.

"Stay away from me, or it'll be more than your car getting busted up the next time," I warned.

I didn't know if it was my words or my flat tone that surprised him, but he hesitated.

He stared at me like I was someone he didn't know.

Chapter 35

I'd gotten out of there before anyone had a chance to torment me more. Once I jumped in my truck and sped off, my phone started lighting up with calls and texts. K.C. dialed every thirty seconds, and I got nothing from Jared.

Good. He knew that it was over. He'd gotten what he wanted. I was shamed and humiliated, and his job was done.

The texts, on the other hand, were from random people, most of whom I barely knew.

You look like a good fuck. Busy 2nite? One of the texts read, and I clenched the phone so hard that I heard it crack.

Do u do threesomes? This text came from Nate Dietrich, and I felt my stomach start to turn.

Everyone was laughing at me and hovering around that horrid video, no doubt launching it into cyberspace for anyone to see. Thinking of the dirty old men that would get off from seeing it, or all of the people at school who would look at me now and know exactly what I looked like without my clothes on made my skull ache and my eyes burn.

After two more disgusting messages, I steered the truck to the side of the road and opened the door to throw up. My gut wrenched, emptying everything I'd eaten today. Coughing, I hurled and spit up the last contents of my stomach and shut the door.

Snatching tissues out of the glove compartment, I wiped my face clean of tears and stared out the front windshield, not really wanting to go home.

Anyone who wanted to find me would start there. And I couldn't see anyone right now. I really just wanted to jump on a goddamn plane and go to my dad.

My dad.

I exhaled and dropped my aching head to the steering wheel, forcing in deep breaths.

Son of a bitch.

There was no way my dad wasn't going to find out about this. The video was probably all over the place by now. The school and other parents would find out, and someone would call him.

How could I have been so stupid?! Forgetting for a moment that it was ludicrous of me to believe Jared and trust him, but I had sex with him at a party, in someone else's house!

That damn phone of his. He'd placed it on the dresser to play music, but he'd really set it to record us having sex. He probably thought he'd have to coax me into putting out at the Beckman house when I'd actually coerced *him*. Or so I thought.

Everything was a lie. The way he kept me so close this past week, touching me and holding me. Every time his lips brushed my neck as he hugged me, and all the times he kissed my hair when he thought I was asleep.

All. A. Fucking. Lie.

I wiped my nose and pulled off the side of the road. There was only one person I could be around right now. The only person who loved me and couldn't look at me with pity or shame.

My mom.

The narrow roads—almost like paths—of Concord Hill Cemetery were only wide enough for one lane. Thankfully, I was here on a Monday afternoon, so the whole place was empty and quiet. I breathed a tired sigh of relief when I picked out my mom's grave from the road. There was no one around. I'd be alone, for at least a little while, to escape the world and what had happened this morning.

I climbed out of the car and pulled my fleece jacket over my head, shielding myself from the October chill. The cool breeze was pleasant on my face, though, which still burned from wiping tears. I didn't have to see myself to know I was probably splotchy with puffy eyes.

Traipsing through the well-kept grass, I only had to pass a few graves before coming to my mom's. The shiny, black marble head-stone featured three three-dimensional, hand-carved roses hugging the side of the marker. My dad and I had picked it out together, thinking that the three roses represented our family. Even eight years ago I'd loved black, and the flowers also reminded us of her. She loved bringing nature into the house.

I read the headstone.

Lillian Jane Brandt
February 1, 1972–April 14, 2005
"Yesterday is gone. Tomorrow has not yet come.
We have only today. Let us begin."
—*Mother Theresa*

Yesterday is gone. My mom's favorite quote. She would tell me that mistakes would be made in life. It was unavoidable. But I needed to take a deep breath, put my shoulders back and move forward.

Yesterday lasts forever. Jared's tattoo came to mind, and I quickly shoved it away like a hot plate.

I didn't want to think of him now. Or maybe ever.

I knelt down on the damp ground and tried to remember everything I could about my mom. Little pieces of the times we spent together sprouted up in my mind, but over the years, my memories had dwindled. Less and less of her remained, and I wanted to cry again.

Her hair. I concentrated on an image of her hair. It was light red and wavy. Her eyes were blue, and she had a small scar on her eyebrow from when she'd fell ice-skating as a kid. She loved chocolate peanut butter ice cream and playing tennis. Her favorite movie was *The Quiet Man*, and she made the best Hershey Kiss cookies.

I choked on a sob, remembering those cookies. The smell of our kitchen during Christmas baking hit me like a sledgehammer, and I was suddenly in pain. I hugged my stomach and leaned forward, putting my forehead to the ground.

"Mom," I whispered, my throat tight with sadness. "I miss you."

Crumbling to the ground, I lay on my side and let the miserable tears fall to the earth. I stayed there a long time, being quiet, and tried not to think about what had happened to me today.

But it was impossible. The impact was too great.

I meant nothing to Jared. Once again, he'd tossed me out like trash and everything he'd said and done to lure me in—to get me to love him—was a lie.

How would I survive the vicious taunts day-in and day-out? How could I walk down the hallway at school or look my father in the eye when everyone had seen that video?

"Do you see it, Tate?"

"What?"

"The balloon." Jared took my hand and pulled me across the cemetery. I tried not to think of what was underneath my feet as we crossed the graveyard, but all I could envision were gruesome zombies popping out of the earth.

"Jared, I don't want to be here," I sniveled.

"It'll be okay. You're safe with me." He smiled and looked out over the meadow of gravestones.

"But . . ." I looked around, scared out of my mind.

"I'm holding your hand. What do you want me to do? Change your diaper, too?" he said sarcastically, but I didn't take it to heart.

"I'm not scared." My voice sounded defensive. "It's just . . . I don't know."

"Look at this place, Tate. It's green and quiet." Jared gazed around the grounds with a wistful look on his face, and I was jealous that he could see something here that I didn't.

"There are flowers and statues of angels. Look at this marker." He pointed. "'Alfred McIntyre born in 1922 and died in 1942.' He was only twenty. Remember Mrs. Sullivan said that World War II was between 1939 and 1945? Maybe he died in the war. All of these people had lives, Tate. They had families and dreams. They don't want you to be afraid of them. They just want to be remembered."

I shivered as he led me deeper into the cemetery. We came upon a shiny, black marker adorned with a pink balloon. I knew my dad came here to visit, but he always put flowers on the grave.

Who had left a balloon?

"I brought your mom the balloon yesterday," Jared admitted as if reading my mind.

"Why?" My voice shook. It was nice of him to do something like that.

"Because chicks like pink stuff." He shrugged his shoulders and made light of his gesture. He didn't want attention. He never did.

"Jared," I scolded, waiting for a real answer.

He smiled to himself. "Because she made you." And he wrapped his skinny arm around my neck and yanked me into his side. "You're the best friend I've ever had, and I wanted to tell her 'thank you.'"

I felt warm all over despite the April frost on the ground. Jared filled the emptiness and eased the hurt in a way my dad couldn't. I needed him, and thought for a moment that I'd like him to kiss me. But the idea quickly disappeared. I'd never wanted a boy to kiss me before, and it probably shouldn't be my best friend.

"Here, take this." Jared pulled his gray sweatshirt over his head and tossed it to me. "You're cold."

I slipped it on, letting the remaining heat from his body cover me with a shield of warmth.

"Thank you," I said, looking up at him.

He pulled my hair out from under the collar and let his fingers linger as he stared at me. My skin erupted in chills but not from the cold. What was going on in my stomach right now?

We both looked away quickly, a little embarrassed.

I sat up and wiped my nose with the sleeve of my jacket.

Despite everything, I could see the light in one thing. At least I'd given my virginity to someone I loved. Even though we were done, I had loved him when I gave myself to him. What he took from me was honest and pure even if he thought it was all a joke.

"Tate." A shaky voice whispered behind me, and I stopped breathing. Without even turning around, I knew who it was, and I tore blades of grass from the ground as my fists clenched.

I refused to turn around. And I'd be damned if I listened to any more bullshit from him.

"Haven't you won, Jared? Why won't you just leave me alone?" My voice was calm, but my body screamed for violence. I wanted to lash out. Hit him. Do anything that could hurt him.

"Tate, this is all so fucked up. I—" He started to spew his non-sense, but I cut him off.

"No! No more!" I whipped around to face him, unable to reason with myself. I said I wasn't going to get into it with him, but I couldn't help it. "Do you hear me? My life here is ruined. No one will let me live this down. You've won. Don't you get it? You. Have. Won! Now leave me alone!"

His eyes widened, probably because I was screaming and madder than I'd ever been. When was it enough? Couldn't he just be satisfied?

He gripped the hair on his head, looking like he stopped midway combing his hands through it. His chest rose and fell like he was nervous. "Just stop for a minute, okay?"

"I've listened to your stories. Your excuses." And I walked away towards my truck, feeling my heart breaking. He was near, and my arms still hummed with the desire to hold him.

"I know," he called out behind me. "My words aren't good enough. I can't explain any of this. I don't know where that video came from!"

I knew he was following me, so I didn't turn around. "It came from your phone, asshole! No, never mind. I've stopped talking to you." I kept walking, feeling as if my legs weighed two tons.

"I called your dad!" he blurted out, and I halted.

I squeezed my eyes shut. "Of course you did," I murmured, more to myself than him.

Just when I thought things couldn't get any worse. I thought that I'd have a few days to get my head straight before I had to deal with my dad. But the storm was going to descend sooner rather than later.

"Tate, I didn't send that video to anyone. I didn't even record a video of us." He sounded desperate, but I still couldn't turn to look at him.

He continued, "I haven't seen my phone in two days. I left it upstairs at Tori's party when we were listening to music. When I remembered later, I went back to get it, but it was gone. Don't you remember?"

I recalled him saying something about misplacing his phone that night, but we were all dancing, and it was loud. I must've forgotten.

I sucked in my cheeks and shook my head. *No.* He wasn't getting out of this. His phone was pointed at the bed that night, exactly the position it needed to be in to record a video.

"You're a liar," I retorted.

While I couldn't see his face, I felt him approach, and I couldn't move. Why couldn't I just get out of here?

"I called your dad, because he was going to find out anyway. That goddamn, fucking video is out there, and I wanted him to hear it from me first. He's coming home."

My shoulders sunk. My dad would be home sometime tomorrow then. The thought both warmed and scared me. The fallout from this prank—I hated to even call it that, because it was so much more—would be embarrassing for my father.

But I needed him right now. No matter what, I knew he loved me.

"I love you more than myself, more than my own family, for Christ's sake. I don't want to take another step in this world without you next to me," he said softly.

His sweet words washed over me, but they were like a hand that was just out of reach. I could see it. I wanted to take it. But I couldn't.

"Tate." The weight of his hand fell on my shoulder, and I whipped around, flinging him off. Constant tears, anger, and weariness burned my eyes as I scalded him with my stare.

He ran a hand through his hair again, and I could see the worry lines on his forehead. "You have every right not to trust me, Tate. I know that. My fucking heart is ripping open tight now. I can't stand the way you're looking at me. I could never hurt you again. Please . . . let's try to fix this together." His voice cracked, and his eyes were red.

I told myself a hundred times today that he couldn't be trusted. He was a liar. A bully. But his words were getting to me. He looked upset. Either he was a really good actor, or ... he was telling the truth.

"Fine. I'll play along." I took out my phone and turned it back on.

He blinked, probably confused by my sudden change of attitude. "What are you doing?"

"Calling your mom." I didn't elaborate and dialed Katherine.

"Why?" he drawled out, still confused.

"Because she installed a GPS tracking app on your Android when she bought it. You said you lost your phone? Let's find it."

Chapter 36

I let out a sigh and shook my head as soon as I hung up with her.

School. Not somewhere I wanted to go. Ever again.

"So?" Jared inched closer.

"School. It's at school," I muttered, studying the ground.

"Son of a bitch. She's smarter than I thought." Jared sounded almost impressed with his mother.

What did this mean? Maybe he left his phone at school and was trying to cover his ass. Maybe Madoc or one his pals had it, and they were covering for him. Or maybe it really was stolen.

I'd rather cut off my hair than face those people today. Or any day in the next hundred years. Eating squid or slamming my finger in a car door all sounded more appealing than braving those hallways. A few hours wasn't nearly enough time for everyone to move on to new gossip. I'd be the talk of the town for a long time. How could I even be considering stepping foot back on school grounds today?

"I see that look in your eye." Jared looked down at me and spoke gently. "It's the look you get when you want to bolt. The look you get right before you decide to stay and fight."

"What am I fighting for?" I challenged, my voice hoarse.

He frowned. "We did nothing wrong, Tate."

He was right. I had nothing to be ashamed of. Granted, I hated that people had seen what they did, but I gave my heart and body to someone I loved. There was nothing dirty in that.

"Let's go." I walked to my truck and opened the door.

Jared had parked in front of me, and I cringed when I saw the damage I'd done to his car.

Shit.

If he was, in fact, guilty, then screw him and his dumb car. But if he was innocent, then I didn't even want to think about how mad my dad was going to be when he saw the bill for repairs.

"Is . . . um . . . is your car safe to drive?" I asked timidly.

A tired smile tugged at his lips. "Don't sweat it. It gives me an excuse to do more upgrades."

I filled my lungs with a deep breath, feeling like I'd been suffocated all day. The cool wind danced across my face and gave me a little more energy.

"Stop at your mom's firm and pick up her phone. I'll meet you at school." And I climbed into the truck and sped off.

Everyone was still in their final period, so Jared and I walked silently through the halls without interruption.

"Is it still flashing?" I glanced over to his mom's phone in his hand.

"Yeah. I can't believe my phone is still on after two days. GPSs use a lot of battery." He was looking around, but I wasn't sure what for.

"Well, the video was sent this morning. If what you say is true, then whoever used your phone has probably charged it since Saturday night."

"If what I say is true. . . . " He repeated what I said in a whisper like he was aggravated I didn't trust him.

Part of me wanted to believe him. Desperately. But the other part of me was wondering why the hell I was here. Was I really entertaining the possibility that he didn't have anything to do with this? Wasn't it a little too far-fetched that this was all put together without Jared's help?

"Look," I said, trying to change the subject, "this tracker's only accurate within fifty meters. So ... "

"So start dialing my phone. Maybe we'll hear it."

I slid my phone out of my back pocket and dialed his number, letting it ring and keeping our ears peeled for any noise. But our school was huge, and we had almost no time until last period ended, and the halls flooded with bodies.

Every time his voicemail picked up, I ended the call and redialed.

"Let's split up," I suggested. "I'll keep dialing. Just listen for a sound. I think it's in a locker."

"Why? Someone could have it on them, too."

"With me calling every ten seconds? No, they would've turned off the phone, in which case it would've gone straight to voicemail. It's on, and it's in a locker." I nodded.

"Fine." His voice was hesitant and a little biting. "But if you find it, call my mom's phone immediately. I don't want you in the halls alone, not today."

I started to get my hopes up at his concern for me. This was the Jared from the past week. The one that held me and touched me gently. The one that cared.

In that moment, I wanted to grab him and hold him close.

But then I heard their laughter in my ears again. And I remembered that I didn't trust him.

Hitting "redial," I turned and leapt up the stairs, two at a time.

My boots hit the tiled floor with more of a thud than I would've liked. Trying to lighten my step, I crept along each side of the main hallway with my ear to the lockers. But each time I called Jared's number I heard no rings or vibrating noises.

I passed two students in the hallway, both of whom did a double-take when they saw me.

Yep, they knew who I was, and in no time at all everyone would know I was on campus. My heart sped up as it became more and more obvious that I'd made a mistake in coming back here today.

The phone was in a locker, probably Jared's, and silenced. This was just another trick. My throat tightened.

I breathed hard as I paced each hallway, continuing to punch "redial." Each time the voicemail picked up, I wanted to cry again.

Please, please . . .

I wanted him to be innocent. I could live with the talk and the look in everyone's eyes, knowing that they'd seen the video. I would live with that, because I had no choice.

But I didn't want to be without Jared. I needed him to be innocent.

Because she made you.

His words floated through my mind.

I don't want to take one more step in this world without you next to me.

Neither did I.

I was hoping we could move forward without looking back.

I caught a tear with my thumb before it spilled over, turned a corner and called his phone again.

And froze.

Limp Bizkit's "Behind Blue Eyes" echoed down the hall, close to Dr. Kuhl's classroom. I narrowed my eyes and tilted my head towards the music. When it ended, I tapped the button again to call it back.

Please, please, please.

When the line started ringing, the slow, sad ballad played again from down the hall. I nearly dropped the phone as I took off toward the sound.

I put my hand to locker 1622.

I smiled for the first time since this morning, and with shaky fingers, I texted Jared's mom's phone.

2nd floor, next to Kuhl's room!!

I jerked my head up at the sound of the school bell sounding. My stomach sank. Doors swung open and flocks of students poured out, sounding more like a murder of crows than humans.

A murder.

Yep, that's about what was going to happen right now. But I didn't know if I'd be the predator or prey.

I stood facing the lockers with my back to everyone, hoping that I could get away with it for as long as possible. Out of instinct, I put my head down, trying to be invisible. My heart pounded in my ears, and I felt like a thousand eyes were boring into the back of my skull.

But then the flame of cowardice hit me. More than the shame I felt this morning, I hated the way these people made me want to crawl into a hole.

I used to love people. I loved being a part of things and socializing. Now, I only wanted to be alone. Because alone was the only way I felt safe.

I had done nothing wrong. Those in my school who had passed the video around or gossiped about it were the ones to feel ashamed. Not me.

But I was the one hiding.

Isn't it about time you fought back?

Taking a deep breath and turning around, I leaned back on locker 1622 and looked up, daring them to come at me.

I didn't have to wait long.

"Hey, Tate." Some kid with stringy, blond hair walked past, undressing me with his eyes.

"Whoa, she came back!" another guy taunted.

Others slowed in passing and laughed to their friends. The girls didn't tease like the guys did. They bullied more quietly, with whispers behind their hands. With looks.

But everyone had something nasty to offer.

Until Jared ran up.

And then everyone stopped.

He looked between them and me and took my face in his hands. "Are you alright?" he asked, his eyes full of love.

"Yes." My voice was softer on him now. "The phone is here, in 1622. I don't know whose locker it is, though."

His lips pressed in a thin line, and a scowl crossed his face. He knew whose locker it was.

"Back so soon? Is your porn career a failure already?" A catty voice rose out of the murmurs, and I shut my eyes.

Piper.

I felt Jared's lips on my forehead before he pulled away. I opened my eyes to see him turn around, shielding me, but I yanked his arm back and stepped forward.

I should've known Piper was a part of this. I don't know how she did it, but she was responsible, and I wanted to deal with her. Hell, I'd take pleasure in it!

I briefly noticed everyone in the hall squeezed together, patiently waiting for something.

"Actually, we're just waiting for you." I smiled and kept my tone even. "You know that video that came from Jared's phone this morning? The one that everyone saw? He didn't send it. His phone was stolen Saturday night. Would you know where it is?" I raised my eyebrows in my best condescending look.

She blinked but straightened her shoulders and tilted her chin up. "Why would I know where his phone is?"

"Oh, because . . . " I drifted off and hit "redial." "Behind Blue

302

Eyes" started playing from her locker, and I held up my phone screen to her so she could see that I was dialing Jared. Everyone else saw, too.

"This is your locker, Piper," Jared pointed out after I'd hung up.

"You know, I just love that song. Let's hear it again." As I called his phone, everyone heard the song echo from Piper's locker once more. Now there was no doubt.

Jared stepped forward and bent down into her face. "Open up your locker and give me my goddamn phone back, or we'll get the Dean, and he'll open the locker."

Option A would prove to the entire school she was a thief and a liar. Option B would prove the same thing but also get her into trouble. She was standing there like she had a choice.

"It was Nate's idea," she blurted out, her voice cracking.

"You stupid bitch!" Nate growled from the crowd, and I looked over to see him step forward. "It was your idea."

Jared pulled his arm back and punched Nate across the nose, sending the guy spilling to the ground like a wet dishcloth. The bystanders gasped and backed up, and I tried to resist the urge to do the same to Piper.

At that moment, Madoc pushed through the crowd, wide-eyed with shock at the bleeding Nate on the floor.

"Are you okay?" he asked, looking pissed as he came to stand by my side.

I nodded and turned my attention to Piper. "How did you do it?"

She pursed her lips and refused to meet my eyes. *So we're going to be stubborn today, I see.*

"Your dad's a cop, right? What's his number?" I held up my phone, my fingers primed to dial. "Oh, yeah. 911."

"Ugh, alright!" she gritted out. "Nate took me to Homecoming and then to Tori's party afterwards. When we saw you and Jared head upstairs, Nate took his camera phone and climbed onto the balcony. When he showed me the video later, I saw that Jared had left his phone on the dresser, so I snuck back into the room to take it."

"So the video came from Nate's phone. It was transferred to Jared's before it was texted." I spoke to Piper but my eyes were on Jared. He looked at me, not angry like he should have been, but relieved. Now I knew he wouldn't do something like that to me. I should've always known, I guess.

Shit. I really messed up his car.

"Get Jared's phone, Piper. Now," Madoc ordered, with a scowl I usually didn't see on his face.

She huffed and walked up to her locker, working the combination until the lock clicked. Yanking the door open, she shuffled through her purse while the rest of us waited.

The crowd hadn't dispersed. If anything, it'd grown. I was surprised teachers hadn't come out of the classrooms yet. Jared hovered over Nate, who still lay on the ground holding his nose. He had to remember a night not so long ago that he'd been in the same situation with Jared and probably decided that it was better to just stay down.

Piper finally picked the phone out of her bag and threw it at my chest. Out of reflex, my hands shot up to catch it, but there was a dull ache from where it'd hit. She was scowling at me, and I almost wanted to laugh. Almost.

"We're done," she snapped and waved her hand to shoo me away. "You may go."

Um . . . yeah, no.

"Piper? Do yourself a favor, and get some help. Jared is not yours, and he never will be. In fact, he won't ever look at you again and see anything good, if he even saw anything good in the first place."

Piper's eyes narrowed to slits, and I could tell by the muffled whispers that the crowd was more on my side than hers now. I guess it didn't hurt that everyone knew that Jared hadn't sent that video. Hell, I guess they were really on *his* side.

Oh well, they didn't need to like me, but it helped to not have them against me, too.

I twisted around to pass Jared his phone but was yanked back by my hair. Pain shot through my scalp as I slammed back to the lockers.

My equilibrium was thrown off, and I stumbled to right myself again. *Shit.* That had hurt. What did she think she was doing?

I saw Piper's fist priming for a punch. My eyes nearly bugged out of my head, but I reacted.

I ducked, and her fist caught my hair instead of my face. Shoving her away, I whipped my hand back and smacked her across the face. Before she even had a chance to stumble, I brought my other hand across her other cheek, and that sent her crumbling to the floor.

I registered the audience's sharp intakes of breath and their shocked laughs, but I didn't care. I glared down at Piper, who was trying to hold her face and stand back up at the same time.

Pulling my hand back to deliver another blow—hey, she deserved it—I felt myself being lifted off the ground.

I tried to wiggle out of the grasp of whoever had me, but when I heard Jared shushing me in my ear, I eased up.

"What's going on here?" A male voice interrupted us. I looked over to see Dr. Porter, coffee-stained beard and all, looking between the two heaps on the floor. I grimaced. There was no way I was getting away with all of the damage I'd done today. *And thank you Jared for stopping me before Dr. Porter saw!*

Madoc cleared his throat. "Dr. Porter. Nate and Piper bumped into each other."

Oh, my God. I was convinced. Madoc was an idiot.

"Mr. Caruthers, I'm not stupid." Dr. Porter glanced around, trying to make eye contact with anyone who would talk. "Now what happened here?"

No one spoke. No one even breathed, I think. The hallway was silent, and I merely waited for Nate or Piper to break the silence.

I was going to be in so much trouble.

"I didn't see anything, sir," a male student piped up, giving Dr. Porter a blank stare.

"Me either, Dr. Porter," another student followed suit. "Probably just an accident."

And I was blown away as everyone either lied or remained silent, covering for us. Okay, they were covering for Jared, but I was going to take what I could get.

Dr. Porter looked around, still waiting for someone to tell the truth.

He was right. He wasn't stupid, and he knew something was fishy. I just hoped he didn't call on me. I liked the guy and probably couldn't lie.

He sighed and rubbed his scruffy jaw. "Alright, you two." He gestured to Nate and Piper. "Get up, and come to the nurse. Everyone else. Head home!"

Piper grabbed her purse, slammed her locker shut and stalked off down the hall, while Nate held his bloodied nose and followed Dr. Porter.

As everyone dispersed, no one said anything to me. No one gave me snide looks or cruel snickers. Jared circled his arms around my neck and pulled me to him, enveloping me in the safe, warm wall of his chest. I closed my eyes and breathed him in as a wave of relief flooded me. I had him back.

"I'm so sorry about not trusting you. And about what I did to your car, too," I said into his hoodie.

He laid his cheek on the top of my head. "Tate, you're mine, and I'm yours. Every day you're going to realize that more and more. When you believe it without a doubt, then I'll have earned your trust."

"I am yours. I just . . . wasn't sure if you were really mine."

"Then I'll make you sure." He kissed my hair, and his body started shaking with laughter.

"You're laughing right now?" I looked up at him, confused.

"Well, I was kind of worried about my anger issues, but now I'm kind of worried about yours. You like to hit people." His perfect mouth grinned with pride.

I rolled my eyes and pouted. "I'm not angry. She got what she deserved, and I was attacked first." She got off lucky, actually. After the shit she pulled, Piper was lucky I didn't take a flame thrower to her entire halter-top collection.

He lifted me by the backs of my thighs, and I locked my arms and legs around him as he carried me off.

"It's your fault, you know?"

"What?" Jared asked. His breath hot on my ear.

"You made me mean. And now I pummel poor, defenseless girls . . . and guys." I tried to make my voice sound accusing and innocent.

Jared gripped me tighter. "You might say that I turned metal into steel."

I buried my nose in his hair, kissing the ridge of his ear and joked, "Whatever helps you sleep at night, you big bully."

Chapter 37

Cool air caressed my back sending chills down my arms. My eyes drifted open at the draft, and an uncontrollable smile crept across my lips.

"You better not be asleep." Jared rustled behind me as I lay in bed, probably removing his boots.

A silent laugh escaped my lips as I turned onto my back and faced him. Hovering over me, the moonlight poured over his beautiful face, and his hair glistened with droplets of rain from the light drizzle outside. I couldn't get enough of the sight of him.

"You came through the tree ... in a storm," I stated as he crawled into bed and immediately positioned his body on top of me. He still wore his clothes.

My dad had arrived home last week, and it went without saying that Jared was not welcome for any overnight visits. Of course, Jared and I had already assumed this. I knew my dad loved Jared, but he wasn't going to put up with finding him in my room either. That was understandable.

Resting both arms on either side of my head, Jared gazed down into my eyes. "Yeah, we used to sit in that tree all the time when it rained. It's like riding a bike. I never forget how good it felt."

Tears welled in my eyes. The years that separated us had hurt, but how quickly they'd passed. We were together again. We'd never forgotten how to be together.

"Do you like your car?" He smiled and started nibbling my lips with soft, teasing kisses. Giving me little pause, I could only nod.

Last weekend, after my dad had gotten home, we all took a trip to Chicago and bought my G8. I'd owned the sleek, dark metallic silver car for only a few days so far.

Dad had decided to turn over the rest of the Germany project to his partner, so he could stay home with me. It'd been tough to face him after the video leaked, but after a couple of days and lots of talks, we got the situation under control. He came down on me for making such a dumb choice at a party, and he was slightly uncomfortable with Jared's new role in my life. But, he admitted, he probably wouldn't be comfortable with anyone at any time dating his only daughter.

Jared and I had been online constantly, taking down the video wherever we found it. Our classmates also seemed to be laying off the gossip. But I was sure it had more to do with their respect for Jared than their sense of decency.

A week ago, I thought I'd never live down that storm, but I was already concentrating on other things. I had a list of modifications to perform on my new car, and I hoped Jared, my dad and I could work on it together throughout the winter. Madoc seemed to think he'd be included, too, and I didn't do anything to dispel his little brain fart.

My father agreed to let me take the money for Jared's repairs out of my trust, but I'd have to get a job to replace it. He was very strict that my college fund wasn't a snack dish that I could stick my hand in whenever I wanted. And that was fine. A job was a good idea. I needed something to take up my time now that Dad was limiting my time with Jared. I don't think he was as worried about our intimacy as he was about me losing focus in school.

Jared started a slow grind between my legs as his soft nibbles quickly changed to devouring and caressing. The chill that came into the room with him was replaced by sweat and heat.

Oh. I breathed hard; the pulse between my legs twitched with the friction he was making.

"You know," I gasped. "I want you here more than anything, but my dad will wake up. It's like he's still in the Army or something. He sleeps with one eye open."

He abruptly stopped and peered down at me like I was crazy. "I won't be able to stay away. Not with knowing that your cute little body is curled up in this nice, warm bed without me."

"You would never disrespect my dad. Even I know that."

"No, you're right," he conceded, and then his eyes widened. "Do you want to come over to my house?"

I folded my lips between my teeth to stifle a laugh.

As I guided my legs up and around him, he kissed me harder before whispering against my lips. "I love you, Tate. And I'm here for you always. With or without the sleepovers. I just needed to see you."

I held the back of his neck as he raised himself to look down at me. "I love you, too."

The top half of his body slid off of me, over the side of the bed, as he searched for something on the nightstand. I ran my fingers along his back, barely noticing his scars beneath his shirt. He popped back up with a box in his hand.

"What's this?" I asked.

"Open it," he urged gently.

I sat up, and he leaned back on his feet, watching me. Sliding the lid off, I pulled out a charm bracelet. Not the clunky, jiggling kind that makes lots of noise but a dainty, silver chain holding four charms. My eyes darted up to Jared, but he just sat silently, waiting for something.

Eyeing the bracelet closer, I saw the charms were of a cell phone, a key, a coin, and a heart.

A cell phone, a key, a coin, and . . .

"My lifelines!" I burst out, it finally hitting me.

Jared exhaled a laugh. "Yeah, when you told me on our way to Chicago about how you always wanted your escape plans when dealing with me in the past, I didn't want you to see me that way anymore."

"I don't—" I started.

"I know," he rushed to assure me. "But I want to make sure I never lose your trust again. I want to be one of your lifelines, Tate. I want you to need me. So . . . " He gestured to the bracelet. "The heart is me. One of your lifelines. I took Jax with me today to pick it out."

"How is your brother?" I ran the bracelet through my fingers, never wanting to let it or him go.

Jared shrugged his shoulders. "He's hanging in there. My mom is working with a lawyer to try to get custody. He wants to meet you."

I smiled. "I'd love to."

I didn't know what else to say. The gift was beautiful, and I loved what it represented. But what I loved more was that I was getting to know Jared. We'd missed time over the years, but he had found family in his brother, and I could see the love he had for him.

A tear glided down my cheek, but I brushed it away quickly. "Put it on me?" I handed him the bracelet and blinked back more tears.

He worked the clasp and secured it around my wrist, not letting go of my hand as he sat back and pulled me on top, straddling him.

He brushed the hair away from my face, and I came down, meeting his lips. He tasted like heat and man, and I wrapped my arms around him, savoring the reality of just being here with him.

"Jared." My father knocked on the door, and we both jerked

our heads up. "You need to go home now. We'll see you for dinner tomorrow night."

My heart thumped so hard it hurt.

Crap!

Jared snorted back a laugh and spoke to the door. "Yes, sir."

The heat of embarrassment covered my face, my arms, my toes—hell, everywhere as I saw my father's shadow under the door disappear.

"I guess I need to go."

I clenched his black T-shirt and touched my nose to his. "I know. Thank you for my bracelet."

"I'm going to spoil you." His hands caressed my hair.

I smiled. "Don't you dare. Just do me a favor. Leave your window unlocked. I may surprise you some night soon."

He sucked in a breath, and I crashed my mouth down on his. His tongue touched mine, and he dug his fingers into my hips, bringing me hard against him. I could already feel that I was ready for him.

Damn it. *Must earn father's trust back.* I repeated my mantra.

"Go on. Get out of here. Please," I begged and stepped off the bed. He got up but grabbed me for one more kiss before he walked to the French doors.

I watched him climb safely back through his window, where he gave me one last look before grinning and turning off his light.

I stood there for a minute, watching the rain splatter through the tree.

The thunder rumbled in the night, reminding me of my monologue and how Jared and I had come full circle. We were friends again, and also more.

I was his. And he was mine.

We had never been gone from each other. Both of us were shaping the other even though we didn't realize it.

And now we were complete.

Keep reading for a special preview of
Until You
Available now from Piatkus Books!

I dug my fist into the hard, tiled wall across from Penley's classroom.

Fuck her. Fuck Tate and her pathetic whining.

But even saying those words, I still wasn't calming down. Fuck! Who did she think she was anyway? Acting like she was the victim? Really?

I pressed my forehead to the cool wall and closed my eyes. What had she just done to me in there?

I'd gone stone cold as soon as that monologue started. I knew she was talking about us right off the bat. And I couldn't tear my eyes away from her. She still remembered when I was good to her. And from the sound of it, she still missed me.

Why?

Goddamn, Tate. Don't do this! Don't fuck with my head!

All I wanted when I was fourteen was her. And she wasn't thinking about me when I was fucking screaming for her. She didn't need me. She didn't miss me while I was away. Life went fuckin' on, didn't it? I'd needed her so goddamn much that day, and she wasn't giving me one fucking thought. She was happier without me.

I could barely breathe, and I tried forcing air into my lungs. God, I didn't know what I wanted. Maybe I wanted to leave her alone. Maybe I wanted her to look at me like she used to. Maybe I just wanted to hold her and breathe her in until I could finally remember who I was again.

But I couldn't. I needed to hate Tate. I needed to hate her, because if I didn't have a place to sink all of my energy, then I'd spin out. That's what happened last year after she'd left. I went fucking crazy.

"See ya, Jared."

I twisted around and blinked. Ben had called out to me, and she was with him. Looking at me like I was nothing. Like I wasn't the focus of her life when—fuck—she was the focus of everything in mine.

I stuck my fists into the pocket of my hoodie, so they wouldn't see me clenching them. It was kind of a natural thing for me to do now. To keep my temper in check so that no one would notice what was boiling underneath.

Stupid bitch. She couldn't hurt me.

But the air coming out of my nose was heating up as I watched them fade away down the hall.

She was leaving with him.

She'd just handed me my ass in that classroom.

She was surviving me.

And I clenched my fists tighter until the bones in my fingers ached.

"Give me a ride?"

My jaw instantly hardened as frustration poured out of every hair on my body. I didn't even have to turn around to know it was Piper.

Piper was the last thing on my mind these days, and I wished she'd take the hint and back off.

But then I remembered that she was good for one thing.

"Don't talk." I spun around and grabbed her hand without even looking at her and dragged her to the nearest bathroom. I needed to burn off frustration and Piper knew the score. She was like water. She assumed the shape of whatever container held her. She didn't challenge me or make demands. She was just there for the taking.

It was after school. The place was empty as I barged into a stall, sat down on a seat and brought her down on top of me. She giggled, I think, but to be honest, I didn't fucking care who she was, where I was, or that anyone could walk in on us. I needed to dive deep. So deep into a cave that I couldn't even hear my own thoughts. That I couldn't even see *her* blonde hair and blue eyes in my head.

Tate.

I ripped off Piper's little pink cardigan and attacked her mouth. It didn't feel good. It wasn't meant to. This wasn't about me getting off. It was about me getting even.

I grabbed the straps of her tank top and pulled them down her arms, her bra coming with it, until everything sat at her waist. Her chest was free for me, and I dived in as she moaned.

Nothing hurt if I knew I had you.

I was trying to run from Tate, but she was catching up with me. I pulled Piper harder against me and inhaled her skin, wanting her to be someone else.

I felt sick when I saw you hating me.

My heart was pounding, and I couldn't fucking catch my breath. What the fuck?

Piper leaned back and started grinding on me, and my hands were everywhere, trying to find the escape. Trying to find my control.

And my heart was ripped open. I missed you.

I gripped Piper's ass and attacked her neck. She moaned again and said some shit, but I couldn't hear it. There was only one fucking voice in my head that no amount of Piper or any other girl was going to drown out.

I loved all of those things, and I loved you.

And then I stopped.

All the air had left me.

She loved me.

"What's the matter, baby?" Piper had her arms around my

317

neck, but I couldn't look at her. I just sat there, fucking breathing into her chest, trying to delude myself for even a few seconds that it was Tate I was holding.

"Jared. What's with you? You've been acting weird ever since the school year started." Her whiny-ass fucking voice. Why didn't people ever know when to shut up?

I ran my hands over my face. "Just get up. I'll take you home," I bit out.

"I don't want go home. You've been ignoring me for a month. Over a month, actually!" She pulled her shirt and sweater back on, but she still wasn't moving.

I took a deep breath and tried to swallow down the nerves exploding in my stomach. God, I just wanted to fucking get out of here.

"You want a ride or not?" I said, pinning her with a look that said "take it or leave it." Piper knew better than to ask questions. I didn't tell Madoc shit, and I wasn't going to start with this girl.

By the time I got home, my mood had gone from bad to worse. After dropping Piper off, I just drove. I needed to listen to some music, clear my head and try to get rid of this ache in my chest. It felt like someone was squeezing my heart, and instead of calming down, I'd gotten more pissed off.

Tate was doing this to me. She was always to blame.

And as much as I knew that that wasn't true, it felt better to believe it. Because the truth hurt too fucking much.

The truth was that I wish I could go back to that day in the park. Back to the fish pond when I'd decided that she'd needed to hurt. I would've done it differently. Instead of pushing her away, I would've buried my face in her hair and let her bring me back from wherever I'd gone. She wouldn't have had to say or do anything. Just fill my world.

But my anger ran deeper than my love for her that day. And right now, I couldn't face what I'd done. I couldn't face that she hated me now, that my mother barely wanted anything to do with me, and that my father spent every Saturday reminding me of what a . . .

Fuck it! Fuck them all.

I walked into my house, slammed the door and threw my keys across the room. The place was as quiet as a church as usual, except for Madman's paws scurrying across the floor.

He started clawing at my jeans and whimpering for attention.

"Not now, buddy," I snipped and walked into the kitchen. Madman couldn't calm me down, and I wanted to hit something. As I yanked open the refrigerator, I noticed that my mother had left a note stuck to the door.

Off for the night. Order a pizza. Love you!

And I slammed the door closed again. *Always fucking gone.*

I gripped both sides of the refrigerator and pressed my head into the stainless steel. *It didn't matter,* I told myself. Everything was okay. I had shitty parents, but who didn't? I'd pushed Tate away, but there were other girls out there. I had no idea what the fuck I was going to do with my life, but I was only eighteen—or almost eighteen.

Everything. Was. Fine.

I gripped the sides harder, willing myself to believe the lie.

And then I saw myself, alone in a kitchen, and holding a refrigerator. Telling myself that my life was good.

Fuck.

I started pounding the steel doors. Every muscle in my body felt choked as I slammed my palm against the appliance again and again. Madman yelped and scurried away. All the shit my mom had sitting up on top turned over or shattered to the ground, and I just kept going. Using both hands to slam it time and again against the wall.

Nothing hurt if I knew I had you.

She was fucking with my head. Why couldn't I just forget her?

I stopped, my shoulders slumped, forcing air in and out of my lungs, but it was never enough. I turned around to head up the stairs. If my mom was gone for the night, then there was no harm in bringing out the Jack. Since she was an alcoholic, I kept that shit hidden. But tonight I needed a way out. I couldn't stomach the hurt. I couldn't deal, and I needed to be numb.

On my way up the stairs, I noticed that the front door was open. *Shit.* It must not have latched when I'd slammed it before. And Madman got out, no doubt.

I kicked the door shut. Hard.

Fucking awesome. He can leave too.

Once in my room, I went to my stash in the closet and pulled out a bottle. Madoc and I skimmed alcohol from the liquor store his father had in the basement for his many company parties and gatherings. The guy was hardly ever home and didn't notice shit, so we decided to keep some here for our get-togethers. I flung off my hoodie and shirt, kicked off my boots, and unscrewed the bottle, swallowing massive gulps to drown out her voice in my head.

I couldn't figure out what the fuck was wrong with me. It had sucked when she left for France, but I'd gotten better after a while, staying focused on racing, work, and school. And I knew she'd be back. But now, it was like she was farther away from me than when she was in a completely different country.

Walking over to my window, I instantly stilled. My stomach dropped, and I didn't want to move.

There she was.

Dancing.

Closing her eyes and jumping around.

I almost laughed when she threw the devil ears up in the air and screamed along to the music. My chest swelled with the urge to hold her.

God, I wanted her back so fucking much!

But what the hell was I going to say to her? I couldn't tell her everything.

Not everything.

I brought the bottle back up to my lips, closed my eyes, and forced the bile back down my throat.

There was nothing to say to her. The guy she knew when we were fourteen was gone. They'd left me. She'd left me. I was on my own just like that cocksucker said I'd be.

The stinging nip of hatred and hell crawled its way up my neck and into my head until my nerves burned so badly that I wanted to rip off my skin just to breathe.

I launched the bottle across the room where it slammed against the wall before spilling to the floor.

Goddammit!

Leaving the room and charging down the stairs, I went fucking crazy. I kicked over chairs, smashed pictures, and went to bat with some pottery and crystal. All things my mother loved. It made no difference. I'd clean up the mess before she got home tomorrow or five days from now. But stuff would be missing, and she'd get over it. Because there was only one thing that woman loved more than me or all of this stuff. Herself.

I spent the next two hours lost in a haze as I destroyed every picture she had of me smiling and every fucking figurine that gave the impression that we were a happy household.

When all was done, the house was a disaster. But I was as high as a kite. Nobody could hurt me if I could hurt them.

Sweating and exhausted, I parked myself outside on the back porch with my bottle of Jack and let the rain cool me down. I don't know how long I was there, but I was finally breathing and that felt good. There's something to be said for acting like a five-year-old and breaking some shit. Control had finally settled over me again, and I just sat there and drank, soaking up the quiet in my head.

"Jared?"

I twisted my head at my name and immediately lost my breath. *Aw, Jesus Christ. No, no, no . . .*

She was here? And in fucking shorts and a tank top?

I turned back around, hoping she'd go away. I didn't want to lose my shit with her. Or do anything stupid. I'd finally calmed down, but my head was nowhere near straight enough to deal with her right now.

"Jared, the dog was barking outside. I rang the doorbell. Didn't you hear it?"

Damn, she was so close. I could feel the pull. I wanted to get closer. To sink into her arms until I couldn't even remember yesterday.

She walked around in front of me, and my fingers tingled. They wanted her. Always her.

I glanced up, only for a moment, unable to resist the pull.

Jesus Fucking Christ. She was drenched. And I looked down again, knowing what I would do if I kept looking. Her wet shirt stuck to her body, but she tried to hide it by crossing her arms. Her legs glistened with the water dripping down, and her shorts clung to her toned, wet thighs.

"Jared? Would you answer me?" she yelled. "The house is trashed."

I tried looking at her again. Why? Who the fuck knows? Because every time I saw her, I wanted to bury my heart and body inside of her. What good was that going to do either of us?

322

"The dog ran away," I choked out. *What the hell?*

"So you threw a temper tantrum? Does your mom know you did that to the house?"

And that's when the wall went back up. My mother. Tate looking at me like I couldn't control myself. Like I was weak.

I didn't want to hurt her anymore, but I wasn't letting her in, either.

"What do you care? I'm nothing, right? A loser? My parents hate me. Weren't those your words?" *Yes, this was easier. Just push back.*

She started talking, and I shot back with my usual bark, but it didn't matter. I'd shut her down and shut her out. Like I always did. I didn't need her. I was strong.

She followed me inside, and I tried to tune her out as I dried off the dog. But then she took the control out of hands again when she rushed to empty my bottle down the drain.

"Son of a bitch!" I ran up to her and tried prying the Jack out of her hands. "This is none of your business. Just leave." I didn't want her here to see me like this. She shouldn't care about me. I'd done nothing to earn it. And I didn't need it or her!

I jerked the bottle, and her body came flush with mine.

She was the most beautiful thing I'd ever seen. And angry was even hotter. A fire was in her eyes, and her full bottom lip glistened from the rain. I didn't want to stop this for anything. I wanted to let loose all of my energy on her. In more ways than one.

My head jerked to the side with the sting of her hand, and I stood there for a moment, stunned.

Fuck! She hit me!

I dropped the bottle, because fuck, I didn't give a damn about it anyway and hauled her up onto the counter. I didn't know what I was doing, but it was out of my control. And for once, I had no problem with that.

323

She met my eyes, not looking away for a second, as her body squirmed against mine. I shouldn't be holding her like this. I shouldn't be crossing this line with her. But I had Tate in my arms for the first time in over three years, and I wasn't letting go. The more I looked at her, and the more she let me touch her, I was completely hers. She owned me.

And I fucking hated and loved that at the same time.

"You fucked me up today."

"Good," she challenged, and my hold on her tightened.

I jerked her into me again. "You wanted to hurt me? Did you get off on it? It felt good, didn't it?"

"No, I didn't get off on it," she answered way too calmly. "I feel nothing. You are nothing to me."

No. "Don't say that." I hadn't pushed her away completely. I still had her, didn't I?

I could smell her sweet breath as she leaned in. "Nothing," she repeated, taunting me, and I was instantly hard as a fucking rock. "Now, get off—"

I took her mouth, eating up her sweet little whimper. She was fucking mine, and that was it. Her smell, her skin, everything invaded my world, and I couldn't see straight. My head felt dazed, like I was underwater, weightless and quiet. God, she tasted good.

I sucked on her bottom lip, tasting what I'd been fucking dying to get at for years. And I wanted to taste her everywhere. I went too fast, but I couldn't control myself. It was like I needed to fit in all the lost time right now.

Her chest was pressed into mine, and I was between her legs. I tried to catch my breath between kisses. This is where I wanted to be, and why the fuck didn't I see that sooner? She wasn't fighting me, and I smiled as she stretched her neck back for me, inviting me in. I released my hold and dug my hands into her body, pulling her into my hips, so she could feel how much I wanted her.

She'd wrapped her legs around me, and I ran my hands up her thighs, in complete awe of her soft, hot skin. We weren't going to fucking move until my hands or mouth had been on every part of her.

As I kissed her neck, she brought my face back up to her lips, and I reveled in how she responded. I knew I didn't deserve it. I knew she deserved more. But I was going to bury myself in this girl or spend my life trying. I couldn't get her close enough or kiss her fast enough. I wanted more.

I dove for the little spot under her ear, smelling and aching for her. I felt freer with her body wrapped around mine than I had in years.

"Jared, stop." She pulled her head away from me, but I just kept going. *Nope. You. Me. And a fucking bed. Now.*

I was about to carry her off when she yelled, "Jared! I said stop!" And she pushed me away.

I stumbled back, shocked out of my trance. My body was fucking screaming for her. I stood there, trying to fucking figure out what to say to her to bring her back to me, but she didn't give me a chance. She leapt off the counter and ran out of the house.

Goddamn.

I had no idea what the hell I was going to do now, but one thing was for damn certain.

That would happen again.

And don't miss Madoc's story
Rival

**available now
from Piatkus**